NATIONAL BESTSELLER

"[*Ape House*] is peopled (so to speak) with characters who are meaty and real. . . . A page-turner written with flair, imagination and a sharp sense of irony." —*The Globe and Mail*

"Consider reality TV, meth labs, over-the-top animal-rights activists, Botox, tabloids and Internet diatribes, and you, too, might come to the conclusion: People should be more like animals. Sara Gruen's entertaining, enlightening new novel will certainly leave you thinking so." —*Miami Herald*

"Gruen delivers a tale that's full of heart, hope, and compelling questions about who we really are." —*Redbook*

"Terrific: an incisive piece of social commentary." —*The New York Times Book Review*

"[*Ape House*] hums along with a pop-culture plot full of slick profiteers, sleazy pornographers, idiotic reality TV and gossip rags— with botox and ape sex thrown in for entertaining reading." —*Des Moines Register*

"Gruen has a knack for pacing and for creating distinctive animal characters. Scenes involving the bonobos are winsome without being sappy, and the reader comes to share Isabel's concern for the animals." —*Boston Globe*

"Sara Gruen knows things—she knows them in her mind and in her heart. And, out of what she knows, she has created a true thriller that is addictive from its opening sentence. Devour it to find out what happens next, but also to learn remarkable and moving things about life on this planet. Very, very few novels can change the way you look at the world around you. This one does." —Robert Goolrick, author of *A Reliable Wife*

APE HOUSE

SARA GRUEN

APE HOUSE

A NOVEL

ANCHOR CANADA

Library and Archives Canada Cataloguing in Publication is available upon
request.

ISBN 978-0-385-66445-5

Ape House is a work of fiction. Names, characters, places and incidents are
products of the author's imagination or are used fictitiously. Any resemblance to
actual events or locales or persons, living or dead, is entirely coincidental.

Book design by Casey Hampton

Printed and bound in the USA

Published in Canada by Anchor Canada,
a division of Random House of Canada Limited

Visit Random House of Canada Limited's website: www.randomhouse.ca

10 9 8 7 6 5 4 3 2 1

For great apes everywhere
but especially Panbanisha

Give orange give me eat orange me eat orange give me eat orange give me you.

— NIM CHIMPSKY, 1970s

Gimme gimme more, gimme more, gimme gimme more.

— BRITNEY SPEARS, 2007

APE HOUSE

1

The plane had yet to take off, but Osgood, the photographer, was already snoring softly. He was in the center seat, wedged between John Thigpen and a woman in coffee-colored stockings and sensible shoes. He listed heavily toward the latter, who, having already made a great point of lowering the armrest, was progressively becoming one with the wall. Osgood was blissfully unaware. John glanced at him with a pang of envy; their editor at *The Philadelphia Inquirer* was loath to spring for hotels and had insisted that they complete their visit to the Great Ape Language Lab in a single day. And so, despite seeing in the New Year the night before, John, Cat, and Osgood had all been on the 6 A.M. flight to Kansas City that same morning. John would have loved to close his eyes for a few minutes, even at the risk of accidentally cozying up to Osgood, but he needed to expand his notes while the details were fresh.

John's knees did not fit within his allotted space, so he turned them outward into the aisle. Because Cat was behind him, reclining his seat was not an option. He was well aware of her mood. She had an entire row to herself—an unbelievable stroke of luck—but she had just asked the flight attendant for two gins and a tonic. Apparently having three seats to herself was not enough to offset the trauma of having spent her day poring over linguistics texts when she had been expecting to meet six great apes. Although she'd tried to disguise the symptoms of her cold ahead of time and explain away the residual as allergies, Isabel Duncan, the scientist who had greeted them, sussed her out immediately and banished her to the Linguistics Department. Cat had turned on her legendary charm, which she reserved for only the most dire of circumstances, but Isabel had been like Teflon. Bonobos and humans share 98.7 percent of their DNA, she'd said, which makes them susceptible to the same viruses. She couldn't risk exposing them, particularly as one was pregnant. Besides, the Linguistics Department had fascinating new data on the bonobos' vocalizations. And so a disappointed, sick, and frustrated Cat spent the afternoon at Blake Hall hearing about the dynamic shape and movement of tongues while John and Osgood visited the apes.

"You were behind glass anyway, right?" Cat complained in the taxi afterward. She was crammed between John and Osgood, both of whom kept their heads turned toward their respective windows in a futile attempt to avoid germs. "I don't see how I could have given them anything from behind glass. I would have stood at the back of the room if she'd asked me. Hell, I'd have worn a gas mask." She paused to snort Afrin up both nostrils and then honked mightily into a tissue. "Do you have any idea what I went through today?" she continued. "Their lingo is completely incomprehensible. I was already in trouble at 'discourse.' Next thing I knew it was 'declarative illocutionary point' this, 'deontic modality' that, blah blah blah." She emphasized the "blahs" with her hands, waving the Afrin bottle in one and the crumpled tissue in the other. "I almost lost it on 'rank lexical relation.' Sounds like a smelly, overly chatty uncle, doesn't it? How on earth do they think I'm going to be able to work that into a newspaper piece?"

John and Osgood exchanged a silent, relieved glance when they got their seat assignments for the trip home. John didn't know Osgood's take on today's experience—they hadn't had a moment alone—but for John, something massive had shifted.

He'd had a two-way conversation with great apes. He'd spoken to them in English, and they'd responded using American Sign Language, all the more remarkable because it meant they were competent in two human languages. One of the apes, Bonzi, arguably knew three: she was able to communicate by computer using a specially designed set of lexigrams. John also hadn't realized the complexity of their native tongue—during the visit, the bonobos had clearly demonstrated their ability to vocalize specific information, such as flavors of yogurt and locations of hidden objects, even when unable to see each other. He'd looked into their eyes and recognized without a shadow of a doubt that sentient, intelligent beings were looking back. It was entirely different from peering into a zoo enclosure, and it changed his comprehension of the world in such a profound way he could not yet articulate it.

Being cleared by Isabel Duncan was only the first step in getting inside the apes' living quarters. After Cat's banishment to Blake Hall, Osgood and John were taken into an administrative office to wait while the apes were consulted. John had been told ahead of time that the bonobos had final say over who came into their home, and also that they'd been known to be fickle: over the past two years, they'd allowed in only about half of their would-be visitors. Knowing this, John had stacked his odds as much as possible. He researched the bonobos' tastes online and bought a backpack for each, which he stuffed with favorite foods and toys—bouncy balls, fleece blankets, xylophones, Mr. Potato Heads, snacks, and anything else he thought they might find amusing. Then he emailed Isabel Duncan and asked her to tell the bonobos he was bringing surprises. Despite his efforts, John found that his forehead was beaded with sweat by the time Isabel returned from the consultation and informed him that not only were the apes allowing Osgood and him to come in, they were insisting.

She led them into the observation area, which was separated from the apes by a glass partition. She took the backpacks, disappeared into a hallway, reappeared on the other side of the glass, and handed them to the apes. John and Osgood stood watching as the bonobos unpacked their gifts. John was so close to the partition his nose and forehead were touching it. He'd almost forgotten it was there, so when the M&M's surfaced and Bonzi leapt up to kiss him through the glass, he nearly fell backward.

Although John already knew that the bonobos' preferences varied (for example, he knew Mbongo's favorite food was green onions and that Sam loved pears), he was surprised by how distinct, how differentiated, how almost *human,* they were: Bonzi, the matriarch and undisputed leader, was calm, assured, and thoughtful, if unnervingly fond of M&M's. Sam, the oldest male, was outgoing and charismatic, and entirely certain of his own magnetism. Jelani, an adolescent male, was an unabashed show-off with boundless energy and a particular love of leaping up walls and then flipping over backward. Makena, the pregnant one, was Jelani's biggest fan, but was also exceedingly fond of Bonzi and spent long periods grooming her, sitting quietly and picking through her hair, with the result that Bonzi was balder than the others. The infant, Lola, was indescribably cute and also a stitch—John witnessed her yank a blanket out from under Sam's head while he was resting and then come barreling over to Bonzi for protection, signing, BAD SURPRISE! BAD SURPRISE! (According to Isabel, messing with another bonobo's nest was a major transgression, but there was another rule that trumped it: in their mothers' eyes, bonobo babies could do no wrong.) Mbongo, the other adult male, was smaller than Sam and of a more sensitive nature: he opted out of further conversations with John after John unwittingly misinterpreted a game called Monster Chase. Mbongo put on a gorilla mask, which was John's cue to act terrified and let Mbongo chase him. Unfortunately, nobody had told John, who didn't even realize Mbongo was wearing a mask until the ape gave up and pulled it off, at which point John laughed. This was so devastating that Mbongo turned his back and flatly refused to acknowledge John from that point forward. Isabel eventually cheered him up by playing the game properly, but he declined to interact with John for the rest of the visit, which left John feeling as if he'd slapped a baby.

"Excuse me."

John looked up to find a man standing in the aisle, unable to move past John's legs. John shifted sideways and wrangled them into Osgood's space, which elicited a grunt. When the man passed, John returned his legs to the aisle and as he did so caught sight of a woman three rows up holding a book whose familiar cover shot a jolt of adrenaline through him. It was his wife's debut novel, although she had recently forbidden him from using that particular phrase since it was beginning to look as though her debut novel was also going to be her last. Back when *The River Wars* first came out and John and Amanda were still feeling hopeful, they had coined the phrase "a sighting in the wild" to describe finding some random person in the act of reading it. Until this moment it had been theoretical. John wished Amanda had been the one to experience it. She was in desperate need of cheering up, and he'd very nearly concluded that he was helpless in that department. John checked for the location of the flight attendant. She was in the galley, so he whipped out his cell phone, rose slightly out of his seat, and snapped a picture.

The drinks cart returned; Cat bought more gin, John ordered coffee, and Osgood continued to rumble subterraneously while his human cushion glowered.

John got out his laptop and started a new file:

Similar to chimpanzees in appearance but with slimmer build, longer limbs, flatter brow ridge. Black or dusky gray faces, pink lips. Black hair parted down the center. Expressive eyes and faces. High-pitched and frequent vocalizations. Matriarchal, egalitarian, peaceful. Extremely amorous. Intense female bonding.

Although John had known something of the bonobos' demonstrative nature, he had been initially caught off-guard at the frequency of their sexual contact, particularly between females. A quick genital rub seemed as casual as a handshake. There were predictable occurrences, such as immediately before sharing food, but mostly there was no rhyme or reason that John could ascertain.

John sipped his coffee and considered. What he really needed to do was transcribe the interview with Isabel while he could still recall and annotate the non-aural details: her expressions and gestures, and the moment—unexpected and lovely—when she'd broken into ASL. He plugged his earphones into his voice recorder, and began:

ID: So this is the part where we talk about me?
JT: Yes.
ID: [*nervous laugh*] Great. Can we talk about someone else instead?

JT: Nope. Sorry.

ID: I was afraid of that.

JT: So what made you get into this type of work?

ID: I was taking a class with Richard Hughes—he's the one who founded the lab—and he talked a little about the work he was doing. I was utterly fascinated.

JT: He passed away recently, didn't he?

ID: Yes. [*pause*] Pancreatic cancer.

JT: I'm sorry.

ID: Thank you.

JT: So anyway, this class. Was it linguistics? Zoology?

ID: Psychology. Behavioral psychology.

JT: Is that what your degree is in?

ID: My first one. I think originally I thought it might help me understand my family—wait, can you please scratch that?

JT: Scratch what?

ID: That bit about my family. Can you take it out?

JT: Sure. No problem.

ID: [*makes gesture of relief*] Whew. Thanks. Okay, so basically I was this aimless first-year kid taking a psychology class, and I heard about the ape project and I went, and after I met the apes I couldn't imagine doing anything else with my life. I can't really describe it adequately. I begged and pleaded with Dr. Hughes to be allowed to do something, anything. I would mop floors, clean toilets, do laundry, just to be near them. They just... [*long pause, faraway look*] ... I don't know if I can say what it is. It just... is. I felt very strongly that this was where I belonged.

JT: So he let you.

ID: Not quite. [*laughs*] He told me that if I took a comprehensive linguistics course over the summer, read all his work, and came back to him fluent in ASL he'd think about it.

JT: And did you?

ID: [*seems surprised*] Yeah. I did. It was the hardest summer of my life. That's like telling someone to go off and become fluent in Japanese over four months. ASL is not simply signed English—it's a unique language, with a unique syntax. It's usually time-topic-comment-oriented, although like English, there's variability. For instance, you could say [*starts signing*], "Day-past me eat cherries," or you could say, "Day-past eat cherries me." But that is not to say that ASL doesn't also use the subject-verb-object structure; it simply doesn't use "state-of-being" verbs.

JT: You're losing me.

ID: [*laughs*] Sorry.

JT: So you came back, you blew him out of the water, and you got the job.

ID: I don't know about blowing him out of the water . . .

JT: Tell me about the apes.

ID: What about them?

JT: Seeing you with them today, and then speaking with them myself, and then managing to actually insult one of them—that was an eye-opener.

ID: He got over it.

JT: No. He didn't. But do you understand how strange that whole thing would seem to your average, everyday person? The concept that you can insult an animal in a social situation and have to make it up to him? And possibly fail? That you can have a two-way conversation with apes, in human language no less, and they're doing it simply because they want to?

ID: By Jove, I think he's got it!

JT: I suppose I had that coming.

ID: I'm sorry. But yes, that's the entire point of our work. Apes acquire language through exposure and a desire to communicate, just like human infants, and age-wise there is approximately the same window of opportunity. Although I'd like to branch out a little going forward.

JT: How so?

ID: Bonobos have their own language. You saw that today—Sam told Bonzi exactly where he'd hidden the key, even though they were in separate rooms and couldn't see each other. She went straight for it and never looked anywhere else. We may never be able to use their vocalizations to communicate with them for the same reasons they can't use spoken English—our vocal tracts are shaped too differently, which we think is related to the HAR1 gene sequence, but I think it's high time someone made an attempt to decode it.

JT: About the sex.

ID: What about it?

JT: There's just so much of it. And they're so . . . virtuosic. It's clearly not just about procreation.

ID: Absolutely right. Bonobos—along with dolphins and humans— are the only animals known to have recreational sex.

JT: Why do they do that?

ID: Why do you do it?

JT: Uh . . . Okay. Moving right along.

ID: I'm sorry. That's a fair question. We believe it's a mechanism to relieve tension, resolve conflict, and reaffirm friendship, although it also has to do with the size of the females' clitorises and that they are sexually receptive regardless of estrus. Whether this shapes or reflects bonobo culture is a matter of scientific debate, but there are several related factors: food is abundant in their natural habitat, which means the females aren't in competition to feed their babies. They form strong friendships and band together to "correct" aggressive males, thus keeping those genes from entering the pool, and so, unlike chimpanzees, male bonobos do not practice infanticide. Maybe it's because no male has any idea which babies are his, or maybe it's because the males who are allowed to breed don't care and that trait is passed along. Or maybe it's because the females would rip him to shreds. Like I said, it's a matter of some debate.

JT: Do you think the apes know they're apes, or do you think they're human?

ID: They know they're apes, but I don't think it means what you think it does.

JT: Explain.

ID: They know they're bonobos and they know we're human, but it doesn't imply mastery, or superiority, or anything of the sort. We are, all of us, collaborators. We are, in fact, family.

John clicked off his voice recorder and closed the lid of his laptop. He'd have loved to follow up on the family thing, but since she'd back-tracked immediately he left it alone. It was also interesting that she'd later called the bonobos her family. Maybe he could coax her into opening up in a follow-up interview. They'd definitely made a connection— a connection that he worried might have crossed over into flirtation at one point, although with each passing mile he felt better about that. She was unquestionably attractive, slim-hipped and athletic with straight blond hair that fell almost to her waist, but her charm was frank and earnest: she wore no makeup or jewelry of any kind, and John doubted she recognized her own appeal. Friendly is what they'd been; maybe she'd eventually trust him with her messy family history. It was the sort of detail readers loved, although this piece already promised to have plenty of those. She'd made another interesting comment when she put on the gorilla mask and gave a proper demonstration of Monster Chase. After she "caught" Mbongo, they'd rolled around on the floor tickling each other and laughing (hers was full and high-pitched, his a nearly silent wheezing, but the expression on his face left no question that it was laughter). John was shocked at the level of roughhousing going on, having been given to believe that working with great apes was extremely dangerous. Even though he'd read that bonobos were different, he hadn't expected her to be so physical with them. His surprise must have been evident, because when she stopped she said, "Over the years, they've become more human, and I've become more bonobo," and in that moment he'd felt a flash of understanding, like he'd been allowed to peek briefly through the crack.

2

Isabel leaned through the doorway, her eyes scanning the dinner carts. Only two-year-old Lola reacted to her presence, glancing briefly in her direction. She was tiny, as bonobo babies are, and clung to Bonzi's chest and neck, alternately mouthing her mother's nipple and letting it slide from her lips.

The bonobos lolled on the floor in nests of carefully arranged blankets, watching *Greystoke: The Legend of Tarzan, Lord of the Apes.*

Bonzi was more precise about her nest than the others—she always used exactly six blankets, swirling them over each other and folding the edges under so there was a soft rim all the way around. Isabel, who was prone to a certain precision herself, loved watching Bonzi poke and fiddle with her nest, which had to be just so before she'd invite Lola in, slapping her hands to her chest and signing, BABY COME.

Jelani and Makena lay head to head on their blankets, reaching up with lazy and long-fingered hands to examine each other's faces and chests and rid each other of imaginary bugs. When John Clayton, Seventh Earl of Greystoke, slid Miss Jane Porter's filmy nightdress off her shoulders, they tipped up their chins and exchanged a languorous kiss.

Sam sprawled on his back with an arm behind his head and one leg crossed over the other. His foot bobbed, and he worked a watermelon rind, scraping the last of the sweet flesh off with his teeth. Mbongo had set up his nest across the room and wrapped a blanket firmly around his new backpack to keep Sam from noticing its suspicious girth. Mbongo had punctured his own bouncy ball almost immediately, and so had "borrowed" Sam's. Mbongo flashed impressive canines, his gaze flitting nervously between Sam and his precious blanketed lump. He lifted a corner of the fleece and peered beneath, then hurriedly tucked the blanket back around it. He was enjoying his secret too visibly. It wouldn't be long before Sam noticed.

Not wishing to disturb movie time, Isabel said nothing as she retrieved the empty carts. She rolled them out one by one and passed them off to Celia, a nineteen-year-old magenta-haired intern. When all the carts were in the kitchen, the two of them began to clear the remains of dinner. Celia stacked the plastic soup bowls while Isabel scooped up peels and stems, dumping the fruit and vegetable detritus into the disposal and running water over her hands.

Celia finally broke the silence. "So how did the big visit go today?"

"It was good," said Isabel. "Lots of conversations. Lots of great pictures—the photographer's camera was digital so I've already seen a bunch."

"Anyone we know?"

"They're from *The Philadelphia Inquirer.* Cat Douglas and John Thigpen. They're finishing a series on great apes."

Celia snorted. "Catwoman and Pigpen! Love it. So what did the apes think?"

"I only let John in. She had a virus, so I sent her over to Linguistics instead."

"David and Eric were here? On New Year's Day?"

"They have a fancy new spectrum analyzer. There's no keeping them away from it."

"And how did that go?"

Isabel smiled at the plate she was holding. "Let's just say I owe them one. That woman is a real piece of work."

"Ha! Did Pigpen know ASL?"

"His name is John. And no. I translated their responses." After a moment's pause, she added, "Mostly."

One of Celia's pierced eyebrows rose.

"Mbongo called him a 'dirty bad toilet' at one point," Isabel explained. "I may have paraphrased that one a little."

Celia laughed. "And what did he do to deserve that?"

"A game of Monster Chase gone hideously wrong."

Celia picked up a plastic dish and held it at various angles, trying to determine whether it had been washed or licked clean. "In Pigpen's defense, Monster Chase *is* hard to do through glass."

"It was much worse than that. But we showed him how it's done," said Isabel. "Monster Chase, Monster Tickle, Apple Chase, we did it all. Much to the delight of the photographer."

"Did Peter come in today?"

Well, that was a hard left turn, thought Isabel, stealing a quick look at Celia. The girl stared into the sink, the corner of her lip lifted into a smirk. Apparently Dr. Benton had become "Peter" to the intern at some point over the last twenty-four hours.

"No. I haven't seen him," Isabel said carefully.

At the previous night's New Year's Eve party, Isabel had been uncharacteristically thrown for a loop by a sorry excuse for dinner (four tiny cubes of cheese) and three strong cocktails ("It's a Glenda Bendah!" the host, and husband of Glenda, had exclaimed as he thrust a glass of the iced blue concoction into her hands). Isabel didn't normally drink— had in fact just purchased her first bottle of vodka so she'd have something on hand to offer guests—but this was the first social gathering of the people involved with the Great Ape Language Lab since Richard Hughes's death, and everyone was working hard at the appearance of being merry. It was exhausting. Isabel tried to keep up, but when she staggered into the powder room and encountered her own flushed, intoxicated face in the mirror, she saw something even more frightening than the gorilla mask in Monster Chase was supposed to be: she saw an earlier version of her mother, weaving and pale. Isabel was unused to wearing makeup and had somehow managed to smear lipstick up one cheek. Sections of hair stuck like twigs from her updo. She ditched the remains of her third Glenda Bendah in the sink, dissolved the blue-tinged ice cubes in running water, and tried to creep out before she could embarrass herself further. Peter, who was not only Dr. Hughes's successor but also Isabel's fiancé, found her in the lobby in stockinged feet, slumped against the wall with her high-heeled shoes dangling from a thumb. When she looked up and saw him, she burst into tears.

He crouched next to her. He held a hand to her forehead. His eyes filled with concern. He went back upstairs and returned with a moist, cool cloth, which he pressed to her cheeks.

"Are you sure you're okay?" he said moments later, helping her into a taxi. "Let me come with you."

"I'm fine," she said, and promptly leaned out of the car to be sick. The cabdriver observed this with alarm through the rearview mirror. Peter lifted the hems of his pants to inspect his shoes and leaned forward to examine Isabel more thoroughly. His eyebrows formed a lopsided V beneath a series of wavy lines. He paused, and then decided.

"I'm coming with you," he declared. "Wait while I get my coat."

"No, really, I'm fine." She groped through her purse for a tissue, beyond mortified. She couldn't stand for him to see her like this. "Stay," she insisted, waving a hand in the general direction of the party. "Really. I'll be fine. Stay and ring in the New Year."

"Are you sure?"

"Completely." She sniffed, nodded, and straightened her shoulders.

He watched a moment longer and said, "Drink lots of water. And take Tylenol."

She nodded. Even in her inebriated state, she could tell that he was considering whether to kiss her. She took mercy on him, pulled the door shut on her taffeta dress, and waved the driver onward.

Isabel had no idea what happened after she left. The party hadn't quite reached the lampshade stage, but that was certainly the trajectory—veiled grief, an endless supply of alcohol, and resentment on the part of a select few over Peter's appointment made for a strange and unpredictable atmosphere. Peter had been at the lab for only a year, and there were some who felt the position should have gone to a person with a longer investment in the project.

Nearly twenty hours later, Isabel still felt wretched. She leaned her belly against the edge of the counter and snuck another fleeting glance at

Celia, whose shoulder-to-wrist tattoos were displayed in full glory because she was wearing an orange "Peace" tank over a bright purple bra—in January. It wouldn't surprise Isabel at all if Celia had attempted a bit of political maneuvering at the party. A little dancing, a little flirting, maybe even sidling up to Peter when the ball dropped, angling for a midnight kiss.

Isabel sighed. It wasn't as if she could take it personally: her relationship with Peter was not yet public. He had proposed only a few days earlier, after an accelerated and passionate courtship—Isabel had never fallen so fast and so hard—but for various reasons, including an ongoing and rancorous custody battle with his ex-wife and concern over how it would be perceived by the department, he felt it best to keep things quiet until they moved in together. Besides which, although Celia apparently had no idea, Peter disliked her.

"What?" Celia stopped digging vegetable peelings out of the bottom of the sink and glanced down the length of her arm.

Isabel realized she'd been staring at the tattoos. She turned her eyes back to the dishes. "Nothing. I just have a headache."

Bonzi rounded the corner and ambled up to them. Lola rode on her back, jockey-style, tiny fingers laced over her mother's shoulders.

Celia looked over her shoulder and called out, "Bonzi, did you try to kiss the visitor?"

Bonzi grinned gleefully and spun on her behind, propelling herself with her feet. She touched her fingers to her lips and then her cheek, twice, before crossing both hands over her chest, signing, KISS KISS BONZI LOVE.

Celia laughed. "And what about Mbongo? Did he also love the visitor?"

Bonzi considered for a moment and then wiggled her fingers beneath her chin and swept her hand downward, signing, DIRTY BAD! DIRTY BAD!

"Did Mbongo think the visitor was a dumbass?" continued Celia, stacking clean plates.

"Celia!" Isabel barked. "Language!"

This was precisely why Peter had been unhappy when Richard

Hughes had bestowed the coveted internship on Celia over a half-dozen other deserving candidates. He was worried about her colorful language. If one of the bonobos picked up an offensive phrase and used it the requisite number of times in proper context, it would have to be included in the official lexicon. It was one thing when a bonobo came up with an insult like "dirty bad toilet" on his own, and quite another to acquire "dumbass" from a human.

Although Bonzi had been conversing with Celia, she was now looking intently at Isabel. Her expression shifted to worry. SMILE HUG, she signed. BONZI LOVE VISITOR, KISS KISS.

"Don't worry, Bonzi. I'm not mad at you," Isabel said, speaking and signing simultaneously. She threw an accusatory glare in Celia's direction to drive her point home. "Don't you want to watch the rest of the movie?"

WANT COFFEE.

"Sure, I can make coffee."

WANT CANDY COFFEE. ISABEL GO. HURRY GIMME.

Isabel laughed and assumed a posture of mock offense. "You don't like my coffee?"

Bonzi sat on her haunches, looking sheepish. Lola climbed over her shoulder and blinked at Isabel.

"Touché. Neither do I," Isabel conceded. "You want a caramel macchiato?"

Bonzi yipped excitedly. GOOD DRINK. GO HURRY, said her hands.

"Okay. You want marshmallow on that?" said Isabel, using Bonzi's term for the sweet froth on the top.

SMILE SMILE, HUG HUG.

Isabel threw the damp dish towel over her shoulder and wiped her still-clammy hands on her thighs.

"You want me to go?" Celia said.

"Sure. Thanks." Isabel was surprised by the offer, and also grateful, on account of her lingering headache. Celia's shift had technically ended almost a quarter of an hour earlier. "I'll finish up here."

Celia waited as Isabel lined the carts up against the wall. "Ahem," she said finally.

Isabel looked up. "What?"

"Can I take your car? Mine's in the shop."

Mystery solved. Isabel nearly laughed out loud. Celia wanted a ride home at the end of the night.

Isabel patted her pockets until a lump jingled.

GRAB PICTURE, said Bonzi.

"Take the video camera," Isabel said, tossing the keys in a perfect arc. "And make sure you ask for decaf. And skim milk."

Celia nodded and snatched the keys from the air.

All the bonobos—but especially Bonzi—loved watching videos of humans carrying out their requests. The bonobos used to ride along on limited errands, but all that stopped two years ago on the day Bonzi decided to steer the car and nearly wrapped it around a telephone pole. She'd simply reached across and grabbed the steering wheel. Isabel managed to brake before impact, but not before running off the road. This happened less than a week after Dr. Hughes's car was swarmed at a McDonald's drive-through when the driver of a passenger van in front of them glanced in his rearview mirror and spied Mbongo—who had successfully talked his way into a rare and cherished cheeseburger— riding shotgun. Moments later adults and children alike mobbed the car screaming, "Monkey! Monkey!" while trying to thrust their arms through the windows. Mbongo's response was to dive beneath the back- seat as Dr. Hughes closed the windows, but that, followed by the Bonzi- steering episode, sounded the death knell for public outings.

The bonobos missed their contact with the outside world (although, when asked, they were absolutely firm in their belief that the double electric fence and moat around their outside play yard was there to keep people and cats out rather than bonobos in), so now Isabel and the oth- ers brought the outside world to them by video. At this point, the local shopkeepers thought nothing of being filmed for the viewing pleasure of the neighborhood apes.

"Try to run over some protesters while you're at it," said Isabel.

"There's nobody out there," said Celia.

"Really?" said Isabel. There had been a gaggle of protesters outside the gates every day for almost a year, silently holding placards that showed great apes undergoing terrible procedures. Since the protesters obviously had no clue as to the nature of the work being done at the language lab, Isabel always ignored them.

Celia opened the viewfinder of the video camera and then flicked the switch to check its battery. "Larry-Harry-Gary and Green-Haired Freaky Dude were there before dinner but they were gone when I went out for a smoke."

" 'Green-Haired Freaky Dude'? This from the girl with hot pink hair?"

"It is not hot pink," Celia said, fingering a pixie curl in front of her ear. "It's fuchsia. And I have nothing against his hair color. I just think he, himself, is an asshat."

"Celia! Language!" Isabel whipped her head around and noted with relief that Bonzi had wandered back into the TV room, thereby missing this opportunity to enrich her vocabulary. "You have *got* to be more careful. I'm serious."

Celia shrugged. "What? They didn't hear me."

Isabel felt her eyes wander over to Celia again. The intern's body art fascinated and repulsed Isabel almost equally. A labyrinthine swirl of nudes and mermaids tumbled down her shoulders and frolicked along her forearms, their hair and breasts entwined with the scaly limbs and tails of creatures borne from hell. A smattering of horseshoes and daisy-eyed skulls rained down on the whole, which was sharply rendered in reddish pinks, yellows, purples, and ghostly bluish greens. Isabel was only eight years older than Celia, but her own brand of rebellion had been to bury her nose in books and ride the scholarship train away from home as far and fast as possible.

"Okay. I'm off," Celia declared, tucking the video camera under her arm. Isabel went back to the dishes, listening as Celia's footsteps receded down the hallway.

A moment later, the door creaked open. Isabel spun on her heels. "Wait! You do have a valid driver's—"

The door slammed shut. Isabel stared at it for a moment, then tucked a bottle of Lubriderm under her arm and went in to watch the end of the movie.

Sam had reasserted ownership of the ball, and Mbongo was sulking in his nest, the picture of desolation. He wore his new backpack, whose concave shape betrayed the ball's absence. His shoulders slumped forward, and he hugged his arms across his chest. Isabel knelt beside him and put a hand on his shoulder.

"Did Sam take his ball back?" she asked, signing and speaking at the same time.

Mbongo stared forlornly ahead.

"Do you need a hug?" asked Isabel.

At first he didn't respond. Then he signed with a flurry: KISS HUG, KISS HUG.

Isabel leaned in and took his head in both hands. She kissed his creased forehead and straightened his long black hair. "Poor Mbongo," she said, wrapping her arms around his shoulders. "I'll tell you what. Tomorrow I'll get you another ball. But don't carry this one in your teeth. Okay?"

The bonobo pulled his lips back in a smile and nodded quickly.

"Do you need some oil? Let me check your hands," said Isabel, reaching for his arm.

Mbongo obligingly stretched it toward her. Isabel took his hand and ran her fingers over it. Although the lab had humidifiers going all the time in the winter, the air still couldn't compete with that of the bonobos' native Congo Basin.

"That's what I thought," she said. She squeezed a glob of Lubriderm onto her palm and massaged it into his long, heavily knuckled hand.

As one, the bonobos turned to face the hallway.

"What is it?" Isabel looked from face to face, puzzled.

VISITOR, signed Bonzi. The rest of the apes remained motionless, their eyes trained on the door.

"No, not a visitor. The visitors left. The visitors are gone," said Isabel.

The apes continued to stare down the hallway. Sam's hair rose until it stood on end, and a pricking like tiny spiders crept over Isabel's neck and scalp. She rose and muted the TV.

Finally she heard it—a muffled rustling.

Sam pulled his lips back and screamed, *"Whah! Whah! Whah!"* Bonzi scooped baby Lola under her arm, grabbed a hanging fire hose with the other, and swung onto the lowest of the platforms that jutted from the walls at various heights. Makena joined them, grinning nervously, clinging to the other females.

The rustling stopped, but all eyes—human and ape—remained on the hallway. After a moment, the rustling was replaced by a muted jiggling.

Sam's nostrils flared. He turned to Isabel and signed urgently, VISITOR, SMOKE.

"No, not a visitor. It's probably just Celia," Isabel said, although she couldn't hide the apprehension in her voice. Celia hadn't had time to get the coffee and return. Besides, Celia would just come in.

Sam stood up and swaggered a few bipedal steps.

The females swung to an even higher perch and backed against the wall. Mbongo and Jelani darted around the corners of the room on all fours.

Isabel let herself out through the partition that defined the bonobos' inner sanctum and stopped to check that it was locked behind her. In eight years of daily contact, she'd never seen the bonobos act like this. Their adrenaline was contagious.

She flicked on the light. The hallway looked as it always did. The noise, whatever it was, had stopped.

"Celia?" Isabel asked tentatively. There was no answer.

She walked toward the door that led to the parking lot. When she glanced behind her, Sam galloped silently past the doorway of the group room, a dark and muscled mass.

Isabel reached for the doorknob and then retracted her hand. She leaned in close to the door, her forehead nearly touching it.

"Celia? Is that—"

The explosion blasted the door entirely out of its frame. As it carried her backward, she processed that she and the door were being propelled down the hall by a billowing, rolling wall of fire. She felt lucid and detached, parsing the events as though examining consecutive frames of a video. Since there was no time to react, she recorded.

When she slammed into the wall, she noted that her skull stopped moving before her brain did. When the door came to a stop against her, trapping her upright, she observed that the left side of her face—the side she'd had pressed against the door—took the brunt of the impact. When her eyes filled with stars and her mouth with blood, she filed these facts away for future reference. She watched helplessly as the fireball whooshed past the door and rolled onward toward the apes. When the door finally tipped forward and released her, she crumpled to the ground. She couldn't breathe, but she did not appear to be on fire. Her eyes shifted to the empty doorway.

Shadowy figures in black clothes and balaclavas swarmed in and spread out, strangely, frighteningly silent.

Crowbars swung and glass flew, but the people didn't speak. It wasn't until one of them knelt briefly by her head, with oversized rubber-band lips mouthing the word "Shit!" that she realized she couldn't hear. And still she couldn't breathe. She fought to keep her eyes open, fought the crushing weight in her chest.

Black-and-white static, the roar of a million bees interrupted by the fluttering of her own eyelids. A vision of boots running past her. She lay on her back with her head tilted to the right. She moved her tongue, fat as a sea slug, and pushed one, two, and then three teeth from the corner of her mouth. More static, longer this time. Then blinding light and crushing pain. She was suffocating. Her eyes drifted shut.

Time passed—how much, she didn't know—but suddenly she was being yanked around. An acrid latexed finger swept through her mouth, and a bright pinpoint of light illuminated the veined landscape of her inner lids. Her eyes sprung open.

Faces hovered over her, speaking urgently to each other. She heard them as though through surf. Gloved hands scissored roughly through her T-shirt and bra. Someone suctioned out her nose and mouth and covered them both with a mask.

"—respiratory distress. No breath sounds on the left."

"She has a tracheal shift. Get a line in."

"I'm in. Any crepitus?"

Fingers massaged her chest. Something inside cracked and popped like bubble wrap.

"Crepitus present."

Isabel tried to gasp, but succeeded only in producing a rasping wheeze.

"You're going to be okay," said the voice attached to the hand attached to the oxygen mask. "Do you know where you are?"

Isabel tried to inhale, and the pain was like a thousand knives. She mewed into the mask.

A male face appeared above hers: "You're going to feel something cold on your skin. We have to insert a needle to help you breathe."

A freezing swipe of antiseptic, a long needle flashing above her and then down and into her chest. The pain was excruciating, but accompanied by instant relief. Air hissed through the needle and her lung reinflated. She could breathe again. She gasped and sucked so hard the mask inverted against her face. She clawed at it, but the hand holding it stayed firm, and Isabel discovered that even though it flattened against her face, it still delivered oxygen. It stank of PVC, like cheap shower curtains and the type of bath toys she avoided buying for the bonobos because she'd read that they exuded fake estrogens when the material began to break down.

"Get her on a backboard."

Hands maneuvered her sideways, holding her head, then eased her onto her back. A radio sputtered in the background.

"We have a female, mid- to late twenties, victim of an explosion. Tension pneumothorax—needle decompression performed in the field. Breath sounds present. Facial and oral trauma. Head injury. Altered level of consciousness. Ready to evacuate—ETA seventeen minutes."

She let her eyes drift shut and the bees swarmed again. The world was spinning, she was nauseated. When the crisp night air hit her face, her lids snapped open. Each movement of the gurney was amplified as its wheels crunched through the gravel.

The parking lot was full of flashing lights and sirens. Velcro straps prevented Isabel from turning her head, so instead she turned her gaze. Celia was off to the side, screaming and crying and pleading with firemen to let her past. She was still clutching a cardboard tray of grande caramel macchiatos. When she caught sight of the gurney, the tray and drinks splattered to the ground. The video camera swung from a strap on her wrist.

"Isabel!" she wailed. "Oh my God! *Isabel!*" and only then did Isabel have a concept of what had happened to her.

When the front wheels of the gurney met the back of the vehicle and folded beneath her, Isabel caught a glimpse of a dark shadow at the top of a tree, and then another, and then another, and she bleated into the mask. At least half the bonobos had made it out.

The ceiling of the ambulance replaced the starry night and her eyes flickered shut. Someone yanked them open, first one, and then the other, and shone a light into them. Against the ambulance interior she saw faces and uniforms and gloved hands, bags of intravenous fluid and crisscrossing tubes. Voices boomed and radios hissed and someone was calling her name but she was helpless against the riptide. She tried to stay with them—it seemed the polite thing to do, given that they now knew her name—but she couldn't. Their voices echoed and swirled as she sank into a chasm that was beyond the bees and darker than black. It was the complete absence of everything.

3

John opened his front door and came to an abrupt halt. It was the scent of Pine-Sol that startled him.

Nine weeks earlier, the death of their cat had pushed his already-teetering wife into an abyss from which she seemed unable to emerge. It was the end of a long progression that had begun more than a year earlier, before they moved from New York City to Philadelphia for John's job at the *Inquirer*.

John had known moving wouldn't be easy for Amanda. She was still reeling from the near-simultaneous loss of both her book contract and her agent—what was euphemistically termed "an economic downturn" turned into a mudslide that swept away her entire publisher. Her agent was so disenchanted she left the business to start a natural-fiber yarn boutique, leaving Amanda a literary orphan.

John did his best to infuse Amanda with enthusiasm for Philly—who wouldn't love its food, its neighborhoods, its architecture?—but she wasn't swayed. She missed her friends. She missed the city. She even spoke wistfully about their tiny six-story walkup, seeming to forget that it had been infested with mice. John had hoped their new house in

Queen Village with a private garden and alley would cheer her up, and
it did give her new energy: she was so determined to snatch victory from
the jaws of defeat that she immediately holed up with her laptop to finish her second novel. She worked in complete isolation, prompting John
to suggest that she volunteer at the animal shelter. He had hoped she
would meet some people and make new friends, but the inevitable and
alarmingly swift result was that she fell in love with a cat.

Although named Magnificat, the creature in question was an ancient
twenty-three-pound one-eared Maine coon with a permanently crooked
tail. He also had a flaking skin rash that left him scaly and bald in places,
which might have been bearable except that he also insisted on sleeping
between their heads, spreading his considerable heft between their pillows and batting at their heads if they didn't pet him enough. Amanda
didn't understand why John got so upset about a bit of dander on his pillow, and John didn't know how to explain that he had fully expected she
would adopt something, but that he had assumed it would be a sweet little baby something, not a monstrous beast with a weepy eye whose
tongue stuck out perpetually because he had no teeth left to hold it in
place. And yet, eight months later, when Magnificat's kidneys failed and
they had to have him put down, John was as shattered as Amanda. They
wept over the empty cat crate in the car, clutching each other for a full
twenty minutes before John felt composed enough to drive. Back home,
Amanda drew the blinds, crawled into bed, and stayed there for three
days. It killed John to see her like that: she had no friends within a hundred miles, her writing career was in tatters, her cat was dead, and there
was nothing he could do about any of it. His suggestion that they get another cat was met with a look of horrified betrayal. His suggestion that
she see a therapist went over even worse, although even John could see
that she was clinically depressed.

She ate barely anything. She couldn't sleep, although it took her
longer and longer to get out of bed in the morning, and when she finally
did, she rarely got dressed. She moved from bed to couch, lying under a
quilt with her laptop on her knees and the curtains firmly drawn. The
only light in the room was the ghostly blue glow of her monitor.

John hadn't realized just how much of the housekeeping Amanda had been doing until she stopped. Clean underwear and socks no longer appeared in his drawer. The pile of shirts remained in the corner of the closet until he gathered them and took them to the cleaners. Greasy cobwebs sprouted along the undersides of furniture and reached with filmy fingers to ensnare the baseboards. The hall table all but disappeared under towering piles of bills, catalogs, and credit card offers. John had taken over the kitchen to some degree, but there were always stacks of dirty dishes in the sink, and usually on the counter too. At this point, Amanda's efforts were limited to spraying lemon Pledge in the center of the powder room and turning the towels around if someone threatened to come over.

Alas, "someone" was always his parents. Their proximity was something he had failed to factor in when considering their move, an oversight for which he and Amanda were paying dearly.

For almost a year after they moved, Patricia and Paul Thigpen tried to persuade John and Amanda to join their church. If it had been anybody else, John might have considered it simply because it would force them to meet people, but the idea of his parents being even on the periphery of whatever social circle he and Amanda eventually assembled was unthinkable. The elder Thigpens had apparently given up, but now they inexplicably showed up at noon each Sunday to recount the sermon and wax on about how darling, how *adorable,* the children in the nursery were. The mournful sighs and static-filled silences made John want to curl into a ball and weep. Amanda tolerated them with an aloof grace (whether resigned or icy, John knew and cared not—he was just grateful, since her own family's brand of conflict resolution tended toward the throwing of crockery).

Patricia's thin-lipped and accusatory glares grew more overt in perfect correlation with the decline of the house. Sunday after Sunday John watched as Patricia shot smoldering blame rays in Amanda's direction. John knew he should do something to shield his broken wife, but his family dynamic was not such that he could address his mother's assumption about who was responsible for either the slide toward squalor or the lack of babies without risking an epic maternal sulk, and if the Thigpen males were united on any one front, it was the absolute necessity of Not

Upsetting Mother. (John's brothers, Luke and Matthew, didn't realize how fortunate they were to live on other continents. Or perhaps they did.)

Now, with ice in his veins and a hand on the door frame, John sniffed again. In addition to Pine-Sol, he identified scented candles, seared beef, and the lingering odor of pomegranate bath bubbles. He steeled himself, entered the house, and pulled the door shut behind him.

Amanda was leaning over the coffee table in the living room, arranging shucked oysters on a bed of crushed ice. Two bottles of Perrier-Jouët and crystal flutes sat off to the side, along with a tiny, perfect mound of Osetra caviar in the center of a small piece of their wedding china. Amanda stood barefoot on fresh vacuum tracks, wearing the silk nightgown John had given her for Christmas. It was a hopeful, desperate gift, a clumsy attempt to address her increasing reluctance to get out of bed. As far as John knew, this was the first time she'd worn it. He felt suddenly light-headed. The last time he'd come home to such a scene, she'd just sold *The River Wars*. Had she found another agent? Had someone bought her second book, *Recipe for Disaster*?

"Wow," he said.

She swung around, beaming. "I didn't hear you come in." She grabbed a bottle and came to him. Her hair, a mass of unruly spirals in a shade he referred to as Botticelli gold and she as Ronald McDonald orange, was arranged in a disheveled knot at the nape of her neck. She was wearing lip gloss. Her toenails were painted an opalescent shade that matched the pink silk. Something glittered on her eyelids.

"You look amazing," he said.

"There's a beef Wellington in the oven," she replied, kissing him and handing him the bottle of champagne.

As John fumbled with the foil, tiny silver flecks drifted down to the carpet. He balled the rest up in his palm and loosened the wire cage. "What's up?"

She smiled coyly. "You first. How was the trip?"

A bolt of joy displaced his apprehension. He tucked the cold bottle under his arm and dug his cell phone from his pocket. "Actually," he said, fumbling with the touch screen, "it was kind of exciting. . . ." He held the photograph triumphantly forth. "Ta-dah!"

Amanda squinted. She leaned closer and cocked her head. "What is that?"

"Hang on," he said, taking the phone back. He zoomed in on the image of a real live stranger reading *The River Wars*. "Here."

When Amanda realized what she was looking at, she snatched the phone.

"A sighting in the wild!" John popped the champagne. He watched Amanda with an expectant smile.

She held the phone with both hands and stared at the screen without a hint of jubilance. John's smile faded. "Are you okay?"

She sniffed, wiped the corner of one eye, and nodded. "Yes. Yes, I am," she said in a tight voice. "Actually, I have something to tell you. Come sit."

John followed her to the couch, where she sat with a straight back and clasped hands. His eyes moved nervously from her profile to the spread. There was no mistaking this for anything other than a celebration dinner, yet she appeared to be on the verge of tears. Was she pregnant? Probably not, as there were two glasses set out for the champagne. He tried to ignore the metallic tang of fear that blossomed in the back of his throat, and leaned forward to pour the champagne. He left the glasses on the table and reached for her hand, interlacing their fingers. Her fingertips were cold, her palm moist. She stared at the table's edge.

"Honey?" he said. "What's going on?"

"I found a job," she said quietly.

John winced. He couldn't help it. He forced his features to relax and breathed deeply, steeling himself. He did not know whether to pretend to be happy about the job or to try to talk her out of it. All she'd ever wanted to do was write novels, and he knew she'd recently completed *Recipe for Disaster*. Surely this was the worst time to give up. Then again, perhaps a reason to get up in the morning would be a good thing. Contact with the outside world, an opportunity to make new friends, to not be pummeled relentlessly with rejection letters—

Amanda blinked at him, awaiting his response.

"Where? Doing what?" he finally said.

"Well, that's the complicated part." She looked back into her lap. "It's in L.A."

"It's what?" John said, unsure if he'd heard correctly.

She shifted to face him and clutched his hands in a death grip. "I know this is going to sound crazy. I know that. And I know you're going to want to say no at first, so please don't answer right away. Maybe even sleep on it. Okay?"

John paused for the space of several beats. "Okay."

Her eyes lifted and stared earnestly into his. She took a deep breath. "Sean and I wrote a treatment for a show, and he had a pitch meeting with NBC last week. Today we got the green light. They're producing four episodes. And then, we'll see."

The room came unmoored. The ceiling swirled like toilet water. John dug his heels into the carpet to remind himself that he was anchored. Sean the who-what? And what was a treatment?

Amanda explained: she had connected with someone in an online chat room for writers, she said. His name was Sean, and they'd been corresponding for weeks. John didn't need to worry—she knew all about the dangers of online chat rooms and had set up a Hotmail account with a fake name. They had exchanged real information only after she was sure he was legitimate. Sean had worked with the major networks for years, matching scriptwriters with various television projects. This time, the project was his, and he wanted Amanda onboard— he'd read *The River Wars* and was a huge fan, thought it criminal that it hadn't gotten the review attention it deserved, because if it had, she would have been picked up by another publisher the second she was cut loose. She had the perfect voice for this project, which involved forty-something single women and a good deal of bed-hopping and was sure to hit the pulse of an enormous audience (apparently the boomer generation preferred to think of itself as in its forties rather than in its sixties). They'd collaborated on the treatment—a five-page description of the project—and Amanda stood to earn fifteen thousand an episode if NBC decided to keep it going after the initial four episodes. She hadn't mentioned anything to John before this because she didn't want to get his hopes up.

John realized she'd stopped talking. Her eyes bored into his, seeking a reaction.

"You don't want me to do it," she finally said.

He struggled to form an answer, trying to give his mind enough lead time to race through the implications. "I didn't say that. It's a surprise, that's all."

She waited for him to continue.

"What about *Recipe for Disaster*?"

"I've been rejected by a hundred and twenty-nine agents."

"But that was to letters asking for permission to send the book, right? Nobody's actually read the thing."

"It doesn't matter. No one's going to. Apparently."

"Tell me why you want to be involved in this series."

"I want to write. It's a way of writing."

"Books. You want to write books."

"And I've been rejected by every legitimate agent in the business. It's over."

He stood abruptly and began pacing. What if she was right? He hated the idea of her giving up, but there was some point at which persistence became masochism.

"Let's think this through. What would I do in L.A.?" he said. "No newspapers are hiring. I'd never find another job. I'm lucky I still have this one."

"Well, that's the thing." She paused long enough that he knew he wasn't going to like whatever came next. "You wouldn't have to right away. You can keep working here. You know, until we know for sure they're going to continue the series."

John's lips moved for a full three seconds before he managed to form words. "You want to move to L.A. without me?"

"No, no," she said vehemently. "Of course not. We'll commute on weekends."

"All the way across the country?"

"We can alternate weekends."

"How would we afford all that flying? And what about your rent? You'd have to get an apartment. And a car." John's voice rose along with the tally.

"We could dip into our savings—"

He shook his head. "No. Absolutely not. And what happens if NBC decides to keep the series going? We continue to live apart?"

"Then you join me out there. If they pick it up, I'll be making enough that we could get by while you looked."

"What's the advance?"

Amanda dropped her gaze.

"There's no advance?"

"Scripted shows cost so much to produce they just don't have the funding . . ."

"Are you kidding me?"

"It's because of reality TV. It costs almost nothing to produce, compared to almost three million per episode for scripted shows. Networks used to produce a dozen dramas or comedies, hoping one might take. Now they produce a couple and fill up the rest of the time slots with stupid shows about stupid people apparently trying to find true love by having sex in a hot tub with a different person every night while the cameras roll. I know they should pay me. But if I say no to this there are thousands of other writers just dying for a shot at it."

John threw his hands in the air. They landed with a smack on his thighs. He hoped this was some kind of hallucination, that his wife was not suggesting they live on opposite sides of the country so she could follow a Hollywood chimera that, for all he knew, came attached to a piece of spam—these writers' boards were filled with desperate people, some of them malicious, and Amanda was particularly vulnerable. He wondered whether she had paid anything to this Sean person. There was nothing, absolutely nothing, about this that smelled right.

John's cell phone rang, piercing a silence that had long since grown uncomfortable.

Amanda picked it up. "Hello?" After a moment she held it out to John. "It's your editor."

John raked a hand down his face and reached for the phone.

"Hey, Elizabeth. No, it's fine. Yeah, really." His eyes widened. "What? Are you kidding me? Jesus God. And what about . . . ? Is she going to be okay? . . . Uh-huh. Of course. Okay." He hung up and closed his eyes. Then he turned back to Amanda. "I have to go back to Kansas."

"What happened?"

"The language lab got bombed."

She brought a hand to her mouth. "The place from today? With the bonobos?"

"Yes."

"Oh my God. Who would do such a thing?"

"I don't know."

"Are the apes okay?"

"I don't know," said John. "But the scientist I interviewed was badly hurt."

Amanda laid a hand on his arm. "I'm so sorry."

John nodded, hearing her as though from a distance. His brain flashed through images of today's visit—following Isabel to the observation area, noticing how her hair swung as she walked. Watching, rapt, as the bonobos plucked "surprises" from their backpacks, as eager as children emptying Christmas stockings. Sitting in Isabel's office, watching her eyes flit nervously between him and the voice recorder, and registering his own physical yearning with a dreadful, guilty pang. Mbongo and his gorilla mask. Bonzi smooching the glass. That sweet infant with the naughty streak and irresistible eyes. Isabel was now in critical condition, and although Elizabeth had no details on the apes, every terrible possibility flashed through John's head—

"We can't do this," he said abruptly. "It's impossible. Please tell me you realize this is not going to happen."

Amanda stared at John until he had to look down. Then she walked past him and up the stairs. A few seconds later, their bedroom door clicked shut.

I am a fucking cad, John thought as he sank to the floor by the coffee table. He poked an oyster and watched it quiver in its shell. He stared glumly at the Osetra, which he knew he should put in the refrigerator because he had a general idea of what it had cost. He imagined Amanda, upstairs, climbing into bed and pulling the covers up to her ears, and knew he should go to her. Instead, he took the open bottle by the neck and alternately took swigs and rested it on his thigh, which was soon dotted with wet circles.

The series seemed like too much of a fluke to be real, but what if it were? His own career was a fluke—he had intended to follow in his father's footsteps and become a lawyer until he got the internship at the *New York Gazette*. He was twenty-one and found the atmosphere intoxicating—everyone around him was so smart, so sophisticated, and so wholly and unabashedly bizarre that he wanted to remain a part of it. He got to talk to important people and ask any question he wanted and then got paid to write. *Paid to write?* Growing up that had never even occurred to him. And every day the job changed and he met someone new, heard another story, and got another chance to either entertain people or expose something that needed to be seen. "The business of a newspaper is to comfort the afflicted and afflict the comfortable" was one of the aphorisms his boss liked to quote. Of course, newspapers themselves were now among the afflicted. But who was he to deny someone else's unexpected opportunity?

It should be easy enough to confirm if the series were real—there would be a letter of offer or a contract—but then what? Everyone knew that long-distance relationships eventually fell apart. John had spent almost half his life with Amanda, and in many ways she defined it. The thought of being without her terrified him. The thought of her being surrounded by predatory males terrified him even more. She was beautiful, and so vulnerable right now, like a nerve scraped raw.

John picked up the little spoon from the plate of caviar and examined it. It was mother-of-pearl. Amanda must have bought it for the occasion. He dug it into the glistening mound of caviar and put some in his mouth. It didn't seem right to just swallow something so expensive and of which there was so little, so he held it in his mouth for a moment and then popped the eggs between his tongue and palate. The result was so exquisite he realized he must be doing it right. He took another little scoop. And then another.

It couldn't take too long to produce four episodes. She could be safely home in six months. Not that he wanted her to fail; she deserved success more than anyone else he knew.

After graduating summa cum laude with an insightful thesis on the sociological consequences of the industrial revolution as reflected in the works of Elizabeth Gaskell, Amanda had spent almost the entire time between graduation and their move to Philadelphia writing catalog copy for an online outdoor-sports outfitter. She worked eight-hour days laboring to find new and inventive ways of describing mukluks and all-weather parkas ("top notes of Ugg with a soupçon of Piperlime, and guaranteed 100 percent cat-fur free!"). She joked that her situation could have been worse—her best friend, Gisele, who had graduated first in their class, had taken a job painting house exteriors and had recently married a man who taught sound healing to a group of raw-foodists—but John knew she was simply putting on a brave face. In her spare time, she worked on her first novel, although she was too shy to show it to John until it was complete.

When she finally gave it to him, John flipped through the pages with a growing sense of unease. He hoped earnestly and with his soul that he was wrong—after all, his own guilty pleasures included Dan Brown and Michael Crichton—and yet he couldn't shake the feeling that the novel was missing that crucial *something*. Her prose was beautiful and polished and swept him along, but by the time he reached the end she had not blown up a single thing. There was no car wreck, no murder, no secret brotherhood or international plague. It was psychological and literary and while John understood that there were people who enjoyed such books, he wasn't one of them, which was exceedingly unfortunate given that his wife had just written one and wanted his opinion. When his silence finally grew conspicuous, he lied copiously and through his teeth.

As the manuscript made its way around New York publishing houses, Amanda—his steady, strong, unsinkable Amanda—began to crack. She developed insomnia. She gnawed her cuticles until they bled. She cooked ever more complicated meals and ate virtually nothing. She developed headaches and, for the first time ever, complained about her job. ("What's wrong with 'tufts of skunk'? They wanted edgy, I gave them edgy. How was I supposed to know it really was skunk? And if it was, why all the secrecy?")

Four and a half months passed. A handful of rejections trickled in, followed by radio silence. And then, on Amanda's thirty-fourth birthday, her agent called. A publisher had made an offer for *The River Wars* and Amanda's as-yet-unwritten second book.

Amanda's was a modest advance, but it allowed her to give up copywriting. Chinese cat fur be damned! With the exception of being required to publish under a pseudonym, John had never seen Amanda so happy. ("Nobody is going to buy a novel by Amanda Thigpen," her editor had explained. "Now Amanda LaRue, on the other hand . . .") The night of the book sale was the first appearance of Osetra in their household, and for that one night everything felt possible—bestseller lists, foreign editions, movie deals. John had never been so happy to be wrong.

If the lead-up to the release of *The River Wars* was a frenzy of excitement and anxiety, the weeks that followed were devastating.

There was no launch party. In retrospect, John realized that he was probably supposed to have arranged one. There were no reviews, because it had been published in paperback rather than as a hardcover, a prejudice John and Amanda didn't understand but felt someone should have explained. Her "tour" consisted of three local signings.

John drove Amanda to the first because she was too terrified to be counted on to steer, and when he reached across the gearbox for her hand she clung so tightly that his palm was pitted with nail marks. She practiced deep breathing in the parking lot before going in, and her hands trembled so violently that she expressed doubts about her ability to sign her name.

The bookstore had a small table set up with a semicircle of folding chairs in front of it. Amanda's books were piled beside two Sharpies, a plate of chocolate-chip cookies, and a bottle of water. Amanda took her seat behind the table and waited.

Halfway through her allotted hour, a man wandered to the middle of the semicircle and settled into a chair. John hovered nearby, watching as Amanda first went pallid and then apple-red, and then smiled and steeled herself to say something. Just as she gathered breath, the man stuck his legs out, crossed his arms, and closed his eyes. Within seconds he was snoring. The color drained from Amanda's cheeks and John nearly couldn't contain his urge to walk over and dump his hot coffee on the man's lap.

The bookstore's Events Coordinator spent the rest of the hour gamely collaring customers and dragging them to Amanda's table. Trapped, they'd pick up the book and pretend to read the back cover, muttering and looking uncomfortable until they managed to break eye contact and wander off. At the end of the hour, the cookies were gone and the books remained. Amanda was the color of chalk.

She insisted on driving herself to both her other signings. "Oh, fine," she said cheerily when John asked how the second one went. Her smile lasted a couple of seconds before she dissolved into shoulder-wracking sobs. After the third signing, she was more pragmatic. "I'm screwed," she proclaimed calmly, while filling a tumbler with equal parts vodka and orange juice.

As the months went by a couple of foreign editions sold (her book was briefly the number-two bestseller in Taiwan, which would have been amusing if it had hit even a single list in the States). And then, out of the blue, both publisher and agent were gone. Although clearly it was through no fault of her own, she obsessed about what she might have done differently. If she'd published under Thigpen instead of LaRue, her real estate in the bookstore would have fallen somewhere between Paul Theroux and Dylan Thomas (it was widely speculated on Internet writers' communities that Joshua Ferris's sales were strong because of his proximity to Jonathan Safran Foer). She could have sent herself on a real tour, armed with a GPS, and signed every copy of her book on the Eastern Seaboard. She could have created an interactive Web site, run contests, started a blog. John watched helplessly as she worked herself into a frenzy. Then, as suddenly as it had begun, the self-flagellation ended. She called her old boss, was reinstated in her cubicle, and went back to work extolling the virtues of Gore-Tex, which turned out to have been their financial salvation, because shortly thereafter, John lost his job.

While devastating, John's layoff was not unexpected: every major paper had suffered massive layoffs, and the situation was particularly dire at the *New York Gazette*. Management announced its plans to cut a quarter of the newsroom months after everyone took what was euphemistically called a "wage concession" to avoid exactly that. A cheery memo followed, assuring them that if they all pulled together they'd be able to "do more with less!" The next memo implored them to "transform the business," "generate content" (John wondered what, exactly, management thought the reporters had been doing), and concentrate on "packaging." Charts! Visuals! Design! These were the way of the future. One buffoon of an executive actually declared that a perfectly designed page should cause readers to spill their coffee. It made John yearn for the days when Ken Faulks was at the helm, but Faulks, a media mogul with sandy hair and a crooked smile, had long since moved on to the greener pastures of porn. John had no particular fondness for the man—as John recalled, he had the people skills of Genghis Khan—but at least he'd kept the company solvent.

After several months of searching, John took a staff job at *The Philadelphia Inquirer,* or "the *Inky,*" as insiders called it. It was a fine job, a great job, but it nearly killed John to accept it because it was a direct result of his father calling in a favor from a fellow Moose Lodge member. And so John was taken on, reporting to Elizabeth, who resented his very presence, even as other *Inky* employees were being encouraged to walk the plank with early retirement packages.

Under any other circumstances, his work would have redeemed him: John's investigation into a fire at the zoo's ape house in 2008—on Christmas Eve, no less—had uncovered gross incompetence. Fire alarms had gone off and been ignored. People smelled smoke and never investigated. There were no sprinkler systems. All told, twenty-three animals died, including an entire family of bonobos. A week ago, on the one-year anniversary of the fire, a toddler scaled a wall and fell twenty-four feet into the new gorilla enclosure. The only gorilla who had survived the fire, whose own baby had died of smoke inhalation, swooped in through the gaggle of other curious gorillas, cradled the child in her arms, and carried him to the door of her enclosure, where she handed him to zookeepers. This astonishing act of empathy, caught on video and aired across the country, was dismissed by several right-leaning outlets and pundits as simple training. Simple training for what, John wondered? Were they suggesting the zoo had been dropping dolls into the gorilla pit to practice for just such an occasion? John found this reactionary denial almost as fascinating as the gorilla's response—was it because empathy was supposed to be a purely human response? Was the discussion really about Evolution?—and this led to his proposing a piece on the cognitive studies being performed at the Great Ape Language Lab. At this point Elizabeth suddenly decided he needed to share the byline with Cat Douglas. She offered no explanations, but John had two theories: either she was still so angry about having to hire him that she was shackling him with the most abrasive woman alive, or else she wanted to associate her star reporter with a series that was beginning to smell like potential Pulitzer material. (Early in her career, Cat had become something of a celebrity in the newspaper world when she caught a Pulitzer Prize–winning reporter in a lie about a made-up eight-year-old crackhead, and then scored a Pulitzer herself for breaking the story. She had also stirred up controversy by allegedly faking a romantic interest in her rival reporter and going through his files when she was alone in his apartment.)

John realized with a start that he had eaten every last dot of the Osetra. There was a tiny bit of champagne left in the bottle, but he didn't want to change the flavor of his mouth. What he wanted was more caviar. He ran his finger across the plate and licked it.

Then he hauled himself off the floor and locked the front door. As he passed the hall table he noticed the message light blinking on the house phone. Fran, his mother-in-law, had left multiple messages, each more forceful than the last. Apparently Amanda had been screening her calls. John could not have been more sympathetic. Their mothers were polar opposites, but equally challenging. Where Patricia would retreat into a glacial silence, Fran would be upstairs sorting your socks. She disguised Schadenfreudic glee as helpfulness, malice as concern, all while harvesting information to share with the rest of the clan. With Fran, nothing was off-limits.

John deleted her messages.

It was two in the morning before John remembered the beef Wellington, and he remembered it then only because he thought the house was on fire. His eyes sprang open at the first hint of smoke. Amanda remained in a dead sleep.

John bounded down the stairs and into the kitchen. Smoke poured from the edges of the oven. John shut it off and opened the window and back door. He picked up a dish towel and snapped it like a matador's cape in an effort to direct the smoke outside.

The beef Wellington was a charred rectangle solidly attached to the bottom of the roasting tin. The winding pastry vine Amanda had carved and applied to the top was the least burned, so John plucked off a leaf and ate it. He examined her artistry—each leaf was scored exactly six times, and the stem wound in and around itself, a perfect pastry kudzu.

At the beginning of their cohabitation, Amanda had given them both campylobacter poisoning from her improvisations with canned soup. Her remorse was grand and her declarations grander: she wanted to become a gourmet chef. John hadn't thought much of it at the time, but in retrospect he felt that this was the first time he'd truly seen the sheer force of her will. She bought all of Julia Child's books, pored over them, and obeyed every command. ("If Julia says peel the broccoli, you peel the broccoli," she'd said bashfully the first time John caught her doing it. He'd roared with laughter, but after tasting the result never again questioned any bizarre kitchen ritual.)

Tonight, she'd left a fistful of raw puff pastry and all the leaves that hadn't passed muster wadded up beside the cutting board. Bits of egg and shell were dried onto the counter along with smashed garlic skins and strips of waxed butter wrapper. Flour coated the floor. Every utensil she'd used was abandoned at the precise spot where she'd ceased to use it.

John turned on the water, and waited until it got hot. Although he was tired, he wanted Amanda to encounter a clean kitchen when she rose the next morning.

4

sabel drifted in and out of a swirling rush. It wasn't sleep, because she was aware of things happening—people speaking, but not understandably, swooshing noises as she zoomed from tunnel to tunnel—this one orange, this one blue, this one green. Hands manipulated her body and her face, and she suffered the occasional discomfort of being punctured. But reacting or moving didn't occur to her, and it was just as well, because it wasn't a possibility. Finally the colors and noise submerged into a merciful, vacuous black.

A high-pitched beeping and intermittent wheezing disturbed her rest, stirring and prodding from the depths. She tried to ignore it like she would a fly, but like a fly, it was insistent. Finally, she surfaced.

She blinked several times and found herself looking at pressed ceiling tiles. Her peripheral vision was obscured by her own swollen flesh.

"Look who's awake."

Peter's face appeared above her, smiling. His eyes had dark crescents beneath them and his chin was flecked in stubble.

"The nurses said you were coming around." He pulled a chair up and sat next to her, reaching through the bars in the bed rail. His hand was warm and familiar to her: he was missing the first two sections of his left index finger, bitten off by a chimpanzee while he was doing graduate work at a primate center in Rockwell, Oklahoma. She tried to tighten her fingers around his, but was too weak. He reached through with his other hand and stilled hers.

Isabel mumbled, but her mouth wouldn't cooperate. Her tongue moved, but her teeth wouldn't budge.

"Your jaw is wired. Don't try to talk."

She lifted a hand and found it encumbered by a finger clamp and loops of IV tubing. She freed the other from Peter's grasp and gingerly investigated her face. Her fingers met a maze of plaster, gauze, and tape, the tender lumps of swollen lip and lines of wire crisscrossing the brackets that had been glued onto her remaining teeth. Her eyes swung to Peter. She signed, TELL ME.

"Your jaw is broken and you have a concussion. They had to reinflate your lung, so you have a chest tube, and your nose—"

NOT ME. THE APES.

Her efforts were truncated and awkward. She fumbled through the spelling of words that usually took two hands to sign, and improvised others.

"Ah," he said.

PETER?

"They're . . . okay." The corners of his lips twitched upward in an attempt to smile, but his eyes gave him away.

A cry escaped Isabel's wired mouth.

INJURED?

"No. I don't think so. But we're not sure. They're still in the trees. In the parking lot. They won't come down."

ALL OF THEM?

"Yes." He stroked her hand and spoke calmly. "Everyone is working on it. The fire department is there. The Humane Society and Animal Control are there. I've been going back and forth."

Isabel let her gaze drift to the ceiling, and then to the window. Sleet drummed the pane, fat droplets of near-hail that coated the black glass. Her eyes welled with tears.

"It will be okay. I promise you," he said. He took a jagged breath and let his forehead rest on the bed rail. "Thank God you're awake. I was terrified . . ."

TAKE ME THERE. PLEASE. IT'S TOO COLD. THEY'LL DIE.

The beeping of her heart monitor sped up.

"Isabel, I can't."

MAKENA IS PREGNANT.

"I know, and I promise I'll make sure she's okay."

WHO DID THIS? WHY?

"Extremists. The bastards claim they 'liberated' the apes. Wait till you see the video statement. Very Al Qaeda. It's all over the Internet." He clenched and unclenched his jaw, his eyes fixed on some point beyond the wall. He suddenly seemed to realize she was watching and softened. "I'm sorry," he said. "I'm just . . ." He looked down and was silent. A moment later, she realized his shoulders were heaving. He was crying.

After a while he collected himself, wiping his eyes with the backs of his hands. "When you're up to it, the police want to talk to you."

She blinked deliberately to indicate assent.

"There's something else you should know. Celia has been taken in for questioning."

Isabel's eyes snapped open. OUR CELIA? ARRESTED?

"No. Not exactly. But she's being held as a 'person of interest.' Apparently she has a background in animal activism. I wish I could say I'm surprised."

Isabel's mind raced back over Celia's time at the lab. Although Isabel had shared several of Peter's concerns over language, she had never doubted Celia's devotion to the bonobos.

NO. THEY'RE WRONG. I DON'T BELIEVE IT.

Peter looked on sadly. Isabel closed her eyes, sending tears down her cheeks.

A silence stretched between them, broken by the patter of hail and all it implied for the tree-bound apes. When she opened her eyes again, Peter was staring at her. He exhaled, and raked a hand through his hair.

SHOW ME.

He nodded reluctantly. "Are you sure?"

YES.

He looked around the room, in the bathroom, and then went into the hall. After a few minutes, he came back with a hand mirror. He stood by the bed, pressing the reflective side against his sweater.

"This is all very fresh—you know that, right? You have the best plastic surgeons in the city. You're going to look fine. You're going to *be* fine."

Isabel stared, waiting.

Peter cleared his throat and positioned the mirror above her. He tilted its flashing surface until a face came into view.

Isabel found herself looking at a complete stranger. The scalp and cheeks were swathed in gauze. The nose was broad and smashed, with an absurd nose diaper taped loosely beneath the oxygen piping to catch the bloody runoff. Its flesh was swollen and blue, with specks of reddish purple. The eyes were slits between swollen pads of flesh and the white of one was scarlet. Trembling fingers appeared beside the face, and these were indisputably hers. The mirror disappeared.

Isabel took a moment to absorb what she'd seen. She looked to Peter for comfort but he was still clenching and unclenching his jaw.

MY HAIR? GONE?

"For now. You have fifty-some stitches in your scalp."

TEETH?

"You lost five, I think. You can get implants. And the stitches, all under the hairline. When it grows back no one will know. Really, it could have been so much worse. You could have been burned."

The clock ticked, the sleet pelted.

DID YOU CALL MY MOTHER?

"I did."

AND?

Peter paused and reached for her hand. He brought her fingertips to his lips. "Oh, sweetheart. I'm so sorry. I really am."

———

The police came by that afternoon, two plainclothes detectives in dripping shell jackets. They stood some distance from the bed as they waited for the ASL interpreter, and were clearly uncomfortable. Isabel remembered the vision in the mirror and understood their reticence.

When the interpreter finally arrived, Isabel shook off her oxy-pulse finger clip and let loose with a flurry of double-handed signs.

The interpreter watched her hands and then spoke. "Are the apes still up in the trees? Have they had any water or food? It's too cold for them. They're delicate. Prone to pneumonia. Flu. One of them is pregnant. Who is with them?"

The detectives exchanged glances. The older of the two asked the interpreter, "Can you please tell her we need her to answer some questions?"

"Speak to her," he replied, cocking his head toward Isabel.

"All right," said the detective. He shifted his reluctant gaze to Isabel, who blinked expectantly. He cleared his throat and practically shouted, leaving a space between words and phrases. *"How many . . . people . . . entered . . . the lab . . . after . . . the explosion?"*

I AM NOT DEAF, she replied. As an afterthought she added, FOUR, MAYBE FIVE.

"Did you recognize any of them?" The cop's brow glistened and his eyes swung between Isabel and the interpreter, clearly unsure about whether to look at the hands that created the words or the mouth that uttered them.

NO. THEY WERE WEARING FACE MASKS.

The other cop spoke: "Is it true that Celia Honeycutt exited the lab immediately before the explosion?"

YES.

"Was she acting strange in any way?"

NO.

"Nervous? On edge?"

NO. NOTHING.

"The people who entered after the explosion—did any of them say anything?"

COULD NOT HEAR. EXPLOSION.

"You didn't hear or see anything—"

COULD NOT BREATHE. COULD NOT HEAR.

"Dr. Benton said an animal rights group usually has a presence right outside the lab. Were any of them in the lab that night?"

DON'T KNOW. FACE MASKS. I ALREADY SAID.

"What do you know about them?"

ALMOST NOTHING. THERE'S A GUY NAMED HARRY, LARRY, OR GARY. MIDDLE-AGED. TALL. WELL-DRESSED. AND A GREEN-HAIRED KID. THERE'S ONE TATTOOED KID AND A FEW WITH DREADLOCKS AND SMELLY PONCHOS. A COUPLE OF PREPPY TYPES. MOSTLY THEY JUST LOOK LIKE STUDENTS.

"Have they ever threatened you?"

NO. THEY WAVE SIGNS WHEN WE DRIVE PAST.

"Have they identified themselves as part of an organization?"

I DON'T KNOW. HAVEN'T SPOKEN TO THEM.

"You've never heard them say anything about the Earth Liberation League?"

NO.

"Did you notice anything strange last night?"

YOU MEAN OTHER THAN BEING BLOWN UP?

The detective scratched his forehead with stubby fingers. "Before that. Did you see or hear anything out of the ordinary?"

NO. BUT THE BONOBOS DID. THEY KNEW SOMEONE WAS OUT THERE. THEY SMELLED SMOKE. ASK THEM WHEN THEY COME DOWN.

"What?" The detective froze with his pen pressed to his pad. "No, never mind," he said. He sighed, put his pad and pen in his shirt pocket, and massaged his temples. "Okay, well, thank you for your time," he said, addressing a portion of wall between Isabel and the balding interpreter. "I hope you feel better soon."

GET THE APES DOWN, said Isabel. AND TALK TO THEM.

She stared resentfully as the police thanked the interpreter and left. She knew they had no intention of speaking with the apes, even though it was clear the apes knew more than anyone. She knew the police thought she was nuts. She had encountered this reaction more times than she could recall, but never, never, had she felt so desperate about it.

———

A nurse brought Isabel's dinner, which consisted of clear liquids. Juice of some sort, and a brown plastic thermos of clear broth with stiff green flakes sprinkled on the surface. The nurse, Beulah, turned to Isabel.

"You're looking much better. Ready for some dinner? I know, it doesn't look like much, but your doctors want us to take it slowly. How about some TV?"

Beulah raised the head of Isabel's bed and flicked on the television. She took a seat by Isabel, dropped the bed rail, and reached for the juice.

"Don't try to lean forward. I'll come to you," she said, guiding the straw to Isabel's lips.

Isabel sucked some apple juice through the straw. It was almost painfully sweet. Her tongue was huge and clumsy, and she was suddenly aware of stitches along its side, poking out like the stiff spines of a caterpillar. It took a couple of tries to coax the liquid down her throat.

"You all right?" asked Beulah, looking momentarily back at Isabel.

Isabel nodded weakly.

"I can't stand the news anymore," said Beulah, reaching for the remote control. "Everything's so depressing. The economy, that oil spill, the war . . ."

Isabel touched Beulah's hand to still it. The scene had just cut to the parking lot of the language lab, with a newscaster standing out in the drizzle. She wore a yellow hooded raincoat, her shoulders hunched against the cold. People crowded around the edges of the parking lot beyond brightly painted barricades.

". . . continuing drama playing out at the Great Ape Language Lab at the University of Kansas. The public is urged to remember that while these apes have a peaceful reputation, they are still wild animals, many times stronger than adult male humans, and capable of inflicting grievous injury, even ripping off limbs . . ."

Isabel's eyes shot open.

The camera panned past the tops of the trees, where the bonobos sat miserable and wet, huddled against the trunk, seeking protection from the wind.

"Many groups have converged in an effort to save the endangered animals, which have been stranded in the treetops since an explosion last night destroyed the building that housed them and critically injured one of the scientists. Today the home of the university president was vandalized. The animal rights extremist group Earth Liberation League has claimed responsibility for the attacks in a video released on the Internet, but the authorities have yet to . . . Oh! My goodness!"

A crack resounded, and the camera swung to a man with a gun on his shoulder and then to the top of a tree. At first, there was nothing. Then one of the bonobos began to sway. Amid screeching and yipping, the others plucked the tranquilizer dart out of his thigh and tossed it to the ground, but it was too late. The stricken bonobo—was it Sam or Mbongo? It was too dark and too distant for Isabel to tell—collapsed and dropped from the ring of hairy black arms that tried to keep him upright. Another crack, another bonobo. This one seemed to split in two midfall, the parts spinning and tumbling through the tree branches. One landed in the center of a piece of round canvas held at its edges by firemen. The other part—Lola, Isabel now realized—hit the frame and bounced back into the air. There was a collective gasp from the crowd and news crew alike as the firemen lunged forward with outstretched arms.

Isabel let out a muffled cry and struggled to get upright. She knocked the juice from the nurse's hand, spilling it across both of them. The insulated brown thermos slid across a puddle of condensation, as if pushed by an invisible hand, the broth sloshing from side to side.

"Stop. You'll hurt yourself! Stop!" said Beulah, and when Isabel did not, she pressed the red call button and held Isabel's wrists and shouted for help, which came pattering down the hall in the form of other uni-formed figures and a syringe that was emptied into the valve on Isabel's intravenous line.

Well, thought Isabel, when she realized what had just happened, *at least they didn't shoot me out of a tree.* The television and its falling bono-bos was clicked off, and shortly thereafter Isabel sank back against the lowered bed, her panicked desperation neutered by the blissful numbing of drugs.

5

John had finally booked his flight for the next morning (inexplicably, all the flights that day were full) and was watching footage of the apes falling from trees when someone started banging on the door. The banging continued with such vehemence that it occurred to him it might be the police. Of course they would wish to speak with him; he had been at the language lab only hours before the explosion. But the vigor and relentlessness of the banging worried him. Surely they didn't consider him a suspect?

When he swung the door open, it all made sense, even though she was supposed to be safely six states away—

"Fran?"

"Where is she?" demanded his mother-in-law, inserting herself between John and the doorway and entering the front hall. Bulging supermarket bags swung from her hands and wrists. John was sure he saw the outline of a box of Velveeta.

"I think she's in the . . ." John's voice trailed off, because Fran was already marching toward the kitchen.

John turned back to the doorway. His father-in-law was climbing the stairs with two suitcases, old-fashioned hard-sided ones without wheels or retractable handles. They had purple ribbons tied around the handles, presumably to tell them apart from all the other pieces of thirty-year-old luggage coming around the carousel.

"Hello, John," said Tim, pausing at the doorway.

"Hello, Tim." John swung his head around toward the raised voices coming from the kitchen. "Did Amanda know you were coming?"

"I don't think so. When Amanda didn't even call to say 'Happy New Year' Fran got it in her head that something was wrong."

John sighed and took the suitcases from the old man. He carried them into the guest room, which was really Amanda's office. It had been in a state of suspended animation since Magnificat's untimely demise, at which point she had been polishing *Recipe for Disaster* and sending query letters to agents. The room looked like a paper mill had exploded. Chunks of her manuscript, marked up in her own hand, littered the bed and were scattered around it. They were mixed in with dozens of rejections: "Hard to market literary fiction . . ."; "Not for me . . ."; "Not taking on new clients at the moment . . ." John picked up a piece of paper that was lying facedown. It was one of Amanda's own query letters, which had been returned to her with the word *NO* scrawled diagonally across it in enormous red letters. He imagined her standing with trembling fingers, ripping open the envelope that she herself had addressed and stamped, hoping that this time, this time, someone had written to say, "Yes, please send the manuscript, I'd love to read it," and instead finding . . . *this*. He let the page fall to the floor. The surge of anger he felt was overwhelming. He'd never felt so impotent.

His mother-in-law's voice sailed in from some other part of the house and John pulled himself together. He couldn't do much—even if the room were neat, it would not be clean enough to please Fran—but he shuffled stacks of paper together and moved them into the closet along with the printer and stepped into the wastepaper basket to squash its contents. As a final touch, he smoothed the bedspread, which still had a fine coating of cat dander.

There was no rescuing Amanda from Fran, and adding his own presence to the mix could only make things worse, so John parked himself in the living room with Tim and the television and a bottle of Bushmills. After a while Fran came through on hands and knees, scrubbing the wall and baseboard, complaining in equal parts about her creaking knees and Amanda's housekeeping. Amanda followed, swabbing half-heartedly with a wad of moistened paper towel. Her deficiencies were grievous: what kind of a woman didn't keep her guest room made up? And why didn't she have shelf paper in the kitchen? Fran promised to furnish some, since it was clear Amanda didn't care, and Lord only knew where that came from, since she, herself, was a meticulous housekeeper. Once, when John was absolutely sure Fran's back was turned, he made a yapping motion with his hand. Amanda responded by holding a finger gun to her own forehead and pulling the trigger.

Through a whiskeyed haze, John endured Velveeta-laced scalloped potatoes, a pile of tasteless green beans, and pork chops dressed in Shake 'n Bake. The Caesar salad, drowning in Kraft dressing, had been carefully denuded of all the crisp white pieces of the romaine, which were John's favorite. Fran herself consumed three quarters of a basket of heat-and-serve dinner rolls, all while continuing to berate Amanda: she needed to take a good, hard look at her life. She wasn't getting any younger, you know. Forty was closer than thirty now, and she still didn't have a career or family to speak of, and while it was fine to have one or the other, Amanda had neither, in case she hadn't noticed. She'd given the book thing a go but now it was time to think of the future. How could she even think of leaving her husband and moving to L.A.? She'd end up being a waitress, that was what, and she was too old to spend that much time on her feet. She did realize that varicose veins ran in the family, didn't she?

John watched with amazement as Amanda blandly "Yes, Mothered" her way through the onslaught.

When Fran got up to clear the table, Amanda stood and calmly gathered plates. Tim Matthews patted his stomach, rose, and toddled off toward the room with the television. God bless him, thought John, following in such a hurry he nearly knocked his chair over.

———

In the privacy of their room, Amanda's inscrutable veneer dropped like a carton of eggs.

"This is unbelievable," she said, flopping onto the bed. "They 'dropped in' from Fort Myers. Who 'drops in' from Fort Myers?"

"Did she say how long they're staying?"

"No." Her voice had an edge of panic.

"My flight leaves first thing in the morning. Will you be okay?"

"I don't know."

"You were brilliant tonight," he said. "How did you do that? Not that she didn't manage to have a fight with you all by herself anyway."

"I tuned her out. Or at least I tried to. It's hard to do. I don't know how long I can keep it up. She—" The strain of whispering was too much. Amanda sat forward with a sudden cough.

John hauled himself up on an elbow and rubbed her back. "You okay?"

"Mm-hmm," she managed. "Just swallowed the wrong way. I'll be fine." She cleared her throat and nestled back against him.

Down the hall, the guest room door creaked open. There were footsteps, moving past the bathroom, and down the stairs, followed by a rattling in the kitchen. It sounded like the cutlery drawer, but that made no sense, unless someone was having a midnight hankering for scalloped potatoes. But no, that could not have been the case, because now, too soon for a plate to have been made, came the unmistakable sound of someone ascending the stairs.

And down the hall.

To their room.

The door crashed open, hitting the wall behind it. John yanked the blankets up to his chin. Amanda let out an "eep" as she struggled to do the same.

Fran stopped at the end of the bed, squinting to make out the figure of her daughter among the shadows. "There you are," she said, coming around to Amanda's side of the bed.

In the near-colorless glare of the moonlight, John saw the flash of a spoon. Amanda sat forward obediently, clutching the covers against her naked body with both hands. Her mother poured cough syrup onto the spoon and Amanda opened her mouth like a baby bird.

"That'll sort you out," Fran said with a nod. She turned on her heel and left the room, closing the door behind her.

John and Amanda lay in stunned silence.

"Did that just happen?" John said.

"I think it did."

John stared at the ceiling. A car drove by; the headlights flashed across the length of their bedroom wall and disappeared.

"Come with me tomorrow," John said. "We'll get you on standby."

Amanda flopped back onto him and adjusted the covers so that only their necks and heads were exposed. "Thank you," she said, clinging to him like a spider monkey and breathing warm eucalyptus across his face. "Because if you leave me here with her, I think I might have to kill her."

The next morning, John lay perfectly still until he heard the sounds of the television downstairs. It was a reliable indicator of when his in-laws began their day.

Amanda was asleep with her arms thrown over her head. Her hair, corkscrew curly, tumbled over her pillow and beyond her pale wrists. It was what had struck him the first time he laid eyes on her, in a hallway at Columbia, standing between him and the sunlight within a glowing halo of curls. It was always out of control, even when secured in its customary knot. She never used elastics; she used chopsticks, pencils, plastic cutlery, and anything else she could poke through it. Very early in their relationship, John had learned to check just what was in there before letting her lay her head on his shoulder so he wouldn't lose an eye. But no matter how tight the knot or how recently done, bits of hair always sprang free.

He leaned over and buried his nose in her hair. He breathed deeply, and then nibbled her collarbone, which gave way to soft curves and heartbreaking dips. God, how he loved her. It had always been Amanda.

For eighteen years, it had been Amanda. He'd never even been with another woman—unless you counted the unfortunate incident with
Ginette Pinegar, which he did not.

"Mmm," Amanda said, swatting him away.

"It's time to go," he whispered.

Her eyes opened wide. She smiled as he pressed a finger to her lips.

With a rerun of *The Price Is Right* as their soundtrack, Amanda piled
folded clothes on the bed while John snuck to the hall closet for a suitcase. Not a word passed between them, but when their eyes met, they sti-
fled giggles. They crept down the stairs and stood by the front door.

"Good-bye! We're leaving!" John called loudly.

Sounds of muffled confusion floated down the hall, followed by fast
footsteps.

Amanda pressed a fist against her mouth to suppress a laugh and
zipped her feet into shiny high-heeled black boots that were very much
the opposite of mukluks. John gazed admiringly, but not for long—
Fran's solid feet slid into view, encased in Isotoner slippers.

"What do you mean, you're leaving?" she said. She stood with arms
akimbo, eyes flashing. "Where are you going?"

"Kansas," said Amanda.

"L.A.," said John at the exact same moment. "House-hunting," he
added. Amanda paused momentarily, then resumed struggling into her
pink belted coat. Large sunglasses already hid her eyes.

Tim ambled down the hall toward them.

"Bye, Tim! Thanks for coming," John called cheerily.

"You're welcome," the old man replied in a baffled tone.

John pulled the door open.

"Wait!" Fran's voice sent chills through John's body. It was a reflex—
her tone demanded obedience. He girded himself and turned to meet
her steely glare. "Yes?"

"Nobody said anything about this last night."

"It was very last minute. No choice. The Realtor was very busy—"

"Very busy," added Amanda. She tied the sash of her coat while trying to remain hidden behind John.

"You only said you were thinking about moving, not that you had
decided. When are you coming back?"

"No idea," said John, ushering Amanda through the door. She headed for the car at a near-run. John followed with the suitcase.

"And what are we supposed to do?" Fran cried from the porch.

"Stay as long as you like," said John. "Good-bye, Fran. Good-bye, Tim!"

"See you at the wedding!" Amanda called over her shoulder. She climbed into the car and slammed the door.

John glanced behind him. Fran was marching down the walkway, a one-woman armada, her bosom an impregnable force resting on a shelf of gut.

By the time John hit the driver's seat, Amanda had pulled down her sunshade and was pretending to search through her purse. "Gun it, baby," she said, without looking up.

John did, screeching backward into the road and then forward and out. Somewhere down the road, as he finally did up his seat belt, he asked Amanda, "What wedding? What are you talking about?"

"My cousin Ariel is getting married in three weeks."

"That's awfully fast."

"It's of the shotgun variety, although officially we don't know that. Are we really going to L.A.?"

"No. We're going to Kansas."

"Oh."

"But after that, you can go to L.A. If that's what you really want."

"Oh God." Amanda dropped her head back and stared out the windshield. They pulled up at a stoplight, and she was silent for the entire red. "Are you sure?" she said when the light finally changed.

"As long as you're really sure this is what you want."

John glanced at her a couple of times, the second time in alarm, because tears were streaming down her face. But when she reached over and laid a hand on the back of his neck, her expression became almost beatific.

"I do. I really, really do. But are you sure you're okay with this?"

"Yes."

They were both reflective for a moment. Then John reached over and patted her thigh. "Yes. I am."

6

John and Amanda's one-hour layover in Cincinnati was extended first by twenty minutes, then by ten, and then by another fifteen, until eventually it stretched to six hours. Weather was the first excuse given, although the sky was perfectly clear. Traffic in O'Hare was blamed next, although John pointed out to the gate attendant that they were not at O'Hare. It did not matter—apparently the logjam of holiday fliers had a domino effect. John was apoplectic: he was now two full days behind in starting his investigation.

As a final insult, Cat had somehow managed to arrive the night before even though John had booked the first available flight. She immediately informed Elizabeth of her coup, copying John on the email: "Here and settled. Will make contacts while awaiting John." She must have flown standby on the red-eye. John had visions of some hapless salesman trussed and gagged in a maintenance closet at the airport, bereft of his boarding pass.

Cat was leaning against the brick wall near the cozy fireplace in the lobby of the Residence Inn when John and Amanda arrived. It was the hotel's "social hour," and Cat was taking advantage of the free wine while emanating waves of unapproachability. It was as though she had an invisible cloaking device: other guests would wander too close and suddenly veer off, looking stunned.

"Cat."

"John."

"You remember Amanda?"

"Of course," Cat said, examining Amanda and offering a limp hand. "So nice to see you again. Do you have family here?" She cocked her head slightly and smiled.

"No," said Amanda.

Cat blinked a few times, inviting Amanda to elaborate. Amanda blinked back.

Cat finally tore her gaze away. "Well, I should let you get checked in," she said, and wandered off in search of a refill.

John sighed. Undoubtedly Elizabeth would know of Amanda's presence by nightfall, and his expense report would be examined accordingly.

After a very quick discussion about whether to invite Cat, they went in search of a reasonably priced place to eat (Elizabeth had made it clear that since the hotel rooms had kitchenettes, the paper wouldn't cover restaurant meals).

"So," Amanda declared over margaritas and wings, "do you know what my mother said to me last night?"

John sawed his overdone steak. "That I'm a no-good lout and you should leave me?"

"Quite the contrary. She told me I should get on with it because my eggs are getting past their sell-by date. Can you believe that?"

"Yes. Absolutely."

Amanda's eyes widened. *"What?"*

John recognized his mistake instantly. "No," he said emphatically. "No, of course not. I mean I believe your mother said that. She would, wouldn't she?"

Amanda sighed in agreement and reached into the basket of wings. She extracted one, holding it between two fingers like a miniature corn-cob. She surveyed it carefully and then took a bite.

"So you don't think they are?"

"What, your eggs? No, I don't."

She chewed for a second, looked far away, and dragged her glass toward her. It was absurdly huge, the size of a fishbowl. She ran the tiny red straw around and through the ice cubes. "When we have kids, do you suppose I'll turn into my mother?"

"You could never turn into your mother," he said through a mouthful of steak. "Your mother is a horror. Your mother is Godzilla. And you, my dear, are perfection." He pointed at her with his fork. It was the kind of establishment where you could do that.

"But they say that, don't they? About women turning into their mothers?" She slurped the last of her margarita, and, after looking furtively to each side, let her tongue dart out to the salted rim. "God, I hope I don't." She swirled the straw again.

"You won't."

"I think I want one," she said. "A baby."

John watched her carefully. She had barbecue smudges on both sides of her mouth. Was this a temporary confluence of Fran and tequila, or was she serious? The topic had come up periodically over the years, usually after Amanda had been to a baby shower or family gathering. So far, to John's relief, the subject had faded away again fairly quickly. Babies appeared to be a lot of work, and he was worried that having one might change things between him and Amanda. Also, a baby would almost certainly mean a whole lot more Fran in his life, not to mention his own mother.

"Do you think it's a good idea if you're about to move across the country?" he said cautiously.

"By the time it happens, either I'll be back in Philly or you'll be in L.A. Besides, what if my mother is right? What if we've been avoiding it for all these years and it turns out we've waited too long?"

"Women are having babies into their sixties these days."

"Yeah, *freakish* women." After a pause, she added, "I don't want to be one of them. I don't want to be an old mother."

John reached across the table and took her hand.

It was true they were both thirty-six. He certainly didn't feel thirty-six. How and when had that happened?

"This is Cat. Leave a message."

"Me again," said John. "Call me."

This was the third message John had left, and while he was trying to give her the benefit of the doubt—perhaps she was in the shower, or had left her cell phone in her room while grabbing breakfast—an uneasy feeling spread through him. They were already two days behind; or at least he was. Who knew what Cat had been up to?

Amanda had risen early, declared the hotel's coffee undrinkable and their pastries concrete, and left on foot for a nearby grocery. She was distracted and agitated, and John felt responsible because he'd flopped and turned through most of the night.

John called down to the front desk and asked to be connected to Cat's room phone.

"Hey, Cat. I think maybe your cell is dead. Call me. We need to get together and figure out our plan of attack."

John called the university and was informed that there would be absolutely no individual interviews. They were holding a press conference later in the morning, their first since the attacks, and would be issuing no statements until then. John found the delay odd, since reporters had been staked out for days.

John then called the hospital, which first asked him if he was a family member, and then refused to confirm or deny Isabel Duncan's presence. He didn't argue, although he knew she was there: it was the only Level 1 trauma center in the vicinity, and if she wasn't there, why ask if he was family? He then left a voice mail at her home number.

"Hi, Isabel. This is John Thigpen. We met . . . uh, well, I'm sure you remember."

He blathered on a little longer than he should have, but he wanted to convey that he really was concerned with how she was and was not just angling for an interview. And it was true: his fractured sleep had been haunted by images of her. He was waiting for her in the hallway of the lab. She came up behind him, silently, and brushed his hand with hers. "Come with me," she whispered, and his whole body tingled. Her lips almost touched his ear. Her breath was like lemon sherbet. Then he was following her, watching her hips and how she placed one foot exactly in front of the other, like an Indian tracker. He caught sight of flitting shadows and stopped dead. And then, in an instant, he knew exactly what was going to happen and cried a warning. He leapt for her, arms outstretched. She turned to him, face forming a question, but before she could say a word she was blown backward and up into a wall of heat so white it was as though she had fallen into the sun. She disappeared in stages: her rounded back went first, followed by face, thighs, and arms. Her long hair, blown forward around her head, went next, then her hands and feet. John woke shaking and drenched in sweat, his heart pounding. He was disoriented: it took him a few seconds to figure out he was not in his own bed. Amanda leaned over him, placing her hand on his chest.

"Christ, baby—are you okay? Your heart is racing like a gerbil's."

"I'm fine. I just had a bad dream."

She switched on the lamp.

"Gah!" he said, shielding his eyes.

She felt his forehead and studied him intensely.

"I'm not having a heart attack. Really."

She turned the light off and lay back down. "What was it?"

"What?"

"The dream."

He shook his head. "Too weird to explain."

John lay awake, eyes open with worry. Had he shouted Isabel's name? Probably not, since Amanda curled up behind him and stroked his shoulder until he went back to sleep. But by morning he was less sure.

John realized he was staring at the radiator. He shook the cobwebs from his brain and dialed Cat again. This time, he didn't bother leaving a message because if he had, it wouldn't have been a nice one. If she didn't respond in ten minutes, he was going to strike out on his own. If they duplicated their efforts, it would not be his fault.

He sipped the coffee Amanda had gotten from the lobby (she was right—it was truly terrible) and booted up his computer. He typed the search string "Earth Liberation League University of Kansas lab" into his browser, hit Enter, and watched with amazement as the results loaded.

There were thirty-two pages of Google hits. The video message had gone viral, showing up on sites as diverse as YouTube, personal blogs, and animal-activism message boards. John had seen it several times before, but it still filled him with fascinated horror.

A man in a black balaclava sat at a metal desk in a room without windows or adornment. The walls were white-painted concrete bricks. His hands were gloved and rested on the desk's surface. The grainy footage was overcast with olive and yellow, like a home video from the 1970s.

He referred to a piece of paper that lay flat beneath his hands, appearing to read it all the way through. Then he addressed the camera. He started by naming the "agents of horror": Peter Benton, Isabel Duncan, a few other people associated with the language lab, and Thomas Bradshaw, who was the president of the university. The man recited their home addresses, complete with telephone numbers and ZIP codes.

"You are all equally despicable and equally guilty, those of you who administered the torture, and those of you who made it possible, sitting so comfortably in your offices miles away from that depraved lab, where your mad scientists performed perverted research on innocent and unconsenting primates. We will no longer allow it. You will be held accountable, as was Isabel Duncan. Your addresses are now public. Who knows what someone will decide to do? Thomas Bradshaw, this time we flooded your home, but what's next? A firebomb, perhaps? Maybe your family will be inside, as trapped and innocent as those apes you tortured in the name of science. Or maybe something will happen to your car. You won't know until you're driving it, and then it will be too late. What will you say to your children then, Thomas Bradshaw? You'll finally be as helpless as the apes you've imprisoned in that sick and evil lab for all these years."

The man consulted the paper again. When he raised his face to the camera, there were traces of a hard smile through the mouth hole in his ski mask.

"For now, the research has stopped. We made it stop, but it's up to you to keep it stopped. Because now you know what will happen if you don't. We will liberate the apes again, and again, and again, and we will come after you—personally, each and every one of you—again, and again, and again. We don't back down. We are the ELL. We are everywhere, and we don't give up. Expect us."

The picture froze. John stared at the final image for several seconds before realizing he was gaping.

Torture? Mad scientists? Unconsenting apes? Even from John's short visit it was clear that everyone associated with the lab went to great lengths to ensure that the bonobos had as much control over their surroundings as possible. The entire premise of the project was that the apes were communicating because they wanted to. Was it possible that these people—these terrorists—had bombed the building simply because the project contained the word "lab"? Would all of this have been avoided had it been called the Great Ape Language *Project* instead?

How badly hurt was Isabel? He wondered if he closed his eyes and concentrated hard enough whether he'd get some kind of telepathic feeling. He tried. It didn't work. And then he felt guilty.

John drained his coffee, and grimaced when he sucked in a mouthful of grinds. He held his head sideways under the tap in the kitchenette, swishing his mouth with water. Then he set out for the university. The hell with Cat.

7

Isabel spent the day waiting: for orderlies to wheel her from place to place, for tests and procedures, for doctors and consultations. Most of all she waited for Peter and news of the apes.

Were they hurt? Dehydrated? Where were they being housed? The televisions in various waiting rooms showed repeats of the other night's footage along with a terrifying clip of the video that had been released on the Internet. The clip was very short, and always shown over the shoulder of an anchorperson. The lips behind the balaclava moved, but Isabel could not hear what they said.

She was devastated at the thought that Celia was involved. Although wary of her own reaction to human beings, Isabel trusted the bonobos implicitly, and they adored Celia. After her first day at the lab, Bonzi had signed, CELIA LOVE! BUILD NEST. HURRY CELIA COME BONZI LOVE.

As the day wore on, another, more primal longing crept up beside Isabel's desperate loneliness. It was an irrational, wrenching desire, since Peter had all but said her mother wasn't coming. Isabel had been meting out her family history in digestible bites, although, since they intended to marry, she knew she eventually had to disclose exactly what lurked in her gene pool. So far, he knew about her father's exit and her mother's decline into alcoholism, and also that the two events might not have happened in that order. He knew about the welfare fraud. He knew that her brother had been expelled from school by fifteen, and had also been carried off on the current of addiction; Isabel didn't know if he was alive or dead. He knew something of Isabel's tortured school years, and that none of her nascent friendships had survived the first bloom because when the parents of the other children saw the state of her house, no further visits were allowed. He knew generally about the schoolyard taunts because of thrift store clothes and bizarre lunches, but he didn't know specifically about the canned corn sandwich and how it had prompted Mrs. Butson to start sending an extra lunch each day with Michele, or how that misguided act of kindness had cemented Isabel's status as a pariah. He did not know about the day Marilyn Cho leapt around behind Isabel in the playground, mocking her silently and with cruel precision, unaware that Isabel could see every movement in the shadow on the pavement in front of her. And he certainly did not know about the "uncles," or how her mother would race for the powder room to apply a pucker of pink lipstick and shoo the children into the basement as though each rendezvous were some kind of fun secret. He didn't know that Isabel watched *The Muppet Show* and after-school specials with her brother while trying to ignore what was happening upstairs, or that after the man left, her mother would disappear into the bathroom for prolonged periods to weep.

And yet Isabel could not help imagining that her mother was on her way right now, that she had somehow found the strength to pull herself together and was going to walk through the door at any moment. She would fold Isabel in her arms as though she were a little girl and tell her that she was sorry, so sorry. She'd gotten help and things would be different from now on, and everything was going to be okay. And Isabel would believe her, because what was the alternative? To believe that she was lying alone in a hospital bed without a single family member or friend to sit with her?

In the afternoon, Beulah poked her head through the door, beaming. "You have a visitor," she said.

Tears sprang to Isabel's eyes. She had come.

"It's your sister," Beulah continued.

Isabel's eyes snapped open.

Cat Douglas strode through the door. "Dr. Duncan, nice to see you again. How are . . ." She stopped. Her eyes widened. "Wow." She pulled a digital camera out of her pocket, snapped a shot, and palmed it again.

Isabel let out a cry and lurched forward, hands seeking the pad and pen she'd been using to communicate with the nurses. She accidentally knocked the pen to the tiled floor, then threw the pad overhand at Cat. Its pages flapped and separated and it dropped to the ground like a crumpled fledgling.

Realization, and then horror, crossed Beulah's face. She spun to Cat. "You said you were her *sister*," she hissed. "How dare you? Get out of here!"

Cat leaned forward at the waist, scanning Isabel's face. "That's some serious hardware. Can you even speak with all that?"

Peter's voice boomed from behind them. "Who the hell are you?"

Isabel signed frantically with both hands: GET HER OUT OF HERE, GET HER OUT, GET HER OUT. Tears streamed down her face.

Peter grabbed Cat's upper arm and swung her toward him.

"Get your hands off me!" Cat shrieked. "That's assault!"

Peter pulled her close and put his mouth against her ear. "So sue me," he said. His eyes were glinting, his smile hard. She raised her chin and stared right back. He shoved her, hard enough that she stumbled, but because of his grip on her arm she remained upright. "Call the police," he said to Beulah.

"Fine. Fine, I'll go," said Cat. She took a moment to compose herself and lowered her gaze to look at the fingers encircling her arm. Her eyelids flickered as she registered the missing joints of his first finger.

"Damned right you will," said Peter. "Come on." He yanked her toward the door.

8

Half a dozen news crews were waiting outside the university's administrative offices, along with a handful of reporters. John knew several of them. One was a classmate from Columbia who had married a homely girl with old money and a summer home in the Hamptons. He had subsequently landed a job at *The New York Times*. Philip Underwood. He'd been present the night of the Ginette Pinegar incident, had held John's legs toward the ceiling while someone else held the funnel to his mouth. It was all so fuzzy, and it was never going to get any clearer. After all these years, John was still so embarrassed he didn't want to face anyone who had witnessed it. Another familiar face was an old-timer John had worked with at the *New York Gazette*, a man known for writing warning messages on masking tape and affixing them to his lunches in the communal refrigerator in case anyone was thinking of stealing them, as well as for peppering his speech with outdated terms such as "burying the lede" and "nut grafs." He was gaunt yet paunchy, and gray in all respects—hair, clothes, complexion. A few years ago he'd gone through a divorce that had sucked the life, color, and possibly a decade right out of him. He was wearing a battered trench coat, his shoulders rounded against the wind.

John came up beside him. "Hey, Cecil."

Cecil glanced over at John, took one last drag from a cigarette, and flicked it to the ground. It rolled away from him, the end still glowing. He rubbed his reddened hands together and blew on them. "Hey, John."

"Hope you have a sweater on under that," said John.

"Nope." Cecil shrugged and stared straight ahead. "So, still with the *Inky*?"

"Yup. Still with the *Gazette*?"

"Yup."

The banter that followed was as ritualized as a mating dance—each of them trying to figure out what the other knew without giving anything away himself.

Eventually Cecil dug his hands in his pockets and rocked back on his heels. "You've got nothing, do you?"

John shook his head. "Nope. You?"

"Not a thing."

They nodded slowly, in commiseration. John saw no reason for Cecil to know that he'd met Isabel and the apes on the day of the explosion, and he wondered what Cecil was keeping from him.

There was a buzz of excitement, and the building's double glass doors were pushed open by two large men. A petite woman in business attire and towering heels made her way down the stairs to the standing microphone. The men came down and flanked her.

She pushed her glasses up her nose and smoothed her hair. Her manicured hands shivered in the cold. "Thank you for coming," she said, looking around.

News crews jostled to get their overhead microphones into place, and reporters began shouting questions:

"Was the Bradshaw family home at the time of the attack?"

"How is Isabel Duncan?"

"Were the apes injured?"

"Has anyone been arrested?"

The woman scanned the faces in front of her. Flashes from the cameras reflected off her glasses in bursts. Fuzzy black microphone cozies surrounded her face like monster caterpillars suspended from the sky. She closed her eyes for a moment and drew a breath.

"The police are holding several persons of interest, although they are not being described as suspects at this time. We are also told that as of this morning Isabel Duncan's condition has been upgraded to stable, and her doctors are hopeful that she will make a full recovery. The home of the university president was vandalized in connection with this incident, and although he and his family are safe, the Earth Liberation League is designated by the FBI as one of the foremost domestic terrorist groups, and therefore any and all threats are being taken extremely seriously. The apes are uninjured, but, for their own safety, have been transferred to another location."

She was interrupted by another volley.

"Who are the persons of interest?"

"What type of facility are the apes in?"

"Are they still on campus?"

She lifted a hand to silence them. "I'm sorry, but I cannot provide specific answers to those questions. We have every confidence that the perpetrators will be found and prosecuted to the fullest extent of the law, and we encourage anyone with any knowledge of the incident to speak to the authorities. In the meantime, we have done—and are continuing to do—everything in our power to ensure the safety of our students and faculty. Thank you."

She squared up the edges of her note cards and kept her gaze turned downward. Clearly, she was preparing to leave. The shouts grew louder.

"The Bradshaw flooding happened almost twenty-four hours after the bombing—what actions has the university taken to prevent further attacks?"

After a moment, she put her hand on the standing microphone and said, "We have taken definitive measures to ensure that nothing like this will ever happen again. Please direct any further inquiries to the press office. Thank you." She turned and wobbled her way back up the stone steps.

"Isn't *she* the freaking press office?" muttered Cecil.

From there, John went to the lab. A couple of bored-looking policemen walked the perimeter, keeping an eye on photographers and making sure they didn't duck under the reams of yellow tape (where was Osgood, anyway? John guessed Elizabeth had decided to run Associated Press photographs to avoid paying his airfare).

John had thought he was prepared for the sight of the lab, but actually seeing it was like taking a cannonball to the gut. Three days ago he had climbed those steps and held that handrail. It had been painted bluish gray; it was now blistered and dark. He had followed Isabel Duncan through that doorway and been allowed into the rooms that housed the apes. The door was gone, its absence a gaping hole in an epicenter of black, the exterior wall scorched with angry spikes. He could see only a few feet into the hallway, but insulation and wiring hung from sooty ceiling panels, and the sickly scent of burned plastic lingered.

John cast his eyes over the parking lot: here, where John, Cat, and Osgood had climbed into the cab, the pebbles were littered with shards of glass. It was almost certainly here, too, that an ambulance had received Isabel Duncan. And here, beneath the tree where the apes had sought refuge, broken branches lay like an enormous and messy bird's nest, evidence of the bonobos' failed struggle to stay at the top. John turned away in a fruitless attempt to stop the mental image of their unconscious bodies dropping into the night.

Next he drove to Lawrence City Animal Control, a one-story building with rows of chain-link dog runs extending from the back end. The cinder-block walls of the reception area were painted green, and, from the smell of it, the linoleum floors had been recently bleached. An operatic canine howl came from behind the swinging door leading to the back.

"Sounds like a Wookiee," said John.

"He just came in," said the woman behind the desk. "He's not very happy. Better off here than where he was, though."

"My name is John Thigpen, and I'm with *The Philadelphia Inquirer.* I was wondering if—"

She held a hand up to stop him. "The apes aren't here."

"Were they?"

She eyed him, sizing him up, then spoke. "Briefly. A truck rolled up in the dead of night, the guys tranq'ed them, and off they went."

"They shot them again?"

"They said it was the only way. It's not like we have crush cages here. Mostly we get dogs and cats. The craziest thing we've ever had before this was an alligator. Some guy bought a hatchling in Florida and next thing he knew it was seven feet long and he was throwing turkey legs down the basement stairs and aiming a hose at various kiddie pools he'd tossed down there. That worked fine until his furnace broke and he needed a repairman."

John stared at her, wide-eyed. Then he shook his head. "The apes—were you here when they were taken away?"

"Yup. We're short-staffed. A bunch of our volunteers got picked up in that sweep yesterday. One of them is an intern at the lab."

John perked up. "Really? Can I have his number?"

"*Her* number. Since it's all over the Internet anyway, I can't see why not. I think she's still in custody, though." She pulled a book from a drawer and flipped through its pages before copying a name and number onto a scrap of paper. She slid it across the counter at John.

Celia Honeycutt. She had been named in the ELL video, which John found odd, given that she was apparently under suspicion. Had the ELL included her in an attempt to cover their tracks? He folded the paper and put it in his pocket. "Do you know why they picked her up?"

"No idea. What time is it, anyway?" She looked at her watch and gave a despairing sigh. "Oh God, I've been here sixteen hours."

"Who took the apes?"

She shook her head. "No clue. They even covered the truck's license plate. All I know is they had deeds of sale, so I had to hand them over."

"What?" Then, as realization hit, John closed his eyes. He suddenly understood the university's statement that they had taken steps to ensure that this would never happen again. He wondered if Isabel knew yet, and experienced a physical pang at the thought.

Family, she had said.

He leaned on the counter and rested his forehead on his arm. "Tell me you saw the buyer's name on the deed."

"It was a corporation number."

"Tell me you kept a copy."

"You don't seem to get it—I was here alone. I had six *apes* in the back, as well as all the other animals. Those guys had a lawyer with them as well as a rep from the university. What could I do? They owned them." She fell silent for a moment, then added, "Do you know, sometimes when I was at Starbucks, Celia or someone else from the lab would come in and order skinny lattes for the apes. They always brought a video camera. Apparently the apes liked to watch afterward. The people behind the counter always spoke to the camera like the apes were right there. I always thought that was kind of cool. Supposedly they understand English."

"They do. I've met them," John said quietly, lifting his head. He sighed and knocked his knuckles on the counter a couple of times. "Okay. Well. Thank you, you've been very helpful."

John called Celia Honeycutt from the car, but, as he expected, there was no answer. When he got back to the hotel, he could smell Amanda's handiwork from the lobby.

The door to their suite opened directly onto the tiny kitchen area, where an enormous pot bubbled furiously on one of the electric coils. Amanda stood at the counter meticulously removing the topmost epidermis of mushroom caps. The rest of the counter was obscured by celery leaves, onion skins, chicken carcasses, cans of stock, wine bottles, shreds of cheesecloth, scraps from leeks, and bunches of flat parsley.

He kissed the back of her neck. "What's this?"

"It's chicken pot pie filling. I figured if there's no crust you can just call it soup."

"Okay." After a moment he added, "But the crust is my favorite part."

"I can make crust. It's just there aren't any pie tins here, or even a rolling pin." Her eyes scanned the counter. "I guess I can soak the label off a wine bottle and use that to roll it out. The grocery probably has foil pie tins."

John picked up a square plastic food container from a large stack by the fridge and examined it.

Amanda glanced over. "I got those because they're dinner-size and I figured you could just grab one out of the freezer and nuke it"—John's heart sank because he instantly registered that she was talking in the singular—"and I made beef bourguignon as well so you'd have a little variety. There's egg noodles in the cupboard, or you could boil potatoes to go with it. And I got some of those steam-in-the-bag veggies. You don't even have to pierce the bag. Just pop them in the microwave." She piled the mushroom caps onto one end of a cutting board, moved them one at a time to the center, and deftly quartered them. When she was finished, she scooped them into the pot, set the lid on it, and turned the burner to its lowest setting.

"There," she said, wiping her hands on her thighs. Her face was flushed. Wisps of curly hair stuck to her forehead and temples. "Want a glass of wine? I opened a decent red for the beef."

"You're beautiful," John said.

She smiled, wiped her hair from her face, and picked up the bottle. "I'll take that as a yes?"

They walked the ten feet to the so-called living room and settled on the couch. Amanda tucked her feet beneath her and nestled into John's armpit. "You're really okay with this? With me going to L.A.?"

"I am."

"Because I reserved a flight for tomorrow morning."

"Wow. That's . . . fast."

"Yes." She shot him a nervous look. "It's just that if I am going to do this I have to do it right away, and it didn't make any sense to fly all the way back to Philly first because it's in the opposite direction, and even though we'll lose the return portion of this last flight it's still cheaper to—"

John pulled her to him and buried his nose in the top of her head. She smelled of burgundy and all things good. He kissed her. "It's okay. Really, it is."

She smiled, took a deep breath, and looked up at him. "So, how was your day?"

"You know what?" John said, "There's a hot tub downstairs. Let's discuss it there. Then I've either got to find Cat or file a report on my own."

Amanda glanced over at her simmering pot, had a visible, fleeting moment of doubt, then vanished into the bedroom to change.

———

John was holding the glass door to the pool enclosure open for Amanda when he caught sight of the back of Cat's head. She was alone in the hot tub, resting with her arms stretched out on the rim. Amanda looked back at John and whispered, "Speak of the devil."

John gritted his teeth and stared straight ahead. "Indeed."

While Amanda got towels, John stood by the edge of the hot tub and gazed down at Cat. Her head was resting on the rim, her eyes closed, and the sides of her neatly angled dark brown bob hung slightly above the tiles. She looked either dead or asleep. John cocked his head, considering. If he hadn't known her, he might have found her attractive—the sharp collarbone, the defined upper arms and chiseled fingers, the tidy little nose. But he did know her, so that was that.

John turned to survey the room. In the pool beyond the hot tub, three families' worth of kids splashed and shrieked in preternaturally blue water. Their parents lounged poolside, the fathers slouching forward in dry swim trunks, scowling at their BlackBerries and occasionally sipping beer from cans. The mothers reclined on towels in equally dry bathing suits, knees slightly bent and arms flung overhead, as though sunbathing. One of them was reading a glossy tabloid—the *Weekly Times*—and had a bendy straw in her plastic wineglass so that she didn't have to lift her head to take a sip. Paintings of palm trees and sandy beaches adorned the concrete walls, peeling slightly beside the air vents. Oversized ice cube trays of artificial light flickered overhead.

Amanda returned with a stack of white towels, set them on a nearby table, and caught John's eye to make sure he was looking. She ran her gaze dramatically up the sun umbrella that sprouted from the table's center and laughed. Then she peeled off her coverup.

Two of the three fathers with cell phones lifted their heads, noses crinkled like bloodhounds'. Within a split second, Amanda was locked in a collective tractor beam. As she approached the hot tub, one of the men banged his knee against the leg of the third, oblivious one, alerting him to the situation.

In your dreams, thought John, and his sudden and irrational rage caught him off-guard. Men had always looked at Amanda, everywhere, and until this moment, John had kind of liked it.

Amanda descended the stairs of the hot tub. When her thighs were underwater, she mouthed the words "Hot! Hot!" before pushing off and submersing herself to the shoulders. She took a seat along the edge, let out a deep breath, and looked expectantly at John.

"You coming?"

John threw a last fierce look at the middle-aged dads. Now that Amanda's body had disappeared into the well of the hot tub, they were back to emailing and ignoring their wives and children.

John followed Amanda into the steaming, swirling water and sat next to Cat. "So," he said, "where were you today?"

Cat lifted her head and opened one eye with great suspicion. "Oh. It's you," she said, laying her head back down.

"You didn't answer any of my calls."

"Phone was dead. Sorry."

"We're supposed to be working together."

"I said sorry."

"Well, plug it in, for Christ's sake!"

"I will," she said, sounding irked. She stirred the water with the fingertips of one hand. "Of course."

A new game began in the pool behind them, and the children's voices echoed off the concrete.

"Marco!"

"POLO!"

"Marco!"

"POLO!"

There was the slap-slap-slap of wet feet on concrete, followed by a child's plaintive cry, "No fair! Fish out of water!"

"Oh, Jesus," Cat said, sitting forward angrily. She cupped her hands around her mouth, yelling toward the parents. "Could they *be* any noisier?" She fell back and once again let her head loll on the rim. "Their spawn will be in here before you know it, splashing and peeing, and the parents won't do a thing about it. Oh, great," she said, rolling her eyes as another family with young children entered the room. "Here." She flicked the backs of her hands at John and Amanda. "Spread out so we take up all the space."

"They're just having fun," Amanda said, although she scootched in the direction Cat indicated.

John stayed put and settled himself against a jet. "So," he said, lifting his arm and resting it on the edge, "what *did* you do today?"

Cat shrugged. "I interviewed Peter Benton and saw Isabel Duncan. What did you do?"

John sat forward and glanced quickly at Amanda. "You saw Isabel?"

"Yes."

"How is she?"

"Extremely grumpy. And her jaw is wired so I didn't get much out of it. Except, of course, an introduction to Peter."

"How did you get in?"

Cat waved a hand dismissively. "Psh, it was easy."

John stared at her as it dawned on him. "Oh, no, you did *not*."

"Of course I did. How else was I going to get in?"

A round-bellied toddler blasted past, squealing in joy, pursued closely by her father.

"Is that a swim diaper?" Cat said, screwing up her face. "Those things aren't even waterproof. What's the point?"

"I think she's adorable," said Amanda. "Did you see the daisies on her bathing suit?"

John shot her an alarmed look.

"So what did Benton have to say?" he said, tearing his eyes away from Amanda, whose face had turned to follow the baby's trajectory.

"I think academics need to get out into the sun more. They're a surly lot."

"So you didn't get anything out of him."

Cat shrugged. "I asked him about his missing finger—I mean, it's not like he's trying to hide it or anything—and he went totally berserk on me. There's obviously a story there."

John sighed and rubbed his forehead. "Okay. Look. We have to cobble together some kind of report. Want to do it now or after dinner?"

"Already done."

"What?"

"It's already done. I sent it an hour ago. Relax."

John sat forward angrily. "You just assumed I'd get nothing?"

"Did you?"

"The university sold the apes. Did you know that?"

Cat's brow creased.

"And one of the lab interns is in custody. Did you know that?"

Cat looked at him, irritated, then turned away. "I'll send an amendment."

"No," John said firmly. "I will send the amendment. I assume you copied me on the original?"

Cat began stirring the water again, watching her own fingers. "I'll forward it to you."

John stared in disbelief. This was so entirely unacceptable he couldn't form a response. Was his byline even on it?

An elderly man appeared at the edge of the hot tub. "Got room for another?" he asked.

Amanda slid over.

He climbed down the first two steps, glanced around at the three of them, and winked at John. "Looks like you've got your hands full. Want me to take one off your hands?"

"Be my guest," said John, tipping his chin toward Cat.

Cat turned her head slowly and fixed the man with a look so withering, so devastating, that he backed up the steps and went to sit on a lounge chair instead.

"Perv," said Cat.

"I think he was just trying to be friendly," said Amanda.

"And I think you just like everybody," said Cat.

"Well, *almost* everybody," Amanda said archly. She wiped her face and stood. Water slid from her hips and dripped back into the steaming hot tub. "I'm going back to the room." As she ascended the steps, John looked in alarm at the collection of dads, who were once again staring openly.

John leapt upright, leaving chop and angry whirlpools in his wake. He took the steps two at a time, grabbed the nearest towel, and wrapped it around Amanda.

"Oh, thanks, baby," she said. She fixed the towel, picked up her coverup, and headed for the door.

John followed. As he pulled the door open, he looked back at the men, who were still staring. He pointed first at her and then at his wedding band, and mouthed the word "Mine."

———

They made love that night in a way that left John gasping and quivering. He'd felt like an animal, desperate with need, desperate to lay claim, and she had responded in kind.

Until tonight, John had felt a sense of pride that other men found his wife attractive. Tonight, he had wanted to kill them. He had never been as keenly aware of their real intent. Married men, men with children, men whose wives and children were *right there*. How could he let her go to L.A. without him?

Yet there was something that frightened him even more, something that was so terrifying he didn't even want to think about it. John considered himself as faithful and devoted as they came. There was nothing he wouldn't do for Amanda. If she needed his liver, she could have it. An eyeball? Hers. And yet right now, with his beautiful, perfect, coveted wife lying naked beside him, he couldn't keep his thoughts from drifting across the city toward Isabel Duncan.

9

Bonzi crouched in a dark corner with Lola clinging to her chest. She was the first to hear the jingling of keys and screeched a warning to the rest of her family: the men were back.

The fluorescent lights flickered spasmodically and then finally buzzed to life.

In the cage opposite Bonzi and Lola, Sam screamed, *"Whah!"* and sprinted around the small confines of his cell. He stopped to sign, BAD VISITOR! BAD VISITOR! then leapt onto the front of his extruded metal cage and shook it violently with hands and feet. When he jumped backward, his right thumb was bleeding. Oblivious to the wound, he perched near the front of his cage, his hair bristled and head cocked, on full alert. The other bonobos sat waiting, watching.

Human footsteps followed, heavy-soled steps that echoed in the concrete hallway. As they approached, panic flooded Bonzi's body. She could never see them until they were immediately outside her space.

Jelani, Sam, and Makena were in cages across the aisle from Bonzi, so she could see all of them and they could see her, but they could not see each other because the walls between them were concrete. Nobody could see Mbongo, but they knew he was there. He was the only member of the family out of sight of all the others, and the strain of this situation was clear in his vocalizations.

The clomping got louder until the men came into sight. There were two this time. Bonzi recognized only one—he was the food giver, coming through the halls twice a day to slide trays of tasteless, homogenous pellets through the slots in their cages and refill their water with a hose. He never made eye contact. He never spoke to them, but was always in deep, angry conversation with some invisible other.

The second man was new. He had light hair, gray eyes, and a crooked, joyless smile. "These look like chimps," he said.

"You're the one who wanted them," the food man said with a guffaw.

The stranger turned his gaze on him.

"I'm just saying," said the food man, lowering his eyes, "we could have got chimps a lot cheaper."

The alpha male, having asserted himself, stood with hands on hips and did what Bonzi could not: he moved his eyes across her family members and evaluated them.

"Are they eating and whatnot?" he said.

"They appear to be."

PEARS, signed Bonzi. GOOD PEARS. BRING PEARS.

"Because I want them to look healthy. They can't appear to be mistreated." The alpha male crouched down outside Bonzi's cage and looked her straight in the eyes. "Which one is this? Is this the matriarch?"

ME BONZI, BONZI ME, she signed. GIMME PEARS. EGGS. GOOD EGGS. SAM HURT.

"What the hell is that? Is that some kind of monkey voodoo? It's creeping me out," said the food man, averting his eyes.

Bonzi held the alpha male's gaze and raised her left hand in a fist, which she flicked off her ear. Then she bounced her pointed index fingers off each other in front of her chest.

"Shut up, Ray. She's trying to tell us something."

SAM HURT, repeated Bonzi, more urgently. SAM HURT. NEED GOOD PEARS.

"What the hell is she doing?" said the nondominant.

The alpha continued to watch Bonzi, who repeated her assertions in ever more urgent motions. "She's saying something."

"What?"

"I don't know."

BONZI OUT KEY GIMME HURRY YOU.

The nondominant's voice rose. "I don't like it. It's not right. Are these things even natural? Are they genetically engineered or something? Anyway, aren't they supposed to have sex all the time? They haven't done it once since they got here."

"They're caged separately, you imbecile."

The food man shifted from foot to foot, looking uncomfortably up and down the hall.

"But you wait," said the alpha. "This is going to revolutionize everything." He leaned closer to the cage. "Are you my girl?" he whispered.

Bonzi, whose response for no was simply not to respond, remained still.

"You're my girl, aren't you?" he repeated. His voice was a hiss of rank breath between his teeth.

Bonzi stayed motionless.

"I'm going to move you soon."

He rose and addressed the other man. "Come on. Let's go."

On his way past, he double-whacked the front of Sam's cage with an open palm. The clash reverberated through the cement hall, and Sam shrank into a corner.

10

Amanda had brought so few clothes to Kansas that when she split her things out from John's they all fit into her backpack.

"I don't suppose you'll be going back to Philly anytime soon?" she asked ruefully, as she rolled up her fourth and final shirt.

"I don't know," John said. "It depends entirely on what happens with the story."

"I wasn't thinking about clothes when I decided to leave from here." She zipped the backpack and stood staring at it. "I guess I could ask your mom to put some things together, although I really don't like the idea of her rummaging through my underwear drawer."

John snorted. "Better than *your* mom."

She slapped his chest. "Ha! True, that."

John checked his watch. "Well, I guess it's time."

They grew quiet as they approached the airport, and quieter still when they parked the rental car. By the time they got into the security line, it had been minutes since either of them had said a word. They held hands, shuffling closer and closer to the point where they would have to part. Amanda suddenly swung around and pressed herself against John's chest. He cupped her face in his hands and raised it to his. He could see that she was trying not to cry.

John wiped her eyes with his thumbs. "Are you sure you'll be okay?"

She sniffed and nodded. "Uh-huh," she said, too brightly. "I'll be fine." She dug a tissue from her purse and blew her nose. "We're not going to see each other every weekend, are we?"

John hesitated, and then shook his head. He would have given anything to provide a different response, but he had spent much of the previous night awake, analyzing their new financial situation. They had been barely surviving on his salary as it was. There was not a chance they wouldn't be dipping into their savings, even before taking into account any travel. "Not unless we win the lottery. But we'll talk every day, and Ariel's wedding is only two and a half weeks away."

Amanda was now second in line.

"It's going to be okay," John said encouragingly. "Between now and then I'll figure something out. We might be able to swing a visit every two or three weeks. That isn't too bad, as long as it's temporary."

Amanda brought her hands to her face and ran them over her forehead and cheeks. Then she said, "Am I doing the right thing?"

"I think so," said John. "I hope so. Anyway, we're in it together. We're a team, remember?"

The man in front of Amanda passed through the checkpoint.

"Boarding pass and ID," said the TSA officer.

Amanda handed them to her and turned back to John.

"I guess this is it," she said, kissing John. "Good-bye."

"Bye, baby," he said, squeezing tight. "Call me the second you get there."

"Will do."

The TSA officer looked from Amanda's driver's license to her face, squiggled something in highlighter on her boarding pass, and handed both back to Amanda, who flashed a tight, brave smile and disappeared.

John walked around the glass wall until he could see her again. He watched as she took off her boots, purse, and laptop and placed them in gray bins on the conveyor belt. He watched as she was reprimanded, and removed her boots and purse from the bins and laid them directly on the belt instead. He watched as she stood in her stockinged feet in front of the metal detector waiting to be waved through, and then she was truly gone.

"Bye, baby," he said quietly.

———

His cell phone rang just as he was pulling into a parking space at the Residence Inn. For a fleeting moment he dared hope Amanda's flight had been canceled, or at least delayed. Even if it just gave them a final meal together—

"Hello?" he said.

"Hey, it's Elizabeth."

"Hi," he said, trying not to sound disappointed. "Did you get the amendment?"

"Yeah. Hey, listen, I need you back in Philly. How soon can you arrange it?"

"What? Why?"

"I need you to cover something."

"I'm already covering something."

"Yeah, but that whole ape thing is becoming more like Cat's kind of thing—"

"The hell it is!"

"—and you two don't seem to be working too well together anyway—"

"What did she say to you?"

"It doesn't matter. I need you here."

"What . . . did . . . she . . . say . . . to . . . you?"

"It doesn't matter. Frankly, I don't have the resources to keep the two of you out there anyway, and she's more than capable. And I need someone to cover another column. So get back here as soon as you can." She hung up.

John flipped his phone shut and threw it on the passenger seat. He parked the car and sat clutching the steering wheel with both hands, grinding his teeth and staring at the dog-poo station that was just outside the hotel entrance.

She's more than capable.

And you, sir, are not. John felt as close to murdering someone as he ever had in his life. It was his series, his story, his idea, and Cat had extracted it from him as deftly as a prankster whipping a tablecloth from beneath a Thanksgiving spread.

Ta-dah!

———

Fran and Tim's rental car was not in the driveway, but they could have just been shopping. It wasn't until John checked the guest room that he knew for sure they had left.

Evidence of Fran's occupation was everywhere: lace antimacassars, shelves lined with paper, drawers rearranged, towels and sheets refolded, and everything ironed. John found it droll that she'd ironed his jeans and undershirts; he found it less amusing when he discovered his boxers were also pressed.

The table was set with good linens, so John took his Hungry-Man frozen dinner to the couch, turned on the television, and put his feet up. As he spooned the gluey potatoes into his mouth, he couldn't help thinking of Amanda's version, mashed with rivers of butter. His mind then turned to all that beautiful food she'd prepared for him that was rotting in a dumpster behind the Residence Inn at that very moment. It had felt like an act of betrayal to throw it out—the sensation was almost painful—but there was no way in hell he was going to offer it to Cat. If Cat were drowning, he wouldn't toss her a straw, and that was before he'd seen the photo. What he should have done was track down Cecil, who probably hadn't had a home-cooked meal in years, but that option didn't occur to John until he was already on the plane.

He flicked through the channels, automatically bypassing sports stations until he remembered that Amanda wasn't home to object. God, how he wanted her home. The house felt empty and huge without her. She had commiserated with him by phone about his new assignment, but he wanted to wrap his arms around her, to draw some comfort from her physical presence.

Elizabeth had recalled John to take over a weekly column called "Urban Warrior." The real "Urban Warrior" had just had twins, who were apparently colicky little monsters, and as a result she was severely sleep-deprived and going on leave. Very unwarriorlike, in John's opinion. Stick a kid on each boob in one of those sling-type contraptions and go out and measure your own damned potholes. This was not just sour grapes. This was the actual nature of his assignments. Profiles on the crazy guy who patented a device to measure and compare potholes around the city, the valedictorian at the most troubled high school, Philadelphia's most beloved doorman. Counting the number of abandoned cars on the expressway, and scoping out the city's most trash-laden street. This week, he was supposed to conceive of and conduct a sting operation on dog owners who didn't pick up after their pooches in Fairmount Park and Rittenhouse Square.

And then there was the photo. John had gone to the *Inky*'s Web site to look up previous versions of "Urban Warrior" and had found Cat's initial report from Kansas under a photograph of a catastrophically injured Isabel Duncan. He felt physically ill. He hadn't even recognized Isabel—it wasn't until he read the caption that he realized who he was looking at. He studied the picture closely, but the resolution was poor and there were too many bandages for him to get a real sense of what had happened to her. There was absolutely no way she had given permission for that photograph to be taken.

He didn't know when and he didn't know how, but someday karma was going to catch up with Cat.

11

"Ready?" Peter kissed Isabel's forehead and handed her a pile of clothes.

She nodded and stared at the motley assortment. An unfamiliar ski toque sat on top, the price sticker still attached. She peeled it off, rolled it into a neat cylinder, and set it on the edge of the bedside table.

"For your head," said Peter. Under different circumstances she might have found his remark amusing, but Isabel thought she might never laugh again. Sixteen days before, Peter had walked into her hospital room and told her the bonobos were gone—sold, like toasters or snowblowers, like so many items at a garage sale. She had fallen completely apart, to the point that they'd sedated her again, and she suspected that the sedation had continued for several days. She was furious—with Peter, who had promised to look after the apes; with the university, for betraying them instantly and apparently without a second thought; with the world, for considering these creatures nothing more than property. Peter withstood her rage, comforting her when she'd let him, and swearing he'd find out what he could. So far the trail had ended abruptly against a wall of bureaucracy. One of the contract conditions was that the buyer remain anonymous, and, out of concern for campus security (and no doubt, contract violation), the university's in-house counsel was hell-bent on honoring it.

"We'll get some pretty scarves," Peter said, as Isabel continued to finger the hat. "It didn't occur to me until I was almost here that you'd need something now, to wear home. So I stopped at the first place and this is what they had."

Isabel felt perfectly capable of walking, but Beulah was having none of it and so Isabel was wheeled from her room and past the empty chair in the hall, which until an hour before had been occupied by a policeman. He had been assigned to Isabel after the incident with Cat Douglas, although as far as Isabel knew, Celia was the only other person who had tried to see her, and she had been turned away on Peter's orders.

She sat silently at the curb while Peter pulled the car around, aware that people were staring. She couldn't blame them. She was painfully thin, deeply bruised, and sporting an improbable plaster cast on her nose. She had the toque pulled low, but it merely accentuated the fact that there was no hair to cover.

It was a typical winter day in Kansas, with a bright sky and gray earth, and the air cold enough to sting the insides of her nostrils. The rhinoplasty had been the worst of the surgeries, not because of the pain, but because the relief of finally having her jaw unwired had been instantly displaced by having nostrils packed with gauze. The surgeon had taken some liberties and was clearly pleased with the outcome: the slight bump on her bridge was gone, and the tip refined, almost angular. It was a nose worthy of Hollywood, he'd said with obvious pride. Isabel would have preferred that he hadn't done anything but repair her septum, but there didn't seem much point in complaining after the fact.

Peter pulled up to the curb, left the car idling, and came around to the passenger side. Beulah leaned over and snapped the feet of the wheelchair upright.

"I bet you'll be glad to be home," she said.

"You have no idea." Isabel grasped the arms of the chair and stood up.

"Oh, I think I do. Now go on. I don't want to see you around here anymore." Beulah waved her off with mock severity.

Isabel tried to muster a laugh.

Beulah leaned in and hugged her. "Take good care of yourself," she said. As she pulled away she wagged a finger at Peter. "And *you* take good care of her too."

"You'd better believe it," he said. He took Isabel's elbow, steadying her as she lowered herself onto the seat of his Volvo. Beulah handed him the clear plastic bag that contained her belongings. There was not much: her purse, some magazines, and *The River Wars,* a novel she'd picked up in the waiting area of the radiology department. She'd meant to set it free for some other patient to find, but somehow hadn't gotten around to it. Other than hospital socks, there were no clothes in the bag—everything she'd been wearing when she arrived had been cut off and taken away to be examined for traces of explosives.

"Anything special you want to do?" Peter asked as they pulled away from the curb. "If you're up to it, we could go ring shopping."

Isabel shook her head.

"Movie on demand? We can order in—soft food, of course. Lentil curry? Saag paneer? Gulab jamun? We can have a picnic on the bed . . ."

"It doesn't matter," she said. "I just want to get home."

Peter glanced over and laid a hand on her thigh. Isabel turned to stare out the window.

As they rode the elevator Peter held her hand, but when the door opened she pulled away so she could walk the hallway as she always did—treading the center line, feet hitting the same piece of pattern each time—hoping this familiar ritual would bring comfort. Everything about the building looked and smelled the same, yet it was all different. It was as though the whole world had shifted by a few degrees.

She stood off to the side as Peter opened the door, pushed it inward, and let her pass.

Her eyes swept the room. Her plants were shriveled wisps, collapsed and clinging to the outsides of their pots as though, in the throes of death, they'd tried to crawl to safety. A pizza box, uncharacteristically left out by Isabel on the morning of the explosion, was untouched, as was the crumb-covered paper towel from which she'd eaten. A teacup sat beside it, contents evaporated but for a desiccated milky scum that resembled the edge of a pudding skin. Stuart, her Siamese fighting fish, was a fuzzy and colorless lump sucked up against the intake of the water filter, which sputtered valiantly in an attempt to keep operating.

Peter disappeared into her bedroom with the plastic bag. When he returned, Isabel was sitting on the couch.

"Can I get you anything?" he asked, perching on the edge of the coffee table so they were eye to eye. "A glass of water?"

"No," she said, turning her head.

"Are you okay?"

She was so tired, so empty, that she didn't feel like talking. Then she looked again at the remains of Stuart, and turned back with a flash of anger. "No. I'm not okay. I really liked that fish, Peter. I know you think that's stupid, but I really liked him. I had him for two years. He interacted with me. He came to the front of the tank to see what was going on whenever I . . ." She began to cry.

Peter looked quickly at the fish, and his eyes widened.

"Oh, please," she said, nearly hysterical. "You didn't notice that he's dead?"

"I fed him. I swear I did."

"You fed a corpse. For three weeks."

"It wasn't three weeks. He was alive just . . ." He threw the tiny body another glance. "Recently."

"You have no idea when he died, do you? And my plants. You know what? I liked them too. You owe me an oxalis. And a Norfolk pine. And a whatever the hell that was," she said, sweeping a hand toward a magnificently dead plant.

"Sure. Of course. Whatever you want." He tried to put a hand on her shoulder. She whacked it away.

"You really don't get it, do you?" she said.

Peter didn't answer. He stared into her eyes. She could well imagine the mental acrobatics he was using to let himself off the hook. Good to know all those degrees in psychology weren't going to waste.

"Stop looking at me," she said.

"You're distraught. It's understandable. You've been through hell."

"Oh, shut up."

"Isabel . . ."

"You promised me, Peter. You promised!"

"I'm sorry about the fish—"

"The *apes,* Peter. The *apes.* You swore you'd look after them."

He took her hands and lowered his voice. "Listen. It's a terrible shock. I know it is. Everything we worked for, everything we achieved, down the drain. But we can start over."

"What?" Isabel said after a stunned pause.

His voice took on a desperate tone. "Together. We'll get new apes. We'll find funding. I'm not happy about it. It won't be easy. I'm not pretending it will be. I'm forty-eight years old—I'll be ancient by the time we get back to where we were a month ago, and God knows where we'll get infant bonobos, but you—it's different for you. You're young. You can be the star. Carry the torch."

Isabel stared at him. "You can't be serious."

"I am. There's no reason we can't do this. We'll share the credit. Hell, your name can come first on papers."

"We can't just replace the bonobos."

"Why not?"

"Because they're not hamsters! We're talking about Lola, Sam, Mbongo, Bonzi . . . Peter, they're family! I've known them for eight years. Don't you feel anything? Makena is pregnant—pregnant!—and they're probably at a biomedical lab right now, having God knows what done to them."

"Of course I feel something. I'm devastated. But we have to accept that they're gone. You know we will come to love the new ones. How could we not?"

She rose abruptly and headed for the kitchen.

"Where are you going?" Peter said.

"To get a fucking drink," she called back. "Unless you somehow managed to kill my vodka."

He stood in the doorway and watched as she pulled the vodka from the cupboard and poured two fingers' worth in a glass.

"Are you sure you want to do that?" he asked.

"Sweet Jesus, Peter. You're going to judge me now?"

He leaned against the door frame, watching.

She fingered the glass, but left it on the counter. "How could you do it, Peter? How could you let them be taken away?"

"I didn't," he said quietly. "I had nothing to do with it."

"But you didn't stop it, did you?"

She picked up the glass. Her hands were shaking.

"Isabel?" he said. He was gazing at her with such concern it made her want to beat him with her cast-iron skillet, which was frighteningly close to hand.

"Get out," she said.

"You're tired. Let me help you to bed."

"No, I want you to get out. And I want you to leave my key."

"Your key is in your—"

"*Your* key. *Your* key to my place. I want you to leave *your* key."

"Isabel—"

"I mean it, Peter. Leave your key and get out."

He stared at her for a while before finally turning away. The second he rounded the corner, she poured the vodka down the sink. At the very same moment she slammed the glass back on the counter, she heard the key hit and skid across a surface in the other room. She waited to hear the door, but didn't.

"I mean it!" she screamed.

After what seemed like forever, the door shut with a precise little click. She immediately ran to it, bolted it, and put the chain across.

———

She'd been too hard on him. Even in her distressed state, that was clear to her. She knew she should call immediately and ask him to come back. It wasn't as though he hadn't also been through hell—he had stood by her bedside during those first few days wondering if she was even going to live, and then, while helping her recover, he had learned about the sale of the bonobos. It was his bad luck that he had to be the one to tell her. When it came right down to it, Peter had as many reasons to feel traumatized as she did, perhaps more—after all, he was conscious during the time she had been blissfully out of it. And while it was true that she cared about the fish, she didn't really care about the plants. Her frustration and grief had been mounting from the moment she'd found out the bonobos were gone, and when she'd finally erupted, Peter had happened to be the closest target. She looked across the room at the phone; in her mind, her fingers were already punching in his number. But she didn't do it. Even if her anger was misplaced, it was real.

Isabel couldn't bring herself to deal with Stuart just yet, but she did turn off the tank light and unplug the water filter.

Her voice mail was full to capacity with messages dating back to immediately after the bombing:

"Hi, Dr. Duncan. This is Cat Douglas. We met yesterday. I'm really hoping I can—"

"Hi, Isabel. This is John Thigpen. We met . . . uh, well, I'm sure you remember. I called the hospital, but they wouldn't tell me anything. I hope you're okay. I'm so, so sorry. I just can't imagine. My wife and I are staying at the—"

"Yeah, hi, my name is Philip Underwood. I'm a feature writer with *The New York Times* and I would really appreciate—"

"Good afternoon, Miss Duncan. I'm calling from the offices of Bagby and Bagby. We were wondering if you had talked with anyone yet about your injuries. The attorneys at Bagby and Bagby have more than twenty years' combined experience helping people like you get the money they—"

There were none from her mother, none from her brother, none from acquaintances or neighbors, or even colleagues, with the exception of Celia, who had plenty to say about being turned away from the hospital. Isabel deleted them all.

She picked up the pizza box, remembering how she'd sat cross-legged in front of the coffee table the morning of the explosion and choked down a single leftover slice of pizza. She closed its lid and tossed it like a frisbee at the front door.

Out of the corner of her eye she caught sight of a dissymmetry that stopped her in her tracks. Her computer, unlike the pizza box, was not exactly where she had left it. When Isabel set a glass down, it was perfectly placed along the outside edges of her place mat. When she folded towels, or even fitted sheets, their edges were aligned exactly. And when she set her laptop on her desk, it was always precisely two inches from the front edge and absolutely parallel. She hesitated, staring at its silver case. She took several deep breaths, sat down at her desk, and reached for it with icy fingers.

The "recent documents" list revealed that someone had gone through her email, documents folder, pictures, and trash.

Had the FBI searched her hard drive? She scanned the room again, mystified. Wouldn't they have left a mess of everything else as well? Drawers overturned, couch cushions toppled, closets emptied?

She opened her browser and found that someone had added a bookmark. It led directly to the ELL video. This was the first time Isabel had seen it.

When it came to a close, leaving the final, menacing image onscreen, Isabel was frozen, leaning forward with hands pressed to her cheeks. They had been here. It was the only thing that made sense. The bookmark was a calling card.

After a couple of seconds, she turned her head quickly, checking that she had put the chain on the door. She went from window to window, yanking the blinds down and pulling the curtains closed; and then from room to room, collecting chip clips, hair clips, and safety pins, and affixing them with trembling hands, making sure the edges of all the curtains were completely sealed. She turned off all but one table lamp in the corner of the living room, and withdrew to the couch to perch, hugging her legs and pressing her chin to her knees.

An hour later, she had not moved. She lifted her chin and gasped, as though coming to.

She scanned the room. Almost every surface in the room was adorned with framed photos of the bonobos—Mbongo, putting together a marble run; Bonzi, playing an electric keyboard with a rock star to whom she famously signed, SIT DOWN! BE QUIET! EAT PEANUTS! after becoming impatient with his entourage; Sam, using a computer to play Ms. Pac-Man; Lola, riding on Isabel's shoulders as they walked in the woods, clutching Isabel's chin with one hand and using the other to point to where she wanted to go. Richard Hughes and Jelani, sitting under a tree, earnestly discussing a hard-boiled egg in ASL. Makena, exchanging a kiss with Celia, both of them with lips extended and eyes closed. Isabel stared at this last one for a long time.

Isabel heard the ding of the elevator and froze, looking toward the door. Within a second she lunged for the table lamp, nearly knocking it over in her hurry to turn it off. She ended up curled into a ball on the floor by the end table.

There was a shuffling of plastic bags, the closing of the elevator, and then an interminable silence. Finally footsteps began. They came to her door, paused, and continued.

Isabel sat in the dark, breathing so fast she was lightheaded. She closed her eyes and lifted her chin, willing her heart rate to come down.

After several minutes she sat up and switched the table light back on. She reached for the phone. Her fingers paused above the keypad as she contemplated numbers. Finally, she chose.

"Hello?" said the voice at the other end.

"Celia?" she whispered into the receiver. "It's me. I need you. Can you please come over?"

12

When Amanda came through security, she ran to John, who lifted her and spun her around. People stared and John didn't care. The scent of her skin, the feel of her hair—he might never let go.

"Oh, John," she said, laying her head in the crook of his neck in a gesture of trust so absolute it slayed him. "God, I've missed you."

"Me too, honey. Me too."

When he finally set her down Amanda glanced around and self-consciously straightened her clothing. Her cheeks were flushed.

John reached for her backpack. "Is that all you brought?"

"I'm only here for three days."

"Don't remind me."

"Are you sure you can't take tomorrow off?" she asked.

"Can't. The column runs on Sunday."

When they got home, their lips were locked before the door was even latched. John dropped her bag to the floor.

"Careful!" she said breathlessly, between kisses. "Laptop!"

"Sorry!" he gasped, struggling out of his coat as she unbuttoned his shirt.

Minutes later, at the critical moment, Amanda leaned in and whispered, "Let's make a baby."

The effect was immediate and horrifying. Despite Amanda's best ministrations—and she was in fine form—John could not recover. Eventually she gave up and rolled off.

"What's the matter?" she asked after several minutes of silence. The candles she had paused briefly to light flickered against the wall, their wicks grown long, their shadows deep.

"I don't know," he said. "It just happens sometimes." He wished the mattress would swallow him whole. Glurp, just like that. One tiny sinkhole in the universe. Was that so much to ask?

"It's never happened before," said Amanda. "Is it because of what I said?"

"No, of course not," he assured her. *Yes, of course it was,* screamed the voice in his head.

"Do you want to employ a little . . . help?" she said playfully.

When John was young, his mother used to go to Tupperware and Avon parties. Later, she had gone to Top Chef and candle parties. By the time Amanda was invited to such a party by friends in New York City, it was for lingerie and sex toys. Amanda, having been plied with cheap wine by her hostess the entire evening and then taken into a "consultation room," came home giggling and tipsy and handed John a bag of items that left him speechless, a little bit horrified, and entirely intrigued. Very soon, he had come to realize their usefulness. After eighteen years together, variety could be good.

"Mmm," he said. "Sure."

"Any special requests?"

"Nope. Surprise me," he said. He stretched his arms out over his head while Amanda opened the top drawer. She reached in and patted around. After a moment, her expression became quizzical and the patting more determined. Finally her hand hit something that crinkled. She flipped over to investigate. Then she shrieked. She began making yakking noises similar to those Magnificat had made immediately before discharging a hairball, and bolted from the room.

John raised himself on his elbow and looked in the drawer. Everything in it had been placed in individual Ziploc bags and sorted by size against the back.

John flopped back on the bed. His retinas hurt just from thinking about Fran opening the drawer and realizing what she had found. He could picture it so clearly: smug in her discovery; enjoying her shocked outrage as she cleaned, bagged, and sorted; her prurient delight in imagining their reaction when they discovered what she had done. John could only imagine how Amanda felt. In fact, he could hear how Amanda felt. She spent ten minutes in the bathroom wracked by dry heaves. By the time she returned to bed, the sex toys and lubricant were buried deep in the downstairs trash and the candles extinguished.

"You okay?" he asked.

"No," she said, sliding into bed and under John's arm. She was sniffling, either from crying or because she was congested from hanging her head over the toilet. "She probably expects me to thank her for that, along with her stupid antimacassars."

John stroked her hair, smoothing it down her back. "Yes, I expect she does."

———

Ariel's wedding did not seem at all as though it had been thrown together at the last moment. In fact, it looked rather as though Amanda's aunt and first cousin had been planning this moment for every second of Ariel's thirty-three years on this earth. John looked in astonishment at the bushels of flowers and ribbons, the swags of tulle that connected the pews on the aisle.

He and Amanda had arrived minutes before the ceremony started, stifling giggles over a sign they had just passed. (GUNS 'N' WAFFLES, it had read. John said, "Sounds like a Ma and Pa operation, doesn't it?" and Amanda had retorted, "Yeah, only in my family, Mom would be responsible for the guns.")

At the church, they were ushered hastily to their seats. Fran glared briefly in their direction before lifting her chin and turning majestically away. Amanda sighed, all merriment dissipated, and John squeezed her hand.

The ages-old pattern of fallings-out between Amanda and Fran was carefully choreographed: Fran sulked until Amanda broke down and tearfully apologized, at which point Fran folded her to her bosom and blamed everything on John before graciously forgiving him since they were, after all, family. This last was usually accompanied by a direct stare at John that would have caused her to be burned at the stake in previous centuries.

Amanda had never before held out this long—it had been three weeks since the Great Escape—and Fran's face was nothing short of armored.

Ariel's tuxedoed groom took his place at the end of the aisle, looking for all the world like a panicked deer. John half expected to see a stream of urine leaking down his leg.

When the procession started, Ariel was preceded by four bridesmaids wearing ill-fitting sea-foam-green dresses. By comparison, Ariel was a vision of loveliness. The combination of waist-length veil and trailing bouquet almost succeeded in hiding the baby bump.

Many of the women wept, dabbing their eyes discreetly so as not to disturb carefully applied makeup. But not Amanda—halfway through the procession, John saw her eyes darting from person to person, frowning. She was doing mental arithmetic. Later, in the car on the way to the reception, John discovered why.

"She's got them all turned against me. I didn't apologize, so she's been recruiting for her side."

"What are you talking about?"

"Janet is a second cousin. I'm a first cousin," she said. "They didn't even invite me to the shower! She must have had a shower. Of course she had a shower! I'm so stupid."

John's mental cogs chomped and masticated, finally spitting out a pellet of possible explanation. He glanced quickly at his wife. "You wanted to be a bridesmaid?"

"Of course not! No one *wants* to be a bridesmaid, but it would have been nice to be asked. I know exactly what happened," she said, thumping her seat. "Mom told Aunt Agnes all about how I ignored her advice and abandoned her at the house and was ungrateful for all the crap she did and now nobody's talking to me. But you can be sure they're talking *about* me." She slapped a hand over her mouth, stifling a cry. "Oh my God. The sex toys. If she told them about the sex toys I'm going to die."

John wished he could reassure her, but he'd been part of the family too long.

She spun to face him, eyes gleaming, fingers splayed on the seat. "Let's ditch it."

"What?" John gripped the wheel tightly and glanced over several times, trying to gauge her expression.

"The reception. Let's ditch it and go home."

"Are you serious?"

"Yes. Nobody's going to talk to us anyway. And how can I face all my relatives knowing what they know?"

"You don't know what they know."

"Oh, I think I do. Want to bet Aunt Agnes hands me a thank-you card to give to Mom?"

Again, John wanted to reassure her, but this very thing had happened two years before, when Amanda was apparently not grateful enough for some other "favor" provided by Fran.

"Let's do it," she said, growing increasingly animated. "Turn around here. Here!" She jabbed her finger at the window. "We'll mail their gift."

John was tempted by this proposition—so tempted, in fact, that it was hard to force the next words from his mouth. "We have to go. If you don't, it will just give your mother more ammunition, and then it will be even longer before you two make up."

When he looked over again, Amanda was staring fiercely out the windshield.

"I don't want to make up," she said.

"Yes, but you know you will eventually."

Amanda dropped her head against the side window.

"Baby, if you really want to skip it, we'll do it. But it's not something you can take back, and I think you'll regret it."

She continued to lean on the window. She sighed wearily. "Okay. Fine. We'll go. But I'm not apologizing."

"I never said you should."

"Fine."

He glanced over at her, hoping that this wasn't turning into an argument. They were both on edge: last night's reunion was hardly what they'd hoped for, and John got the sense that Amanda was not very happy in L.A., although she hadn't said anything specific. For John's part, he was increasingly bitter about losing the ape story to Cat. Her reports about the ongoing investigation appeared regularly in the front section; meanwhile, John's latest "Urban Warrior" assignment was to experience firsthand the city's new efforts at flushing out vagrants, meth-heads, and other undesirables from the places they congregated by spraying them with skunk oil. He had been perfectly amenable to the idea of following along with police and city employees as they tested this technique, but Elizabeth decided that would be boring and predictable. Oh no, she said—how much more effective this would be if written from the perspective of a homeless man! And so John had gone under-cover and been skunked out of a doorway earlier in the day. Three tins of tomato juice later, and the scent still lingered.

———

"Amanda! My dear! Lovely to see you," said Uncle Ab, the proud father of the bride. He was in clear violation of orders, but drunk enough to be impervious to the look of searing reproach coming from his wife and her female relatives.

Fran sat stiffly at a table across the room, emanating silent fury beneath the flashing glint of a disco ball. Tim looked defeated, and played with his swizzle stick. The sound system belted out Sister Sledge's "We Are Family" as people old enough to know better flung themselves around with drunken abandon. Arms flew into the air, stayed for a moment, and then were yanked back down as the owners realized they had no idea what to do with them.

Uncle Ab was weaving a little. He hugged Amanda and planted a wet one on her cheek. As she wiped her face with a cocktail napkin, he shook John's hand. Ab's nose crinkled in disgust and the corners of his lips turned down. "What's that smell?" he said, bobbing his head from side to side and sniffing in the general vicinity of John.

"It's skunk."

"It's what?"

"*Skunk,*" John said firmly.

"How the hell did you manage that?" asked Ab.

"Ariel looks wonderful," said Amanda, sipping her drink. She gazed at the dance floor over the rim of her glass.

"She should look good," replied her uncle. "Do you have any idea how much that cost? The nails, the makeup, the eyebrow waxing! Eyebrow waxing!" He wagged a finger for emphasis. Held his breath and nodded sagely. Leaned forward conspiratorially, floppy jowls reeking of cologne, pie hole reeking of Red Label.

"You know, I've always admired that about you, Amanda. You never felt the need to do any of that nonsense."

Amanda's eyebrows shot up. Her hand flew to cover them.

Rank lexical relation indeed, thought John, staring at the old man with pure, unadulterated hatred.

When they got home, Amanda tossed her beaded purse onto the hall table and rushed into the bathroom. A moment later she wailed.

"What's the matter?" John asked. He was headfirst in the fridge, getting a beer.

"He's right!"

John closed the refrigerator door. "Who's right?" He went into the bathroom and stood behind her. She bent forward until her face was inches from the glass, holding her hair back with one hand and using the other to point at the space between her eyebrows.

"Look."

John leaned in close, scrutinizing the area. "There's nothing there."

"There are hairs. Uncle Ab saw them."

"That is not what he said."

"It was between the lines. He said I was hairy and unkempt."

"No, he didn't. And anyway, since when do you take fashion advice from a man who wears Old Spice?" John wrapped his arms around her shoulders. "You're sexy. And so are your eyebrows."

"You mean my *eyebrow,*" she said, twisting free.

He followed her into the living room, where she flopped onto the couch.

"Why are you letting this get to you?" he said. "It's Uncle Ab, for Christ's sake."

Amanda leaned forward and cupped her face in her hands. "Something happened last week."

John sat next to her, trying to contain his alarm. "What?"

She shook her head.

"Amanda, what is it?"

She sighed, and closed her eyes. It felt like ages before she spoke. "The NBC execs took Sean and me to the Ivy for lunch. It's full of celebrities. Paparazzi everywhere."

John watched, waiting.

"So I ordered quiche."

After a long silence, John said, "I don't get it."

"Apparently women in Hollywood don't order quiche. They order undressed salads, or plates of strawberries."

"I still don't get it."

"So at first nobody said anything, but it was like someone had passed gas. The atmosphere got very weird. Then the executive producer finally piped up and told me how refreshingly different I am from the average Hollywood woman."

John paused. "You are. That's a good thing."

"No. Apparently it's not. One of his eyebrows was raised. What he really meant was that I'm not *enough* like the average Hollywood woman."

John didn't know what to say. She started to cry and he pulled her to him.

The next morning Amanda went to her regular hair salon and returned with a different head. The stylist cut her hair and blew it straight before passing her along to an aesthetician, who shaped her eyebrows and gave her a lesson in the application of makeup. When Amanda came home, she had smoky eyes, cupid-bow lips, and flawless skin. She was also clutching glossy pink bags with gilt lettering and slick rope handles.

"He said he'd always wanted to blow my hair out," Amanda said sheepishly when John did a double-take. The difference was astonishing, and he felt an unexpected rush of pleasure, for which he immediately felt guilty, because it was the newness, the difference, he found exciting.

"It'll go back to the way it was, won't it?" he said, running his fingers through her hair. Its texture was completely different, like silk, or water.

She laughed. "Yes. Next time I wash it, unfortunately."

John poked through the layers of pale green tissue that puffed from the tops of the bags and discovered mysterious elixirs in boxes sealed with gold stickers.

"How much did all this cost?"

"You don't want to know," she said. She shot him a guilty glance, and added, "I needed the haircut anyway, and the eyebrows cost fifteen bucks. But now that they're done I can maintain them myself. And the makeup will last at least a year."

"Huh," John said, admiring the dexterity with which she had avoided revealing the grand total.

She ran her hand through her hair. "Since I'm having a good hair day that will only last until my next shower, do you want to take me to dinner?"

"If I do, can I have my wicked way with you later?" he said.

"Absolutely. And I promise not to mention procreation."

She apparently didn't realize that by mentioning it now, she had doomed John to thinking about it later. He had already been thinking about it—a lot, actually. He had always supposed they'd eventually have children, but given their current circumstances he was having trouble believing this was the right time.

They went to their favorite sushi restaurant. It was a splurge, but Amanda was returning to L.A. the next morning and it was very possible they might not see each other for another three weeks. Amanda wore the dress she'd bought for Ariel's wedding, along with new shoes. To John's right was the fully stocked bar, which was illuminated from behind by lights that changed color every fifteen seconds.

"You okay?" said Amanda. "You seem kind of quiet."

John realized he had been twirling his sake cup. "I'm sorry. I just can't stand the thought of you going back. I miss you." He paused, looked quickly up and back down, then added, "And I hate my job."

She looked stricken. "Oh, honey—"

"It's true. I used to love reporting. I used to feel I was making a difference. The ape series was groundbreaking on so many levels—language, comprehension, culture. Evolution, a fundamental redefinition of the way we view other animals, extremists on both sides, but reasonable people in between. I felt like I was contributing to an important discussion." He heaved a deep sigh. "Do you know what my next 'Urban Warrior' assignment is?"

She shook her head.

"I'm doing a piece on stay-at-home moms who double as hookers. They turn tricks while their kids are taking afternoon naps."

Amanda's mouth fell open.

"Yeah," said John. "I have an appointment with one on Wednesday. Candy is her name. Supposedly. She didn't believe me when I said my name was John. Said that's what they all say."

"They probably do," Amanda said.

"Anyway, she asked me to park around the block and go through her backyard so her neighbors don't see me—oh, and get this, this is the best part, she lives two blocks from my parents—and then I'm supposed to look through the window to see if the kid's still up. He watches *Sesame Street* and has a snack right before he goes down, so if the high chair is empty I'm supposed to just let myself in the back door."

"Oh my God. I want to cry," said Amanda, and for a moment she looked as though she might. "She doesn't know you're a reporter?" she eventually added.

"No, she thinks I'm a john."

"Do you think she'll talk to you when she finds out?"

"I hope so. Otherwise I have to find another one and start over."

Amanda swirled her miso, which had separated, and then stared at the vortex of seaweed and tofu.

He reached for her hand. "Amanda, you haven't said much about L.A. except for that asshole at the Ivy—is everything okay? How are things going?"

"Meh," she said, shrugging. "The work is okay. Except the executives keep changing the script, which is hugely annoying when you're trying to build threads."

"Have you made any friends?"

"Sometimes I go out with Sean." She registered John's alarmed look and added, "Don't worry. He's gay."

"Oh. Good."

She scooped her purse from the padded bench and got up. "I'll be back in a minute."

"Sure," said John. As soon as she passed behind him, he slugged his tiny cup of sake. What he really wanted was a Valium.

Amanda's landlord had required her to sign a six-month lease, so they were committed to paying the mortgage as well as rent on the L.A. apartment for at least that long. They had lived on ramen noodles before, and could do it again. He just wanted to feel that this move had actually made her happy, and so far that didn't seem to be the case.

"Ohhhhhhh, look at you!" a familiar voice squealed. John turned to see Li, their usual waitress, standing behind the bar. Her face was glowing, her eyes and mouth wide in an exaggerated smile. John whipped around and saw Amanda returning from the washroom.

Amanda stopped and checked over each shoulder to see if she was the one being addressed. Having apparently decided she wasn't, she continued walking.

"You look so *good*!" sang Li. "I didn't recognize you!"

Amanda realized Li was indeed talking to her. She paused, her face frozen into a mask of horror. After a moment she said, "Thank you," and walked stiffly back to the table. When she sat, she leaned toward John, her eyes bright with hurt. "You know, I have to believe she meant that as a compliment, but I don't think there's any good way to take it."

"It didn't come out very well," said John. "But I'm sure—"

"Oh my God!" said Li, appearing directly beside them. "I still can't believe this!" She clapped her hands in delight and slid onto the bench beside Amanda. She waggled a finger at John. "You're going to have to be very careful tonight because all the men will be looking at your beautiful wife!" She turned to Amanda. "You know, we have a saying in Chinese: there are no ugly women, only lazy women. And after seeing you, I totally believe it! Look at you! The makeup! The hair! And all dressed up!"

John looked with dismay from his wife to Li, his fractured mind trying to process why the waitress in their favorite Japanese restaurant was quoting Chinese sayings, and how on earth he was going to glue Amanda back together at the end of it all.

Amanda stared at her chopsticks. "I got my hair cut."

"And straightened!" Li reached out and fondled it, letting it slip through her fingers. "And you're wearing makeup! You're going to have to keep this up, you know, now that he knows what you *really* look like . . ."

"Li!" the manager barked from behind the bar. He motioned toward some customers who had just walked in.

Li called over to him. "Look at Amanda! Look how good she looks! Can you believe it?"

"Li!" yelled the manager.

"Got to go. See you!" Li leaned in for a one-shoulder hug and floated off.

For a long time, Amanda didn't look up. "Okay," she finally said. "Okay." She was nodding rapidly. She picked her napkin up from the table and smoothed it on her lap, all without looking up. "That's good to know. I'm not ugly. Just lazy."

13

Celia arrived with a backpack and duffel bag.

"Good God. Look at you," she said, pausing in front of Isabel. Then she turned and tossed her bags on the floor. She leaned over and began rummaging through them, removing shoes, wadded-up clothes, and plastic bags of toiletries, which soon littered the carpet around her. A portion of her back showed above her cargo pants, displaying a tattoo in Asian characters that ran up her spine and disappeared under her shirt. "So I thought you weren't talking to me. They turned me away at the hospital."

"That wasn't me," said Isabel. "I think it's because you'd been arrested." She watched Celia carefully, feeling the nagging seeds of doubt. Had she just invited an ELL member into her home?

"Not arrested—detained. And what kind of bullshit was that? I could have gotten killed too. Not that anyone got killed, but you know what I mean. I was there minutes before it happened. No, apparently my crime is that I'm a vegetarian and I volunteer at an animal shelter. My God—they took in people simply for belonging to the Humane Society. Hey, you're a vegetarian. Why didn't they arrest you?" She walked over to the fish tank and stared into it. She crinkled her nose and drew back. "Eww. What happened here?"

"Don't ask."

Celia went to the kitchen and returned with a tablespoon, with which she removed Stuart's body. She cupped a hand around the spoon and said, "Don't look," as she passed Isabel on the way to the bathroom. Moments later, the toilet flushed.

Isabel wanted to laugh. Celia was so transparent she didn't seem capable of hiding murderous intent, or anything else.

As the contents of Celia's bags continued to spread across the floor, Isabel realized she was taking over the living room. Isabel assumed Celia had an apartment or dorm room somewhere, but Celia was vague on the details and Isabel didn't want to press the issue because, as the days passed, she decided she wanted Celia to stay. In fact, she was so grateful for the company she didn't mind all the things Celia did that would normally drive her crazy, like leaving wet towels on the floor, or squeezing toothpaste from the center of the tube. Isabel even caught Celia using her deodorant. Isabel was about to say something, but then she noticed that a second toothbrush had appeared in the mug by the sink and decided that as long as her toothbrush was safe, she could live with sharing her deodorant.

The day after Celia moved in, Isabel called Thomas Bradshaw and begged him to tell her where the apes were.

He insisted that he did not know. Moreover, he did not want to know. He had a family to protect, a life to rebuild. He and his family had been away the weekend the ELL had broken the windows to their house and fed hoses into their living room and kitchen. Did Isabel know that he, his wife, and three children had returned to almost six inches of water, and they'd had to rip out not just the floors but also all the drywall up to ceiling level? That there were hundreds of thousands of dollars' worth of damage? He knew nothing about the bonobos or their private benefactor. He suggested that if Isabel knew what was good for her, she didn't want to know either.

Isabel spent the next few days contacting the big zoos and primate sanctuaries, but none of them had taken in any bonobos. She called the places that hawked "animal actors" and pretended to be a customer. She was offered the services of macaque monkeys, mandrills, and a two-year-old chimp, but she insisted she needed several mature great apes for her advertising campaign. One agent said she might be able to scrape up a few more chimps, although they would all be juveniles, and bemoaned the tragic loss of the entertainment industry's last two orangutans a little more than two years before. (Isabel knew that the orangutans had gone to the Great Ape Trust in Des Moines to live in a state-of-the-art complex with other orangutans, but the agent spoke as though some dreadful fate had befallen them.)

She lurked on Internet sites filled with messages posted by people willing to pay tens of thousands of dollars for a baby chimpanzee. There were even more posts by people with chimps on offer, all of them at the age of puberty, which meant they were starting to assert themselves and their owners were trying to dump them before anyone got killed. "Please take my baby," begged the typical ad, citing the owner's health problems as the reason the "baby" had to go. More likely, the chimp had started to topple the refrigerator, dismantle built-in bookshelves, and bite. But there was no sign of anyone seeking multiple great apes, and certainly not mature ones.

She called all biomedical facilities that used primates, and every one of them refused to provide any information at all. She then called a lawyer, who dedicated 7.3 hours of billable time before concluding that Isabel had no legal basis upon which to learn the whereabouts of the bonobos because they were private property. Isabel scraped together a retainer for a private investigator, who cashed her check and never called back.

She called the FBI, and an increasingly exasperated agent explained anonymous proxies and why it was possible to post something untraceable on the Internet. She didn't believe him. If they could trace the ink or imprint of a letter to a specific typewriter, how was it they could not follow an electronic trail?

Celia hovered in the background, listening to this last phone call with interest. When Isabel hung up, she said, "I've got some friends who might be able to help."

Isabel threw her an irritated glance.

"What?" said Celia.

"If the FBI is stumped, what makes you think your friends can do anything?"

"They break into business networks all the time. Once they even got into a bank."

"Oh my God! What kind of people are you hanging around with?"

"It's not like they're creating viruses," Celia said, somewhat indignantly.

Isabel and Celia locked eyes. Eventually, Isabel threw her hands in the air and turned away. "Okay. Fine. Ask them for . . . help."

Joel was a lanky kid with a long nose and pasty skin that seemed like it should be blemished but wasn't. Jawad was compact, with tightly curled dark hair and eyes the color of roasted almonds. They were students in the computer science department and self-described "weekend hackers."

They parked themselves on Isabel's sofa with their laptops and began tippy-tapping away. They were apparently also instant-messaging each other, as they would occasionally snort and jab each other in the ribs for no apparent reason. Celia got fed up, hung her head out the window, and lit a cigarette. "Don't," she said sharply, sensing the look Isabel was aiming at her back. "I already have a mother."

Isabel sighed and turned away. If anyone on earth understood that one mother was enough, it was Isabel. Instead, she wandered and fidgeted. She picked up each photograph of the bonobos. She stared at their faces, their hands, the shapes of their ears, recalling specific details to keep them fresh in her memory. She picked up a picture of Bonzi and stared into her eyes.

I will find you. I will.

Where she would take them she had no idea, but she would worry about that later.

She set the picture down and aligned all of them so that their frames were at the exact same angle relative to the table's edge. She paced the living room, swinging her hands back and forth and letting them slap in front of her until Joel looked up in irritation. She disappeared into the kitchen and scrubbed the vegetable crisper. She made herbal tea, and when she set the cups down on the coffee table tried to peer around the edges of Joel's and Jawad's laptops to see what they were doing. They hunched forward protectively, angling the monitors down.

"These guys are badass," said Joel a half hour after all previous conversation had ceased.

"I think we know that," said Celia. She and Isabel were lying on their backs on the living room floor with a bowl of blue corn chips between them. "They bombed the lab."

"No, I mean really badass—there's this family that raised guinea pigs. Lots of guinea pigs. Anyway, the ELL started targeting them because they thought some of the guinea pigs were going for biomedical research."

"Were they?" said Celia. She popped a chip into her mouth, crunched it, then sucked the salt from each finger.

"I don't know. Maybe. That's not the point. The point is that they terrorized the family for years. When the grandmother died, the ELL actually dug up her corpse and held it hostage for three months until the family agreed to stop raising guinea pigs."

"They stole a dead body?" Isabel said around a mouthful of corn chips.

"And hung on to it for three months," reiterated Joel. "The family gave up the guinea pigs, and Grandma got dumped in a forest and retrieved. Can you imagine the shape she was in?"

Celia and Isabel looked at each other and simultaneously stopped chewing.

"Listen to this," said Jawad. "Five months ago some of their operatives broke into an animal shelter, stole all the animals, killed them, and dumped them in a bin behind a supermarket. Seventeen dogs and thirty-two cats."

"And these people call themselves pro-animal?" said Isabel.

"Why are you surprised? They bombed the bonobos," Celia said. "And you." She had apparently recovered from the image of the dead body, because she licked her finger and ran it around the bottom of the empty bowl.

"Their so-called rep said it was more humane for the animals to be dead than in a shelter," said Jawad.

"Why 'so-called'?"

"These guys operate in cells, so no one group ever really knows what any of the others is up to. It's a way of protecting themselves. Because of that they've been accused of claiming responsibility for things they didn't do. Hamas-style."

"What about the Webcast?" Isabel said wearily. "Can you find any-thing?"

"No," said Jawad, "and I don't think I'm going to. I've been tracing the IP addresses of each mirrored copy, but I don't think the original is even up anymore, and the copies have bounced between proxies from Uzbekistan, Serbia, Ireland, and Venezuela, all via Nigeria. Good luck getting subscriber info from them."

Isabel thought of the final sentence spoken by the frustrated FBI agent: "If it were that easy, we'd have bin Laden."

"Excuse me," she said, climbing to her feet. From the corner of her eye, she watched Celia wipe her fingers on the carpet.

Isabel made her way to the bedroom, leaving the students alone in the living room. She flopped face-first onto the bed.

Six great apes could not simply disappear. They could pick locks with straws, dismantle heating ducts, pull bolts from door frames, break through drywall, and remove window casings—all of which meant that wherever they had gone had been prepared to receive them. Since it wasn't a zoo or a sanctuary, it had to be a biomedical lab.

She felt a sudden stab as she realized that Peter hadn't been back since she threw him out. It was true she'd turned off her cell phone and yanked the other phone's cord from the wall, but if he loved her, shouldn't he just come?

When she eventually went back into the living room, the students were sitting cross-legged around the coffee table with a bottle of tequila, slices of lime, and a salt shaker. Jawad glanced up. He'd already put salt on the webbing between his index finger and thumb, and had a lime slice at the ready. He offered her the filled shot glass.

"I can't," she said, staring at it. Her fingers twitched, wanting to reach for it. "I can't," she repeated, with more conviction.

Jawad's eyebrows rose into a question mark. Then he shrugged, licked the salt from his hand, tossed the tequila down his throat, and jammed the slice of lime between his teeth.

Isabel went back to her bedroom and found a sitcom on TV.

———

A week later, Celia drove Isabel to her final surgery, which was the most unpleasant of all: getting dental implants to replace her five missing teeth.

This time she was grateful when the nurse wheeled her to the curb, because she had been heavily sedated during the procedure and hadn't quite come around. Her limbs and head felt like bags of concrete.

"You good?" said Celia, straddling Isabel's legs in order to do up her seat belt.

Isabel nodded with her eyes closed. She was obediently biting down on rolls of gauze.

Within a few hours, when the sedation and anesthetic had worn off, Isabel was lying in abject misery in bed. She tossed sleeplessly, sandwiching her head between two pillows and propping bags of frozen vegetables—replaced by Celia as soon as they began to thaw—against her jaw.

Celia had a strange but charming bedside manner. She flung herself onto the duvet beside Isabel, appropriated half the pillows, and flipped through the channels until she found comedies to distract Isabel from her pain. She brought Jell-O and Gatorade, and although her culinary knowledge did not extend much further than that (even the Jell-O was pre-made), Isabel was almost pathetically grateful. She remembered her childhood ear infections, when her mother was extraordinarily solicitous during the early part of the day—allowing Isabel to watch television in bed, and bringing her paper dolls and juice—and then increasingly absent as the wine kicked in. By midafternoon, Isabel was left to fend for herself.

The next day, when Isabel ventured from her bedroom and found that Celia had removed the dead plants and bought African violets from the supermarket, she burst into tears. The white stickers with their bar codes were still stuck slapdash across the terra-cotta-colored plastic.

"What?" said Celia, looking a bit alarmed at the sight of Isabel with a hand over her mouth, crying. "It's no big deal. It was the loss leader."

"It is a big deal," said Isabel. "Thank you." She immediately peeled the stickers off the pots and rolled them into cylinders.

Celia laughed. "You're a complete neat freak."

"And you're completely . . . not," said Isabel, also laughing.

That afternoon, Celia persuaded Isabel to plug her phone back in. It rang within minutes. Celia jumped from the bed to answer it, and Isabel muted the TV so she could listen.

"Oh, hey!" she said brightly. After a pause she said, "It's Celia." After another pause she said, "C-E-L-I-A." Her voice had taken on a different tone. "What do you mean? . . . I'm helping Isabel out for a while. . . . Helping her out, like looking after her. . . . What? . . . What are you talking about? . . . No, I haven't said anything. Why would I?" Celia's voice rose dramatically. "Oh my God. You stinking rat. I get it. I get it entirely. . . ." From here on out she was yelling. "What makes you think you get to tell me what to do? I'll do what I like. . . . Are you trying to threaten me? Really? What are you going to do, fire me from the lab? . . . No, I think maybe *I'll* talk to her first."

Click.

Celia returned to the bedroom and threw herself down on the bed. She and Isabel lay side by side, staring at the muted television set.

"So," Celia eventually said. "It seems I slept with your boyfriend on New Year's Eve."

"Fiancé," said Isabel. It was the only word she could choke past the aching lump that had risen in the back of her throat.

On the television, a bumbling actor swung his arms wildly before falling backward over a sofa.

"I'm sorry," Celia said. "I had no idea you were together."

Isabel covered her eyes with her hands.

"Do you hate me?" asked Celia.

Isabel shook her head, unable to speak.

"Want to be alone?" asked Celia.

Isabel nodded, still covering her eyes. When she heard the bedroom door click shut, she rolled over, pressed her face into a pillow, pulled her knees to her chest, and wept silently, heaving sobs until long after the last rays of sun had disappeared.

———

The next day, a large box of cut tulips appeared in the hallway. The phone rang shortly thereafter.

"Yup, still here," Celia said casually, holding the phone with one hand and using the other to cup her elbow. "No, I put them down the garbage chute. . . . Yes, I'm sure they *were* expensive, and yet somehow I don't think she wants armfuls of decaying plant genitals from you. . . . No, I don't see that happening anytime soon." And then she hung up.

"I'm right, right?" she said, turning to Isabel. "You don't want to see him?"

Isabel thought for a moment, biting her lower lip, perilously close to tears. She glanced around the room at the multiple containers of tulips that, despite Celia's claims, had never been anywhere near a garbage chute. "Not yet. I really don't think I can."

Two days later he finally showed up in person. Isabel was padding into the kitchen when an ungodly pounding started at the door. Celia glanced quickly at Isabel, who ducked into the corner behind it. Celia opened the door, but left the chain on.

"I want to see Isabel," he demanded.

"She's not available," said Celia.

"I know she's here. Her car's in the lot. I want to see her."

"I don't think she wants to see you."

His voice turned vicious. "What did you tell her, you little slut?"

Celia let out a short bark of a laugh. "Little slut? That's inventive. I expected better from someone involved in language studies. Anyway, I told her we fucked."

"I was drunk. You were available. It meant nothing."

"You got that right."

"Isabel!" he roared.

Isabel, squatting against the wall behind the door, cringed.

"Isabel! I need to talk to you! Isabel!"

"I'm going to close the door now," Celia said calmly. Then she sighed and shook her head. "You know, it's funny, but sticking your foot in the door doesn't seem to have any effect on the chain."

Isabel looked down at the brown shoe tip, the only part of Peter that was visible from her vantage point. She half expected him to reach through the crack and grab Celia. After a couple of seconds, the shoe disappeared and Celia shut the door.

"He is such an ass," she said, sliding the bolt. "Want a drink?"

"No," said Isabel.

"Well, I do." Celia disappeared into the kitchen.

Isabel felt used and betrayed and foolish. It had all happened too fast—she could see that now. The animal attraction, the heady mix of endorphins and pheromones that left all logic turned to mush—all of it had led to the sense that she was protected, would never have to face anything alone again. She had given herself to him too quickly, too completely, and in return he had dashed her world to pieces. Although she hadn't disclosed everything about her background, he knew enough to be aware that betraying her on a personal level was much larger than that. He was betraying her trust in the world in general, undermining her faith in everyone. She knew he thought he could talk his way back into her heart and her bed—he had great faith in his abilities in all things, and that confidence was part of his allure—but this time he was wrong.

———

The day Isabel was fitted with flippers—false teeth that were attached to a retainer because the titanium pegs would need to heal for several months before her new teeth could be screwed in—she came home and discovered that her refrigerator was virtually empty. So was her apartment, as Celia had moved back out.

Over the course of her stay, the vagaries of Celia's living arrangements had become somewhat clearer. Celia, along with Joel, Jawad, and three other students, rented a large ramshackle house near the university. When it came to light that Celia was sleeping with three of them (Joel, Jawad, and an unnamed girl), a brief power struggle had ensued, during which Celia announced that if they couldn't live with it, she wanted none of them and was going to couch-surf for a while. Isabel's predicament had created a perfect symbiosis. Since then, the roommates had made peace, and Celia had moved back in. Isabel didn't ask for details. It was just another of the mysteries that was Celia, who sometimes seemed more bonobo than human. Isabel missed her, so she took the absence of any food other than lime chutney, canned peaches, and ramen noodles as an excuse to treat Celia, Joel, and Jawad to dinner.

The restaurant was a small vegan place called Rosa's Kitchen. Isabel was giving her retainer a test run, having been warned by the denturist that it would take a few days for her to get used to it and speak clearly. The students conspired to make her say things with esses and then laughed uproariously at the resulting lisp.

Isabel was about halfway through her green curry with eggplant when she caught sight of someone at a table in a darkened corner of the restaurant. She recognized him instantly—he was the oldest of the protesters, the one Celia always referred to as Larry-Harry-Gary. He was sitting with two other men, leaning in on his elbows, the jacket from his blue-black suit hung over the back of his chair, his tie loosened. He was deep in conversation, apparently unaware of Isabel's presence.

The smile dropped from Isabel's face and her eyes hardened. "Excuthe me," she said, leaning forward to spit her retainer into her hand.

Celia's head whipped around to see what Isabel was looking at. "Uh-oh," she said.

Isabel rose, pushing her chair back with a screech. She walked to the table and stood in front of it.

Larry-Harry-Gary stopped laughing and looked up. "Can I help you?" he said, a smile lingering at the edges of his mouth.

"Are you happy?" said Isabel, narrowing her eyes.

He shook his head, confused. "I beg your pardon?"

She leaned forward and shouted, *"Are you happy?"* A stray piece of basmati rice flew from her mouth.

He sat back, alarmed. "What are you talking about?"

As he continued staring, realization dawned on his face. Although he had waved signs at her every time she had driven into the parking lot for almost a year, he hadn't recognized her.

"My God," he said quietly.

"My God is right," she said, lowering her tone to match his, and nodding rapidly.

"Are you okay?"

"Do I look okay?" She gestured toward her face and head, voice rising like a siren. She turned to address the rest of the stunned diners, some of whom had forks poised in front of open mouths. "You're dining with a terrorist! In case you're interested!"

"Uh, Isabel?" said Celia. She came up behind Isabel and laid a hand on her arm. "I really don't think—"

Isabel shook Celia off and swung back to Larry-Harry-Gary. "Congratulations! You 'liberated' the apes! What a huge, enormous favor you did them. They're so much better off at a biomedical lab. What good work you people do!"

A handful of waiters gathered. The manager elbowed his way through them. "I'm sorry, ma'am," he said, "but I'm going to have to ask you to keep it down."

"I had nothing to do with it," said Larry-Harry-Gary. "On my mother's grave, I had nothing to do with it. None of us did."

Isabel leaned over, eyes blazing, and knocked a bowl of curry from the table. It hit the floor, its contents skidding and splashing.

"That's it. Let's go," said the manager. He grabbed Isabel's arm and spun her toward the door.

A male voice bellowed from behind them: "Get your hands off her!" Isabel was startled to discover it belonged to Larry-Harry-Gary. He rose and took a step forward, face flushed with anger. "For Christ's sake, leave her alone! Can't you see she's been injured?"

Everyone froze. Isabel's chest was heaving from the effort. Her eyes bored into the manager's, and then moved to Larry-Harry-Gary's. His dark brown eyes met her gaze and matched it.

Isabel walked back to her table, put her teeth back in her mouth, retrieved her purse, and headed for the door. She felt every pair of eyes watching her retreat, and, just as surely, examining the long, crooked gash on the back of her nearly-bald head. She raised her chin and kept walking.

The next afternoon, there was a tentative knock on Isabel's apartment door. When she looked through the peephole, she saw Larry-Harry-Gary.

She slammed her body against the door and struggled to get the chain on. "I'm calling the police! I'm not alone in here!" She was, of course. Her fingers trembled so violently it took several tries to get the chain on the door.

"I'm sorry," he said, his voice muffled. "I didn't mean to scare you. I just want to talk."

"I've got my phone in my hand! I'm calling the police. Right now! I'm dialing!"

"Okay! All right. I'll go."

Isabel eyed her cordless phone, which sat out of reach on the coffee table, next to her teeth. When his footsteps receded down the hall, she lunged for the phone and returned to the door. She pressed her ear against it until she heard the ding of the elevator. Then, with phone in hand, she opened the door as far as the chain allowed.

"Wait!" she said. "Come back."

After a moment's pause, the footsteps returned and Larry-Harry-Gary leaned against the far wall, hands raised in supplication.

"I still have my phone in my hand," she said through the crack in the door.

"I can see that."

"How did you find out where I lived?"

"The Webcast."

"Oh. Right. Of course."

"Which I had nothing to do with." His words tumbled out. "Look, I'm sorry. I wouldn't have come if I thought it would scare you."

"What do you want?"

"I just wanted to know if you're okay."

Isabel simply stared.

"All right. I know you're not okay. I can't imagine what you've been through. I'm so sorry."

"Great. Thanks."

"I also wanted you to know that our group had nothing to do with the explosion. Harming animals—including people—is against everything we stand for. Every one of us was taken in by the police and cleared. Peaceful protest coupled with education. That's all we do."

Isabel centered herself in front of the narrow opening. "Okay, fine, maybe you didn't blow us up, but what in God's name were you protesting? All of our research was performed in a collaborative setting. There were no negative repercussions, ever. There were no cages, no coercion. Those apes ate better than most people I know."

He shifted from foot to foot. "You'll have to ask your friend about that one."

"What friend? What are you talking about?"

"I think you know what I'm talking about."

"Actually, I have no clue."

"Well, you should."

An uncomfortably long silence followed, during which he rocked back and forth on his heels. Eventually he said, "Do you really think they went to a biomedical facility?"

"Yes. Because nobody will tell me anything, and if they went somewhere decent, why would it be a secret? I've contacted everyone I can think of, and nobody's admitting to knowing anything about them. So, yes. I think they went to a biomedical lab."

"Let me see what I can find out."

Isabel laughed. "You'll find out nothing is what. Those apes were the closest thing I had to family and nobody will tell me a damned thing."

He pulled a card from his pocket and held it forth. When she didn't reach for it, he laid it on the floor in front of her door. "My name is Gary Hanson. Please call if you need anything."

Isabel crouched and snatched the card from the carpet. She glanced at it. An architect? He was an architect? She looked at him again. He'd always looked surprisingly normal, but somehow she didn't expect this.

Gary Hanson watched her for a moment longer. "I mean it," he said. "If you need anything, call." He ran a hand through his dark hair, pulled his coat collar up, and walked down the hall.

Isabel clicked her door shut and stood clutching her phone. When she heard the elevator doors slide open and then shut, she checked to make sure the hall was truly empty.

What friend could he possibly be talking about? Celia?

Four days later, Isabel was lying on the couch in the dark, running her hand back and forth across the sheared velvet of her hair. It felt like the patch glued to the heads of G.I. Joe dolls. Although she was no longer completely bald, when she held a hand mirror up to see the back of her head the jagged scar was still angry. It would be conspicuous until her hair was long enough to fall rather than stand. She supposed she should get a wig, or maybe some scarves, as Peter had suggested.

The phone rang, startling her.

Isabel dropped one leg to the floor and swung around to a sitting position. "Hello?"

"Hello, Isabel," said a female voice.

The connection, the tone, everything was all wrong. Isabel sat forward, on alert. "Who is this?"

"I'm a friend," said the woman.

A chill flashed outward from the pit of Isabel's stomach. She glanced at the curtains, which, since Celia's departure, were once again held together with chip clips and safety pins, and then at the door, which was chained. "I have caller ID. I'm recording this call," she said, although her caller ID was registering a solid line of ones. Isabel's mind raced back through all she'd learned about IP addresses and Internet anonymity—did it work the same way for telephones?

"Don't be scared," said the woman.

"What more do you want from me? You've already taken everything." Her voice, raised in false bravado, betrayed her panic.

"I'm a friend of a friend," said the woman, "and I think I know where the bonobos are."

Isabel grasped the phone with both hands, her breath coming in short bursts. Her heart was racing so fast she thought she might faint. She closed her eyes for a moment, and rocked back and forth.

"I'm listening," she said.

14

John checked his watch. It was nearly two o'clock. According to his research, the credits to *Sesame Street* should be rolling right now and Candy's tyke would be in bed shortly thereafter.

Given the alarming proximity to his parents' house, John was parked almost a mile away but he wasn't kidding himself—he was still in grave danger of being recognized. To this end he was wearing a knit hat pulled low and a peacoat with the collar turned up. He drummed his fingers on the steering wheel and checked his watch again. He thought about the child, maybe in footsies pajamas, maybe sucking his thumb, being tucked under a quilt while a mobile dangled stuffed animals above him and plinked out a lullaby.

John could not believe he had been reduced to this.

Exactly what he had been reduced to had been driven home yet again that morning, when the first section of the *Inky* featured another report from Cat in which she pretended that *she* was the one who had visited the lab the day of the explosion, that *she* was the one who had brought presents and backpacks to the bonobos. It was extremely carefully worded—technically nothing was an outright lie, but she had made great use of the Royal "We" and the passive voice. The photographs Osgood had taken ran with the piece—images of Sam playing the xylophone, of Mbongo holding the gorilla mask and looking desolate, of Bonzi opening her backpack, and then another of her leaping up to kiss the glass. John had been carefully cropped out of this final one. Frankly, he was surprised that Cat hadn't been Photoshopped in. Meanwhile, John was sitting in his car dressed like a hoodlum waiting for a part-time hooker to put her child to bed so they could begin their "party."

He waited an extra ten minutes, since he had no idea how long it took for a kid to fall asleep, and then slunk through the alley to the back of Candy's townhouse. There was only one window on the main floor, which he assumed was the kitchen. He took a deep breath, looked around at the surrounding houses, and slid behind the holly bush to hoist himself up and check if the high chair was empty.

He was clinging to the window ledge with strips of paint lodged beneath his nails and his nose pressed to the glass when the sound of rapid footsteps shuffled through the gravel behind him.

"Get down from there, you . . . you . . . *reprobate*!" said a voice both wavery and sharp. "I have pepper spray!"

John's fingers slid from the sill and he toppled into the holly. He thrashed his way out and landed facedown in the gravel.

"We all know what's going on in that house," the woman cried, "and we won't have it. This is a respectable neighborhood!"

John turned his head and found himself facing orthopedic shoes, opaque stockings, and a tweed skirt that fell well below the knee. He was also facing a can of mace.

"Don't you move!" The tiny canister trembled violently in the clutches of arthritic fingers, one of which hovered over the red trigger button.

"Please," John said, trying to recover his breath. "Please don't."

"Give me one reason why I shouldn't!"

"Because it's backward. You're pointing it at yourself."

The mace disappeared and John rolled over. He sat up and wiped off the gravel that was embedded in his cheek. Both his hands were bleeding from the holly. He tested his left wrist, which had been overextended and was quite possibly sprained.

"John Thigpen? Is that you?"

He looked up. After a moment of sickening confusion, he realized he was looking into the face of Mrs. Moriarty, his childhood Sunday-school teacher.

"Oh, Jesus," he said, dropping his head into his injured hands.

"Oh, for shame, John Thigpen, for shame!" she scolded. "What *will* your parents think?"

———

"What the hell happened to you?" said Elizabeth, giving him a dismissive once-over as he entered her office. She had risen to answer the door, become visibly irritated at the sight of him, and sailed back behind her desk. "You look like something the cat dragged in."

"Don't ask." Although not invited, he took a seat.

Elizabeth surveyed him dubiously. "If you say so." She flung herself onto her spring-loaded chair. "So what's up?"

John pulled off his ski hat and held it on his lap, flicking off random bits of yard debris. "I've decided to take the buyout."

She froze. "You what?" she said, leaning forward.

"The buyout. I'm taking the buyout."

Her eyes narrowed, drilling into him. "You're taking early retirement? Are you insane?"

"The buyout," John said firmly. The terminology was important to him. He was thirty-six. He was not retiring.

Elizabeth cocked her head. "Really. And when, exactly, did you decide this?"

"Just now."

"And may I ask why?" said Elizabeth.

"Does it matter?"

"Yes."

John stared straight at her, feeling the storm cloud of his combined humiliations swelling within him. He had intended to come in, calmly announce his decision, and leave. Suddenly he found himself shouting. "Because in the last few weeks I've been sprayed with skunk oil, I have personally taken samples of random dog poo in parks for goddamned DNA testing, I have measured the depth of rotting trash in gutters and estimated what percentage of it was used condoms. I have hidden in doorways recording the license plates of the people who pick up tranny hookers, and today I was *nearly maced by my Sunday-school teacher*!" He thumped his fist on her desk to punctuate this last indignity.

Elizabeth's eyes were wide. He did not blame her; he had shocked himself. He knew he should try to collect himself, but at this point he had nothing to lose.

"The ape story was mine," he continued, pounding his chest. "I know you didn't want to hire me in the first place, but I've done damned good work, and my reward for that is . . . *this*." He flashed his hands, which were crisscrossed with lacerations. "You took my story—my series—and gave it to Cat Douglas the second it started to look like Pulitzer material."

Elizabeth's eyes narrowed to pinpricks. She began tapping her pencil on her desk.

"Cat Douglas, for Christ's sake!" he reiterated. "Did you even read what she wrote this morning? She was never in the room with the apes. They wouldn't let her in because she was sick. She was briefly in the building with them, but she never laid eyes on them. And that picture she posted of Isabel Duncan? Unconscionable. I hope she gets sued!"

Elizabeth didn't respond. *Tap, tap, tap,* went the pencil.

John sighed and sank back in his chair. When he continued, his voice was lowered. "Amanda has an opportunity in L.A. I'm going to join her there. Hell, you should be relieved. Now you have one less person to get rid of, right? Make the executives happy?"

Elizabeth sat forward suddenly and grabbed her phone. She punched four digits and waited.

"Yeah, it's Elizabeth Greer. I need an HR rep up here now. And a packing box. And someone from security."

"I can carry my own box," John said.

"Yes, right away," Elizabeth said into the phone.

———

When John told Amanda what he had done, there was a pause long enough that he wondered whether the line had gone dead. Then she said, "Oh. My. God. You did *what*?" Only then did he truly comprehend the enormity of it. He had just done away with their only source of income. Regret was useless—being escorted from the *Inky* by security guards almost certainly precluded any possibility of slinking back and begging for reinstatement.

He began to babble, trying to convince Amanda—and himself—that they would be okay. He would put the house on the market immediately and come to L.A. His buyout was only one month's salary, but if they were thrifty they could survive until he found work, which he would do immediately, even if it meant flipping burgers. They would have to dip into their nest egg, but not by much, and no matter what, they would be okay. They always had been, even in the lean student years.

When they hung up, John hugged his knees and rocked.

Over the next few days they rallied, or at least John thought they did. Amanda seemed more cheerful on the phone, although it finally dawned on him that it was an act. She relayed funny stories from the studio (ha! ha! ha!) that he later realized weren't funny at all. Apparently the actors were now required to walk around carrying Vitaminwater bottles at all times, label out, because studies had shown that the new trend was for audiences to record shows to watch later, allowing them to skip past commercials, and so the studios had to find new ways of integrating commercial endorsements into the shows themselves. When John finally picked up on Amanda's level of horror over this, he wanted to shrink into the earth. They had been apart only a few weeks and already he was having trouble reading her.

While packing boxes, John found the edited manuscript of *Recipe for Disaster* in the guest room closet. Fran had collated it, stacked all the rejections on top, and secured the lot with two rubber bands going in opposite directions. The rejection with the enormous red *NO* scrawled across it was uppermost; this was what she had chosen her daughter to see the next time she opened the guest room closet.

John sat cross-legged on the floor, peeled off the rubber bands, and began reading.

An hour later he had not moved, and it was more than two hours before he turned the final page. It was good, really good—and by good he meant that she'd blown things up, or at least set them on fire. She had incorporated a number of aspects of her real life—such as her passion for cooking and poor old Magnificat. Somehow she hadn't felt the need to exact revenge on certain family members by way of cameo performances. John was not at all sure he himself could have risen above temptation, given the richness and abundance of available material, but he was grateful nonetheless. Perhaps she had been tempted, as she'd gone to some effort to kill off the mother before the story began, and then killed the father within a couple of pages.

John picked up the stack of rejections and flipped through them, marveling at the many ways people found to say no. No, they couldn't be bothered to have a look, not even at the first few pages. No, they weren't interested. No, they weren't accepting new clients except by referral.

No, no, no, no, no.

John set the rejections on the floor. He didn't count them, but he had no reason to disbelieve Amanda's claim that there were 129. The stack was nearly half as thick as the manuscript itself. No wonder she had taken to her bed.

15

sabel stood on a residential street in Alamogordo, New Mexico, behind a panel van with a woman who called herself Rose. Rose had a job as a technician inside the Corston Foundation, a primate research facility, but she was actually working undercover for an animal advocacy group. They were just beyond its dimly lit parking lot.

The Corston Foundation had acquired six new chimpanzees. Many people, including research scientists, had trouble distinguishing bonobos from chimpanzees. This gave Isabel hope and despair in equal parts, since the Corston Foundation was notorious for flouting USDA and NIH requirements for primate care. They had been cited eight times in the past year alone for violations in cage size and basic care, and two years before that had been fined for leaving three elderly chimpanzees outside in unventilated crates in the summer sun with the predictable result that they died of heatstroke. Because these were cast-off Air Force chimps, their deaths had caused a small blip of media interest and public outrage. Buddy, Ivan, and Donald had been celebrities in their day, media darlings whose enormous grins—as they were plucked free from their space capsules after crashing into the sea—were splashed across

magazine covers nationwide. What the American public didn't know
was that the grins were actually grimaces of fear. They also didn't know
that Buddy, Ivan, and Donald had been acquired in the way of all "wild-
caught" chimps, which is to say yanked from the bodies of their mur-
dered mothers, or that they had spent their first five years in captivity in
enormous centrifuges and decompression chambers designed to test the
rigors of space travel on the human body. Nor did they know that the
chimps were used as crash-test dummies and slammed repeatedly into
walls at high speeds to develop seat belts that would effectively restrain
human astronauts during reentry into the atmosphere. Indeed, until
they were left to expire in the sun, the public didn't know that while the
human astronauts were greeted with ticker tape, confetti, and hero pa-
rades, the Air Force decided that Buddy, Ivan, and Donald were no
longer useful and leased them to the Corston Foundation, where they
were renamed 17489, 17490, and 17491 respectively, infected with hepatitis, caged individually, and subjected to regular liver biopsies. Ferdi-
nand Corston surely breathed a sigh of relief when the surge of gossip
about a major celebrity's marital infidelities swept his own bilge out of
the media's eye. The Corston Foundation was the very last place Isabel
would want the bonobos to end up. On the other hand, knowing where
they were was the first step in rescuing them.

Isabel stood beside Rose at the van's tailgate. The looming concrete
building was surrounded by gravel, chain link, and razor wire. Isabel
tried to imagine the more than four hundred chimpanzees imprisoned
inside.

"I don't know how you stand it," she said.

"I have to," said Rose, tossing a pair of rubber boots at Isabel's feet
and then laying a jumpsuit, rubber gloves, and surgeon's mask with full
face shield on the tailgate. "If we don't have someone on the inside, we'll
never know what's going on. They're not exactly forthcoming about
what they do in there."

"I know," said Isabel, recalling her recent attempts at gathering information. She glanced at the hazmat outfit. "Is this really necessary?"

"Yes. They spit and throw shit. Many of them have been infected
with diseases that are transmissible to humans. Malaria, hepatitis, HIV.
So put these on."

Isabel stared at the squat building with a renewed sense of horror. The behavior Rose was describing was typical of apes who had suffered severe psychological trauma.

Rose watched her, as though assessing. Finally she spoke. "Last week they infected three baby chimps with leukemia by poisoning the formula in their bottles. Others are subjected to lawn treatments, cleaning chemicals, cosmetics—you name it. Some are addicted to drugs, some are locked in unventilated rooms filled with secondhand smoke. One chimp had his teeth smashed out so someone could practice dental implant techniques on him."

Isabel's hand flew to her still-tender jaw.

If Rose noticed, she didn't say anything. She was busy pulling on her hazmat gear. Isabel did the same, in shame-filled silence.

Isabel and Rose both held flashlights as they entered. A long concrete corridor stretched before them, a windowless expanse of cages that hung from the ceiling. The cages were the size of small elevators, and each held a single chimpanzee, who crouched or slept on the chain-link floor. There were no blankets, no toys—nothing except stainless-steel water bowls that refilled automatically. The cages were suspended a couple of feet from the floor, which sloped toward a trough against the wall. Isabel supposed this was for cleaning purposes—a high-powered hose would do it, although now, several hours after the last human had left, feces and urine lay in lumps beneath the cages. The stench was nearly unbearable.

The chimpanzees were mostly quiet, huddled in the corners of their barren cages. A few rushed to the front and displayed, shaking the chain link with hands and feet and splattering Isabel and Rose with water, urine, spit, and worse. Their angry screeches echoed down the hall, amplifying the silence of the others. Most of the quiet ones had their heads turned to the wall, but the ones who faced forward looked through Isabel and Rose with deadened eyes. Their bodies were present, but their spirits gone. A couple had metal bolts coming from the tops of their skulls. Several were missing fingers and toes.

Rose followed Isabel's gaze. "They chew them off from stress."

When they finally turned a corner, Isabel leaned up against the wall to catch her breath.

She would not cry. She would not. Crying would help no one.

Rose waited, but offered no comfort. Did she think Isabel condoned this? Surely not. If she did, she wouldn't have tried to help find the bonobos, would she?

When Isabel finally composed herself, they began walking again. As irrational as it seemed, Isabel thought they were going through the laundry facility, but after passing a few extra-large front-load dryers, she realized that behind the thick round portholes were baby chimpanzees.

"Oh no, oh no," she cried. She sank to her knees in front of one and rested her forehead against the glass, grasping the edges of the porthole with her gloved hands. The infant inside, who should have been with his mother for at least four more years, did not respond. He already had the glassy-eyed stare of the lost. Isabel sobbed openly. She turned to Rose. "Why?" she demanded. "Why?"

Rose responded with a look that spared nothing and said, "They're not much further."

Isabel followed. Because of her surgeon's mask she could not even wipe her nose or eyes, although her gloves were so filthy with feces and spit she couldn't have anyway. She walked past one isolette after another, each containing a lone, infected baby.

At the end of the hall, Rose punched a combination into a keypad beside the door. She went through first and held it open for Isabel.

"This is where they quarantine the new ones. These six are the recent additions."

Isabel stepped inside, heart pounding, blood rushing through her ears. She stopped in the center and turned by degree until she had viewed the occupants of all the cages. As she shone her flashlight on them, they raised their arms to shield their weary faces. They shifted on their haunches, perching uncomfortably on their wire floors. A female clutched her baby against her and turned her back to them.

"No," Isabel said, nauseated with disappointment. "No, these are *Pan troglodytes*. Common chimpanzees. Bonobos are slimmer, with flatter features and black faces."

"Okay." Rose turned to leave.

"Wait—" said Isabel. "If they just arrived, where did they come from?"

Rose shrugged. "Could be from a breeding facility, but we don't know. Not even sure they all came from the same place, so some of them could have been pets. Or used in entertainment. Although they still have their teeth and the males aren't castrated, so probably not."

Isabel looked from chimp to chimp. Had they been raised as people only to be discarded when it became clear they were not simply amusing, furry stand-ins for human babies? Had they worn pink tutus or ridden tiny bicycles to make people laugh? Or had they been kept as breeders, to suffer the serial devastation of having infant after infant taken away immediately after birth?

"Isn't there anything we can do for them? I mean . . . They're still here. I mean, *here*," she said, knocking her gloved head against her temple. "You can see it in their eyes."

"No. Not tonight," said Rose. "Someday, I hope, but not tonight."

Back in the parking lot, they peeled off their protective clothing and dropped it into a bin in the back of the van. Rose handed Isabel a container of antibacterial wipes, and although she had been wearing gloves, it was only after using several of these that she dared dry her eyes.

Rose snapped the lid onto the bin and slammed the van's back doors. "I'll drop you back at your car," she said.

"Rose?"

"Yes?"

"I didn't know."

Rose shot her a scathing look. "Really."

"I had a general idea, but no. I never imagined . . . "

"Your scientific director—or should I say boyfriend? You should ask him about his time in Rockwell."

Isabel's eyebrows shot up as Rose disappeared around the side of the van. When she climbed into the driver's seat and slammed the door, Isabel scrambled around to the other side. She slouched against the interior door and neither said another word until they reached the rental car that would take Isabel back to the airport.

"Thanks," said Isabel, leaning to gather her scant belongings from the floor.

"Uh-huh," said Rose, without turning her gaze from the windshield.

———

When Isabel got home, a Norfolk pine sat outside her door along with an oxalis and a purple passion. All were adorned with velvet ribbons. She recognized the handwriting on the envelope, so she didn't bother opening the card.

Isabel tucked the plants under her arms, took the elevator up a few floors, and left them in front of a neighbor's door.

The African violets had died a terrible death—Isabel didn't know she wasn't supposed to water them from the top, so their leaves and stems had turned to mush. She thought maybe this was from lack of water, so she had done it again and now the plants were slimy and brown. Isabel realized her mistake only when she pulled the plastic tab from the soil and read the care instructions. Isabel—who had rescued crushed snails in her childhood and kept them in shoebox hospitals filled with leaves and twigs, who had captured and released spiders while her mother shrieked for their deaths, who had rescued discarded poinsettias from the curb the week after Christmas—took the violets to the tiny room beside the elevator that housed the garbage chute and dropped them down one at a time. She waited for each thud before releasing the next. Once she heard them hit the dumpster, she exhaled in relief. She returned to her apartment, locked herself in, and put the chip clips back on the curtains.

The phone rang periodically, but she didn't answer it. Celia came but Isabel pretended she wasn't there.

"Isabel?" said Celia, rapping on the door. "Are you in there?"

Isabel sat absolutely still, clutching a couch cushion to her chest.

"I know you're in there."

Isabel still didn't say anything.

"Are you okay?"

Silence.

"Can you please open the door? I'm worried about you."

Isabel pressed the cushion against her mouth and rocked back and forth.

"Okay. Fine. But I'm coming back," said Celia. "I bet you don't even have any food in there."

After Celia left, Isabel paced, trying to calm down. She threw herself on the bed, but ended up punching her pillows. She swept all the books from her dresser onto the floor, and then smashed a mug against the wall. Its handle snapped off, which was no good, no good at all, and so she screamed and pushed the television off the edge of her dresser. It landed on its side with a *thunk,* but nothing imploded, nothing smashed, so she picked up her laptop and raised it high. She stood like this for several seconds, her chest heaving. Then she lowered the laptop and hugged it to her chest.

She set it on the corner of the bed, opened it, and sat cross-legged on the floor while it chirped happy booting noises. Her lip twitched involuntarily. Her desktop shortcuts loaded against her desktop wallpaper, which was an image of Bonzi driving a golf cart in the woods—Bonzi never had quite gotten the hang of steering, and reliably drove better in reverse. Isabel caught her breath and held both hands to her face as though in prayer. She surfed to the folder that contained video files, selected one, and double-clicked.

She was looking at her former self, the one she still somehow expected to see in the mirror each morning. The one with the slightly hooked nose and nostrils that flared at the bottom ("as much nose as you can handle, but no more" was the verdict of one long-ago boyfriend, who seemed surprised—and even a little hurt—that Isabel didn't consider this a compliment). Her long, pale hair, straight as boiled fettuccine, was parted in the middle and tucked behind her ears. She'd given up bangs, and then layers, when she finally accepted that haircuts, at least for her, were a semiannual event at best. When they first met, Celia had compared her to Janice of Electric Mayhem. Isabel had managed a weak smile, because of course Celia had no idea that any mention of the Muppets dredged up memories of time spent in the basement waiting for various "uncles" to leave.

In the video, Isabel and Bonzi were in the kitchen. Celia had recorded them surreptitiously on her cell phone.

GOOD DRINK. ISABEL GIMME.

"You want a drink?" said Isabel. "How about some juice?"

Bonzi opened and closed her fist in front of her chest, and then brushed her chin with her index and middle fingers: MILK, SUGAR.

"No, Bonzi. I can't give you milk and sugar. You know that." Bonzi had recently been declared overweight by Peter and put on a diet.

GIMME MILK, SUGAR.

"I can't. I'm sorry. I'd get in trouble."

WANT MILK, SUGAR.

"I can't, Bonzi. You know I can't. Here, have some milk."

ISABEL GIVE MILK, SUGAR. SECRET.

Isabel threw her head back and laughed before slipping a little sugar into Bonzi's milk. She looked at the camera and held a finger to her lips, making Celia complicit. The clip ended abruptly.

Isabel opened another file.

In this one she was laughing, leading a team from *Primetime Live* to the observation room. She walked down a corridor, turning occasionally to walk a few steps backward, smiling at the camera.

As her onscreen self swung around, Isabel caught sight of her profile and thought, It was a good nose. Not perfect, but good. And her teeth too. She'd never had the luxury of braces, but in a land of perfect occlusion her teeth had personality. Her hair, which hung well beyond her shoulder blades, had taken years to grow.

Cut.

She sat cross-legged on the cement floor now, facing Sam. The cameraman was behind Plexiglass, but from the footage you'd never know it. The glass was invisible. The camera panned in, first to Sam's face, and then to hers.

"Sam, I want you to open the window now. Can you do that for me?" she said sweetly, signing simultaneously.

Sam's hands moved: SAM WANT ISABEL GIVE GOOD EGG.

"But Isabel wants Sam to open the window. Please? Now?"

NO. SAM WANT ISABEL GIVE GOOD EGG.

"Please open the window."

NO.

Her eyes flashed to the camera. She was clearly working hard to suppress a grin.

"Yes," she said emphatically. "Sam. Please make the window open."

YOU—

Isabel cut him off. "Sam, please open the window."

YES.

Isabel sighed with visible relief, but Sam did nothing. He sat sullenly, scanning the people around him, worrying his toes with his fingers, and finally averting his gaze.

"Sam, please open the window," she said again.

SAM WANT JUICE.

"No. Isabel wants Sam to open the window."

NO. SAM WANT ISABEL MAKE WINDOW OPEN.

At this, Isabel burst out laughing, and Sam got his juice and egg. The camera crew was thrilled by this exchange, but after they left, Peter turned to Isabel in a rage.

"Every other day he opens the damned window. This time, with a national television crew here, he can't open the window? And you *re-warded* him?"

Isabel had never seen this side of Peter and was startled. "Of course I rewarded him. He disagreed and argued his own point. If anything, that is an even more valid demonstration of using and understanding language than following orders. Not to mention that it proves definitively that he's not simply trained."

Peter's eyes were hard, his jaw set. "I told them he would perform specific tasks."

"He chose not to. He did nothing wrong. In fact, I think he was brilliant and I think we're extremely lucky this was captured on film."

Peter put his hands on his hips and exhaled so hard his cheeks puffed out. Then he ran a hand through his hair. His face softened. "You're right. I'm sorry. You're right. Look, I'm going to take a little walk, okay? Sort myself out. Back in a bit."

Isabel's memory lingered on this flash of temper. It was the only time she'd seen it, but now, combined with the curious comments from Gary and Rose, it made her wonder exactly what Peter had done during his time in Rockwell. The Primate Studies Institute had a terrible reputation—the owner was an imposing man with a salt-and-pepper beard known to subdue chimps with cattle prods and even a shotgun. But several leading primatologists had put in time at PSI as grad students, largely because there were very few programs in the country that provided access to primates. Most came out vowing that PSI had taught them how not to do things. This had always been Peter's line.

Isabel booted up her laptop and searched the Internet. His dissertation came up immediately: "Why Apes Don't Ape: How Motor Patterns and Working Memory Constrain Chimpanzee Social Learning," as did another article that had gotten him national recognition: "Cooperation or Joint Action: What Is Behind Chimpanzee Hunting and Coalitionary Behavior?" There were no surprises here—Peter's cognitive studies had been the primary reason Richard Hughes had hired him. There was certainly nothing to warrant Rose's comment.

Isabel called Celia.

"Glad to hear you're alive," said Celia. "Have you eaten?"

"I need a favor."

"You didn't answer."

"Celia, please."

"Okay. What?"

"You said at one point that Joel and Jawad can access private networks."

"Yes. And you were pretty horrified, if I remember correctly."

"Yes, well." Isabel cleared her throat. "Can you see what they can dig up about Peter, and what he was doing when he first went to PSI?"

"That's quite a turnaround."

"Please, Celia?"

"Okay." Celia sounded nonplussed. "I'll call you back."

Forty minutes later, she did. "Check your email," she said without salutation.

"Why? What did they find?"

"Please. Just check your email." Celia's voice was shaking.

Isabel's inbox was full: Joel had forwarded dozens of articles, abstracts, and briefs from Peter's days as a research assistant. He had participated in studies on the effects of maternal deprivation in chimpanzees, and, later, stress caused by immobilization. He had removed infants from their mothers at birth and placed them in cages with either a wire or a terry-cloth "mother" and clocked the differences in how long it took each group to die. He had placed chimpanzees in wooden chairs with their heads, hands, feet, and chest restrained, and had kept them there for weeks at a time, all to come to the stunning conclusion that this resulted in increased stress.

Isabel stared at images of chimpanzees strapped upright with a sickening sense of déjà vu. She knew these pictures. They were the same ones Gary and company had waved on sticks. The arrival of the protesters the year before suddenly made sense—it coincided with when Peter was hired.

Peter had always glossed over his time in Rockwell, dismissing his studies as noninvasive. She supposed that technically they were noninvasive—as long as all you meant by that was not drilling bolts into apes' brains or removing pieces of their internal organs. He had been sterner with the bonobos than the other researchers at the language lab, but she had always thought it was an alpha-male thing. And then she was hit by a wall of guilt, because it was this very quality she had found attractive.

She had fallen in love with a kidnapper, torturer, and murderer. She had opened herself up to him, made love with him, had been preparing to share her life with him, even to bear his children. He had told her what he wanted her to believe about his work, and naïvely, she'd believed it.

No wonder some chimp had taken off most of his finger. Isabel wished it had taken off his testicles instead.

————

That night she had vivid dreams: of Bonzi clipping her nails while Lola climbed all over her head. Of Makena wearing an inside-out blouse and gazing at herself in a mirror, alternately applying and nibbling lipstick. Of Jelani picking up branches and displaying in fearsome style, waving them over his head and staggering bipedally, then suddenly growing introspective. He came to Isabel on all fours, picked up her foot, and quietly unlaced her shoe. He removed it, and then her sock. His big hands, with their callused knuckles and hairy fingers, held her foot as he worked deftly, and oh-so-gently, searching between her toes for invisible nits.

In a flash she was in the other building. Men in hazmat suits marched down the concrete hall under glaring fluorescent lights, leaving a trail of screaming primates behind them. One pushed a gurney; another held a gun. When they slowed their pace the screams became even more deafening. They came to a stop in front of a cage, and the female inside realized they had come for her. She flew from side to side, trying to climb the walls, to find some way of escaping, but she had no chance. The man with the gun leveled it at her and shot her in the thigh. The men waited, chatting, while she staggered and fought the loss of consciousness. They continued chatting as they loaded the ape onto the gurney and secured her hands and feet with thick rubber straps. Several of her fingers and toes were chewed to nubs.

Isabel woke screaming. Her sheets were slick and cold with sweat, her heart pounding.

The next morning, she rose and solemnly turned all the framed pictures of the bonobos facedown. From a distance the downturned frames looked like a row of shark fins. She began sleeping on the couch under an afghan her grandmother had made.

She worked her way through the last of the food, eating peaches from the can, lime chutney from the jar. She ripped packages of ramen noodles open, set aside the seasonings, and broke off strips of long, uncooked noodles, which she crunched between her temporary teeth. When she ran out of all other options, she microwaved mugs of water and made broth from the seasoning packets.

She was pondering the tiny bottle of colorful flakes that had been the defunct Stuart's staple when there was a great pounding next door. Isabel jumped—red, yellow, and orange flakes flew everywhere, drifting on the air currents like snow.

"Jerry? Jerry! Open the damned door!" shouted her neighbor's lover. "I know you're in there! *Jerry!*"

Isabel dropped her head back and let her jaw drop. She then melted against the wall until she reached the floor. Stuart's food was scattered like confetti on the carpet.

Had she really been considering it as soup base?

———

Isabel finally accepted that she had to go buy food. She showered first, because she hadn't been dressed since her excursion to Alamogordo. Just before she stepped into the running water, she caught sight of herself in the mirror and stood back to survey herself.

She was gaunt, her face hollow and shadowed, her hip bones sticking out like the blades of a plow. The lines between her nose and mouth had deepened, and, of course, she still had virtually no hair. She raised a hand tentatively, tenderly, to her new nose and her delicately bristled scalp, and then stepped into the steaming water.

On a whim, Isabel took a right instead of a left on her way back from the supermarket. Her food was in the back, most of it frozen and actively melting, but she suddenly, desperately, needed a new Stuart. She needed something alive in her apartment, something she could feed, something that would look back at her.

She was nearly at the mall when something flashed in her peripheral vision. It was a digital billboard, its picture changing every few seconds.

A portion of a familiar black face (Was that Makena?) blended into a profile (Dear God, was that Bonzi? BONZI! Yes! She was sure!), and then two dark hairy hands clasped together.

The car beside her honked in panic as Isabel swerved into its lane. She yanked the wheel back and rammed the guardrail. Her side panels crunched rhythmically for the length of a few rails before the rear spun out. When she came to a stop, the chassis still bouncing and the engine ticking, she was facing a long line of cars with startled drivers. Several of them were already reaching for their cell phones.

I'm fine, she gestured with her hands. Everything's okay.

She held up her cell phone and pointed to it to indicate that she was calling for help herself.

———

As she waited for the tow truck, she studied the billboard. It was cycling pictures of the bonobos, but otherwise displayed only a date, time, and what appeared to be the address of a Web site: www.apehouse.tv.

Isabel had heard of dot coms, dot orgs, and dot nets, but dot tv?

When she arrived home she immediately turned on her computer and entered the address: the Web site turned out to be identical to the billboards, except that it had a clock ticking down toward the date and time, which was just a week away. Isabel studied the pictures of the bonobos carefully—they seemed to be in decent physical condition, but the stark white background offered no clues as to where they were or how they were being housed. Mbongo was displaying a stress grin, but at least Bonzi was holding Lola.

She called Celia, who consulted with Joel and Jawad, who traced ownership of the URL back to the corporate headquarters of Faulks Enterprises. From there, she didn't know what to expect. Faulks was apparently a pornographer. Isabel knew the sexual habits of the bonobos better than anyone, and wondered with increasing alarm how Faulks might intend to incorporate their behavior into his oeuvre. Information regarding the project appeared to be carefully guarded, but the "mystery meat" campaign was pervasive—viral, even—not only on billboards, but on television commercials and automatically generated Internet ads that clicked through to the same mysterious site. Animal activist boards were overrun with speculation about where the bonobos were and what Faulks was up to. No one had proof of anything, and since the information posted on such sites was dubious at best and the date on the official billboards, advertisements, and Web site was only a week away, Isabel decided to wait. Although the radicals had already mobilized, Isabel saw no point in wasting valuable resources on a false alarm.

The moment she had seen the billboard, her entire core hardened with resolve. Where she had been weak, now she was strong. Somehow, some way, she and the bonobos would be reunited.

16

James Hamish Watson just wanted the screaming to stop.

He'd been driving a forklift for thirty-some years and had never felt so desperate before. All he wanted to do was park and climb off.

The way his brother-in-law had described it, it was supposed to be a simple and fast job, damned close to a free lunch. All he had to do was lift a steel cage off a truck, drive it into a house, leave it there, and collect a day's wages. But when he'd done the required dry run (which he'd thought stupid at the time, but Ray had advised him not to argue with the boss man), there were no protesters to push past, no apes in the cage.

It was the apes that were giving him grief, not the protesters. He discovered that if you were willing to run over a few feet, protesters would get out of the way. But the apes shrieked and screamed, hurling themselves from one side of the cage to the other, clinging to the bars until the whole cage teetered dangerously on his pallet forks. He tried to right it with the side-to-side, but he grabbed the tilt lever by mistake. In thirty-two years, that was a first.

After nearly tipping the cage off the forks, he simply lowered the teeming, screeching mess to the floor. It was nowhere near flush with the wall and he knew he'd catch hell for that, but his head didn't feel right and he wanted to go home. He'd *pshawed* his wife's concerns about the job, but now he thought she was right—they might only be animals, but this was the Devil's work and he was sorry he'd gotten involved.

He studied the cage and its occupants with something akin to panic and inhaled sharply. Thin purple veins snaked around the base of his nose, anchoring it to his ruddy face like the knotty roots of a banyan. Sweat seeped between his frown lines, stinging his eyes.

Enough. He was finished.

He pivoted to face the door, cranked into gear, and jolted tank-like across the empty room. He paused in front of the open door and the swath of moving color that was the outside world, gritted his teeth, maneuvered through it, and was immediately sucked into the vortex of angry shouts, jabbing placards, bobbing television cameras, and blinding flashbulbs.

As the forklift exited, someone waiting in the anteroom pushed the door shut behind it.

The slam resonated through the house before warbling off into silence. A second slam marked the closure of the outside door.

Within the house, dozens of cameras affixed to junctures of ceiling and wall sprang to life, blinking red and swiveling silently.

Isabel sat rapt, watching the clock on the Web site as it ran down through the final seconds. When the counter reached zero, a message flashed, instructing people to turn their televisions to a specific station.

Isabel knocked her chair over in her rush to get to the TV. She fumbled with the controller, hitting the wrong combination of numbers twice before finally landing on the right channel.

She found herself looking at a vivid splash screen of a house that was meant to look like it was drawn by a child—squiggly primary-colored crayon marks that formed a square structure with peaked roof, four windows, door, and chimney. A minivan bounced and chugged up to the house, and six smiling apes hopped out. They jumped up and down, scratching their heads and armpits, while an obviously human voice hooted, *"Hoo hoo hoo haa haa haaaa!!"* The cartoon apes went inside and closed the door with such vigor the whole house shook. Moments later, smoke billowed from the chimney and apes waved at the windows before yanking the gingham curtains shut.

"Welcome to *Ape House,*" boomed an exaggerated baritone voice, "where the apes are in charge and you never know what's coming up next! Fifty-nine cameras! Six apes! One computer, and unlimited credit! And unlimited . . . Well, you *know* what they say about bonobos"—the voice paused long enough for the double-squonk of an old-time bicycle horn—"or *do* you? Find out what our 'Kissin' Cousins' get up to next, right here, on *Ape House*!"

The cartoon house disappeared in a poof of cartoon smoke, and suddenly there they were, the real apes, huddled together in the corner of a steel cage, a hairy black mass of long arms, long fingers, and even longer toes.

Isabel was breathless, kneeling on the floor with fingers pressed against the edges of the screen. Her stomach turned somersaults, contracting around a nugget of ice. She tried to count, to make sure they were all there, but it was impossible to tell where one ended and the next began.

The "Morning Mood" theme from *Peer Gynt* began, implying that the bonobos were about to wake from a peaceful slumber.

———

The bonobos clung together in silence. A lone peep rang out, followed by a series of high-pitched squeaks, which bounced off the empty walls. Bonzi extracted her callused and dark-knuckled hand from the mound to pat reassurance. She raised her head and met Sam's worried eyes, which darted from blinking camera to blinking camera, taking it all in.

A rasping buzzer preceded a definitive metal *thunk*. The apes shrieked and once again receded into themselves. The door of the cage began to rise, powered by hydraulic pistons, and came to rest in a groove at the top.

Once again, silence filled the building's interior.

For a long time, the only signs of life from the ape heap were the rise and fall of rib cages and occasional outbursts of primate distress. Finally, Sam and Bonzi extracted themselves. The others screamed and reached

for them, trying to pull them back, but they patiently peeled fingers and
toes from their hairy limbs. Bonzi handed Lola to Makena, paused to examine the pistons beside the cage door, and—after a moment's consideration—slowly, slowly ambled forth on her knuckles. Sam stood guard
by a piston and watched, his face the picture of attentive concentration.

Bonzi made her way to the center of the room and pivoted, taking
everything in. Lola and Makena hovered near the exit of the cage, wanting to be near her, but not enough to trust the pistons. They yipped high-
pitched warnings.

Bonzi went to the front door and sniffed it, touched it, ran her fingers along the seal at the bottom. She looked through the peephole
(which happened to be at ape height), and scrunched up her face. She
tasted the doorknob. She turned the deadbolt this way and that with
both hands, and then lay on her back and tried it with her feet. She
toured the perimeter of the room, which was empty but for the cage.

At the far end of the room, she found a doorway that led into another
all-beige room. When she entered, her eyes lit on a computer. She let
out a piercing shriek and loped over on all fours. She swung onto the
stainless-steel stool, her eyes glinting. Her large-knuckled fingers slid
beneath the Plexiglass shield and poked at the touch-sensitive screen,
finding and selecting, finding and selecting.

———

Isabel leaned even closer to the TV screen, trying to make out the symbols Bonzi was pressing. It was a bastardization of the software they
used in the lab. How in the hell had Faulks gotten hold of that? But
while the lexigrams in the lab allowed for complex utterances, this one
merely displayed categories of abstract nouns with the ability to drill
down to specific items. Bonzi chose among symbols that stood for food,
electronics, toys, tools, and clothing, navigating subcategory after subcategory without pause. Isabel was transfixed. In spite of herself, the scientist in her registered with relief that all of this was being recorded.

While Bonzi got to work, the other bonobos left the cage and tentatively began exploring the house ape-style. Isabel did a head count. They
were all there, all seemingly okay. She could see they were vocalizing but
couldn't hear them—what was being broadcast was the type of canned

music, sound effects, and laugh track associated with shows like *America's Funniest Home Videos*. The television screen separated dynamically to reflect areas of activity in the house. Bonzi remained in the center slice, parallel to a growing shopping list that was rendered as puffy handwriting, white crayon on red. Mbongo, in a square on the bottom left, went into each of the three bathrooms and turned the faucets on full blast. He relieved himself in the toilet and then stood flushing it over and over. Sam, in the square above Mbongo, explored the refrigerator and freezer, which were empty but for an automatic icemaker. He popped ice cubes into his mouth, one after another, until his cheeks bulged, at which point he shot them individually at various targets. On the right side of the screen, Jelani took running jumps at the wall, flipping backward when he reached the ceiling, while Makena looked on with an expression of adoration. Occasionally one of the other bonobos would drift into the room where Bonzi was and peep excitedly (Isabel could tell by their respirations and the way they shaped their lips) or even sign a request, which Bonzi dutifully entered. All the while Lola sat on Bonzi's head, peering at the screen and reaching out with tiny hands to press symbols of her own. The "handwritten" list grew until it began to scroll:

Eggs
Pears
Juice
M&M's
Onions
Milk
Blankets
Wrench
Doll
Screwdriver
Magazine
Bucket

Bonzi stared thoughtfully at the screen, carefully making her selections.

In the control room, Ken Faulks pumped his fist at the bank of monitors and jumped into the air. "Yes!" he screamed.

The room erupted into cheers. Champagne corks popped against a backdrop of joyous whooping.

A squat man with a black headset thrust a bottle toward the ceiling. "We did it! Congratulations, everyone! *Ape House* is live!"

"Long live *Ape House*!" a woman bellowed from the back.

"Long live *Ape House*!" yelled a chorus of voices.

Faulks's face was flushed. He was uncharacteristically passive when accepting handshakes and back pats. His hands even shook as he held out his glass so someone could fill it with champagne. With cheeks marked by lipstick and fingers curled around a flute of mostly bubbles, he turned away from his jubilant crew and back to the wall of monitors. They showed the house's interior from every conceivable angle: here the bathroom and its gleaming white porcelain; here the kitchen, with its maple cabinets; here the female ape, squatting on the stool in front of the wall-mounted computer, knees folded up beside her earnest face, baby perched on her head. The soundtrack being broadcast to the world, along with the actual noises coming from the house, were piped into the studio simultaneously.

Faulks leaned in close. A blinking green light indicated that this was one of the views streaming live—anyone tuned in was face-to-face with Bonzi (and according to Nielsen, anyone was potentially a great many people). The ape's bright eyes darted back and forth as she tracked the cursor on the screen in front of her. She paused to emit a series of emphatic peeps over her shoulder.

Faulks raised a hand and traced the outline of her jaw on the glass with the back of his finger.

"That's my girl," he whispered.

"Hey—hands off my screen," muttered the only engineer who hadn't left his post. He was hunched over his controls. After a moment of nonresponse he did a double-take, registering Faulks's steely look. "I mean, please," he said. "Sir."

17

John yanked his tie loose while waiting for the garage door, which jerked arthritically upward. His left hand dangled out the window, grasping the black plastic garage door opener and tapping it against the side panel of the car. When the garage door finally reached the top of its track, John aimed the clicker and pressed again. Then he slapped the whole thing against the padded steering wheel so the button would unstick. Left to its own devices the door would go up and down forever.

He was convinced the commute was killing him: an hour and twenty minutes each direction in bumper-to-bumper traffic, stewing in filthy emissions so he could spend the day writing shampoo copy for Procter & Gamble in a cubicle that shook each time the elevator went past. They had just offered to extend his contract by three weeks, despite being obviously underwhelmed by his first efforts, which included such gems as "Head & Shoulders, Won't Be Snowing Boulders" (although he had meant that as a joke, and was beyond mortified when a colleague presented it at a meeting).

He knew he should be grateful. He was not flipping burgers. He was not measuring garbage, or potholes, or counting stripped car frames on the side of the highway. But he was also not in Lizard, New Mexico, covering *Ape House.*

The day after John arrived in L.A., he had looked through the windshield and done a double-take. A quarter of a mile ahead, on thirty-foot posts, was a digital billboard cycling photographs of the bonobos. A hairy hand here, a whiskered chin there. Unchanging red text across the bottom gave the address of a Web site and a date, nothing more. It didn't take long for him (and Cat, and various other of the reporters from major papers still assigned to the story) to figure out that Ken Faulks, John's old boss from the *New York Gazette,* was behind it. John was now obsessively following the reports.

Apparently Faulks had acquired the apes and built them an ape-proof house with a courtyard in a remote area of New Mexico best known for its third-rate casinos and "gentlemen's clubs." The house contained cameras designed to catch every angle of every room, but was otherwise entirely empty except for a single computer and a stool so the apes could reach it. Faulks installed the apes, switched on the cameras, and had been broadcasting the results live ever since.

A handful of animal rights activists had been present at the house from the very beginning, but no one really believed the endeavor would last more than a couple of days. Surely even the notorious Ken Faulks— who had made his fortune on porn series such as *Busty Lusty Ladies, Jiggly Gigglies,* and *Crazy Cougars*—wouldn't let endangered great apes starve to death in an empty house on live television.

But it turned out that Ken Faulks was the only person who did not underestimate the bonobos. They used the computer to order food. Then they ordered blankets and kiddie pools and play structures and beanbag chairs. They even ordered televisions. They didn't technically order the installation man, but they let him do his thing before showing him the door. John had seen the news footage of his exit: ashen and shaken, the man had staggered from the front door and fallen into the arms of the nearest protester in a dead faint. Apparently some sort of intimate kissing had been involved, although the actual kiss had not been broadcast on *Ape House* because of "technical difficulties."

In the five days since, the show gave every indication of becoming the biggest phenomenon in the history of modern media, and not simply because of the astonishing language and computer skills of the bonobos. It was the sex. Having witnessed it firsthand, John was not surprised, but apparently the rest of the world was. The bonobos incorporated sex into every aspect of their lives, and as a result, human audiences were hooked. The bonobos had sex to say hello. They had sex before eating. They had sex to alleviate tension. They had sex in so many combinations, so frequently, and in so many positions that after three days the FCC forced the show off the air. But Ken Faulks was no stranger to the FCC: he had a secondary system set up and ready to go, and without a second's interruption in broadcasting, *Ape House* was made available by satellite and the Internet, beyond the FCC's reach, and—not coincidentally—only to paying subscribers.

At last count, more than 25 million people had called in their credit card numbers. John was one of them.

———

When John entered the living room, he found Amanda sitting in the middle of the carpet with one leg chicken-winged beneath her and the other sticking out straight. Her laptop was in front of her, causing her to hunch over as she typed. Crumpled paper dotted the floor around her. The TV was blaring in front of her.

The screen was a collage of small squares, each displaying a different view from inside *Ape House*. One ape admired himself in a mirror and picked his teeth. Others swung from doorjambs and scooted across floors. Another lolled in a kiddie pool, repeatedly filling his mouth from a hose and spitting jets of water. In the top right frame, two wildly grinning females joined in a passionate embrace and began rubbing together their swollen genitals, which looked like large wads of chewed bubble gum. A Klaxon horn blew three times as this frame enlarged and slid to the center of the screen. It grew an outline and digital shadow. HOKA-HOKA!!! said a garish and flashing bright-red subtitle. The whole thing was accompanied by frenetic clown music and canned sound effects—whistles, pings, and boings.

"What's up?" said John.

Amanda looked up. Her hair, newly blond and perfectly straight, swung back to reveal a thick white paste smeared across her upper lip. It had a crystalline appearance, sugary and alchemic.

"I'm bleaching my mustache," she said. "Not sure I can do it after my appointment tomorrow, and apparently it's another of my many flaws."

A few days ago one of Amanda's new bosses—the one who had called her "refreshingly different"—had given her the name of a dermatologist and suggested in a tone Amanda interpreted as an order that she get injections of Restylane, a popular face plumper, along with Botox and some sort of laser treatment to get rid of her freckles. John couldn't fathom why a writer needed to look like a movie star, but it seemed to be true: recently there had been a scandal involving a nineteen-year-old scriptwriting ingenue who was feted and celebrated until she was discovered to be thirty-five, at which point she could no longer find work. Although Amanda's latest round of transformations were clearly traceable to this one specific idiot's mutterings about the Hollywood "type," in his heart, John blamed Uncle Ab. If only the scotch-addled old man had kept his yap shut at the wedding—

"I mean what's up in general," said John.

"Oh," said Amanda, rising to her feet. "You should probably look at the fridge."

"Why?" said John, staring at the television. The genital-rubbing apes had gone their separate ways and were relegated back to the bottom left corner. One was now wearing a bucket on her head. In another square, an ape lay on a beanbag chair with his legs crossed, casually flipping through a magazine.

Arroogah! Arroogah! The Klaxon horn sounded as a different square enlarged and slid to the center of the screen. A male walking upright presented his long, pointy erection to another ape.

"I just think you should," Amanda said, disappearing into the bathroom. John sighed, dragged a hand down his face, and went to the kitchen. The last thing he needed to deal with was a broken refrigerator.

As he opened its door to investigate, a neon pink Post-it note came unstuck and fluttered to the ground. He stooped to pick it up. He stared at it for a moment and then called into the hallway. "Amanda?"

The bathroom door opened and Amanda sailed out. She had

changed out of her drawstring pants and was wrapped in a fuzzy white robe, her upper lip scrubbed pink. She passed between John and the refrigerator and reached inside for a beer.

"Yes?" she said, handing him the bottle.

He twisted the cap off and handed it back to her. "What did the *Times* want?"

"A job interview, I assume," she said, and broke into a wide grin.

John stared at her for a moment, then whooped in joy.

———

"Pendleton Group. How may I direct your call?"

John's brow furrowed. He glanced down at the Post-it note, which was stuck along the length of his forefinger. The *Los Angeles Times* was owned by the Tribune Company. Everybody knew that.

"Topher McFadden, please," he said, reading the name from the Post-it. John had not heard of him; he must be an editorial assistant, or a new addition.

"Which division?"

"The *Times*. Editorial," John said.

"One moment, please." There was a click, followed by waterfall noises and birdsong. It cut off abruptly after several seconds.

"Yes?" said a languorous male voice.

John propped the phone between his ear and shoulder and set about detangling the coils of the cord. "Hello. This is John Thigpen. You left a message for me earlier today?"

"Oh, yes. So I did. I have your résumé here." The sound of paper rustling. "Pretty impressive. Internship, and then eight years at the *New York Gazette*. A year plus at *The Philadelphia Inquirer*. Some freelance work for *The New York Times*."

"Thank you."

"So what brings you to the City of Angels?"

"My wife is co-writing a series for NBC."

"What's it about?"

"Single women navigating the jungle of urban relationships."

"Like *Sex and the City*."

"It's similar. I guess."

"So she's ripping it off. Like *Cashmere Mafia,* or *Lipstick Jungle.*"

John swallowed loudly. "Not at all. It's got its own . . . twists."

"Sure it does," said Topher McFadden. "So, do you want to come in tomorrow? Maybe at ten?"

"That would be great," said John.

"Good. Bring a double-shot grande skinny latte. Two sugars."

"Would you like a dusting of Madagascar cinnamon with that?" said John, smiling at his own little joke.

This was followed by a devastating, cricket-filled silence. John's smile reversed itself. Either the man had never watched *Frasier* or he had no sense of humor. John's instincts leaned toward the latter.

"Do you know where we are?" McFadden finally said.

"Yes. Of course. You're on West First."

"Huh? We're what?" A pause, and then, "Wait—are you shitting me? With Simon Bell at the helm? You think they're hiring? You're shitting me, aren't you?"

"No," said John. "No, I'm afraid I wasn't."

———

John descended the stairs slowly. Amanda had a selection of pots and pans out on the counter and was crushing garlic cloves with the flat side of a knife. A copper pan was on the stove behind her, a generous lump of butter melting within.

She glanced up at John. "Was that the *Times?*"

"Yes."

She turned to swirl the saucepan with both hands, making sure the bottom was evenly coated. "How did it go?"

"They want an interview." He paused, watching as she tipped the pan from side to side.

"Oh! That's great!"

"The only thing is, it's not the *L.A. Times.*"

Amanda reached for a wooden spoon from a canister on the counter. "What do you mean?"

"It was the *Weekly Times,*" John continued. After a moment he added, "I didn't apply to the *Weekly Times.* It's a tabloid."

She stopped stirring for a second, and then resumed.

"Amanda?"

"Yes?" she said cautiously. The distribution of butter had suddenly become utterly absorbing.

"Is there something you want to tell me?"

She tapped the spoon against the edge of the pan and set it on the counter.

"How did they get my résumé?" John continued.

She closed her eyes for a moment and leaned against the counter. "I might have sent it."

"You *might* have sent it?"

"Okay. Yes," she said, turning to face him. "One of the producers said he knows an editor at the *Times* and he said he'd put in a word for you, so I emailed your résumé."

John stared with an open mouth.

"What?" she said. "I don't understand why you're angry."

"It's a *tabloid*! I can't write about stars in rehab and stupid skinny blond girls and who's boinking them."

"I didn't know," she said. Her voice had taken on an edge. "I also thought it was the *L.A. Times*."

John opened his mouth and then snapped it shut again. He swiped the car keys from the counter.

"John! Wait!" She was suddenly behind him, holding his wrist. "What's going on here? If you don't want the job, don't go to the interview. Nobody's forcing you. I was just trying to help."

"You think I can't get a job by myself? Is that what you think?"

"What is wrong with you?" she said.

Finally, she let go of his wrist. He went back to the garage, coaxed the Jetta's engine to turn over, and screeched down the street, bypassing third gear altogether and leaving the garage door in the mostly-up position.

———

John had no idea where he was going. He headed toward the Santa Monica Freeway with the vague notion of streaming down it until his fury dissipated, but traffic was jammed from the moment he got on the entrance ramp. By then, he was already committed. He had no choice now but to bake in the smog and creep along toward the next exit.

The *Weekly Times* was the rag that people surreptitiously thumbed through while their groceries crawled along the belt in the checkout lane. John tried to remember if he'd ever seen anyone openly reading it—occasionally in an airport or a hotel, cloaked by anonymity. Maybe at the dentist's, but even then it was only because the alternatives were *Forbes* or *Golf Illustrated.*

If he worked for them, that would be the end of his credibility as a reporter. That, or he'd have to fake a hole in his résumé when and if they left L.A., which would be almost as bad as admitting he'd been with the *Weekly Times.*

John blinked rapidly, bringing himself back into the moment. The cars began moving again, requiring him to shift from first gear to second to first again, keeping one foot poised over the clutch. He rolled up the window and turned on the air-conditioning.

His cell phone buzzed against his thigh. He dug it out and flipped it open. Amanda had sent a text:

U THR?

John held his phone up above the steering wheel so he could see the traffic beyond and thumb-typed: NO.

He snapped the phone shut and tossed it onto the passenger seat. He turned his gaze back to the highway, although the traffic wasn't moving. He focused on the thin wisp of blue exhaust coming from the tailpipe of the convertible in front of him.

The phone buzzed again.

Y R U MAD? PLS TALK 2 ME.

He didn't answer, because he didn't have an answer to give.

A horn blared from behind, and John looked up to see a three-car gap in front of him. In the rearview mirror the driver behind him gesticulated wildly. John raised a hand in apology and pulled up.

John glanced at the phone, hoping she would text again and then realized that no, of course she wouldn't, because he was being a complete jerk. It also became entirely clear to him that he was not angry with her. He was terrified. He had been methodical and relentless in his job-hunting, spending two hours a night at it, keeping spreadsheets and notes in three-ring binders. So far, he hadn't gotten so much as a nibble from anywhere he actually wanted to work. And, of course, the very first place he had applied to was the *L.A. Times*.

Was writing for the *Weekly Times* really worse than writing shampoo copy? It would certainly be more secure than a temporary job, assuming they even wanted him. If Amanda was serious about having children— which she appeared to be—they needed an income they could count on.

Another horn sounded. John eased up on the clutch and the Jetta was actually in motion before he looked up and realized that the car in front of him hadn't moved. He slammed on the brakes so violently his engine stalled and his phone dropped to the floor. Against the blaring of horns, he laid his head against the steering wheel, and then reached down to retrieve the phone from the floor pads that were still stained with salt from the streets of Philadelphia.

———

It was past midnight before he cut the engine and coasted into the garage, Garp-style. All the lights were off.

Amanda was asleep in the center of the bed with her arms thrown over her head. The television was on, and an electric guitar ground out a primal soundtrack while bald security guards held two fantastically obese women apart as dry ice wafted around them. Their fists flew, their legs spun like egg beaters. Both were down to their bras and black-wired microphones, although one of them still had the tattered remains of her shirt tucked into the waist of her Tweedle Dee stretch pants. She brandished a wig torn off the head of her rival and shrieked a string of obscenities that were rendered as solid bleeps. The apparent object of dispute was a lanky man slouched in a chair behind them. He sat with knees spread and eyebrows raised in a combination of annoyance and boredom. Look at what I put up with, his expression seemed to say. Jerry Springer arranged his features into a look of unspeakable sadness, shaking his head as the camera panned past.

John switched the television off and undressed in the dark. He sat on the edge of the bed and stared down at Amanda, who was milky-blue in the pale glow of the streetlight. She stirred and opened her eyes.

"Hey," she said, rolling over to make room for him.

"Hey," he replied.

He slipped between the sheets and tucked his knees into the space behind hers. When he draped an arm over her rib cage she took his hand in both of hers and squeezed it beneath her chin.

"I'm sorry," she mumbled. "I shouldn't have sent your résumé. I was just trying to help."

"I know," he said. "And I'm sorry I was such an ass. I'm going to go to the interview."

After just a moment, John pressed his nose into her hair. It was smooth and slick, unlike her old hair, but it still smelled like her. He took a deep breath and held it in, taking an olfactory snapshot. He kissed the back of her head and closed his eyes.

18

Five days before, Isabel had spent the night of *Ape House*'s debut glued to the television. It didn't take long for her to figure out the premise. In fact, it took Isabel about as long as it took Bonzi.

After Bonzi had poked lexigrams representing various objects and clearly decided her actions were having no effect, she left the computer. Shortly thereafter, a doorbell rang. Although what Isabel could hear through the TV was a sound effect (like the rest of the soundtrack), something actual had happened within the house because the bonobos gathered in the main room, their heads swiveling suspiciously.

Ding dong!

Sam and Mbongo rushed the front door several times, pounding it with hands and feet before leaping back. Then they kept guard from a dozen feet back. Their hair bristled, making them look larger.

Ding dong!

Sam approached the door and lined an eye up at the peephole. After a moment's scrutiny, he flung the door open and jumped back. Immediately beyond it sat several crates, brimming with the goodies Bonzi had ordered.

A celebratory orgy ensued, set against a canned laugh track. The sex was followed by feasting and mutual grooming.

Isabel watched from her place on the floor until the bonobos formed nests out of their new blankets, surrounded by discarded fruit boxes, milk and juice jugs, candy wrappers, and other detritus. An unbearable ache seized her heart when she realized that Bonzi had gathered exactly six blankets and was folding their edges as she always had. Then she called to Lola, who was investigating the hinges of a kitchen cabinet with a wrench. When Lola looked, Bonzi signed, BABY COME! and Lola bounded over and into the nest to let Bonzi groom her into slumber. Isabel wondered if any of the viewing audience had any idea what they had just witnessed: one of the most exciting discoveries to come from the language lab was that once bonobos acquired human language they passed it on to their babies, communicating with a combination of ASL and their own vocalizations.

Isabel didn't move until all the bonobos were asleep. The frenzied soundtrack had been replaced by a synthesized version of the Brahms lullaby with an occasional human snore or whistle tossed in. The cameras zoomed in on the rise and fall of chests, the pucker of a whiskered chin caught on the exhale. Only then did Isabel go to bed herself, leaving the television on. Several times during the night she awoke and sat bolt upright, checking the screen to make sure she hadn't made the whole thing up. But there they were, snoozing in their nests.

The next day, after a CNN broadcast confirmed that the show was airing from Lizard, New Mexico, Isabel was on a plane to El Paso. She rented a car, drove to Lizard, and settled into the Mohegan Moon, a hotel next to the largest casino. With *Ape House* playing on the flatscreen TV, she gave her sheets a couple of spritzes of Spirit of Ylang Ylang—the hotel had provided a variety of essential oils designed to promote relaxation—and collapsed on the bed, fully dressed.

The feather duvet was soft, and she slipped her arms beneath the pillows. She didn't intend to fall asleep, but at some point she realized that not only was it morning, but also that six hours had passed since she'd last checked the apes.

In the center square of the television, Makena and Bonzi performed a quick genito-genital rub before splitting a banana. Makena was wearing an inside-out fleece shirt and carried a doll in the crook of her arm.

She would give birth soon, and Isabel felt a stab of panic: she had no reason to believe that the producers even knew Makena was pregnant. It wasn't the same as looking at a woman in her eighth month; to the untrained eye, a bonobo pregnancy could easily go undetected.

Isabel rose immediately, and, without bothering to change her clothes, covered her baldness with a pale blue mohair beret. She then asked the concierge for directions to where *Ape House* was filming.

The place was teeming with protesters, many of whose issues had only tenuous connections with the apes. Certainly animal rights and activist groups were represented, but so were Christian Right protesters, anti-war protesters, Intelligent Design protesters, gay pride groups, Support Our Troops protesters, people on both sides of the abortion fence, and one particularly large and odious family calling themselves the Eastborough Baptist Church, who demanded the deaths of all homosexuals, human or otherwise. Camera crews surfed the perimeter, sampling the groups as though they were dim sum. Isabel caught snippets of the carefully rehearsed sound bites:

"Make love, not war! Be one with your inner bonobo! Harness pleasure for peace, and peace for—"

"—proving yet again that homosexuality is a naturally occurring phenomenon in the animal kingdom, and discrediting the basis of any and all politically and religiously motivated—"

"—maybe *you're* related to monkeys, but I'm certainly not. The Bible clearly states that man was created in God's image and that we have dominion over all of God's creation, including apes. He put them here on earth for our use and entertainment, whatever form that may—"

"—nothing more than prime-time pornography. This is typical of the kind of so-called 'entertainment' that corrupts the minds and morals of our youth. We pray, O God, for the souls of the sinners and pornographers who willfully expose our nation's children and young people to wanton fornication and senseless acts of—"

"—intelligent, curious, and highly social animals that deserve to be treated with the same dignity and respect we demand for our—"

Isabel made her way through the crowd. When a body shifted, she slipped into the gap, moving forward until she was finally within sight of the building. She stopped and drew her breath, aware that she was within a hundred yards of the bonobos. She felt a sensation like a fist tightening around her heart.

The real Ape House looked nothing like the cartoon drawing. It was a single-story, flat-roofed building with no windows, like a smaller version of the Corston Foundation. Its walls were concrete and uninterrupted except for the front door, which was wide enough for a small vehicle to drive through, an occurrence Isabel observed three times in close succession: everything the bonobos ordered was delivered in crates on the front end of a forklift. The crowd always turned as one, standing on tiptoe and trying to catch sight of the apes, but they never did. The forklift dropped the goods off in an anteroom, which was closed before the apes accessed them through an inside door. Speculation about what the crates contained usually subdued the crowd temporarily, and there was nearly universal laughter when a kiddie pool arrived. But when the front door closed and the forklift retreated, the fight for attention and airtime resumed.

—

Isabel was about to go back to the hotel when the buzzing began. At first she thought it was in her head—she was overwhelmed by the crowd and felt nauseated, as if she'd had too much sun. But when other people's heads started turning and the yapping mouths lost track of where they were mid-rant, she realized the noise was external. The buzz soon became a *thwackity-thwackity* with a vibration so deep Isabel felt it through her entire body. Black-suited security guards wearing noise-reduction headsets herded the crowd backward and erected sawhorse barriers along a portion of the wall. A helicopter appeared, dangling a large and ungainly object that twirled at the end of its cables. Isabel glanced up at it, squinting into the blindingly bright New Mexico sky—there was wood, rope webbing, and yellow plastic tubing, all of it spinning and swaying. The helicopter hovered directly over Ape House and slowly lowered the play structure behind the walls of the courtyard. The cables were detached and retracted, and the helicopter swooped away.

The people around the house, most of whom had crouched and covered their ears, were momentarily silent. They rose one by one, shielding their eyes with their hands. After the helicopter disappeared from sight, anchors once again began earnestly addressing cameramen, and protesters, as though roused from sleep, resumed poking their boards and flags into the air. A few people gathered around laptops and BlackBerries, trying to figure out via the Internet what they had just witnessed.

Isabel decided they had the right idea. She would learn far more from watching what was being broadcast from within Ape House than by standing outside it.

The hotel bar was crowded and the restaurant empty, which Isabel attributed to the fact that the former was playing *Ape House* on the overhead televisions and the latter was not.

She spotted the last available stool between two burly men, and slid onto it. Both men nursed beers while keeping their eyes on the television, where the apes cavorted on their new play structure in the courtyard. Mbongo walked out with an erection and two oranges. Bonzi approached, rubbed her hips up against him, and left with both pieces of fruit.

"I dropped them off in there," said the man on Isabel's right.

She couldn't tell who he was talking to, as he continued to face forward. His cheeks were ruddy to the point of discoloration, the base of his nose surrounded by plum-colored veins.

When no one else responded, Isabel said, "Who? The apes?"

"Yep," he said. He looked down at his kielbasa-like fingers. "Drove 'em right in on my forklift. Put up a real fuss, they did. Could've had the delivery job too, but my wife—that's Ray's sister—she don't like the whole idea. Says she won't have it on our TV at home, so I have to come here to watch."

"Oh, really?" said Isabel. "She doesn't approve?"

"It's because of all the other stuff Ray helps out with." He glanced over quickly, his potatoey face looking unexpectedly boyish and bashful. He lowered his voice to a whisper. "*Porn.* He works on movies with Ken Faulks. He doesn't do, you know, *that,* but he helps out on the sets. Does special effects—dry ice, pyrotechnics, that kind of stuff."

Isabel leaned in closer, feeling immensely grateful that she had put on a pretty hat that morning. She smiled with demurely closed lips, because although she had her teeth in, that was only by virtue of having accidentally fallen asleep with them in place.

19

The day of the job interview, John was shaved, showered, and drinking coffee at the counter with his tie thrown over his shoulder before Amanda appeared.

She was in her robe with a towel turban on her head. She padded over and got herself a cup of coffee, her very aura subdued.

John set his coffee down and went over to her. "Hey," he said, rubbing her lower back. "You okay?"

She nodded. "Yeah." Then she put her mug on the counter and shuddered. "Actually, no. I'm terrified. I can't stand the thought of getting needles in my face. What if I move and make him slip?"

"So don't get it done. You don't need to. That guy is a complete idiot."

"Even if he is, he's also the executive producer." She took a deep breath. "No. I'll be okay. Everyone says it's not that bad." She kissed John quickly, distractedly, and picked up her coffee. "Good luck with the interview."

"Thanks," he said, and watched helplessly as she disappeared into the hall.

John pushed the door to the building open with his hip, clutching the corrugated cardboard sleeve of the double-shot grande skinny latte. He stepped into the lobby and stopped to absorb it, his preconceived notions shattered. Apparently somebody bought the *Weekly Times*. Lots of somebodies.

The reception area was high-ceilinged and airy, graced with red leather sectionals arranged in semicircles. Glass-topped cherrywood tables displayed perfect fans of the most recent issues of the *Weekly Times*. Square candles in sugared glass glowed on either end of a glass-topped reception desk, and a large slate waterfall burbled peacefully against the end wall. Above it was a super-size magazine logo.

John breathed the scented air deeply, trying to shift his attitude. He'd suffered humiliation at the hands of a barista only minutes before, having mangled the wording of his order. His mind had been on Amanda and her face full of needles, and he'd stuttered something that, while inelegant, had apparently been functional, since he'd ended up with the correct beverage. When the barista gave John his change, she also gave him a pitying smile and reminded him that it was actually called a double-shot grande skinny latte.

John approached the reception desk. The polished young woman behind it looked up. "May I help you?" she said, smiling without showing teeth. Her skin was flawless and entirely smooth. John wondered if he was looking at evidence of Restylane. A little apple-plump about the cheeks, a pillowy *je ne sais quoi* about the upper lip.

"Uh, yes. I have an appointment with Topher McFadden at ten." John set the latte on the counter. The woman's eyes followed it. A dribble of coffee pooled at its base. He snatched it up again, leaving a ring.

"Your name?"

"John Thigpen."

"Thigpen?"

"Yes. Thigpen."

"I'll let him know," the woman said in the reverent hush of a librarian. "Please have a seat."

"Thanks," said John, lowering his own voice accordingly.

He set his briefcase on the floor and perched uncomfortably on a red furniture arrangement. After a moment, he dug a tissue from his pocket, folded it, and used it as a coaster for the latte so he wouldn't besmirch the beveled glass.

The receptionist looked into his eyes and flicked her perfectly manicured fingers against her shoulder. John knitted his brows. She repeated the gesture. John glanced down and found his tie still tossed safely over his shoulder. He flushed and smoothed it against the front of his shirt. No wonder the barista had thought he was a bumpkin.

The receptionist took a phone call, and John trained his eyes on the door to the street and the legs that paraded beyond its vast panes—the starched creases, the sheer stockings, the teetering stilettos. The combat boots, oxbloods, and running shoes. Waddling legs, strutting legs, purposeful legs—furry legs that lifted so a stream of urine could hit the corner of the stone before the leash above yet another set of legs gave a firm tug.

John's heart was pounding.

On the table beside him was an array of glossy magazine phantasmagoria—tousled hair extensions, bubble dresses, and impossibly high heels with red soles. White veneers peeked between lips that looked like platypus bills. Surgically enhanced faces balanced on necks as skinny as stems.

DIET OR SURGERY? shrieked the headlines.

THE FEUD GETS NASTY!

CAUGHT!

HOLLYWOOD NANNIES TELL ALL!

BOOB JOBS GONE *BAD*!

John glanced up and found the receptionist flirting with a FedEx man. He picked up one of the magazines.

A morbidly obese blond-bouffanted drag queen named Madam Butterfly offered quips on the worst of the week's red-carpet disasters. Tiny starlets hid behind Sputnik-sized sunglasses, and pencil-thin women gazed mournfully over their shoulders at phalanxes of cameras.

John had one leg straddled over the other, completely absorbed, when someone called his name.

The newsroom was enormous, with waist-high cubicle walls that allowed for no privacy but nearly equal access to natural daylight. Monitors streaming news stations hung overhead, and young, thin, well-coiffed people rushed through the aisles with armloads of paper, proofs, and photographs.

As John entered a corner office with floor-to-ceiling glass panes, Topher McFadden stood to greet him. He was expensively and colorfully dressed, in an apple-green shirt and periwinkle silk tie, a combination that should not have worked but did. His glasses and shoes were chunky and square. He was fit and tanned, with a thatch of blond hair, and could have been anywhere from twenty-five to forty-five. John hoped he was closer to forty-five, given the obvious differences in their situations. They shook hands.

"Have a seat," said Topher McFadden, gesturing toward a couch. He retreated behind his desk.

John sat and toppled downward into the buttery leather. He struggled to the front—no small feat while balancing a hot drink, as it involved a fair bit of scootching and an unfortunate chair fart. He balanced carefully on the edge. The differences in furniture rendered him almost two feet shorter than his interviewer.

"Uh, here," said John, stretching forth to set the skinny ultra double-freaking la-ti-dah on the desk.

Topher McFadden grabbed the coffee. He located the drink hole and sucked long and hard.

"So. Brass tacks," he said, reaching for John's résumé. "I see you interned for Ken Faulks. Were you friendly?"

"He's Ken Faulks," John explained, although he perked up at the mention of Faulks's name.

"Huh," said McFadden. He swung his feet up onto his desk and made a steeple with his fingers. "Have you seen his new project? With those monkeys in that house in New Mexico? It's huge, unprecedented. And it's going to get bigger. I want someone out there, someone with an edge."

John's heart skipped a beat. He caught his breath. He tried to hold back, but before he knew it, he was rambling.

"That was my story at the *Inky*. Never mind just interning with Faulks at the *Gazette,* which I did, of course—I've also met the apes. I was in the language lab literally hours before it got bombed."

"Really?" said McFadden. He shifted slightly, changed the angle of his head, examining John more closely.

"Really. I know the history of those apes. I know their names. I know the work they were doing—hell, I *talked* with them. I *talked* with them—a two-way conversation. And the scientist who got hurt. And I worked for Faulks. I'm good. I'm hungry. I want my story back, and I'm the best person for it. I'll do anything to get it. You won't be sorry."

Topher McFadden looked at John long and hard. His fingers were once again undulating like a jellyfish. "So why did you leave the *Inquirer* again?"

John stared and tried not to grind his teeth. "Let's just say a colleague there threw me under the bus, and I had very strong reasons for wanting to be here."

"Your wife?"

"Yes. My wife."

McFadden smiled and swung his feet down from his desk.

"Well then. Looks like the *Inky*'s loss is our gain. How soon can you leave for Lizard?"

———

John's cell phone rang while he was pulling out of the parking garage. It was Amanda.

"Did you get the job?" she said.

"You're a goddess! A genius!" he said, propping the phone between his ear and his shoulder so he could pay the attendant.

"I am?"

"Yes! I'm back on the ape story!"

She shrieked, so loudly he nearly dropped the phone. "Oh my God! Honey! I'm so happy for you!"

"Did you get your face done?"

"Yes, but never mind that. Tell me about the assignment."

"It means I have to go to New Mexico almost immediately, but I'm—"

"Oh, shit," Amanda said, cutting him off. "That's Sean on call-waiting. Sorry, babe. I have to take it. Which reminds me, we're going to a party tonight. See you soon. Pick up champagne!"

———

John went home with champagne in hand and found a note from Amanda on the fridge explaining that she would be at a series of appointments in preparation for the party and didn't know how long she'd be out. She asked him to be ready by eight and signed it with exes and ohs.

She walked through the door at five minutes to the hour, took one look at John, and said, "You're not wearing that, are you?"

Her hair was swept up in a pile of loose blond curls of the kind achieved by hard work, hot rollers, and hairpins. Her perfect toenails peeked out of open-toed high-heeled shoes whose crimson soles sent a warning chill up John's spine (he had seen celebrities teetering on similarly red-soled shoes earlier in the day in an issue of the *Weekly Times*). Her body was encased in a black knit sheath dress that went over only one shoulder.

She blinked expectantly. He remembered her question.

"I was planning to, yes," he said, looking down at himself. He was still in his interview garb, minus the tie.

"I'm in Christian Louboutins," she said by way of explanation. John had no idea what that meant.

"You want me to put my tie back on?" he asked.

She shook her head and smiled. Clearly he was hopeless.

"Here, let me look at you," he said, going over and tilting her face up to the light. She turned obligingly.

The contours of her face looked exactly the same to him as they had that morning. "Remind me—what's supposed to be different?"

"I'm a little fuller here," she said, indicating the area between her nose and mouth, "and here." She pointed toward her lips. "He also injected a little bit under my eyes, and my freckles are gone. And in a few days apparently I won't be able to frown."

"How will I know if you're mad at me?"

She laughed. "Oh, you'll know."

"How much did it cost?"

After a slight pause she said, "Eleven hundred dollars."

John blanched. *"Eleven hundred dollars?"*

"But on the bright side, if I keep it up I'll never get wrinkles," she said quickly. "The muscles will atrophy. And I think we can write it off . . . maybe."

At that moment, the doorbell rang.

Amanda turned and ran her eyes over John.

"Look, why don't you just go without me?" John said. "I'm not all that good at schmoozing anyway."

"Are you sure?" she said, swiping her tiny sequined purse from the hall table.

"Yeah," said John, although he was more than a little curious about this world of celebrities his wife was starting to inhabit.

"We'll have the champagne when I get back," she said.

"Okay," he said.

She kissed him good-bye and opened the door long enough to reveal Sean, who appeared to have gone to great effort to look like a greasy and unshaven addict. Sean muttered something to John and raised a hand in greeting as Amanda lurched out on what had to be five-inch heels. The door slammed.

John stared at the back of it for a few seconds.

Eleven hundred dollars?

Eventually he took his laptop to bed to dig up everything he could find on the apes. So far, nobody had succeeded in getting an interview with Ken Faulks, any of the university's board members, or any of the scientists involved in the project. Peter Benton was actively eluding the media, smugly invoking the usual clichés as though he were some kind of celebrity: "No comment," he'd say from behind dark glasses, or lifting his hand to block the camera's lens. As for Isabel Duncan, she appeared to have fallen off the face of the earth. She had never granted an interview, and had never returned to the university. He remembered her cryptic comment about family and hoped that wherever she was, she was okay.

———

Amanda was home three hours later, a dark shadow slipping into the bedroom.

"Party over already?" John said. He was half asleep, his glazed eyes fixed on the late show. He'd watched *Ape House* until the bonobos were asleep.

"No!" she spat, hurling her purse against the wall and sending its contents—a lipstick, compact, credit card, and driver's license—flying.

John jumped out of bed. "Whoa. What happened? Are you all right?"

"No, I'm not all right." She threw her shoes overhand into the corner, one after the other.

Bang.

Bang.

The tiny black point of one stiletto left a dent in the drywall.

"Baby?" John said, approaching as though she were a crazed horse. He tentatively reached for her arm. When she didn't strike out, he began to stroke her. "Amanda? Baby? Talk to me. Tell me what happened."

"First of all, we waited an hour in line behind velvet ropes while they let other people past. More important people, I gather. Then it started to rain, and my hair curled until I looked like Medusa and my feet were killing me. Have you ever tried to walk in five-inch heels? Those shoes cost seven hundred and sixty dollars and now they're ruined because I had to stand there in a greasy puddle. And my feet are ruined too."

"Did you say seven hundred and sixty dollars?"

"And then, when we did get in, the place was swarming with goddamned celebutantes like Kim Kardashian and Paris Hilton! Oh, Paris was swanning around like she was *born* in five-inch heels! What have any of them ever done? Seriously? What contributions have any of them made to culture or life or even entertainment, except maybe racking up

DUIs and doing token jail time? At least Kim and Paris have sex tapes to their credit." Amanda shifted into an imitation of Paris Hilton, thrusting her hips forward and shoulders back, arms akimbo, and tilting her head so her hair fell over one eye. "Hello, Mirror! I'm hot!"

John sank down to the edge of the bed. "You saw Paris Hilton's sex tape? When did you see Paris Hilton's sex tape?"

"And then we caught up with our group, and everyone was checking out my face because I guess it's no secret that I got it done this morning, and some bug-eyed balding ass in shoe lifts said, 'You know, I've got just the guy for your nose.'"

John's back straightened instantly. *"What?"*

"Yes. It sparked a conversation. Apparently my nostrils are 'protrudey.' Someone actually used that word. Everyone thought it was very funny, *ha ha ha.*"

"Oh, shit."

She shook her head violently and dropped onto the bed beside him. Her eyes were wild. "I'm not going to do it, John. I won't do it. I will not be turned into a Hollywood bot."

She inhaled deeply and closed her eyes. John could sense there was more to come.

"And then they told me that they may change the age of the actors on our show so that they're just under twenty rather than in their mid-forties, which basically means we'll be ripping off *Gossip Girl* instead of *Sex and the City*. And I will have to start over with the scripts. Which will still have to include Vitaminwater in every scene, only now I have to fit in a mention of Macy's too. At least that's only once per episode. Apparently there has to be a clear shot of their shopping bag as well, but that's the scene director's problem." She opened her eyes and stared at the ceiling. John lay next to her, propped on an elbow, watching her.

"I hate this place," she said. "I hate this job. I even hate myself. I can't believe I did this to us. I've completely ruined our lives."

She got up and went into the bathroom, shutting the door behind her.

John lay on the bed listening carefully, wondering if he should be worried—he hadn't seen her this upset since Fran had forever ruined sex toys for them.

He got up and put his ear against the door of the bathroom. He heard the sound of running water. "You okay?"

"Yes," she said. "Just soaking my stupid feet. Can you check and see if the shoes are ruined?"

John retrieved the shoes from the corner. There was a nick halfway up the crimson inside of one heel, a tiny ripple in the leather. John smoothed it out with his thumb.

"Well, they're not exactly returnable, but they're not destroyed."

"Good. I'm going to sell them on eBay. Along with the dress."

"Do you want me to get you a glass of wine or something?"

"No."

"Do you want a foot rub?"

"No, but thank you. I think I'm just going to soak for a while."

He was dozing when she finally came to bed, but that didn't last. She flopped from side to side and rearranged her pillows every time John began to fall asleep.

"You're rattling and hemming," she said.

"Sorry." He rearranged himself obligingly, moving from his back to his side. Seconds later, she added, "No, actually it's more of a snorking and whistling."

"Mmm."

She fell mercifully silent, and once again John felt himself drifting.

"Now you're grumbling and rumbling, with more of a mumble on the exhale—"

John's eyes popped open. "Amanda."

"Yes?"

"Only a writer could describe snoring the way you do."

"I'm sorry. I'll stop."

He got up.

"You don't have to leave," she said, rolling onto his side of the bed and burying her face in his pillows.

He watched her inert form.

"Amanda?"

"Mm-hmm?"

"I don't know if it registered earlier when I told you on the phone, but I'm going to New Mexico."

Amanda shifted onto her elbows and looked stricken. She stared at him for several seconds. "Oh my God. I really am a horrible human being." And then after another pause, "I can't believe I haven't even asked you about that yet. I'm the most self-absorbed person on the planet. I'm already becoming one of them."

"You were distracted. With good reason."

"Do you want to talk about it now? Open the champagne?"

"I think it's a little late for that," he said, glancing at the clock. "I may be leaving as early as tomorrow. Will you be okay on your own?"

She sank back onto the pillow. "I'll be fine," she said in a tiny voice.

"Because I'm a little worried about you right now . . ."

"I'll pull myself together. I really will. This is just . . . Nothing here is what I expected. It's all plastic and Botox and nose jobs and people sizing you up all the time for things that have nothing to do with your job. Please come back to bed. I promise I'll let you sleep."

He gazed down on her for a moment. "No. You sleep," he said, leaning over to kiss her forehead.

John went downstairs, poured a glass of wine from an open bottle, booted Amanda's computer, and downloaded a copy of *Recipe for Disaster* onto a thumbnail drive. He found a spreadsheet in the same folder that listed agents, presumably in order of preference, as they were graded with numbers of stars. The file recorded when she had queried them and what their response had been. About a third had not bothered to reply at all. He put a copy of that file on the thumbnail drive as well.

At just past two he slipped back upstairs. She was still on his side of the bed, snoring softly. The sight caused a stab of tenderness so exquisite it brought a lump to his throat.

20

Because lists and order helped Isabel make sense of the world, she dissected the problem into three main obstacles. The first was getting Faulks to surrender the apes, and to this end she had enlisted the help of Francesca De Rossi and Eleanor Mansfield, world-renowned primatologists and founding members of the group People Against the Exploitation of Great Apes. PAEGA had been instrumental in securing basic human rights for great apes in Spain the year before, and they continued to lobby on behalf of apes trapped in the entertainment industry and biomedical facilities. They were on their way to Lizard at this very moment.

The second obstacle was finding temporary housing for the apes once Faulks did surrender them, and while Isabel was making some progress on this front (she was in discussions with the San Diego Zoo), it led directly to the third—and most worrisome—obstacle: acquiring a permanent home for them. Building a suitable facility would cost millions of dollars, and even if Isabel could find a university willing to fund the project, she would never again allow the bonobos to be in a position to be sold, even if that meant owning them herself, a concept she found abhorrent.

Celia was also on her way to Lizard, despite Isabel's protests that she would miss her exams and lose the semester. But Celia didn't seem to care about that: she was more concerned about the impact leaving Lawrence would have on her protracted tormenting of Peter, which had started as soon as they learned the details of his research at the Primate Studies Institute. Isabel was almost relieved when Celia set about making his life miserable. She'd been half afraid Celia would flat out do him in.

Isabel didn't ask the details, but Celia was proud of her progress and kept her up to date. And so Isabel knew, for example, that Peter was running over more than his fair share of dog poo these days. ("It's a public service," explained Celia. "I pick up turds from playgrounds and redistribute them to more deserving locations. Sharing the wealth, if you will.") Isabel was also given to understand that enough unordered pizzas, chow meins, and burritos had been delivered to Peter's door that his name had been added to the DO NOT SERVE list taped to the wall beside the telephone at virtually every takeout and delivery restaurant in the city.

Although Isabel made a point of discouraging Celia, she secretly admired her resolve. When Isabel herself had learned of Peter's experiments at PSI, she fantasized about cornering him and telling him exactly what she thought of him, but in the end she couldn't even pick up the phone to berate him from a distance. She had a near-pathological desire to avoid confrontation, which made the incident with Gary Hanson in Rosa's Kitchen all the more startling in retrospect.

Celia, however, was of an entirely different nature. She showed no signs of letting up: the longer Peter didn't call the police, the cockier she became. Her greatest achievement to date was the delivery of ten cubic yards of peat moss to the end of his driveway while his car was in the garage. Celia was apparently so committed to the cause she had persuaded Joel and Jawad to continue in her absence. Isabel hoped they might be a little less dogged in their efforts. It wasn't that she felt Peter deserved respite; it was that the students were the closest thing she'd had to family since the abduction of the apes, and she didn't want them to be locked up as well.

Francesca De Rossi called to tell Isabel that she, Eleanor, and Marty Schaeffer, a lawyer who had agreed to work pro bono for PAEGA, were on their way from the airport. They decided to meet at the hotel bar, since Marty, being one of the few people who had not yet tuned in to *Ape House,* wanted to watch the bonobos in action (the restaurant, despite complaints from patrons, declared itself family-oriented and continued to refuse to air the show).

About ten minutes later, Isabel headed downstairs to wait. To her surprise, James Hamish Watson was sitting in the corner. Many of the bar's patrons—indeed many of the hotel's guests—were camera crews, reporters, observers, and even work crews connected with *Ape House.* After speaking to Isabel for only a few minutes five days earlier, he had been swarmed by eavesdropping reporters. He had turned bright vermilion and scuttled off. Isabel had also beat a hasty retreat, but since she hadn't divulged her identity, no reporters tried to follow her.

When she first arrived in Lizard, Isabel worried that someone would recognize her, since she had done many documentaries and news segments about the bonobos before the bombing. But no one at the Mohegan Moon ever gave her a second look. It finally dawned on her that with a new jawline, new nose, and virtually no hair, she looked very different than she had in what she increasingly thought of as her previous life.

Although she was surprised to see him back at the bar, it made sense. He'd already admitted he wasn't allowed to watch *Ape House* at home, and whatever his wife might say about Ray and his role in the pornography business, Isabel was sure it was because of the apes.

Humans were fascinated and discomfited in equal parts by bonobo sexuality. Although the apes' sexual encounters were brief, they were frequent, and their broad grins and facial expressions left little question that they were enjoying themselves. Almost everyone at the bar seemed to think that female-to-female genito-genital rubbing was hilarious, although there was unanimous agreement that the genital swellings themselves were disgusting. How could they walk around with those things? Surely they got in the way. The swellings swung from side to side when the females engaged in "hoka-hoka," the Congolese term for this face-to-face activity. They were so bulbous and colorful that in the first few days of the show a large percentage of viewers apparently mistook them for testicles. Faulks Enterprises narrowly diverted this public relations disaster by labeling the activity with a flashing subtitle and, for added distinction, a Klaxon horn. It seems that the target audience—working-class heterosexual adult human males—were just fine with a bit of hoka-hoka once they realized what it was. Male-to-male contact, not so much. In the bar, the hoka-hoka usually initiated a series of cheers. The less common male-to-male rump and scrota rubbing, on the other hand, resulted in manly groans of disgust, accompanied by embarrassed sluggings of beer and flushing of cheeks. But it was the bonobos' face-to-face copulation, group sex, oral sex, and masturbation that caused the most awkwardness, because it resembled human sexuality so closely. In public, even the rowdiest of spectators burst into nervous laughter or fell silent and averted their gaze. As often as not little red spots bloomed on the cheeks of the armchair scientists, whose faces bore determined expressions of "We will not look away. We are not shocked."

It was this last group that most interested Isabel. Someone in the media had finally clued in to the fact that although the bonobos were no longer in a bi-species environment, they continued to pepper their conversations with ASL, and this—coupled with Bonzi's extraordinary computer literacy (she took frequent breaks from shopping for a round or six of Ms. Pac-Man)—had resulted in a growing segment of viewers who were fascinated by the apes' cognitive abilities rather than their sexual displays. Faulks Enterprises, never known to miss an opportunity, hired ASL interpreters around the clock and began providing subtitles that appeared in thought bubbles above the appropriate bonobo's head.

Isabel worked her way toward James Hamish Watson, who was staring at the monitor in front of him and nursing a beer. When Makena put her arm around Bonzi and led her into a corner for a little hoka-hoka, the Klaxon horn sounded and the subtitle flashed. James Hamish dug into his pocket, slapped some cash on the counter, and made for the door. Isabel had not gotten within twenty feet of him.

Isabel considered following him out to the parking lot, but instinct told her to hold off. Instead, she sat at the bar, ordered an iced tea, and waited for Francesca, Eleanor, and Marty.

They arrived not long after and had just exchanged greetings when Isabel caught the opening strains of "Splish, Splash."

"Here," she said to Marty. "Watch."

All around the room, conversation ceased and faces turned to the monitors.

Within Ape House, faucets at various places near the baseboard sprang to life. Some of the bonobos made for higher ground (Bonzi and Lola chose the play structure in the courtyard, while Sam simply hung by an arm from a doorjamb). Mbongo and Jelani both crouched to the side of a blast, leaned down to catch water in their mouths, and then blasted each other between the eyes before falling backward in paroxysms of silent, gleeful laughter. Makena squatted in front of a jet and positioned herself so that the stream hit her genital swelling. She moved back and forth, adjusting the angle, assisting the stream with her finger.

The floors sloped toward central drains, and the water cascaded toward and then over them, because they were largely blocked by trash—bits of food, waxed cheeseburger wrappers, fruit cartons, and plastic packaging. When the faucets finally turned off, the water was several inches deep. Makena lifted and dropped her arms a couple of times, splashing. Then she grew bored and joined Bonzi and Lola in the courtyard.

The soundtrack switched to another familiar leitmotif, the frenetic opening bars of "Wipeout."

One of the first things the bonobos had done to the house was remove the doors from the kitchen cabinets. Sam, Mbongo, and Jelani now used them every morning immediately after the automated hose-down and resulting flood. They started at the far end of the house and galloped down the hall with a cabinet door tucked under one arm. When they reached the water, they flung the doors to the ground, leapt on, and sailed across the room like the most graceful of surfers. When the doors slid to a stop—or especially if they collided with the opposite wall—they grinned and screeched and swaggered in fine fashion before grabbing their doors, loping back, and doing it all over again. They did this until the last bit of water had dribbled through the blocked drains and the cabinet doors remained disappointingly on the very places where they had been thrown. Jelani gave up before the others and went out to join the females; Mbongo and Sam made a few more attempts before believing the fun was truly over. When it became clear that it was, Sam wandered off like it was no big deal and Mbongo went to sulk in a corner.

"I . . . don't even know where to start," said Marty.

Francesca said, "It's clearly unsanitary. Simply sloshing the place with water once a day is in absolute violation of the guidelines of the Association of Zoos and Aquariums."

"Of which this place is not a member," Marty pointed out.

"True. But we can absolutely prove that the apes are at risk of infection. Adding plain tap water to trash simply speeds the growth of bacteria."

"And unfortunately Mbongo has been ordering mostly cheeseburgers, and then not finishing them," said Isabel. Although Mbongo ate enough of his cheeseburgers that he was getting fatter by the minute, he had begun peeling off and discarding the bottom bun along with the pickles, which he usually flung against the walls.

"They're toilet-trained, yes?" said Marty.

"They use toilets," Isabel explained, "but they don't *clean* toilets."

Eleanor took over: "Never mind the bathrooms. The bacteria level in the food detritus alone must be hugely toxic. We can definitely argue that the pregnant one is in immediate danger. Any biologist and veterinarian will testify to that."

"Which one is pregnant?" Marty asked.

Isabel pointed. "Bottom left square."

"And the baby is due when?"

"Any minute."

Makena was in the courtyard, lying on her back in the sunshine and flipping through a magazine, which she held with her feet. She signed to herself about its contents, which came up instantly as subtitles:

SHOE, SHIRT, LIPSTICK, KITTEN, SHOE.

She turned the page and continued to browse. SHIRT, FLOWER, SHOE, SHOE. Finally she got up and emitted a high-pitched squeak.

Bonzi was across the courtyard playing airplane with Lola. She paused with Lola overhead to *peep peep* in response.

Makena walked over and bumped her fists together in front of her chest. Then she did it again, accompanied by a volley of squeaks. Bonzi handed Lola to Makena, went to the computer, and ordered a pair of women's shoes.

A buzz of amazement ran through the bar. Marty's eyes widened, and he looked from Francesca to Eleanor to Isabel.

Isabel shrugged. "Makena likes to play dress-up."

Marty put a hand over his eyes and gave his head a quick shake. After a moment, he dropped his hand. "Okay. I think the obvious line of approach is that this is animal abuse, based on sanitary issues."

Marty continued. "That doesn't mean Faulks will relinquish the apes, and if he does, it won't necessarily be to Isabel. If we establish personhood, which I think we might be able to do if we can persuade a judge to let them testify—and that is a huge long shot, by the way—we can insist on guardianship and put you forward. But I need to think about this for a while."

"Of course," said Francesca.

"I gather their diet is also an issue?"

Isabel nodded. Mbongo was the one guilty of leaving leftovers to rot, but the only bonobo still making healthy food choices was Sam, who mostly ordered green onions, pears, blueberries, and citrus fruits. Bonzi had switched from hard-boiled eggs and pears to a near-exclusive diet of M&M's. Jelani usually got pepperoni pizza and French fries. Makena and Lola grazed off everything that arrived, simply taking what they wanted from the others.

Marty picked up his briefcase and shook Isabel's hand. As he and Eleanor made their way to the door, Francesca De Rossi gathered her things. She paused and momentarily laid her hand on Isabel's arm. "It's going to be okay," she said.

Isabel composed her face into something resembling a smile and nodded. She was embarrassed to find herself wiping away tears.

"I'll call soon," said Francesca.

———

Within moments of their departure, a woman's hand appeared on the back of the stool next to Isabel's.

"Is anyone sitting here?"

"No. Go ahead," Isabel said glumly.

"Thanks," the woman said, sliding onto the stool. "Campari and soda," she called to the bartender, who had his back to her. "And onion rings. Do you have onion rings?"

The bartender responded by tossing her a menu.

After scanning it, the woman said, "I'll have the basket of fries." She slapped the menu on the counter.

Within seconds Isabel was keenly aware of being watched. The feeling was unmistakable. She glanced over to find Cat Douglas regarding her closely.

"Oh my God. It's you," said Cat.

Isabel nearly choked. She waved desperately at the bartender, signaling for her tab.

Cat continued to stare. "It is. It's you!"

Isabel's cheeks got hot and she turned away. "I don't know who you think I am, but you're wrong."

An outstretched hand appeared in front of her.

"Cat Douglas—remember? From *The Philadelphia Inquirer*?"

Isabel kept her face turned to the wall.

The hand was retracted and replaced a moment later by a Black-Berry displaying the picture of Isabel, oozing and battered in her hospital bed. "You can't tell me this isn't you. The nose looks good, by the way. Very nice work."

"Oh dear God," Isabel said. "Will you *please* leave me alone?"

Cat Douglas laid her phone on the counter, sighed, and pulled her lips into a smile that crinkled the corners of her eyes. Her posture softened and she tipped her head slightly in an attempt to make herself look approachable. "Okay. I'm sorry. Let's start over. What happened to you and the apes was horrifying, and obviously you have a totally unique perspective on it. I would really love to hear what you think of what's going on here. Just a few quick ques—"

"I don't give interviews." Isabel spun her barstool so she was facing Cat and added, loudly, "And particularly not to people who would do something like *this*!"

She flicked the backs of her fingers against Cat's BlackBerry, grabbed her purse, and left, registering with a sickening feeling that as a result of her outburst she was no longer invisible to the other bar patrons.

21

Ken Faulks sat in the boardroom, slumped deep in his Aeron chair and dragging a finger in greasy circles on the table's gleaming surface.

It was approximately an hour before dawn. His executives, six men and two women, were sleepy and disheveled. Their shirts were crisp and clean, but from the collar up they were bleary and puffy.

Faulks lifted his finger from the table and observed the pattern he'd left on it. He leaned forward and breathed fog on it before using the underside of his silk tie to restore its perfect shine. He considered the end of his finger, and then ran it across his lips in a distracted fashion as his chief financial officer clicked through a series of PowerPoint slides. The red line on a chart zigzagged up and then sharply down.

"Bottom line," said the beleaguered CFO, "is that even though we're offering discounts on long-term subscriptions, viewers aren't biting."

"And short-term subscriptions?"

"Fine. Great. Brilliant, even. But with only a day's commitment the whole thing could go tits up in a ditch pretty much instantly."

"Make them buy a week, minimum. Make the subscription renew automatically unless they opt out."

"We can't. Virtually all our sales are now in twenty-four-hour increments—businessmen at conferences, etcetera. They're changing hotels daily."

"What about computer subscriptions and home viewers?"

"They don't want to commit."

"Why?" Faulks demanded.

All eyes landed on one of the producers, who took note, sighed, and propped himself up. "The apes are having a lot of sex and spending up a storm, but basically that's it. So far there hasn't been a single altercation. There's no drama. We have to kick it up a notch."

"How?" asked Faulks, his gray eyes trained on the chart.

"Drama, fun, the unexpected. Fights, coalitions, betrayals. The kind of thing audiences expect from reality TV," said one of the producers. "We need tension." He stood abruptly and walked from the table. He propped his hands on his hips, inadvertently displaying sweaty armpits. "Jesus God. People always turn on each other. So do meerkats, for Christ's sake—Animal Planet kept *Meerkat Manor* going for years. What's wrong with these creatures?"

"How about audience participation?" someone suggested.

"And how the hell are we going to manage that?" said Faulks. "Throw a washed-up celebrity in with them for a week?"

There was an immediate, excited response:

"Ron Jeremy!"

"Carmen Electra!"

"Verne Troyer!"

"All three!"

The possibilities were glorious. They paused to consider. Even Faulks seemed lost in reverie.

"No," he said finally. "We'd never get liability insurance. But clearly we have to do something. Mess with them. Goad them into doing something."

"The whole premise of the show is that the apes are in charge," protested a woman whose chignon was falling down.

"Things change," Faulks said sharply.

The director of marketing began drumming the table with his pen. All eyes in the room turned to him. He stopped suddenly and leaned forward. "How about . . . ," he began and then trailed off. He brought a hand to his chin and gazed at the ceiling. His eyes had a dreamy glow about them.

Faulks leaned forward. "What? How about what?"

"How about," he said again, slower this time, spreading his hands in an expansive gesture: *"Ape House Prime Time."* He gave them all a moment to let their imaginations take flight. "The apes are in charge twenty-three hours a day. Then, once a day, we do something to affect their environment. Something," he said, sitting forward, "voted on by the audience. The paying audience. People who have bought the monthly package. Twenty-three hours of doing whatever they want, and then one hour a day of doing something chosen by monthly subscribers."

"Twenty-three for one."

"Ostensibly, yes."

"Ostensibly?"

"Presumably the repercussions would continue until the next . . . intervention. We throw in a wrench, then make the show available for free for the hour that immediately follows. We hook the audience, then they have to subscribe to see what happens next. A twenty-four-hour package brings them to the next *Prime Time* segment. But if they want to vote on what happens in the next *Prime Time* segment, they need to subscribe to the monthly package."

"We need something to start with," said the CFO, snapping his fingers. "Porn, cap guns, something."

"War footage *and* cap guns. Porn *and* sex toys."

One corner of Faulks's mouth lifted almost imperceptibly and then stuck there, twitching. "Go on," he said.

22

John's heart sank when he saw the lizard statue in the parking lot of the Buccaneer Motor Inn: it was sixteen feet tall, wearing overalls and a straw hat, and had disturbingly human bare feet with bulbous, green toes. Its hands held a marquee sign that read:

QUE EN BEDS AVIL

COLUR TV   RADIO

AIR CNDIT

HBO   APE HSE

LOW RA TE

Beneath it, the "no" part of the "no vacancy" light flickered.

The building itself was cinder block, two stories, with trim the color of Pepto-Bismol. The window air-conditioning units were held in place with plywood and foil, and hummed and excreted water onto the concrete beneath. The gravel parking lot was dotted with beer cans and fast-food wrappers. The vending machine was against the wall, next to a dumpster. Across the street was a small, flat building that housed two businesses: one was clearly defunct, as evidenced by an unlit neon sign reading CHIROPRACTIC CLINIC that hung almost vertically in the window; the other one, a restaurant called Jimmy's, advertised a bento box/pizza combination. John saw a few pairs of shoes thrown over wires. He knew drug gangs did this to mark their turf in urban areas, but here? In Lizard? As his eyes ran the length of the wire, he noticed a pair of stilettos, which had been carefully tied together before being tossed.

There was also a pool, which was suspiciously blue. Four attractive bikini-clad women were spread out on white plastic loungers. Their hair was long, their skin the color of honey. There wasn't a dimple in sight, except on the arms of the woman waddling toward her door on the second floor in a brightly flowered muumuu. She apparently took the presence of the sunbathers personally, as she tossed them withering glances every few feet. She took her ancient husband's interest even more personally, and shoved him into their room with the flat of her hand once he got the door unlocked.

John parked the car, got out, and went into the office. A bell strung above the glass door announced his arrival.

The office was paneled in dark wood, like a basement den. There was a false Christmas tree in the corner, draped with limp garland and cardboard air fresheners shaped like pine trees. Behind the laminate desk, a black-and-white portable TV was tuned to *Ape House*. In the bottom left corner, an ape was roasting a marshmallow over the gas range. In the square above, an ape was happily jamming on a keyboard while another watched admiringly. The right half of the screen was taken up by an ape giving another a haircut. The recipient of the haircut was clipping her own toenails.

"Can I help you?" said a fat man sitting in a swivel chair. His fingers were laced together, resting on the swell of his belly. He didn't bother to rise. An oscillating fan with a few pieces of tinsel tied to it was aimed at his bald, sweaty head. Wiry gray curls sprung from the neckline of his sweat-dappled T-shirt, which had probably started out white.

"I'm checking in."

"Name?"

"John Thigpen."

John waited—if ever someone was going to make a Pigpen joke, this was the guy—but it didn't come. He lifted his considerable bulk from his chair and pulled the only set of keys from the board behind him. He tossed them onto the desk.

"You're late."

"My plane was delayed."

"Shoulda called."

"Sorry." John glanced at his watch and frowned. He had taken a short detour to the Staples near the airport to print and mail half a dozen packages to New York, but it was still only midafternoon.

"Credit card," said the fat man.

"My company didn't call one in?"

"Nope."

"Can you check?"

"Nobody called in nothing. You're lucky I didn't give your room away." The man glared at John from under Brezhnev brows.

John dug out a credit card and sent it skidding across the desk. He'd meant to toss it in an insouciant fashion so that it dropped directly in front of the man. Instead, it traveled like a frisbee. The man plucked it off the edge of the counter, fitted it and a slip into the manual processing machine, and ran the slider arm over it. *Kachunk!* He pushed the carboned slip toward John and dropped a pen from a height of ten inches.

"Sign here. Thirty-nine dollars a night, extra if housekeeping finds anything out of the ordinary. *Capiche?*"

"I, uh—"

"The deposit on your credit card is four hundred bucks. No exceptions. You leave in the night, we keep it. Put this"—he chucked a numbered plastic chip that bounced off John's chest and fell to the floor—"on your dashboard where it can be seen or you'll get towed. We count towels and sheets. You're in Room 142. Follow the wall around the outside."

John put his credit card back in his wallet, bent over to pick up his parking chip from the stained carpet, put the keys in his pocket, and set out to find his room.

As he unlocked his door, one of the women by the pool, a redhead with a wasp waist and something sparkly dangling from her belly button, smiled at him before dropping her head back, allowing her thick pelt of hair to fan out. Red and orange highlights winked in the sun.

John, alarmed by what he thought might be an invitation, turned away, but not before processing that her hair was the color Amanda's had been such a short time ago.

———

John stripped the bedspread off and piled it in the corner beneath the air conditioner, which rattled and vibrated and spat through broken teeth. The carpet was slightly damp from a recent cleaning, and the room was suffused with the scents of rug shampoo and something vaguely sour. John cranked the air conditioner up to speed the drying process.

He looked at the bed and called Topher. "Do you mind if I change hotels?"

"I wouldn't mind at all," Topher said, "but the other hotels are booked solid."

"Seriously? It's Lizard," said John, pacing between the bed and the door. "What's in Lizard?"

"Casinos. And Ape House. My assistant had trouble finding you a room at all."

Of course. Cat and all the reporters from the real papers had swarmed in and spread out like locusts a week earlier, filling the good hotel rooms. John sank to the edge of the bed and stared at the bent slats of the window blinds. He suddenly brightened. He would find a Wal-Mart. He would buy his own pillows and a bottle of Febreze.

"Been to the site yet?" Topher asked.

"I'm about to head out."

"Good. Send your first report by midnight tomorrow. We go to press at three A.M."

"Got it."

John shut his cell phone and set it on the bedside table. He leaned down to sniff the bed and was pleasantly surprised to discover that it smelled of laundry soap. In desperate need of a shower, he stripped off his clothes and walked into the bathroom. It was outfitted in white, which was unfortunate because it emphasized that the grout was orange in places, grayish green in others. A half-dozen dead flies lay belly-up on the windowsill above the tub, looking for all the world like Amanda's crispy pan-fried capers, an association he tried to put out of his head at once. And, of course, the showerhead didn't work. It was encrusted with mineral deposits and shot alternately freezing and scalding water at angles so extreme that the shower curtain was unable to contain them.

He was going to have to add a bottle of Lime-a-way and one of those tentacled rubber bath mats to his shopping list, he thought as he crouched near the faucet and splashed water into his armpits. And a bar of soap. This one had been previously enjoyed, as evidenced by the embedded pubic hair.

Since John had eaten nothing but a tiny bag of airplane peanuts all day, he returned to the lobby to inquire about restaurants. The fat man said the restaurant at the Mohegan Moon—the hotel next to the largest casino—was decent. Also, one of the gentlemen's clubs had excellent wings. John asked about the place across the street advertising the pizza/bento box combination. The fat man shook his head sternly and slowly.

The casino was impossible to miss, being the shape of the Taj Mahal and bedecked from top to bottom with twinkling lights. The lobby of the Mohegan Moon was cool and airy, with marble floors, plush oriental carpets, and red-suited hotel employees pushing brass luggage carts. An enormous claw-footed mahogany table in front of the check-in desk held a flower arrangement that was easily as tall as John. Birds-of-paradise and fronds of palm intermingled with artistically bent sticks and other assorted blossoms, about which John knew nothing except that they smelled good. An older woman with platinum-blond hair walked past, talking to a large pink purse. As John was pondering this, a tiny and fluffy white dog head popped out. Its collar was the same pattern as the purse, and studded with rhinestones. The dog's eyes were glossy and black, its ears triangular. The tip of its pink tongue stuck out endearingly.

Although Topher had already said that no other hotels had vacancies, this whiff of luxury, of cleanliness, found John groveling desperately to the manager, asking if they didn't have some rooms set aside, for emergency purposes, because, really, this qualified as an emergency. The manager regretted that he couldn't be of service. They were entirely full.

John turned from the counter just in time to see Cat Douglas leave the bar and head toward a bank of glass elevators.

The bar was standing room only—servers ran back and forth, turning sideways and raising trays above their heads to move between the bodies, and the harried bartender slung drinks as quickly as he could, more often than not leaving a trail of foam sliding down the sides of pint glasses. John made his way to the very end of the counter, beside the station where servers dumped dirty glasses and plates, and ordered a beer while he waited for a seat.

When a patron pointed out that the bonobos' television was showing human porn, the bartender flipped the channel. When the room filled with angry protests, he turned it back.

One of the bonobos was trying to change the channel, but the remote control didn't seem to work. The other apes wandered in and out of the courtyard and flipped through magazines. There was a blow-up sex doll in the corner that one of the females had covered with a blanket. She periodically pulled back a corner to check for signs of life, then gave up and went to play video games. John realized with a start that it was Bonzi, the one who had tried to kiss him.

Although the bartender left the television on, he muted it, which allowed John to listen to the conversations going on around him. Two reporters drank bourbon and compared notes. Neither had anything earth-shattering, but John filed away the details just in case. Observers from animal protection agencies discussed their lack of options with clear frustration. At a table nearby, three women made a point of identifying themselves to the waitress as eco-feminists. Two were long-haired and lanky, wearing skirts that looked as if they needed a good wash. The third was soft and doughy and stuffed into dark khaki pants. They sat with a skinny and bespotted green-haired boy who John thought would be wise to flee. They were vegan—militantly so—and made sure everyone knew it. Was this ever on the same surface as any animal product? they asked. Are you absolutely sure this was made with vegetable oil? Yes, it matters very much, they said to the server, who had begun throwing desperate glances since she was being summoned by other customers. The oppression of women and animals has been historically interconnected. Didn't she realize that waitressing—or for that matter any job that involved minimum wage and working for tips—was a form of female oppression?

The couple seated at the table next to them left and John dove for a chair, narrowly beating a woman who was hindered by high heels and trying not to spill her martini. John immediately felt bad and said she was welcome to join him, but she rolled her eyes and walked off. This whole exchange got the eco-feminists' attention. They eyed John for a moment and then turned away, murmuring, "disgusting," "pig," and the like. John could only imagine what they would have made of his surname. One of the male servers, presumably unoppressed, came to John's table and took his order—a Reuben sandwich and another beer. John heard further mutterings about murder and factory farming from the table beside him.

Half an hour later, when the Reuben still hadn't appeared, he ordered another beer, and then, twenty minutes later and after hearing from the harassed waiter about how backed up the kitchen was, another. Half an hour and another beer later, he gave up on the sandwich and asked the waiter to just bring the bill.

As it was already getting dark, he gave up on the idea of scoping out Ape House. Getting back to the Buccaneer proved difficult enough, as the sidewalk seemed to veer off in unexpected directions and leave him with scrambled legs. He made his way back to his hotel room, where he called Amanda.

When John woke up, he was covered in bullets of sweat. He jerked on his side to look at the clock. Thirteen minutes past four. Outside his door, gravel crunched under tires as a vehicle pulled up. The impossibly low thumping bass line of some sort of club music rumbled through his chest. The doors of the vehicle opened, and the noise increased fourfold. People yelled and laughed over the music. Were they speaking Russian? Ukrainian? Perhaps it was Latvian. John had no idea. He just knew they were drunk. The car doors slammed and there was a short burst of honking, followed by the thud of a fist or a shoe or a purse hitting a side panel. When the car peeled away, female voices exploded into squealing laughter. They began walking, and John noted with relief that the tip-tapping of their heels was moving away from his room. He heard distant clacking as they mounted the concrete stairs, and then, to his dismay, they returned, entering the room directly above his.

They turned on music—some kind of synthesized foreign techno-pop—and there was thumping, stomping, the shower running, and nonstop talking. The floor and bed creaked. The conversation was animated and loud, punctuated by bursts of laughter.

He'd call the night manager, that's what. And if he wasn't there, he'd call—

John stared at the ceiling with wide eyes. He had just remembered his conversation with Amanda.

She said she had bought a kit that would tell her when she was ovulating. He was tipsy, and made a joke about getting a dog instead because they wouldn't have to change its diapers or pay for college.

And then Amanda hung up and turned off her phone.

He swatted through his panic, trying to identify its source. He'd always assumed they would have kids, had even envisioned Amanda sitting by the window with a swaddled infant, the two of them bathed in rays of golden sunshine. But now that they were moving ahead, a very different image replaced it. This one involved threats to Amanda's health, mutations and cord mishaps, sleepless nights and diapers, and knowing that it didn't end at eighteen, because after that there was college, weddings, and loans for down payments (always forgiven)—and that's if you were lucky, because sometimes they never left your basement at all. Sometimes even if they did leave your basement, they came back. And if they did get successfully launched, they went off and had their *own* children, and it began all over again, with the same level of responsibility. And how much more Fran would there be in their lives if they had a baby? He could imagine it now—all the advice, all the boiling, all the sterilizing. He would stock the fridge with the wrong types of food for a nursing mother. He would use the wrong type and wrong amount of detergent for the baby's clothes. He would be wrong, wrong, wrong. And then, when the baby became a toddler, there would be sighing at random baby carriages, and surreptitious calendar counting, and seductions on specific days. He knew that once he set a single toe on this particular slippery slope, he would disappear forever into the great churning gene pool, a slave to dirty diapers, soccer practice, and orthodontics, and then to worrying about drug use, talk of condoms, and endless tortured nights wondering where, and with whom, and how late.

As the noise above him raged, John stared at the ceiling with his palm pressed to his forehead.

23

The executives filed in, weary and visibly deflated. Faulks apparently lacked circadian rhythm. This time they'd been summoned just after dinnertime, which would be reasonable if they hadn't been last summoned before dawn that same morning.

Faulks gestured angrily until they took their seats. He remained standing. He picked up a clicker and pointed at a monitor on the wall, jabbing its buttons. When the image of *Ape House* came up, he fast-forwarded to the delivery of a large crate.

Ding dong! went the sound effect. The apes, who were lounging in front of their television, were obviously surprised. They hadn't ordered anything. As they turned to look at the door, their television station switched to an early episode of Faulks's wildly successful *Busty Lusty Ladies* series.

"Sir," said the director of marketing. The area around his eyes was grayish purple. He knew what was coming, as did everyone else in the room—they had all watched it live an hour before.

Faulks held a hand up to silence him. Then he turned the volume up as Bonzi and Jelani dragged the crate inside to investigate. Sam stayed at the television, trying to get the channel to change back to *Planet of the Apes* while the others emptied the crate. Lola pulled out a vibrator, turned it on, and began spinning it on the floor. Bonzi dragged out the blow-up sex doll, regarded it with some alarm, prodded it, loped away, returned to prod it again, and then took it into the corner and threw a blanket over it.

Faulks fast-forwarded through an excruciating amount of basically nothing before pressing Pause.

"What the hell was that?" said Faulks.

His executives all stared at the table or wall. Some of them shook their heads.

"I said, what the hell was that?"

"Maybe they're not into breasts," ventured one brave soul. When he looked up, he shriveled under Faulks's glare.

"Anyone want to tell me how many long-term subscriptions this gained us?"

Apparently nobody did. Faulks began pacing.

"How about votes for what to do next?"

Again, silence.

The VP of marketing said, "I've been doing a little research . . ."

"And?"

"And apparently chimpanzees are terrible drunks. A group of chimps has been raiding illegal breweries in Uganda and, well, attacking people. Killing children, in fact. So I was thinking that for the segment with the war footage, we could send in beer along with cap guns."

A blond woman with her hair in a tight knot cleared her throat and sat reluctantly forward. "But wouldn't that give them more ammunition for the lawsuit?"

Faulks walked around to the head of the table and sat. He leaned back and made a steeple of his fingers.

"Ah, yes," he said calmly. "The lawsuit. Anyone want to address that?"

"It's from a group called PAEGA. They—"

Faulks leaned forward and pounded the tabletop. "*I know who it's from!* What I want to know is what we're going to do about it! Somebody! Anybody!"

The chief financial officer straightened in his chair. "Sir. If I may suggest. Unless we can think of a way of getting subscriptions up drastically I think maybe we ought to start considering exit strategies. We could just let them take the apes . . ."

"And lose a lawsuit? Never. Next?"

Nobody moved. The blonde looked at several of her cohorts for support, cowered preemptively, and said, "Sir, as long as we're talking about legal issues, there's something else we need to discuss. Something that's becoming a problem . . ."

"Is it that shithead from Kansas?"

"Yes."

Faulks thought long enough that his executives began to exchange nervous glances. Then he sat forward. "All right. First step, put out a press release. Inflate the numbers—make it sound like we've got hundreds of thousands of votes for the next *Prime Time* segment. Stir up hype. Make it clear that we're raising the stakes, but don't say how. Wait a couple of days, work up anticipation. Then send in the beer and cap guns, and make sure the hammers are cocked. In the meantime, get rid of the petition."

"How?" said the blonde.

Faulks leaned forward, resting his arms on the table and looking from person to person, eyes burning. "Call the shithead. Tell him if he wants more money, he can earn it. Bring him out here. And in the press release mention that we now have a bona fide ape expert on staff, because our greatest concern is the health and welfare and blah blah blah . . ." He sat back and stirred the air beside his head. "You know the drill."

24

The noise in the room above John finally ceased at 6:48 A.M. When the thrumming music went silent and the bed creaked under the weight of prone bodies, he fought an urge to turn his television on full blast.

Although Amanda wasn't an early riser, John called at the crack of seven.

"Hello?" she said testily, and he realized that it was actually only six her time.

"Baby?"

There was a brief pause before she said, "What?" He heard clattering in the background, like she'd decided to rearrange the bathroom cabinet.

"Baby, I'm sorry about last night. I had a few beers on an empty stomach and you caught me a little off-guard. I know we've been talking about having kids but I hadn't realized that we were at the point of ovulation kits. I mean, I guess I thought we just weren't *avoiding,* and then I panicked, and I tried to make a joke, and it went downhill from there. I'm sorry."

"If you don't want kids, you need to tell me now, before it happens," she said, her voice brittle.

The thought was only slightly less frightening in the morning light. "I'm fine either way," he said, trying to sound calm. From the icy silence that followed, he intuited that she had taken this the wrong way. "Look, if it will make you happy, it will make me happy. We'll have lots and lots of babies and make all our parents ecstatic. Okay?"

"Okay," she said, but there was still something off about her voice.

John frowned. "Are you okay? Did something else happen?"

"Oh, nothing important," she said wearily.

"Nothing important like what?"

She was silent.

"Amanda? What happened?"

"Sean made a little pass at me. That's all."

"He *what*? I thought he was gay!"

"So did I. I've even met his boyfriend. I guess he's an equal-opportunity lech."

"What did the bastard do to you?" John said in a stony monotone.

"Seriously. Nothing. Please don't do anything stupid like come back and kill him."

John, who could make no such promises, said through clenched teeth, *"What did he do?"*

"We were at a party. He had his hand around my waist, which, you know, if he's gay it's no big deal, but then he started nibbling my ear. I told him to knock it off and when he finally realized I was serious about it, he knocked it off. Like I said, no big deal. He'd had a bit to drink. It's just now I feel a little weird working with him. And I suppose if he wanted to, he could have me replaced."

———

When they hung up, John felt physically ill. He knew from personal experience what pigs men could be, because he, himself, had been one.

It was Frosh Week and he was frosh. That was his only excuse. He'd been dropped off at the dorm by his parents just eight days before, and he was testing his newly minted fake ID in a yeasty bar with sticky floors called Nasty Hammer's Taproom, where people shook salt into their two-dollar watered-down drafts. He was doing his damnedest to pretend he knew how to hold his liquor. He most categorically did not.

Ginette Pinegar was waiting tables. She was close to forty, which at the time had seemed ancient, but she had good legs and the dim lighting of the tavern was kind to her. He felt an immediate affinity toward her on account of her name alone: how could a Thigpen not be sympathetic to a Pinegar? (" 'Piss 'n' Pinegar,' " she'd sighed. "All my life. And every fucker who comes up with it seems to think he's the first.") At one point when he went a bit green about the face, she brought him a pink pickled egg from the enormous jar on the counter, presumably because she thought it would settle his stomach. He thanked her profusely and palmed it, because the mere smell launched contractions within his diaphragm that would have measured seven on the Richter scale.

He shuddered. To this day, he had no idea if he'd even managed to have sex with her. He remembered only snippets—things like standing on his head while people held a funnel to his mouth and hollered support while he choked and gagged on the unstoppable flow of beer, and other people dropping shots of whiskey, glass and all, into mugs of beer and then chanting, *"Hoo! Hoo! Hoo!"* while he chugged it. And then suddenly there she was, and oops—there *he* was, throwing up on the bus, and then again, on his knees and clutching a toilet's edge—and then nothing until several hours later, when he awoke to find himself being regaled with stories of all things Pinegar while he earnestly but silently begged the ceiling to stop spinning.

As he inched backward across the bedroom floor collecting his clothes, he told her he would call. He shouldn't have, because he knew he wasn't going to, but he figured you couldn't just say nothing to a woman while leaving her bedroom, and you certainly couldn't say that you had no idea what the hell had gotten into you (other than a dozen boilermakers) and that your most fervent desire was to never lay eyes on her again.

Back on campus, his male friends laughed as though he'd done something admirable. They laughed even harder when he begged them not to tell Amanda, whom he met a few days later. John was leaving class, looked up, and there she was, a silhouette at the end of the hallway glowing in her halo of copper hair. She wore jeans, cowboy boots, and a soft cotton T-shirt in faded plum. She walked slowly, with calm purpose, moving her legs from the hips like a runway model. Her hair bounced with each stride. John was a goner before he even knew her name.

Two weeks later, as they headed out to dinner, John caught sight of Ginette on the opposite side of the street. She caught sight of him at the very same moment and barreled at him straight through traffic. When she reached him, she rolled forward onto the toes of her dirty canvas shoes and unleashed a searing, finger-pointing stream of abuse. Her eyes were wild and spittle flew. After she finished with John, she turned to Amanda and told her that John was a lying scumbag of a worthless snake and that if she knew what was good for her she'd walk away now.

As Ginette stormed off, shouldering people out of her way and leaving Amanda staring aghast, John was forced to admit what had happened. It was the last thing he wanted to discuss on their third date, but Ginette had left him no choice. Why Amanda didn't walk away, John would never know.

The killing of Sean would have to wait because John had work to do. First, he needed to find coffee. A large one. Then, he would head out to Ape House to get a feel for the types of protesters who were there, and why, exactly, they were there, since his impression was that the connection was none too clear in a number of cases. His main goals were to ferret out whether the ELL had established a presence (having "liberated" the apes, surely they must be observing this development with interest, and—quite possibly—intent), and to get an interview with Ken Faulks. He was hoping he'd make a couple of contacts at the site, but if he didn't, that was okay. He'd go back to the Mohegan Moon and work the bar. If there were no Faulks flunkies there, he'd simply phone Faulks Enterprises and ask for an interview. Nobody else had gotten one yet, although Faulks had been appearing randomly in front of camera crews, thrusting the anchor aside, shamelessly flogging his show, and then disappearing without answering a single question. Faulks seemed to be thumbing his nose at all media, but since technically John—like Faulks—had abandoned so-called legitimate media, maybe he had a chance. Maybe if he appealed to Faulks as a fellow maverick, or promised to do a puff piece . . .

John drove to a gas station to get coffee and breakfast. After some contemplation, he bought a desiccated hot dog from the grill under the heat lamp, doused it with ketchup, and drove toward Ape House.

John had seen from newscasts that people were congregating around Ape House, but he was not prepared for anything like this—he was still at least half a mile from the site when the thin line of people trudging along the road began to thicken. Before long, they were solid and unperturbed by the car's presence. He ended up driving among them at walking speed, and finally decided it was time to park when he nearly ran over a bony man with a scraggly ponytail and earth sandals. The only reason he didn't was that the man turned and banged his fist on the hood of John's car.

"Dude! What are you doing?" the man yelled, putting his angry, bearded face up against John's windshield. John raised his hand in a meek apology.

Makeshift vendors had set up shop at the side of the road, selling bottles of water and soda from tubs of ice. Tailgate grills served up burgers, bratwursts, and Polish sausages, chicken kebabs, unidentified kitchen leftovers, and, for the vegetably-inclined, grilled portobello mushrooms. Beer was purveyed from secret locations toward the front ends of vehicles and decanted into blue plastic cups so it might pass for something else. By means of persistent honking, John managed to turn off the road and squeeze his car between a couple of these impromptu shopkeepers. They viewed him with suspicion until they realized he was not also setting up shop. He bought a can of Coke to further establish goodwill and set out on foot.

John estimated the crowd at around four thousand. Simple arithmetic dictated that many of them must be commuting daily for the purpose, since the Buccaneer and the handful of other hotels around the casinos couldn't possibly house so many. Also, there were buses parked everywhere, ranging from sleek and air-conditioned luxury vessels to the type of revamped school buses used by garage bands and church groups.

It was a mob, and had the dangerous feeling of being nearly out of control. As John suspected, most of the groups jostling for camera time seemed to have only the most tangential connection with the apes. The

eco-feminists and the green-haired boy had co-opted an NBC news
crew and were expounding on how the apes represented oppressed
women everywhere. A member of the Eastborough Baptist Church, a
woman with an angular face and mousy hair, was earnestly explaining
to Fox News why the dead soldiers coming home from the war was
God's way of punishing America for enabling "fags" and would stop
only when America enacted a death penalty against them and their soul-
damning, nation-destroying filth. When the anchor asked why they
were picketing Ape House, the woman explained that bonobos had bi-
sexual and homosexual sex, and therefore were fags. She smiled broadly;
from her tone she might have been offering a glass of lemonade. Behind
her, children with twig-thin arms thrust signs into the air that read
YOU'RE GOING TO HELL and GOD HATES YOU.

With the atmosphere so charged, it was the quiet people who caught
John's attention. Three people were scoping out the building and taking
notes. John's first thought was that they might be connected to the ELL,
but when they turned so he could see their faces he recognized two of
them instantly: Francesca De Rossi and Eleanor Mansfield were famous
primatologists, right up there with Jane Goodall. They had been featured in a number of documentaries, many of which he had viewed
while researching his ape series at the *Inky*.

He approached them. "Dr. De Rossi? Dr. Mansfield? My name is
John Thigpen. I'm a reporter. I was wondering if I could talk with you
for a few minutes?"

"Certainly," said Francesca De Rossi. "I'm sorry—who did you say
you're with?"

"I'm out of Los Angeles. With the *Times*," he said.

Liar! Liar! screamed a voice inside his head.

"Oh, the *Times*. Of course," said Dr. De Rossi. She introduced the
third person, a lawyer who was preparing a legal petition to get the apes
removed from Faulks.

"Thank you," said John. "Can you tell me a little about the petition?
By the way, is it okay if I record this?"

"Yes, by all means," said Dr. De Rossi.

John aimed his voice recorder and made encouraging noises. He got
the sense that Francesca De Rossi was not a person who raised her voice;

in fact, she was leaning quite close in order to be heard above the crowd. The bridge of her nose was smattered with freckles the way Amanda's had been before the Fraxel. He had liked Amanda's freckles. They were evenly spaced and sweet, not at all as Amanda had described them ("like someone tossed dirty dishwater in my face").

". . . their behavior is virtually identical to that of humans in this respect. They order all the wrong types of food and in vast amounts immediately after viewing commercials that . . ."

He realized with a jolt that he had not absorbed a single word Francesca De Rossi had said until she began talking about food, and even then it was because the only thing he'd eaten all day was a leathery hot dog. Thank God for his voice recorder.

"Think *Super Size Me,* but with a species even worse equipped to process junk than we are," she continued.

Of equal concern were the unsanitary conditions within Ape House. The timed and forceful sprayings of the concrete floors were incapable of handling the leftover food and accumulating trash. And, because the bonobos had ordered upholstered furniture, these automated hose-downs left the base of the furniture wet, which invited mold and left the bonobos in danger of all kinds of respiratory and immune-system disorders. These issues were at the crux of PAEGA's legal petition to have the bonobos removed. The hearing was seven days away, having been filed on an emergency basis.

"Obviously we're extremely concerned about these particular great apes and the current situation," continued Dr. De Rossi, "but in a more general sense, we need to educate the public about the exploitation of *all* great apes."

John nodded and smiled. He gratefully accepted business cards and scribbled his own name and number on the back of a gas station receipt. Since the good doctors were laboring under the belief that he was with the *L.A. Times,* perhaps it was for the best that he didn't have business cards. He wondered if there would ever be a good moment to inform them of his real affiliation, and decided that no, there probably wasn't.

25

Mbongo sat on the floor between an upended couch and the strange balloon human that Bonzi kept covering with a blanket. He glanced mournfully at his favorite spot to lounge, the beanbag chair, but found it still occupied by Sam, who was watching TV and sucking an orange. Mbongo crossed his arms, resting them on his belly, and stared at his pile of cheeseburgers.

Eventually he picked one up and turned it over. The edges of the yellow waxed paper were sealed with a sticker, which he peeled off. He moved it from finger to finger, contemplating its tackiness, and then affixed it to the top of his belly. He adjusted its position, pressed it a few times to make sure it was secure, and turned his attention back to the burger. He unwrapped it and set it upside down on its square paper wrapper. He removed the bottom bun—flat, and dusted with flour—and tossed it over his shoulder. He gently pried the patty from the top bun and fished out the pickle, which he threw at the wall. This one stuck, joining the pickles that had stuck on previous days. His forehead creased in thought. He aimed his forefinger near the burger's center, and pushed through it. Pleased with the result, he poked it three more times, leaving it pierced like a button. He glanced around hopefully, seeking approval, but the females were all in the courtyard, Sam was absorbed in the television show, and he didn't see Jelani. Mbongo sucked the condiments off his finger. As he worked the minced onions between his tongue and palate, he removed the stickers from the rest of the burgers and placed them on his belly too, arranging them into a pleasing design. He turned once again to look at Sam's orange, then grabbed the human balloon by the arm and dragged it to him. He folded a burger and stuffed it into its round red mouth, poking it in with his finger. It disappeared completely, so he fed it another. He folded a third burger in half and tried again, but this time it wouldn't go in. Mbongo poked it repeatedly with his fingers, even putting some weight behind it, but whenever a bit of burger got inside the mouth another bit came out. He went to get the screwdriver.

Bonzi wandered in from the courtyard. Lola stood on her shoulders, grasping her mother's ears. Bonzi walked up to Sam and casually extended her hand. He gave her the orange without ever taking his eyes off the television screen. Bonzi handed the orange to Lola and returned to the courtyard.

Mbongo, sitting beside the now-deflated human balloon, brought a fist to his mouth and made squeezing motions, signing, ORANGE, ORANGE, to no one in particular. He stared out at the courtyard for a while, then deconstructed the rest of his burgers and began finger-painting with mustard.

Makena lay on her back in the sun, her face turned to the side. She had been washing a doll in a bucket until she grew tired, and both bucket and doll remained beside her.

A tiny brown bird swooped down over her, low enough that it startled her, and she tipped her head to follow its progress. It came to a smashing halt against the Plexiglass door of the courtyard, leaving a tiny smudge of down at the point of impact. Makena sat up and scootched around. The bird sat in a crumpled heap, unmoving.

Makena approached slowly and crouched in front of it, arms resting on thighs. After several minutes, when the bird had still not moved, she reached out and nudged it. It made a ruffling motion, squeaked, and toppled sideways.

Makena scooped it up in both hands and walked upright to the play structure. She cupped the bird to her chest with one hand as she climbed to the highest point. There she held the bird, gently spread its wings to their fullest span, and tossed it into the air. It disappeared over the wall.

26

Isabel sat cross-legged on her bed picking at the remains of her room-service salad. After the altercation with Cat, she didn't dare go downstairs. She felt bad about leaving the tab, but she'd been down there often enough that the bartender knew her room number.

Her cell phone rang. She did not recognize the number, but since it was from Lawrence and Celia changed cell phone providers almost as often as she changed lovers, Isabel answered.

"Hello?"

"Don't hang up—" It was Peter.

"Oh my God." She glanced again at the number. "Where are you calling from?"

"I'm using a pay phone."

Isabel went light-headed. She pushed the tray aside and pulled her knees to her chest. "What is it? What do you want?"

"You have to make them stop."

"What are you talking about?"

"The peat moss! The pizzas! The dog shit! And now they've hacked into my email account and changed my password."

Isabel held a thumb and forefinger to her temples and closed her eyes. "I'm sorry, Peter, but I'm not responsible for what they do."

"It's illegal," he said quickly. "Harassment. Probably even a felony. I'll have them arrested."

A chill of fear flashed through Isabel's core. "Peter, they're just kids."

"I don't care. I can't even access my own account."

Isabel hugged her knees tighter and began to rock. "I'll talk to them," she said. "Good-bye."

"Wait," he said quickly.

Isabel did not answer, but she didn't hang up. She fell back onto her pillows.

"How are you?" he said. When she said nothing, he continued. "I saw Francesca De Rossi on the news last night. Just the tail end. Something about court proceedings and that you were involved. What's going on?"

"That's none of your business."

"You don't have to do any of that. The bonobos are going to be just fine."

Isabel sat bolt upright and whacked the bedspread with her fist. "They are *not* fine. They are living in filth and clogging their arteries and doing God knows what else to their health, and Makena is going to give birth any second and apparently you don't even give a damn." Isabel stopped. She breathed deeply, closed her eyes again, and said, "Peter, I just can't talk to you. I really can't."

"Isabel," he said. "For God's sake. I know what I did with Celia was unforgivable, but I'm human. It was a stupid, idiotic mistake but it was a mistake, and I swear it will never happen again." His voice dropped to a near-whisper. "Izzy, please. Can we discuss this? I'm going to be out there in a few days."

"What? Why?"

"I'm coming out to make sure they're taking good care of the bonobos."

Isabel shook her head in confusion. "I'm already here, and they won't even . . ." She clapped a hand across her mouth. "Oh my God. Are you *working* for them?"

"Only to make sure the apes are okay," he said quickly. "Look,

Faulks's people approached me, and what was I supposed to do? I've been watching the show too—I couldn't just let things go on the way they are, especially given the opportunity to do something. Besides, with one of us in there, we have a better chance of dismantling the whole thing, of getting the apes back and picking up where we left off."

Bile rose in her throat as she remembered the pictures of the studies he'd participated in at PSI, never mind his cheating on her. But what could she say? At this point, he was her only possible conduit to the bonobos. If Faulks had offered her a job that allowed her to have contact with the apes, she'd have taken it too.

"When did they ask you?"

"Late last night."

Isabel said nothing, her mind a fevered tangle.

"So can I please see you?" Peter said. His voice was soft, gentle.

She sat up straight and took a deep breath before answering. "I will talk with the kids. Please don't get them in trouble. And please, please, take good care of the apes."

"And . . . ?"

"And I need some time to think about the other."

"Fair enough," he said. "But just so you know, I still love you."

————

Isabel waited a few minutes before calling Celia, hoping that the shaking would subside.

Celia didn't bother saying hello. She answered with, "Yeah, I know, I'm supposed to be there already."

"Peter just called," said Isabel. "He says you hacked into his email. Please tell me you didn't."

"That was Jawad, actually," said Celia. "And if he really didn't want anyone looking at it then he shouldn't have been so stupid about his passwords and security questions. It's supremely easy to Google the first street somebody lived on and figure out their first elementary school. Anyway, Jawad was going through some of his folders and—"

"Celia! This is serious. He's going to have you arrested."

Celia snorted. "I will bet all the money I will ever make for the rest of my life that he won't call the police."

"Why?"

"Because of what Jawad found."

"Stop it. I don't want to know."

"Isabel, quit being an ostrich. You need to know."

"No, I don't."

"Okay, fine."

There was silence at the end of the line, but Isabel could feel it swelling. Three, two, one—

"But you really do want to know this."

Isabel paused, considering how deeply she had buried her head in the past. She had never questioned what he was doing to the chimpanzee that took his finger. She had allowed those very hands to touch her. And since she was wavering about seeing him again, she didn't think she could stand to know more.

"Fine," Celia eventually said. "Be that way. I'll see you when I get there."

"Fine. Celia?"

"What?"

"Please be good in the meantime."

"Okay. And Isabel?" The next part came as rapidly as machine-gun fire: "Peter-sold-the-language-software-to-Faulks-for-his-goddamned-show-buh-bye." And then she hung up.

Isabel stared into the drowned remnants of her spinach salad. It took her a while to get around to closing her phone. When she did, she set it gently on the bedspread beside her. She set her knife and fork neatly across her plate, folded her napkin, and arranged the salt and pepper shakers so that their edges were perfectly aligned with the edge of the tray.

Of course. Where else would Faulks have gotten the language software? As for Peter's claim that Faulks had approached him only the day before—

Isabel threw the metal dome that had covered her dinner against the wall beside the TV.

She was going to break her silence. She was going to expose him for what he was—anonymously, of course. Leave him thinking he still had a chance with her, that someone at PSI had been digging around their archives and stumbled upon these papers, that someone in Faulks's camp had leaked his involvement in the sale of the software. There were eight million reporters crawling around beneath her at this very moment, and any one of them would give a limb to interview her. The problem was that she hated them all.

She thought of Cat snapping a picture of her when her face was broken and she didn't even look human, and how that picture had ended up on *The Philadelphia Inquirer*'s Web site. She thought of how her voice mail and email had filled up with requests that bordered on stalking. They were vultures, every one of them—it would be a matter of choosing the least terrible, and, after Peter, Isabel had no faith in her own judgment.

She picked up the neatly folded napkin and began twisting. She twisted and twisted until it curled like a croissant and could twist no more. She twisted until the ends of her fingers turned deep red. Suddenly, she released it. She'd had a flash of memory.

Mbongo, on New Year's Day, sulking in a corner and refusing earnest and repeated pleas for forgiveness. Bonzi, spinning on her rump in the kitchen, signing, BONZI LOVE VISITOR, KISS KISS.

Bonzi's approval was good enough. Isabel would call John Thigpen— even if he did work for *The Philadelphia Inquirer*.

27

John had only four hours left to write and submit his first dispatch, but the only thing he'd eaten all day was the leathery gas-station hot dog. He didn't feel like eating Cheetos from the vending machine, and he didn't have time to go back to the Mohegan Moon.

He went to the window and pried the slats apart. The pizza/bento box place's blinds were closed, but there was a scattering of cars in the parking lot, so John decided to give it a try.

The sidewalk in front of the building was crumbling and littered with cigarette butts. Jimmy's didn't look particularly open—the signs were unlit—but it also didn't look abandoned, so John tried the door. He found it unlocked and walked in.

There was a shuffle and screech as several men sitting at a small table leapt to their feet. A chair clattered to the floor, arms scooped something off the counter, and John heard the cocking of guns. A pit bull the color of red velvet cake fixed John in its gaze and lunged. Its mouth was alarmingly wet, its teeth alarmingly pointed. A squat, muscular man gave its leash a full-arm yank, dropping the dog to the floor. It continued to growl and eye John, who had flattened himself against the door.

John scanned the room, moving nothing but his eyes. There were five men, all staring at him. Three of them kept their hands hidden, making John wonder exactly how many weapons were pointed at him. A series of old bedsheets were nailed to the ceiling behind the counter, obscuring the back of the building. One had faded pink stripes, another a delicate pattern of blue flowers. A smell similar to Amanda's nail polish remover hung in the air. There was no menu, no cash register, no telephone, and certainly no sign of pizza.

"Are you . . . open?" John finally said.

After a silence that seemed interminable, a dark-haired man behind the counter spoke. He wore jeans, an undershirt, and a black trucker's hat that obscured his eyes. The part of his face that was visible was etched with deep lines. "Open for what?"

"Dinner?"

Another pause as the men exchanged glances. The dog growled, leapt forward, and got dropped again.

"Dinner?"

"Yeah." John gestured feebly toward the window and the sign, being careful not to move too quickly. "I thought . . . Never mind." He didn't want to turn his back to the men, so instead he put his hands down beside his rear end and backed up, pushing the door. It opened a crack. A rush of air swirled in.

"Wait," said the man behind the counter.

John froze.

"Close the door."

John stepped forward and let the door close.

"You came here for dinner?"

"Yes. I'll go somewhere else. No problem."

"No," said the man, cocking his head. "You came here. What do you want?"

"I, uh . . . well, a pizza. Or a bento box. Or a combo," John said, although he had no idea why they were even having this conversation. Were they stalling while they figured out where to ditch his headless, handless torso? Would he end up in the dumpster beside the vending machine at the Buccaneer?

"Pizza. You like pepperoni?"

John swallowed heavily, noisily.

The man, who John had decided was Jimmy (or at least operating in a Jimmy-type capacity) snapped his fingers toward the table. "Frankie, a pepperoni pizza. You heard our customer."

Frankie's eyebrows rose in surprise. He pointed at his own chest.

"Yeah, you," said Jimmy.

Frankie glanced around at the others, and, finding no solidarity, skulked off behind the counter and disappeared between the sheets. John heard a clattering in the back, followed by the opening and closing of a door.

"Have a seat," said Jimmy. He tipped his head toward the table, and the men who were still standing around it.

"No, I'm okay," said John.

"I said have a seat."

"Okay." John's eyes flitted over to the dog, which was no longer growling, but continued to stare with malicious intent.

"Don't mind Booger. He wouldn't hurt a fly."

John moved reluctantly toward the table. One of the men righted an overturned chair and pulled it out in invitation. John sat on its edge, mentally calculating the length of the thick leather leash and the distance between him and the dog. The others remained standing wordlessly, their expressions carefully blank.

"So," said Jimmy, who remained behind the counter. He bent down and set something hard (*ker-clunk!*) on a shelf. Then he leaned over the counter, resting on his hairy forearms. His arms, hands, even the backs of his fingers were covered in black hair. "You from out of town?"

"Yes," said John.

"Yeah? Where you from?"

"Iowa," said John. He had no idea why.

"Really?"

"Really."

"I hear they got good potatoes there."

"I think that's Idaho."

"You sure?"

"Pretty sure."

"Because I thought it was Iowa."

And so it went, for the longest half hour of John's life. Twice, a cell phone rang and was taken behind the sheets to be answered in muffled tones. Twice, men came in and stopped cold at the sight of John. They turned their eyes to Jimmy, who tilted his head in a way that said all was well and led them behind the curtain. Eventually, John heard the back door open and close again. Someone flung keys onto a surface, and Frankie appeared with a small box. He came around the counter and dropped it on the table in front of John. It was from Domino's Pizza.

John stared at it.

Jimmy shrugged. "We recycle boxes. Cuz of the environment and whatnot."

Booger raised his snout, sniffing hopefully.

John, for his own part, smelled the sweet scent of freedom. They were going to let him go. No death! No dumpster! He leapt to his feet. "So, what do I owe you?" he said, patting his pockets.

"Frankie?" asked Jimmy.

"Fifty bucks," said Frankie.

"Fifty bucks, all righty, then," said John. He was giddy, dizzy with relief. He dug his wallet out and tore through it with trembling hands. "I only have twenties," he said, tossing three bills onto the table. "But that's okay. Keep the change."

"Thanks. We'll do that," said Jimmy. "Enjoy your . . . dinner."

John snatched the pizza box and backed toward the door. "I will. Thank you. I—" When he felt the cool metal of the door beneath his fingers he turned, launched himself through it, and ran. He ducked across the highway without looking, causing one driver to swerve and lean heavily on his horn. In the lengthening shadow of the Buccaneer's sign-clutching lizard, John leaned over and rested one hand on his thigh, trying to catch his breath. He'd run only about thirty yards, but he was light-headed, his heart pounding.

When John turned to go back to his room he noticed the women at the pool, who were packing up their things as the last of the sunlight dwindled. They stared in horrified amazement. John forced a smile, indicating that everything was okay, and held the pizza box aloft by way of an explanation.

There was no desk, so he stripped down to his boxers and sat cross-legged on the bed. He opened his computer, and then the file. He stared at its blank whiteness and the strip of menus and tools above it.

At this moment, the story in his head was perfect. He also knew from experience that it would degenerate the second he started typing, because such was the nature of writing.

A portrait of Isabel Duncan, when he first met her at the lab, her long blond hair streaming over her shoulders, her laugh clear and unrestrained in a way that, as the interview progressed, charmed him into an attraction that eventually alarmed him. Her statement that "over the years, they've become more human, and I've become more bonobo," as she rolled around on the floor being tickled by Mbongo, and he'd gotten it—he'd really gotten it. An accessible summary of the language research, set forth not in the impenetrable vocabulary of linguistics but rather in the language of the experience itself, of making eye contact with members of another species and the startling and discomfiting realization that there was something damned close to human in there. Of knowing not only that they understood every word you said but if moved to answer would do so—and in your own language. Of trying to capture the wonderment, near-watershed, of it. It had not escaped John that the bonobos had managed to acquire human language, but that humans had not crossed over in the other direction. It had also not escaped him that Isabel Duncan also recognized this.

And then the seismic shift in fortune: the horrors of the bombing, the terrorist tactics, the complete lack of resolution. The swooping away and unexplained absence, the media circus and parasitic publicity junkies. In his imagination he could picture the story whole—if only he could plug a thumbnail chip into a slot behind his ear and download straight from his brain to his computer. But he could not. He had only the imperfect medium of words.

He typed a sentence, and then another. A few more came out, his fingers banging the keys like scattershot. He read what he'd written, and deleted it.

He examined the pizza for razor blades, sniffed it, blotted the orange grease with a wad of toilet tissue, and ate it. It was cold and tough, but no worse than his breakfast hot dog.

He pulled up Nexis and discovered that there were more stories on Biden's abysmal table-tennis scores than on a newly discovered Justice Department memo from Bush's last year in office that blatantly authorized torture.

He called up the pieces other reporters had written about the apes, and then, in the hope of discovering some fresh angle, also searched the Internet for that ubiquitous and free online content that had buried his chances of working at a real paper. He watched the ELL Webcast again, and called up the press release Faulks had sent out the day after *Ape House* began airing. He opened the notes he'd taken on the plane coming back from Kansas, before he knew about the bombing. He investigated the cost of digital billboards. He typed a little, read it back, and deleted it.

After an hour, he had nothing. Zippo. Zilch.

How could this be so hard? The story had been percolating in his head since New Year's Day. Why couldn't he just open the tap and catch it in a bucket?

It was true he was working on no sleep and the physical aftereffects of sheer terror. An image of Booger's gaping maw flashed through his head in slow motion. Strings of slobber flew from undulating jowls. Of course that amount of adrenaline would be followed by a physical crash. Not an hour before, he had thought he might become dog meat.

He also could not help thinking that Amanda was probably out with The Hated Sean at that very moment, fending off his advances. John tried calling her, but went straight to voice mail.

It was 8:30, and he had nothing written.

He took out his voice recorder and clicked Play. He hoped he hadn't been smiling and nodding the whole time he was tuned out, since Francesca De Rossi turned out to have been explaining that the term *wild-caught ape* virtually always translated into "shot the mother, took the baby," and that all great apes used in entertainment were juveniles, which meant that even if they weren't wild-caught they had been kidnapped, since great-ape mothers are as likely as human mothers to hand over their babies.

John began typing, but his brain hurt and he was pulling words out of all the wrong slots. He needed 800 words by midnight. By 9:07, he had 205 words written. By 10:31, he was back down to 187. He glanced through his notes, made bullet points, and began to flesh them out. The transitions could come later.

He downloaded Boston's "Amanda," and put it on repeat. He picked at his file, wrote a sentence here, moved it there, broke it into pieces, and put it back together. As he replaced a comma for the third time, he thought of Oscar Wilde's remark that he'd spent the morning removing a comma and the afternoon putting it back.

His phone rang and he dove for it. It was Topher, and it was 12:07.

"Where's your piece?" Topher demanded.

"I'm just finishing up. It's coming."

"It better be," said Topher.

The line went dead.

John sat hyperventilating in front of his 422 words. He had never missed a deadline in his life, and this was his very first assignment for the *Weekly Times*.

He discovered he'd said the same thing twice, a paragraph apart. He liked the way he'd said it both times, but knew the drill and deleted one anyway. He wanted to pull his brain out of his nose with a crochet hook—surely that would be easier than finding more words. He borrowed some phrases from Francesca De Rossi, and threw in some advertising statistics. He spoke about the bonobos' sexual habits and their apparent total lack of interest in human pornography as compared to humans' sexual habits and their absolute obsession with the bonobos'. He outlined the differences between chimpanzees and bonobos, discussed the apes' decorating choices, and added a snippet about the upcoming hearing and the pregnancy. And then, quite suddenly, he was finished.

He stared in astonishment and checked the word count—797. He rubbed his eyes, went for an overdue piss, reread the piece, and discovered that it was good. Not just passable, but something he would be proud to turn in anywhere. He ran a spell check, read it once again to make sure he wasn't deluding himself, wished Amanda were there so he could run it past her, and emailed it. It was 12:37. The read receipt came back instantly.

———

He crawled into bed and wrapped his arms around the pillow. He gathered the blanket into a ball and squished it between his legs to cushion his knees. He took a deep breath and slid into a dream that involved Amanda.

Just as things were getting good, the thumper car pulled up in front of his door. Noisy women spilled out of it again, just like the night before. Once again they tippy-tapped up the concrete stairs and made their way unsteadily to their room. At one point John heard a heavy thud, followed by howls of laughter, and then cajoling and scraping, as they dragged the fallen one to her feet. And then, just like the night before, they slammed their door, turned on their music and the TV, ran the shower, and generally continued the party.

John tried burying his head under a pillow. He tried wrapping his head in a T-shirt. After twenty minutes, he pulled on his jeans and went upstairs.

The redhead opened the door. She was heavily made up, and wearing a latex dress the color of maraschino cherries. A cigarette hung from the corner of her vermilion lips. She looked older close up, a fact that was accentuated by the layers of makeup, which highlighted the fine lines at the corners of her eyes and above her lips.

She ran suspicious eyes up and down the length of his body.

"What you want?" she demanded in a thick accent.

Behind her, a brunette lay on the bed, curled like a fetus around a large bottle of vodka. Her nails were long and curved, each bearing a silver comet on a background of midnight blue.

"Can you keep it down? I'm trying to sleep," said John.

The bathroom door opened and another woman came out. Her hair was wrapped in a towel. Other than that she was completely naked. Although she could not have missed the fact that John was standing in the open doorway, she was completely unself-conscious as she walked to the bed, plucked the bottle of vodka from the brunette, and took a long drink.

"We just got off work," said the redhead at the door. She inhaled deeply and blew a stream of smoke straight at John's face.

"It's past three and I have to get up in a few hours."

"This is not my problem," said the woman, shrugging.

"It'll be your problem when I complain to the manager."

"Ha!" She snorted. "I don't think so."

And then she closed the door. She did not slam it; she just set it in motion and turned away. John's last glimpse was of her at the bed reaching for the vodka.

John lay in bed, thrashing and trying to ignore the party raging upstairs. Eventually he gave up and turned on the TV. He flipped through the channels, stopping briefly on *Ape House*. The bonobos were sleeping peacefully in their blanket nests, although the engineers were doing their best to keep things interesting. Cameras zoomed in on faces and tremulous lips, and the soundtrack superimposed snores and cricket noises.

Watching the bonobos sleep was infuriating since John himself could not, so he kept clicking. A desiccated ninety-four-year-old man in a muscle shirt demonstrated a kitchen machine shaped like a steam engine that, as far as John could tell, extracted juice from vegetables and spat all the fiber out the back. The man's eighty-seven-year-old wife gamely swallowed the juice of raw onions and beets, smiling broadly to indicate how much she enjoyed it. On the next channel, a lingerie-clad woman rolled around on her bed while purring and smiling into her phone. Local singles who like to party are just a phone call away, said the announcer. Tiffany is waiting . . . The phone numbers were displayed at the bottom of the screen.

The ruckus upstairs stopped at 5:41 A.M. There were a few moments of mattress coils squeaking as bodies adjusted themselves, and then beautiful, beautiful silence.

When John's alarm went off at 7:30, he wanted to cry. Amanda had just vaporized for a second time, and this time at a crucial moment. He hit the snooze button, jacked off with great effort and misery, hit the snooze button again, ripped the covers back, and went to the bathroom to clean up. He was devastated by lack of sleep, so tired he nicked himself four times while shaving. When he emerged to find his clothes, he still had little pieces of toilet paper stuck to his face.

John's hand was on the doorknob before he turned back. He stood at the foot of the bed, looking first at it, and then at the ceiling. He positioned his laptop in the center of the bed, signed on to iTunes, downloaded Jefferson Starship's "We Built This City," put it on repeat, turned the volume to full, gathered his things, and left, slamming the door behind him.

28

The phone beside Isabel's bed rang, waking her. She had her blackout curtains drawn and was momentarily confused; she reached for her cell phone and said, "Hello?" before realizing it was the hotel phone that was ringing. She propped herself onto an elbow and fumbled for the light switch. "Hello?" she said again, this time into the correct mouthpiece.

"Good morning, Miss Duncan. This is Mario from the front desk. There's a young . . . 'lady' here to see you."

"Pink hair?"

"Indeed."

"Please send her up."

"Yes, miss."

Isabel went into the washroom and splashed cold water on her face. She picked up each of the miniature bottles to see what the housekeeping genie had brought her the day before, noting with keen appreciation the symmetry with which they'd been arranged. She put them back exactly as they had been and was contemplating whether she had time to change out of her flannel pajamas when someone started rapping "Shave and a Haircut" on her door.

Isabel swung it open before the Two Bits. "Celia!"

Celia bounded through and hugged her. "Let me look at you," she said. "Love the pajamas, by the way. Turn around."

Isabel sighed and turned her back to let Celia examine her head. Celia ran her finger across the raised scar tissue.

"It's better. You know what I'd do? I'd get a zipper tattooed over it, or maybe Frankenstein stitches."

"Yeah-huh. I don't think so."

"It would be so cool. You could, like, own that scar."

"I do own it. And I'm going to grow hair over it. How was your flight? It must have been the red-eye," Isabel said, glancing at the clock by the bed.

"I hitchhiked."

"Celia! You're going to get yourself killed."

"Not likely. I caught a ride with a church bus. We sang camp songs all the way here."

"No, you did not. You did not catch a ride that took you all the way from Lawrence to here."

"Okay, so maybe there were a few truckers along the way."

"Celia!"

"They were fine."

Celia squeezed past and disappeared into the bathroom.

"So when did you get in?" Isabel called over the sound of running water.

"Yesterday afternoon."

"Where did you stay? Where's your stuff?"

Celia appeared in the doorway, scrubbed her toe in the carpet, and looked coyly at the floor. "Yeah. About that. I kind of met this guy . . ."

"Oh, Celia, tell me you did not stay with a complete stranger," said Isabel.

"Calm down, Mama Bear. You know I'm careful. And I didn't really *meet* him, meet him. More like met up with again. You'll recognize him."

"So who is he and where are you staying?"

Celia came forward and took Isabel's hands. She led her to the bed, sat, and patted the space beside her. "Sit."

Isabel obeyed, albeit reluctantly.

"We're staying at the campground, but he's downstairs in the restaurant. I want you to come meet him."

"I thought you said I knew him?"

"No," Celia said carefully. "I said you'd recognize him."

———

John stared morosely at his plate. The Mohegan Moon offered an impressive breakfast buffet, but after taking stock of its offerings, he had chosen eggs Benedict from the menu instead. It was one of the first breakfast dishes Amanda had perfected, and was his absolute favorite. He already regretted leaving the song blasting at the motel. He felt petty and immature, embarrassed even. He'd go back after breakfast and turn it off.

That green-haired kid was sitting by himself at a table in the corner. John was caught off-guard finding him here at breakfast—was he staying at the Mohegan Moon? Perhaps he was one of those faux punks, with a tidy little trust fund. Dying his hair and piercing things in an attempt to fast-track his nascent individuality. Somewhere, he probably had a perfectly nice mother pulling her hair out over him.

John was distracted by a white glove flashing in front of his face. The waiter deposited a plate with a silver dome in front of him. When John lifted the dome, two perfect eggs in velvet yellow robes sat alongside crispy applewood smoked bacon and crosshatched golden hash browns. John breathed in deeply and reached for one of the cute little bottles of hot sauce that Amanda referred to as "purse Tabasco." She sometimes joked about having empty ones made into earrings. He was about to put the Tabasco on his potatoes, but on second thought slid the tiny bottles into his pocket to take home to Amanda.

———

Isabel dropped her forehead into her hands. "I can't believe you. How on earth did that happen? You've always called him an ass."

"An 'asshat,' actually. When I got in yesterday afternoon I saw him at Ape House with a bunch of granola eaters and told him something along those lines. And then he told me a few thoughts of his own, and then we got to talking, and it turns out we completely agree on the subject of Peter. Next thing I knew, bam."

"Bam?" Isabel lifted her face from her hands. *"Bam?"*

"Yeah. In a manner of speaking."

Isabel threw herself backward and covered her head with a pillow. Celia was beside her instantly, lifting a corner. "Please come meet him?"

"I can't. Cat Douglas is probably down there. She recognized me."

"If Catwoman comes near you, I'll chase her off."

"I think even you would be outmatched, Celia."

"Then we'll hide." Her voice took on a wheedling tone. "Come on, Isabel. Please?"

John spread his starched white napkin across his lap, and lifted his knife and fork. He dipped the tines into the Hollandaise, which had a bit of a skin, and tasted it. It wasn't quite right—there was something in it that shouldn't be, presumably a thickener of some sort so it would hold in the kitchen without growing salmonella.

Amanda's Hollandaise was pure yolk, butter, and lemon. She wouldn't talk while she "played chicken with the eggs," as she called it, because whisking them over heat until the moment they achieved the consistency of heavy satin required all her concentration. At the precise moment before they scrambled she'd impale a chunk of butter on the whisk and use it to cool both the yolks and the bottom of the pan. She was always high with relief and victory, although he'd never seen her turn a sauce. After she incorporated all the butter, she'd spin to him, dip her finger into the pan, and dab sauce on his tongue. "Is it the best ever?" she'd ask, eyes aglow, and he always said yes because it was always true.

There were other things wrong with his breakfast. The eggs themselves were too round, meaning they hadn't been poached in the classic sense. He wouldn't have known the difference, except that when Amanda converted to the Church of Julia she declared that an egg wasn't poached unless it was set free in water, although some minimal guidance was allowed involving a spoon and a splash of vinegar.

John sliced into the center of the yolk, which was perfectly done. Then he flipped all the toppings over so that the yolk could seep into the English muffin. He found himself looking at a piece of ordinary ham. Amanda would never have settled for that. She would have used either proper Canadian bacon with a peameal crust or imported prosciutto. And she would have tucked either the top halves of three spears of lightly steamed asparagus or else a little packet of sautéed and garlic-kissed baby spinach between the meat and egg. She never did understand why Benedict and Florentine had to be mutually exclusive, and he couldn't agree more.

"Is everything to your liking, sir?"

"Hmm?" John thudded back into the atmosphere. "Oh. Yes. Thank you," he said.

"Very good, sir."

After the waiter moved on, John ate a piece of bacon with his fingers. He wasn't positive it was finger food, but nobody gave him any dirty looks.

Except the kid in the corner. He was still staring at John, eyes narrowed to hateful pinpricks.

———

"You're really going to talk to a reporter?" Celia said, as they stepped into the elevator.

"Yes. But you can't say anything to anyone. About any of it."

"Why would I say anything to anyone?"

"I don't know, but . . . look. This is important. Promise me. Tell no one. Especially this new guy. What's his name, anyway?"

"Nathan. You're going to like him."

"Sure I am."

"Give him a chance. Please?"

Isabel looked impatiently at the padded interior of the elevator.

A *ding* announced their arrival on the main floor. They walked around the towering flower arrangement toward the restaurant. Celia said, "That's him in the corner."

"I can see that," said Isabel. "He's hard to miss."

Nathan got up. He was walking. Stalking, really, with his hands deep in his jean pockets and shoulders hunched forward.

"What's he doing? Did he see us?" asked Isabel.

"I don't know," said Celia.

He paused at a table. The man sitting at it looked up. He was holding half a piece of bacon between his thumb and fingers, like a cigar.

"Meat is murder, you jerk," said Nathan. He slid his hand under the edge of the man's plate and flicked his wrist, sending the dish flying. It fell facedown on the floor and cracked into four pieces. Droplets of Hollandaise splattered the man's shoes and pants.

Celia grabbed Isabel's arm and yanked her behind one of the Corinthian columns that flanked the restaurant's entrance.

Nathan stormed past them and out the main doors of the hotel without ever looking back.

"Wow," said Celia. "That was not cool."

Isabel sucked her breath through her teeth. "Celia," she said.

"What?"

"That guy. That's John Thigpen. The reporter Bonzi wanted to kiss. The one I want to talk to."

Celia looked back. John Thigpen was standing with palms turned outward, staring at the exit in wide-eyed shock.

"Oooooooh," said Celia. "That's Pigpen?"

"Yes," Isabel said through gritted teeth. "That's Pigpen."

29

John was not generally superstitious, but on the off-chance that the breakfast incident was karmically related, he headed straight back to the Buccaneer to turn off the song.

He looked automatically over at Jimmy's, and saw one of the thugs smoking a cigarette while Booger shat on the sidewalk. The guy looked at John; John gave a feeble wave, which went ignored.

As he approached, he saw that the door to his room was ajar. He paused with his ear to the crack, not wanting to disrupt a burglary in progress. The women in the room upstairs were squealing and laughing, which made it difficult for him to hear anything. He nudged the door open with his foot.

The room appeared empty, but he checked under the bed and in the bathroom, ripping back the shower curtain. The milky panes of the jalousie window were cranked wide, and the filthy gauze curtain blew in and out on a breeze. The dead flies had drifted to the bottom of the bathtub.

No one.

With heart pounding, he returned to the bedroom. Only then did he notice that Starship was no longer playing. On the bed, in place of his computer, was a pastel blue Post-it note:

Room 242 ☹

John sighed and glanced at the ceiling. Room 242 was directly above his.

He walked to the end of the building and climbed the staircase. The paint of the handrail had peeled and been covered over several times, leaving it with the gritty texture of papadum.

The door to room 242 was wide open. He found himself looking at the back of his laptop, which was on the bed, open, and playing something that involved an electric guitar and wah pedal.

The red-haired woman had pulled up a chair and was resting her platform shoes on the bed. A blonde stood beside her, arranging bits of her hair with a cordless curling iron. She had hairpins in the corner of her mouth. The brunette was on the other side, watching the screen with interest and occasionally cocking her head to blow a stream of smoke toward the ceiling. Not one of them offered so much as a flicker of recognition that John was standing in the doorway.

"What the hell are you doing?" he said.

The redhead leaned in close to the screen, waggling her cigarette, her eyes growing misty. "Those were glory days," she said wistfully. "Look at that. I *invented* that. Teabagging."

The other women leaned in and sighed.

"Absolutely amazing, Ivanka," said one of them. "Truly inspired."

"Yes. I was star. I traveled in limos. Drank champagne all day long, and the coke! Everywhere you looked, line after beautiful line. And now . . ." She sighed tragically.

"Teabagging?" said John. "*Teabagging?* You're watching porn on my computer?"

"That's not porn," Ivanka said indignantly. "That's me."

"You stole my computer!"

"I would probably say 'borrowed,'" she replied, turning her face to the side and taking a drag from her cigarette. She blew a thin jet of smoke.

"How the hell did you get into my room?"

"Oh, you know. The manager, Victor, he is nice man. You"—she

cluck-clucked at John—"not so much. Very unfriendly this morning."
She sat suddenly forward and stabbed a lacquered nail at the screen.
"Look! Watch this!"

"Stop!" he yelped. "That's liquid crystal!"

"See?" she said, ignoring him completely and dragging her nail
across the screen.

Realizing he was helpless, John came around the bed. Ivanka's red
nail had left an impression around the form she had outlined.

"You see that? Tight as a conga, round as a basketball."

"But with just the right amount of jiggle," said another.

"Well, yes," allowed Ivanka, taking another drag. "But time catches
everyone." Another heartbreaking Russian sigh.

"Excuse me? Do you mind?" said John.

Ivanka turned sharply toward him, suddenly paying full attention.
"Yes. I do. That is why the frowny face."

"The frowny face?"

"Didn't you read note? You interrupt our beauty sleep, and Fat Man
Bob doesn't like us looking tired."

"Fat Man Bob?"

"The manager at gentlemen's club. Where we work."

Ivanka leaned forward and clicked the laptop shut. "But I forgive
you, you naughty boy . . ." She waggled her cigarette and winked. "You
didn't tell me you were big celebrity writer." This last was framed by
fingered quotation marks.

"What?"

"Victor. He give me something else besides key." She cocked her
head toward the bedside table. A glossy magazine lay open displaying a
two-page panorama of panty-less women climbing from cars in micro-
miniskirts. Strategically placed yellow stars covered the pertinent areas.
CROTCH SHOTS SPREADING! screamed the headline. TOP STARS MODEL THE
LATEST STYLES IN "DOWN THERE" HAIR!

John sat on the edge of the bed.

The brunette closed the freshly minted *Weekly Times,* slid it back into
its FedEx envelope, and tossed it onto John's laptop. He took both and
stood up.

"You probably want this too," said Ivanka, handing him a corporate

American Express card embossed with his name. "Was also in package. You're lucky you're Big-Shot Writer. I have weakness for shoes."

John stared at the credit card, slid it into his back pocket, and walked to the door.

As he was about to pull the door shut behind him, Ivanka said, "Tonight, you sleep." She blew a kiss in his direction.

———

Back in his room, he pulled the magazine from its envelope.

There, above his byline, was the title PORN KING PUTS SEX-CRAZED MONKEYS ON AIR! (John's had been BIG BROTHER OR BIG LOVE? REALITY TELEVISION SHOWCASES AMOROUS APES.)

It got worse. John's paragraph,

> Formerly known as pygmy chimpanzees, bonobos were recognized as a separate species (*Pan paniscus*) in 1929. Peaceful, playful, and averse to conflict, bonobos are often called "the hippies of the forest." Their society is matriarchal and egalitarian, and remarkable in its sexual behavior. Bonobos form and maintain social bonds through sex, and the females are as likely as males to initiate sexual contact. Wild bonobos, which are native to the Democratic Republic of the Congo, initiate some sort of sexual contact every four or five hours. By contrast, captive bonobos initiate sex roughly every hour and a half.

had become a bunch of sensationalistic gobbledygook glued together with such statements as "Monkeys have sex every hour of every day!" and "Bonobo babes use SEX to get what they want!" and "Pussy-whipped males kept in line with SEX!"

John's comment on the physical differences between chimpanzees and bonobos

> Bonobos are smaller and more delicate than *Pan troglodytes,* with a refined, slim build and flatter features. Their limbs are long and elegant, and the females have more prominent breasts than any species of ape other than humans.

had been boiled down into a single statement: "The Pamela Andersons of the ape world!"

John's references to their acquisition of human language

> They are as closely related to humans as chimpanzees, sharing more than 98.7% of our DNA. Perhaps not surprisingly, bonobos have an extraordinary capacity for human language and abstract thought. These particular bonobos understand spoken English, and communicate using American Sign Language, having acquired human language in the same manner as human infants and for the same reason—a desire to communicate. They are also more computer-literate than some of their human counterparts.

had been removed completely.

He forced himself through the rest. None of it was his. The legal petition, the pregnancy, gone. The whole thing had been adulterated and sensationalized.

Seconds later, he was on the phone with Topher: "That's not what I wrote! None of it!"

"Ech," said Topher.

"No! Not 'ech.' It's not what I wrote."

"What do you think this is, the *National Geographic*? We have someone covering Lindsay Lohan full-time, for Christ's sake. You're not looking at a Pulitzer here."

"I care because it's *wrong*. They're not monkeys, they're great apes. They're not chimpanzees, they're bonobos. And they're not Pamela Andersons. They're A-cups at most, B, tops. Oh my God. I can't believe I just said that."

"Tell you what—when you turn in a piece two and a half hours before we go to press, you don't get to complain. I, on the other hand, do get to complain. Especially when you hand in something as juicy as a saltine. Frankly, I'm a little worried. You need to unlearn everything you learned at Columbia. Forget *The Philadelphia Inquirer* and think *National Enquirer,* only glossier and with fewer aliens. I want you to memorize every word of this week's issue. I want you to start watching

TMZ and *Access Hollywood*. Go to the blogs: Perez Hilton, Mr Paparazzi. *That's* what I'm looking for. And no more Latin, got it? And another thing. Get that interview with Faulks. And Isabel Duncan. Find shit out. Shit we can use. It doesn't have to be true. There just has to be some tiny thing you can extrapolate from, if you get my drift. And you can always fall back on the old 'sources said' routine."

"You want me to make things up about Ken Faulks."

"And Isabel Duncan. And while you're at it, I want you to remember why you got this job in the first place." There was an ominous silence. "I think we understand each other?"

A single muscle to the side of John's mouth began twitching. "Yeah."

"Good. I look forward to your next piece. Which will be on time and full of juicy tidbits."

"Yeah," said John again.

"Excellent," Topher said cheerfully and hung up.

———

John had settled on his bed with the *Weekly Times* and was trying to undo his education when the foundations of the building were rocked by a deafening *ka-boom,* followed by the tinkle of raining glass. John jerked his knees to his chest and covered his head. Once it was clear the explosion had happened outside the motel, he leapt up and threw open the door.

The building across the street was completely engulfed in flames, a sheath of diaphanous white-blue that tapered to red and yellow at the ends of greedy tendrils. John glanced at his feet. They were surrounded by shards of glass—the windows had blown out with such velocity that pieces had traveled across the street. People on both levels of the Buccaneer had opened their doors and were stepping outside—the strippers, the muumuu woman and her undershirt-wearing husband, the Asian family who had gone hopefully down to the pool on their first night and abandoned it on sight. Several people were already on cell phones, cupping their hands around the mouthpiece so they could be heard over the din. John looked back at the burning building.

A human fireball leapt through what had been the front window and barreled full tilt down the street. A woman on the balcony directly above John began to scream—it was Ivanka, and this familiarity in the midst of chaos jolted him into action.

The human-shaped fire ran and ran, arms flailing and hands slapping at the all-engulfing flames, which trailed behind like the tail of a shooting star. John scanned the exterior wall of the Buccaneer for a fire extinguisher. There wasn't one. He bolted back into his room, swiped the bedspread, and sprinted down the street.

The person collapsed on the asphalt like a marionette whose strings had been sliced. John caught up and threw the bedspread over the form, trying to tuck it around and under, starving the flames of oxygen, patting at stray flicks of fire, and rolling the person back and forth as parts of the bedspread threatened to ignite. With the flames finally extinguished, John pulled the blanket away from the person's head. He dropped to his knees and hovered, unable to tell if the person—he assumed it was a man, although at this point it was hard to tell—was still alive. John held his ear to the charred mouth. He examined the chest for signs of breath. He heard sirens, growing mercifully louder.

"Hang in there, buddy. Hang in there. Help is on the way." He felt powerless. He wanted to hold the guy's hand, or provide some soothing contact, but he could see no part of him that wasn't burned, so John just knelt beside him and murmured comforting things. He had no idea if he was effective. He had no idea if the man even knew he was there.

Two fire trucks careened around the corner.

John leapt to his feet, waving his arms and screaming, "Here! We need help here!" But the vehicles swept past and came to a stop in front of the burning building.

As John stared helplessly after them, a police car pulled up. John lifted his hands in a gesture of desperation. The cop surveyed John through the window, and then climbed out. He was in no particular hurry.

"What happened?" he said to John, glancing at the burned man.

"I was in my room over there"—John lifted a quivering finger at the Buccaneer—"and I heard something that sounded like a bomb and came out to see what the hell was going on and this guy came flying out, just burning up. I chased him until he fell and then I put out the fire with my bedspread, and has anyone even called an ambulance? Why didn't the fire trucks stop?"

From the scorched form came a low, keening moan that progressed to a wail. Once the man started, he did not stop. He pleaded and begged, he swore and cried, he prayed and wept for his mother, although his ruined face barely moved.

Moments later an ambulance pulled up. John stood watching as the ambulance crew removed the charred bedspread and loaded the man onto a gurney. His initial outburst had subsided to piteous moaning.

"I need to know what we're dealing with," said a paramedic, looking into the blackened face. "Do you understand? If you want me to save your eyesight, I need to know if you were cooking meth. Do you understand?"

"They were," John said. "At least, I'm pretty sure." He was hugging himself, shaking violently. It was the smell of burned flesh, the sight of another human being whose life had just changed irreparably, if not ended.

"And why do you think that?" said the cop.

"I thought it was a restaurant. There was a sign. Pizza and bento boxes. I walked in the other day. I was hungry. But there was no pizza. They had guns. And a pit bull. And the place smelled like nail polish remover."

The cop gave John an appraising stare, then went over to the ambulance and spoke to the paramedic, who glanced at John, said something back, and nodded. The cop returned.

"Thanks, buddy. There's a chemical involved in cooking meth that takes two or three days to burn through the cornea, so if the burn victim doesn't fess up right away, well, that's it. I don't know about this guy, though. Can't say his chances look good anyway . . ." He pulled a pad out of his pocket. "What's your name?"

"John Thigpen," John said through chattering teeth.

"And you're staying at the Buccaneer?"

"Yes. Room 142."

"Assuming there's anyone alive to prosecute, we'll need to talk to you again. Did you touch this guy or his clothes?"

"No."

"At all?"

"I don't think so. I think I only touched the bedspread."

"Okay. Good. Even so, I want you to go and have a very thorough shower. Thirty minutes at least. You may have corrosive substances on your skin."

John's eyes widened.

"Yeah, that's what you get for being a Good Samaritan these days," said the cop, turning away and shaking his head. "Like my mama always said, no good deed goes unpunished."

John trudged back to the Buccaneer, still shivering, arms still wrapped around himself.

Ivanka was in the parking lot, jog-trotting toward him in a skintight white Elvis jumpsuit and jeweled platform boots.

"Don't touch me," he said. "I may have corrosive substances on me. I need to shower."

She shouted up at the balcony. "Katarina! Start shower!" She shooed John toward the stairs. "Go. Go. Shower in your room not work. I close your door so no one takes computer."

As he climbed the stairs, John wondered how Ivanka knew that his shower didn't work. He also wondered how he would get back into his room afterward, until he remembered that she had magical powers with Victor and possibly a master key.

As he was about to step into the shower, Ivanka came into the bathroom and set a fluffy pink towel on the edge of the sink. Then she handed him a bar of fragrant milled soap of the kind Amanda used. John got teary as he took the soap.

"Thank you."

After a thirty-minute shower, he emerged with the towel wrapped around his waist. The women were in their professional outfits, applying makeup with hand-held mirrors, spraying their hair into architectural forms.

"You need drink?" said Ivanka, offering a bottle.

He shook his head.

"You good man. Brave man," she said, appraising him. "Married?"
John nodded.

"Of course." Ivanka kissed him on the cheek and then wiped the lipstick residue off with her thumb. She handed him his key.

John went down to his room. Although it was not yet five o'clock, he was so shattered from the whole experience that he simply crawled into bed and turned out the light. On second thought, he turned it back on and called Amanda.

"Hello?" she said.

He burst into tears. She comforted him as best she could as he told her what had happened, but what he needed above all else was bodily contact. He ached to be held.

———

John dreamed of dark and winding caves, of fire monsters, of enormous hairy creatures with fangs and glowing eyes. Beowulfian scenes of warriors and clashing weapons flashed before him, of villages pillaged, of monsters with limbs rent off, of Grendel, and worse—Grendel's mother. Her breath was fearsome and ragged and smelled of leftover canned tuna.

John jerked awake and lay gasping. The dream was so real it took him a moment to realize that it hadn't really happened. Then he remembered what really had happened and felt the bottom dip temporarily out of his world. Then he realized that the ragged and fishy breath continued to snurfle and snuff beside him, and that the mattress sagged down and away from him under the weight of a large mass.

He lunged for the lamp, blindly grasping, searching for the switch. When he finally found it, he whipped his head around just in time to see a pair of red haunches slide from the far side of the bed. John squinted as his eyes adjusted to the light. Was he still dreaming?

A tiny whimpering arose from the far side of the room.

"Booger?" said John.

The whimpering stopped. John climbed out of bed and circled it slowly, as though he were stalking big game. In the corner, in a pathetic, quivering heap, was the red pit bull. The dog looked up at him, ears pressed against his head, blinking miserably. His jowls lay loose, hanging against his snout. They huffed in and out with his breath. His nostrils flared and glistened.

He did not look burned. Had he been out back? Did he have corrosive substances on him? It seemed impossible that he could have made it out of the inferno unharmed.

"It's okay, boy," John said awkwardly. John swept his eyes over the dog, searching for injury. He hesitated, took a step forward, and even extended his hand a couple of times. The dog appeared to be fine—free of soot and any other evidence of fire or physical trauma. John thought he should probably bathe the thing just in case, but for the life of him could not figure out how, so he went back around to the far side of the bed, and climbed in. He turned off the light and lay knees to chest under the sheets.

Within minutes, Booger had slithered back onto the other side of the bed and resumed snoring and farting. John lay wide-eyed in the dark.

30

The next morning, John crept out from beneath the sheets so as not to disturb the great slavering beast, who had rearranged himself to take up a full three quarters of the bed. John shaved and splashed himself under the tap in the bathtub, then snuck past and out, leaving the toilet open so the dog would have access to water. Once outside, he stood staring at the door, wondering what the housekeeper's reaction would be. Would she just close the door and pretend she hadn't seen, or would she call Animal Control? John didn't think Booger stood much of a chance of being deemed adoptable . . . He opened the door a crack, slipped his hand inside, groped until he found the DO NOT DISTURB sign, and hung it on the outside knob.

The door had barely shut when his cell phone rang. He did not recognize the number. He started walking and answered. "Hello?"

There was a crackling noise and no response. John thought the connection had gone dead. "Hello?" he said again.

"Is this John?" said a female voice.

"Yes, this is John," he said, furrowing his brow. The voice sounded vaguely familiar, but he couldn't place it.

"This is Isabel Duncan."

John froze in his tracks. "Isabel! How are you? I mean . . ." He stopped, realizing he was on the verge of babbling. He lowered his voice. "How are you?"

"I've been better," she said. "But I've also been worse."

John thought of the human-shaped fire he'd chased down the street the day before. He took a deep breath. "So you're feeling better?" he said, when what he really wanted to say was, How bad is it? Were you burned? The memory of the man's charred face flashed through John's head—if he survived, he was going to be grievously disfigured.

"When my hair grows back, I'll be good as new," Isabel said. "Better than new, actually. Apparently my new nose is a big improvement."

John blurted out: "But I liked your old nose," then squeezed his eyes shut because he knew he'd just said something inappropriate.

"Thanks. So did I."

Relief, followed by more anxiety, as he listened to shuffling at the other end of the phone.

"So I was wondering if you wanted to talk," she finally said. "I've been kind of avoiding reporters—well, completely avoiding them, actually—but now I'd like to talk to someone, and I remembered how good you were with the bonobos. I'd already decided to talk to you when I saw you at breakfast yesterday, and then Francesca mentioned she'd met you at Ape House. It seemed like kismet. In fact, she gave me your number. I gather you're no longer with *The Philadelphia Inquirer*?"

She'd seen him at breakfast? He had been in the room with her and hadn't even noticed? Then he realized the real implications of her statement. He brought the heel of his hand to his forehead. He had been so close, and now his lie—his pride and his shame, his stupidity—was going to destroy it all. "No, I'm not with the *Inquirer* anymore," he said as evenly as he could.

"Good. Because that picture was unforgivable. Do you mind meeting me in my room at the Mohegan Moon? Cat Douglas recognized me the other day and now I'm kind of stuck here."

"Sure. No problem."

"I'm spending most of today with Francesca and Eleanor. Can you come by tomorrow morning? At nine or ten?"

"Absolutely."

———

John spent the day unsuccessfully hunting the elusive Ken Faulks, who, when he wasn't plugging his show in front of Ape House, appeared to fall off the face of the earth. He was clearly staying locally, yet no one seemed to know where. John had quizzed workmen, the forklift driver who made the deliveries, the security team—anyone who was working in a professional capacity around the building—and they either knew nothing or were afraid to tell. Having worked for Faulks himself, John could relate. Faulks had once decimated his staff at the *Gazette*— actually firing a tenth of his workers—because he had been informed that a full 40 percent of their sick days were being taken on Mondays and Fridays. If his intent was to frighten those who remained into countless hours of overtime and coming to work with the flu, he was successful.

Despite not finding Faulks, John was ecstatic over his upcoming exclusive with Isabel Duncan. She was as good a catch as Faulks. Even Topher would recognize that, which reminded John about his other dilemma. He tried not to think about how she would react when she found out he was writing for a tabloid.

As John approached the Buccaneer, he caught sight of the blackened shell across the street, and suddenly remembered his delayed decision. What in God's name was he going to do about Booger?

John heard the television and smelled the cigarettes even before he got his door open. Ivanka was lying on his bed in a typhoon of perfume and smoke, holding an open bottle of vodka, puffing away. Booger was sprawled beside her, his blockish head pressed up against her thigh. He had left dark, wet nose prints on her satin dressing gown, which was the color of dried blood.

"Hi," said John, emptying his pockets and tossing everything onto the bedside table. The ashtray was nearly full. "What's up?"

"Your dog is opera singer," she said, setting her current cigarette on the lip of the ashtray so she could caress Booger's ears. "He wakes me up—*Awooo! Awooo!* So I take him on walk. And feed him lunch. Where is dog food?"

"I don't have any."

"He is from over there?" she asked, inclining her head in the general direction of Jimmy's.

John nodded.

"Poor thing." She leaned over and planted a kiss on the dog's broad forehead. Booger turned his head to return the favor, but she was already out of tongue's reach. "Thank goodness not hurt."

"You want him?" John said hopefully.

"Ha!" she snorted. "What do I want with dog? No, God sent to you. You keep. But get dog food. I give Philly cheese steak and now, the gas! *Pee-whew!*" She scrunched up her face and waved a hand in front of her nose.

John sighed and sat on the bed, which sagged under his weight. Ivanka took a swig of vodka, straight from the bottle, and rolled over to stub out her cigarette.

"You want a glass?" he said.

Ivanka shook her head.

John leaned in closer, examining her. Her eyes were pink-tinged, her nose raw. "Are you crying?"

"Oh, maybe a little," she sniffed.

"What's the matter?" said John.

She made a frog face and waved dismissively. "Bah," she said. "It doesn't matter."

She kept her eyes trained on the television: a woman with a platinum-blond bob sat on a stage between a man and a woman. The woman wept, going down a laundry list of the man's sexual transgressions. The audience, made up entirely of enraged women, shouted and poked their fists in the air. The helmet-headed hostess clucked platitudes, slid to the edge of her seat to put her hand on the woman's knee, and cast the man a withering glance. The camera swung around to him. Guards grabbed him by the arms and hauled him bodily off the stage into the sea of women, who leapt from their seats and into the aisle, beating him with purses. He didn't even struggle, just scowled and half-heartedly protected his head. When he disappeared into a vomitorium, the show cut to a commercial.

"No, really. I'd like to know," said John.

Ivanka looked back at him, pursed her lips, and rolled her eyes. "Is job. And Faulks."

"Ken Faulks?"

"Yes." She turned her head and pretended to spit twice in quick succession. *"Puh! Puh!"* Booger flinched both times but stayed put.

"How do you know Ken Faulks?"

Ivanka sighed. John noticed that a droplet had formed at the end of her nose and got her a tissue from the bathroom.

She took it and dabbed her eyes and nose. "Thank you. Anyway, he come to Fat Man Bob's. He wants lap dance, private lap dance, you understand. I no used to, but now business is not so good. The suits, they used to tuck fives and tens in G-string. Now they tuck singles. They think we don't notice? We can't count?" Her eyes blazed with righteous indignation for a few seconds, then lost their flare. Her right hand remained on Booger's head. Her continuous caress had lulled him into sleep, or something resembling it. "So Faulks, he sees me, he asks for me. I think it's because he recognizes me, because I was one of the original Jiggly Gigglies, and I'm tired of this, I want to go back to film, make some money, retire. Maybe get married. Maybe have children. Who knows? He has series now, *Crazy Cougars,* you know?"

John nodded.

"So I ask him. And he says no!" She sat forward. "No! He doesn't remember me and I'm too old for cougar! And then he wants lap dance anyway!" She picked up the tissue and used it again. She shrugged, and tossed the sodden wad onto the bedside table. Her eyes brimmed with resignation and tears. "So I do. I just do. You know?" She stared into the distance for a while and then turned suddenly to face him. "Do you think I'm too old for cougar?"

John shook his head. She burst into a fresh round of tears anyway. John moved closer and put his arms around her. She pressed the bottle of vodka against his back and sobbed onto his shoulder.

"Ivanka?" he said when the gulping noises had slowed to hiccups. "Can you do me a favor?"

She pulled back and nodded. She reached again for the tissue, and then, on second thought, wiped her eyes on her sleeves.

"Can you please call me if Faulks shows up at the club again?"

She straightened her spine, mustering composure. "Sure," she said with feigned nonchalance. "Why not?"

John grabbed a pen and began rummaging desperately for a piece of paper upon which to write his number. Ivanka handed him a rhinestone-encrusted red cell phone, and said, "Here. Add to contacts."

———

Minutes after Ivanka left, there was a knock at the door. He opened it a crack and found Amanda.

For a second, he thought he was hallucinating. When he realized he wasn't, he swung the door back and came at her with arms wide open. She let her bags fall to the floor and flung her arms around him. Before he knew it, he was weeping into her neck.

"Hush, it's okay," she said, stroking his hair. For a minute they just held each other.

"What are you doing here?" he finally said, ushering her into the room.

"After last night, how could I not come? I saw what's left of the building across the street. I can't even imagine. It must have been horrifying."

"It was the most awful thing I've ever seen in my entire life. The smell, the way he cried, his face—I wish I could unsee it, unhear it."

"But you saved his life."

"No, probably not." John shook his head quickly, sniffing. "I don't know what happened to him. I should call. I should call, shouldn't I?"

Amanda stroked his cheek. "We'll call tomorrow. Unless you need to know now?"

"No. It wouldn't make any difference anyway, and I don't think I want to know tonight. Especially now that you're here."

She embraced him again, and then stiffened. She pulled away, and John watched her gaze move from the unmade bed to the ashtray full of lipsticked butts. "What's this?"

"The woman upstairs, is, um . . ." He pointed hopelessly at the ceiling. "It's complicated."

Amanda opened her mouth to continue the investigation when she caught sight of Booger. "What the . . . ?"

She swung back to John, her eyes wide, the cigarettes forgotten. "Is this what you were talking about the other day? You already *have* a dog?"

"No. He's from the meth lab. He snuck into my room while the door was open. During the fire."

Amanda turned to stare at the dog. "You didn't say anything about him last night."

"I didn't know he was here. He must have been hiding in the bathroom. He climbed onto the bed in the middle of the night."

"Oh, the poor thing," said Amanda. She walked over and crouched beside the dog.

"Be careful!" John yelped. "He's a meth-lab pit bull, for God's sake!"

Amanda reached out to scratch the dog's chin. "Hey, buddy," she said softly. He rested his snout and liver-colored nose in her hand so that she was supporting the weight of his whole head. His thin tail began thumping the floor. "Poor thing," she said again. "Do you know his name?"

John swallowed loudly. "Booger."

At the sound of his name, Booger turned and licked Amanda's other hand, which was sweeping across his back and haunches. "He wasn't hurt?"

"Apparently not."

"That's amazing." Amanda stood up, wiped her hands on her thighs, and came back to John.

"Do you have any dog food?"

"No," said John.

"Is there a grocery around here?"

"There's a gas station up the street."

She turned back to the dog. "Booger, are you hungry? Do you need some dinner, Booger?"

The dog's ridiculous whiskered eyebrows rose and twitched. His pink tongue made a long tour around the exterior of his jowls, which smacked as he opened and shut his mouth. Amanda leaned over, hands on knees, and looked him straight in the eyes. She held a finger in front of his nose. "Mommy will be right back."

Mommy? John's heart lurched.

She grabbed her car keys and left.

———

Amanda returned with two cans of wet dog food and a package of plastic bowls. In the meantime, John had flushed Ivanka's cigarette butts down the toilet and opened the bathroom window.

"Dinner and breakfast," she explained, brandishing the cans. "I have to go back to L.A. in the morning." She disappeared into the bathroom. John followed, doing the math and hoping he was misinterpreting, although he suspected he was not.

Amanda ripped open the package of plastic bowls. She filled one with water and set it on the floor. "We'll get you proper bowls when we get home," she said, ruffling Booger's ears and confirming John's fears.

"You can't be serious about this," he said.

"Of course I am. You said we should get a dog. And here's a dog." She stood up and struggled with one of the pop-top cans before handing it to John. He opened it and handed it back.

"A junkyard dog. Worse—a meth-lab dog!" he said.

"A homeless dog. A sweet dog. Just look at him!"

And, indeed, Booger was sitting at their feet, back legs splayed appealingly, his expression conveying hope and adoration. His eyes followed the can's every movement.

Amanda emptied the dog food into a bowl and set it on the floor. Booger dove in, tail wagging furiously, but the bowl slid away from him each time he tried to take a bite. Amanda crouched and steadied it for him. The food was gone in seconds. When he lifted his square head, he ran his long tongue up and over Amanda's chin, lips, and nose.

"Good God!" she said, wiping her face and rising. "What was that? Road kill?" She examined the label of the empty can.

John switched tactics. "They're never going to let you put him on the airplane."

"Of course they will. I'll buy a crate. And if I don't find a PetSmart between here and the airport, I happen to know you can FedEx a horse to Hawaii."

"What? What kind of people are you hanging out with these days?"

"Heard about it the other night. An actress wanted her horse with her while she was shooting a movie and refused to show up until they arranged delivery."

"I really think you should rethink this," John said.

"Absolutely not."

"He's a meth-lab dog! What if he turns on you?"

Amanda leaned down and covered Booger's ears. "Stop saying that. You're going to hurt his feelings."

John raised his eyes to the ceiling and sighed.

"He'll be fine," said Amanda, standing and fingering the edge of the sink. She appeared to encounter something and examined her fingertip before washing her hands. She dried her hands calmly, and stood absolutely still, staring into the bottom of the sink. A prescient static filled the air, and John knew what was coming. She turned casually to face him. "So, this woman upstairs. How complicated is it?"

"Baby, you can't possibly think—"

"I don't want to think anything," she said. "But I came here unannounced and found your motel room contaminated by cheap perfume, lipsticked cigarette butts, and an unmade bed. Tell me what I'm supposed to think. What would you think?"

"I admit it doesn't look good, but—"

"No," she said harshly. "It doesn't look good."

John took a very deep breath. "Her name is Ivanka. She's a stripper."

"A *stripper*?" said Amanda, eyes widening further.

"No, you've got it all wrong. It's not like that. She has a connection with Faulks. She might be able to give me a lead."

"And how about you? Does she have any connection with you? Just how far are you willing to go for this story?"

"Amanda, for God's sake," he said.

She gestured toward the other room. "Explain the bed," she demanded.

"I was stashing a pit bull in the room. I put out the DO NOT DISTURB sign. The housekeeper didn't come in today."

They stared at each other for what felt like a lifetime. John finally took a step toward her, cautiously, and she didn't move. When he put his hands on her cheeks, she tilted her head, but stood aloof. A moment later, she was on tiptoe, holding his head in both hands, kissing him almost violently. She pulled his shirt free from his waistband, undid his belt buckle and fly, and slid her hand down the front of his pants. John recovered from his shock, lifted her by the armpits, and carried her to the bed.

When he climaxed, he opened his eyes and found Amanda staring straight back at him, her chin lifted, her lips parted in pleasure. When he rolled off, she threw an arm over his chest. A few minutes later, after they'd both caught their breath, she whispered, "I'm ovulating."

A bolt of panic zapped through John. He reminded himself to breathe.

Sometime later the mattress creaked as Booger crawled up onto the bed behind Amanda.

———

Amanda demanded John's services twice more in short order. When she reached for him again, he said in desperation, "Amanda, I can't."

"You're turning down sex?" she said with surprise.

"I'm not turning it down. I just physically can't. I'm not eighteen."

She nestled up to him and said, "Okay. But we're doing it in the morning before I leave. Speaking of rejections—"

"I'm not rejecting anything! We just did it three times in four hours!"

"—apparently not only am I rejectable, I'm rerejectable."

"You're . . . what?" he said even as it dawned on him that this was of his own doing.

"Yes. Agents who have already rejected me are finding it necessary to reject me again. What I don't understand is how they got my new address."

John lay very still.

She lifted her head. "John? Do you know how they got my new address?"

After a moment of consideration, he said, "There's a PetSmart right next to the Staples in El Paso. Not far from the airport. I'll draw you a map in the morning."

He could feel her staring at him in the dark. After a while, she sighed and laid her head back down. He had bartered Booger for forgiveness.

John awoke with a start at 3 A.M. He had been so distracted by Amanda's unannounced visit and businesslike focus on sex that he'd missed the second episode of *Ape House Prime Time*.

"Sorry," he mumbled as he turned on the light and reached for the remote control. Amanda rolled away and threw her arm over Booger, who released a satisfied groan and otherwise didn't move.

John flipped through the channels. With any luck, he'd find some kind of summary, maybe on *Entertainment Tonight*. If not, he'd boot up his computer and check out the gossip blogs Topher had ordered him to emulate.

As it turned out, he did not have to look far. Faulks had arranged to have beer and cap guns delivered and switched the bonobos' television from the program they had chosen, *Orangutan Island,* to graphic war footage. After discovering they couldn't change the channel back, the bonobos became agitated and threw pizza and cheeseburgers at the screen before giving up and attempting to pry the television off the wall. When Lola accidentally set off a cap gun and sent Mbongo into hysterics, Sam collected them all, went out to the courtyard, and heaved them over the wall into the crowd of people, the majority of whom were not online and therefore mistook them for real guns, which was all the more alarming when several people picked them up and brandished them. This caused a near-riot, and ended with Taser-wielding policemen hauling people off in vans. The news segment ended with a statement from the Chief of Police. He'd had enough of the whole situation and was damned if he was going to let the good people of Lizard pick up the tab for this immoral circus, and by immoral he didn't mean the apes. He planned to bill Faulks Enterprises for all expenses his department had incurred in relation to *Ape House*.

John assumed Faulks was hoping the bonobos would get drunk and do horrible things to each other, as chimpanzees had been known to do.

In fact, after the cap guns were tossed and the channel changer once again became responsive, the bonobos discovered the beer, had a short, happy orgy, and then sipped quietly in front of *I Love Lucy*. Mbongo was the only one to go back for a second. He took it to the beanbag chair, flopped onto it, and crossed his legs, his gut pooching out in front of him as he tipped the bottle to his lips. He looked like the ubiquitous uncle at Thanksgiving, passing the time watching football while waiting for the turkey to appear. They were completely oblivious to the human riot going on just beyond their walls.

It was like the sign John and Amanda had seen on the way to Ariel's wedding: GUNS 'N' WAFFLES. Faulks's mistake had been in thinking that bonobos shared the human predicament of being part chimp and part bonobo, and never knowing which side was going to rise to the surface.

31

John Thigpen looked haggard. He was also an hour late, which Isabel found surprising since he'd sounded so happy to hear from her.

"Hi," she said, swinging the door open. "I was beginning to think you weren't going to show up."

He glanced at his watch and seemed stunned by what he saw. "I'm sorry," he said. "I had a busy night. And morning." He stood awkwardly in the doorway, and Isabel realized she had not yet invited him in. It felt strange, receiving a man in her bedroom. It probably felt strange to him too, particularly as he was married.

"Come in," she said. "Please. Make yourself comfortable." As he walked to the couch, she saw his eyes light on the gas station receipt upon which he'd written his name and number.

Isabel closed the door and stood in front of it, twisting her fingers. "Do you want some coffee? I've got one of those little machines."

"No. Thanks. I'm fine."

Isabel turned the desk chair around so it was facing the couch and sat down. John was staring at her, and she realized that of course he must be shocked by how changed she was. She turned her face so he could see her profile. "See?" she said, running her finger down the bridge of her nose. "It's not bad. It's just not mine. Well, I guess it is now, technically."

Thigpen blinked a few times, then raked his fingers through his hair, leaving it standing in uneven spikes. "God, I'm sorry. I didn't mean to stare. I'm kind of out of it today."

"That's okay," she said.

"Can I get that coffee after all? Do you mind?"

"No, not at all," she said. She was actually grateful for an excuse to leave the room. She stood in front of the bathroom mirror, waiting while the coffee brewed. The last time they'd met, she thought they'd had a rapport. Today things felt weird. Was this a mistake?

The coffee machine finished with a sputter and a hiss.

"Cream? Sugar?" she called out.

"Black is fine," he said.

She took it out to him. He stared into the mug, holding it with both hands, and took a deep breath.

"Look, before we start there's something I need to get off my chest." He paused, and glanced up at her.

Isabel's pulse quickened. In her experience, nothing good ever followed those words.

"I left Francesca De Rossi with the impression that I work at the *L.A. Times*. I do not. I am with the *Weekly Times*. I didn't lie, exactly, but I did fail to correct her, for which I am now extremely embarrassed. The *Weekly Times* is a gossip rag of the very worst caliber, and although I'm doing my best to insert some sort of journalistic integrity, I don't know how successful I'll be. Put it this way—my editor told me to limit the three-headed alien babies in my pieces, but that's my only real restriction."

He stared into her eyes, his lips pulled taut, and his skin so gray she thought he might be holding his breath.

Was that all? He was embarrassed about where he worked? Isabel wanted to laugh with relief, although she did understand—Isabel knew the *Weekly Times*. Her mother had subscribed to it. Probably still did.

"So what happened at *The Philadelphia Inquirer*?"

"Cat Douglas is what happened."

"Ha! Why am I not surprised?" She slapped the top of the desk.

John shot her a quick smile. "And then I moved to L.A., where there are no real reporting jobs."

"Why L.A.?"

"My wife's job."

"What does she do?"

"She's a writer."

"Anything I'd know?"

"She published a novel a little more than a year ago. *The River Wars.* But now she's working as a scriptwriter."

Isabel sat forward. "I read that!"

"Really?" John's eyebrows rose in surprise.

"Yes, at the hospital. I loved it. Is she working on another?"

"Like everything else, that's complicated, but for now she's working on a television series."

"And you're working for a tabloid."

"Yes, and Cat Douglas has my old story and appears regularly on the front page of the *Inquirer.*"

Isabel leaned back against the desk and crossed her legs. She felt a smile seep across her face. "Well, now I'm going to give you something that she really, really wants."

John Thigpen closed his eyes in relief. "Thank you," he said, his voice cracking.

An hour later, after solemnly swearing to protect his sources at all costs, he left in possession of the abstracts and briefs Joel had extracted from the PSI database, as well as a promise that Isabel would forward the emails proving that Peter Benton had sold the language software to Faulks the moment she got them from Celia.

"Who is it?" Isabel called as she approached the door. John Thigpen had left a quarter of an hour before.

"It's me," said Celia.

Isabel put her eye against the peephole and scanned the area outside her door. Celia stood there alone, hands in pockets, looking around. There was something decidedly forced about her nonchalance.

"He's with you, isn't he?" said Isabel.

"Who?"

"Your green-haired friend."

There was a long pause. "No," Celia said, tilting her head and cupping the back of her neck with her hand, like she was trying to crack it.

"He is! I can tell," Isabel said sternly. "He can't come in here."

Celia sighed and rolled her eyes. "Fine, I'll send him downstairs."

"I hardly think he's welcome there either. Frankly, I'm surprised they let him as far as the elevators."

Celia disappeared around the corner. After some muffled discussion, she reappeared.

"Is he gone?" asked Isabel.

"Yes," Celia said wearily. "Can I come in now?"

Isabel opened the door, poked her head out, and craned her neck in both directions, bobbing to see around Celia. "Where did he go?"

"He's waiting for me at the bar. It's darker than the restaurant. And he's wearing a hat." Isabel swung the door open and Celia came in. She went immediately to the couch and threw herself lengthwise across it. "For what it's worth, he came to apologize."

"It's not me he should be apologizing to."

"I know, but I thought Pigpen was going to be here. Anyway, you shouldn't be so hard on Nathan."

"Why not?" said Isabel. She walked over and pushed Celia's legs off the couch to make room for herself.

Celia arranged herself upright and dropped her combat-booted feet on the coffee table.

Clunk. Clunk.

Isabel opened her mouth to protest about filth and germs, but since the table was already contaminated, she decided to just douse it later with hand sanitizer.

"Because you did exactly the same thing," said Celia.

"What are you talking about?"

"To Larry-Harry-Gary. You threw his food. At Rosa's Kitchen. Remember?"

Isabel stood absolutely still, her mouth open. Finally, she dropped onto the couch, eyes locked on the desk in front of her. "Oh my God. You're right."

"He wants to apologize. He got the wrong impression the other night when some of his friends thought Pigpen was being denigrating to women. Hey, can you give me his number? Pigpen's, that is?"

"I'm not giving out his number! At least not without asking him."

"Will you ask him?"

Isabel sighed. If she hadn't just been reminded of what she had done to Gary Hanson's curry, she wouldn't even consider it. "Maybe," she said.

"Okay!" Celia hopped up and went to the desk. She leafed through the newspaper for a few seconds. It was *USA Today,* the one left in front of Isabel's door each morning by the hotel. The story of the cap-gun riot outside the walls of Ape House was on the front page.

"You can take it if you want," Isabel said. "I've already read it."

"So you don't want to join us for lunch?"

"I just ate," she lied. Even if she had also been guilty of throwing someone's food, she wasn't ready to break bread with Nathan.

"Okay." Celia gathered up the newspaper. "Catch you later."

"Celia? Can you forward me those emails as soon as possible? I promised to send them to John right away."

"No problemo," said Celia, bounding out the door.

In the afternoon, Jelani began performing his trademark leaps up and backward off walls. Makena usually danced excitedly and egged him on with high-pitched squeaks. Today, she glanced over her shoulder and remained at the window to the courtyard, staring into the distance. Jelani went over and poked her in the shoulder, but instead of turning and wrestling with him, she ignored him. Jelani finally gave up and tackled Sam instead.

Isabel, who had been alternately pacing and checking her email to see if Celia had forwarded the incriminating messages, suddenly stopped, her internal alarm triggered—when Bonzi gave birth to Lola, she just sat quietly in a corner for four hours before standing and popping the infant out. Isabel pulled the desk chair around to face the television, and although it was not parallel, she sat down anyway. Her eyes never left the screen.

After a while, Makena wandered into the computer room and vocalized a series of peeps to Bonzi. Then she leaned against the wall. This was it—she must be in labor—and Isabel knew enough about Faulks to believe there wasn't a veterinarian hovering nearby. For all his proclamations about having an "ape expert" on staff, Peter was a behavioral and cognitive scientist, not an obstetrician. Neither was Isabel, but having been around when Bonzi was pregnant with Lola, she certainly knew more than Peter. Isabel considered rushing to the site, but knew that Faulks's people would never let her in. Isabel knelt in front of the television.

Bonzi, who had been ordering pizza for Jelani, spun on her metal chair.

Makena leaned against the wall and began signing: she banged the knuckles of one hand against her other palm. It was the sign for "bell," which was how the bonobos referred to Isabel.

ISABEL HURRY. BONZI MAKE ISABEL COME. ISABEL HURRY COME NOW.

Bonzi turned back to the computer and searched in vain. The computer in the lab had included a symbol for Isabel, distinct from the symbol for a bell, but this one did not. Bonzi's dark, callused fingers drilled down through every category, following each path to its end, and even then she did not give up. She started over, methodically searching for a way to order what Makena had requested.

Isabel dropped her head in her hands and wept. Makena, knowing she was about to have her baby, was trying to order her.

———

John was lying in bed, recovering from his sojourn with Amanda and periodically checking his email to see if Isabel had forwarded the messages from Peter Benton.

Ape House was on in the background. He got up to get a glass of water and noticed that Bonzi was sitting at the computer and that Makena was signing to her. The cartoon thought bubble above Makena's head read: BELL COME SOON. BELL BELL. MAKENA WANT BELL HURRY BELL SOON. BELL.

The sound engineers responded by adding Big Ben chimes to the soundtrack, but oddly, a bell did not appear on the shopping list. Bonzi seemed to be searching for something else, something that wasn't there. There was an urgency to Makena's signing that John hadn't witnessed before.

He forgot about the glass of water and sat on the end of the bed.

Makena sank down against the wall so that she was squatting, and adjusted herself into various positions. Then she simply began pushing. The other bonobos gathered around, craning their necks to see, and blocking the view from the ceiling cameras. Makena grimaced a few times, then reached down and pulled an infant to her chest, umbilical cord still attached. It was so tiny its head would fit in a teacup. The other bonobos cheered, peeping in excitement, and took turns having a look at the new addition. Minutes later, Makena reached down and delivered the afterbirth.

John watched breathlessly to see if the baby was alive. Makena kept readjusting its position, so he couldn't tell if the baby was responsible for any of the movements. When Makena finally cradled it against her chest and guided its mouth to her breast, it waved a tiny arm, with perfect, tiny fingers.

John stared in astonishment, feeling the deep ache of relief, but also something else, something more primal.

As Makena suckled her tiny infant, John laid a hand on the television screen.

32

The phones had been ringing off the hook ever since that ape squatted and spat out a baby. Because of the birth, the judge had agreed to hear PAEGA's legal petition the next day on an emergency basis, and the Internet chatter was that animal welfare groups were about to converge on Ape House in numbers that would make all previous activity feel like an intimate gathering.

When Faulks burst into the room, throwing the door forth with such force that its knob left a dent in the sage-green wall behind it, three of his seated executives braced themselves. The others remained slumped in defeat.

Faulks's eyes scanned those present. "Where is he?" he demanded. "I told you to get him here."

"He's on his way," said the CFO. "He had a couple of personal matters to clear up first. Something about peat moss."

"On his way isn't good enough. When I tell you to do something, you do it!"

"Unless I put him on the corporate jet, there was no way—" he glanced up at Faulks, and changed his mind. "Yes, sir."

Faulks paced back and forth for a few seconds, then stopped at the head of the table and slammed it with both fists. Water glasses, pens, and executives all jumped.

"How many long-term subscriptions did we get last night?"

He glared at each of them in turn. Only the director of marketing did not lower his eyes. He said, "The *Prime Time* episode didn't do very well, but we had a sharp rise after the baby was born."

"What?" said Faulks, his eyes wide. He took a seat at the head of the table. He was momentarily without words. "How big a rise?"

"Twenty-one percent."

Faulks's forehead crinkled in disbelief. *"Twenty-one percent?"*

The director of marketing nodded.

Faulks leaned back in his chair. "That's huge. Are any of the others pregnant?"

"Not that we know of."

"Huh."

Faulks thought for a while, and nobody interrupted him. He leaned forward and put his forearms on the table. After a moment, he looked back at the director of marketing. "You're sure it was twenty-one percent?"

The man nodded again.

Faulks considered for a moment longer, then pointed at the chief financial officer. "Okay. You, figure out whether these new subscriptions will cover the cost of what the fucking police department is asking. And you," he said, pointing to the woman with the blond chignon, "find out if the police even have a legal basis upon which to bill us. You," he said, pointing to a man with wet spots under his arms, "get in touch with the ape man—I don't care if you have to get him on the phone in the middle of a flight—and figure out what we need to do to fix everything in that legal petition by tonight. And just in case I don't like any of the answers I get, also get a list of places willing to take these things off my hands. Get offers. In case I'm not being clear, I'm not giving them away. I'm selling them."

The CFO cleared his throat. All eyes turned to him. "Sir, if I may . . ." He glanced at Faulks to make sure the answer was in the affirmative. Faulks's steely gray eyes bored into him, so he continued. "I took the liberty of doing just that after the first *Prime Time* episode."

"Really," said Faulks. "And what did you find out?"

"A place called the Corston Foundation is willing to pay significantly more than anyone else I contacted. It's a research facility. They promise to be very discreet."

A crooked smile played at the edges of Faulks's lips. He nodded his head slowly. "So now we have a Plan B. That's good." He pulled his platinum Montblanc pen from his shirt pocket and pointed it at the CFO. "You have initiative. I like that."

33

At first, Isabel thought it was another episode of *Ape House Prime Time,* but a quick glance at the clock told her it was the wrong time of day.

A truck with a cherry picker pulled up alongside the outer wall of the building and dumped a load of peeled sugarcane—one of the bonobos' favorite foods—into the courtyard. When the apes went outside to investigate and celebrate its arrival, men swarmed the house commando-style, immediately closing and securing the doors that led to the courtyard.

Bonzi, Lola, and Makena—clutching her tiny infant—made for the highest point of the play structure right away, hiding within the top of the tubular slide, while Sam and Mbongo made a ruckus beneath. Jelani wasn't sure which group he wanted to be with, and alternated between screeching warnings at the shatterproof glass doors and scampering up to hide with the females.

Sam and Mbongo screamed and bristled, loping over and jumping against the window, smacking it with their palms and the bottoms of

their feet as the men inside emptied the house. They carried out all the
toys, blankets, and smaller objects, and then brought in dollies for the
furniture. Only then did Isabel realize what they were doing. She called
Marty Schaeffer:

"Do you see this? Are you watching?"

"I am."

The men used shovels and carts to collect the garbage and rotting
food. Men with buckets swabbed the floors and walls and were followed
by other men using push brooms and power hoses.

"Can they do this?" said Isabel.

"They can," said Marty.

"Will it ruin the lawsuit?"

"If they also address the dietary issues, yes. With surgical precision."

It was Peter. How could she have missed it? She had been so blinded
by hope that it didn't occur to her that "taking good care of the bonobos"
meant the court would not remove them from Faulks. Isabel grabbed
the ice bucket from the desktop and threw up in it.

When she looked back up, Sam had stopped displaying. He stared
intently through the doors. His eyes followed a specific target. He began
signing: BAD VISITOR. BIG SMOKE. BAD VISITOR. The thought bubble suddenly disappeared.

Sam continued a flurry of signs, which were no longer being interpreted. He put his hand to his mouth and then flung it away as though
tasting something awful. He tapped his lips with two fingers, touched
his index fingers together in front of his chest:

BAD SMOKE VISITOR. ISABEL HURT. BAD VISITOR THERE. BIG FIRE.

Isabel leaned closer to the television, concentrating on the squares
that showed the men at work. One of them shouted something to another, his lips shapeless and fat.

A memory, a flash: a man kneeling briefly by her head on the floor of
the lab, mouthing the word "Shit!" with oversized rubber-band lips.

"Marty, I have to go," she said and tossed her phone on the bed.

The men installed a pallet-type floor that would allow water to drain
through to the concrete, and were in the process of replacing all the upholstered furniture with new, non-moldy identicals, undoubtedly satu-

rated with Scotchgard. Sam and Mbongo had retreated to a far corner of the courtyard and watched intently, with extreme distrust.

DIRTY BAD, signed Mbongo, scowling. DIRTY BAD, DIRTY BAD, DIRTY BAD.

And then, suddenly, the screen switched to static.

———

Celia arrived within minutes. Isabel reached into the hallway and yanked her into the room.

"Did you see that?" she said. "Did you see?"

"See what?" said Celia, glancing at the TV.

"*Ape House*! Sam and Mbongo just identified one of Faulks's clean-up crew as being there the night of the explosion. It wasn't the ELL. It was Ken Faulks's people! They identified the guy, right on the air. I recognized his mouth. They stopped airing, but not in time. It's got to be recorded somewhere, right? Right? Oh my God, what if they don't let the apes testify?" Isabel clutched a fist to her mouth and spun back to the television.

Celia didn't move. "I missed that," she said slowly. "But they don't need to testify, and it wasn't just Ken Faulks."

Something about Celia's tone made Isabel turn around.

Celia looked at her, long and hard. "Where's your laptop?" she said.

Isabel, whose heart was thrumming so hard she could feel it in her eardrums, went and got it. Celia sat down and took control. Within minutes they were looking at Peter's inbox—or rather, a mirrored copy on Jawad's server.

"I'm going to bookmark it for you. The password is 'huge enormous penis head,' all one word, lowercase. Joel's idea. I thought 'itty bitty swizzle stick' would be more appropriate, but I was outvoted." She pointed at the screen. "Jawad retrieved these today. Peter deleted these messages, but he didn't use Secure Delete, so although they weren't visible in his inbox, they still existed. Jawad got them back, then restored Peter's access to his account. For all he knows, his email was down because of a computer glitch."

Isabel shook her head impatiently, stabbing her finger toward the television. "I already know about the software. You're not listening! Something much bigger just happened!"

"Isabel, *you're* not listening. Or looking. Check out the time stamps on these emails."

Isabel did, and for an awful moment thought she might vomit again.

———

John was still staring at the television. Was it even possible? He had seen only a fraction of what Sam was saying before the thought bubble disappeared and the screen went blank.

His phone rang, and he groped for it without ever taking his eyes off the dead air. "Hello?"

She didn't even identify herself. She simply said, "You want a scoop? I'll give you a scoop. Faulks and my fiancé tried to have me blown up."

An hour later, John walked back to the Buccaneer in a glazed stupor, having just seen the contents of Peter Benton's inbox. He had emailed himself the URL of the mirrored server before leaving Isabel's hotel room.

She was already trying to justify, to ameliorate, and it broke John's heart.

"They were supposed to wait until all the cars were gone from the parking lot," she'd said. "I guess they had no way of knowing I'd loan Celia my car." Although she seemed almost ready to forgive the near-murder of herself, she was entirely unforgiving when it came to the apes: "The charge was specifically designed not to reach their living area, but what if they'd been trapped? What if the thugs with the tire irons couldn't get in to release them? Most fire deaths are from smoke inhalation."

What she was telling him was huge. Massive. And for reasons more personal than John was comfortable admitting, he wanted to blow the story wide open. The problem was, he was going to need something more solid than messages sent through an anonymous email proxy. He needed to prove the identity of the person who had received and answered them.

34

The phone startled John. As he reached for it he caught sight of the clock: 3 A.M. Had the dog bitten Amanda? Had she been in an accident? What if Peter Benton or Ken Faulks had caught wind of the sting and done something to Isabel? Or maybe it was Ivanka—

"Hello?" he said.

"Is this John?"

"Yeah," he said, frowning. He reached over and turned on the light. "Who's this?"

"It's Celia Honeycutt. I'm a friend of Isabel's. We kind of almost met the other day."

John already knew who she was, both from the ELL video, and from the woman at Lawrence City Animal Control. "What's wrong? Is Isabel okay?"

"Yeah, Isabel's fine. I'm calling about Nathan."

"Who?" John said.

"You know, the guy with green hair."

"What about him?"

"He's in jail."

"Good," said John.

"No, it's not good. It's bad. Can you go bail him out?"

"What?"

"I can't call Isabel because she'd just tell me to leave him there."

"What makes you think I feel any differently?"

"You know what?" Celia said testily. "Maybe this was a mistake. Maybe you're not the nice guy Isabel seems to think you are. But you know all that information she gave you today? That no other reporter has and would kill to get their hands on? Guess where that came from. *Me.* I bet Catwoman would be very interested."

John sighed. "What did he do?"

"Underage drinking."

"You don't get arrested for underage drinking. You get a ticket."

"He also had fake ID, and they claim he resisted arrest."

"Well, he would, wouldn't he?"

"Oh, come on, John. Please?"

John cradled his head in his hands. "How much are we talking about?"

"Fourteen hundred."

"Are you kidding? I don't have fourteen hundred dollars lying around."

"You only need to put up seven hundred. Gary put up the rest."

"Who?"

"A protester buddy of his. He already wired it."

John swung his legs off the side of the bed and sat up. "How'd you get my number anyway?"

"I took it off the desk in Isabel's room. Nathan wanted to call you to apologize for the breakfast thing."

John dropped his forehead onto his hand. He couldn't believe he was even considering this. "Okay," he said, standing and looking around for his clothes. "Who do I ask for when I get there?"

"Nathan Pinegar. And don't make any vinegar jokes—he's sensitive about it."

Pinegar? Nathan was a Pinegar?

A teenaged Pinegar?

John reached out to steady himself against a wall.

Behind the counter was a row of monitors, each showing the contents of a cell. Even the toilets were in full view. Nathan was curled on a narrow bed. John stared and stared.

"Can I help you?" the cop behind the desk finally said.

"Uh, yeah." John cleared his throat and stepped up. "I'm here to bail someone out."

The cop snapped his gum and looked suspiciously at John before answering. "Who?"

John had to swallow twice before he managed to utter the name. "Nathan. Pinegar. Him." John pointed.

The cop glanced over his shoulder at the monitor. "You paying cash?"

"Credit card."

"There's a bondsman down the street."

They didn't exchange a word until they'd left the building. Nathan slunk out a few feet behind him, shoulders hunched in what John now recognized was a teenage slouch.

When they got to the bottom of the steps, John stopped and glanced back at the building's faux Greek façade.

Nathan looked both ways down the street. "So can I go?"

"No, I need to ask you something. Where did you grow up?"

"New York City. Morningside Heights. Why?"

"What's your mom's name?"

"Why? You planning on calling her?"

"No, no," John said quickly. "I just . . ." Blood rushed through his ears, a supersonic whooshing of terror. "So, um, do you need a ride anywhere?"

"No, man, I'm good," said Nathan. He was shifting, restless, clearly anxious to get on his way. John nodded.

As Nathan's heavy footsteps rang down the street, John became so light-headed he had to sit on the stairs.

35

sabel lay on her side, hugging her pillows. She'd been awake for two hours, although the sun showed no signs of rising. The television played in the background, muted, because she was hoping that *Ape House* would begin airing again. It had not, and Isabel was pretty sure it wouldn't, because Rose had called her and told her that the Corston Foundation was readying the isolation unit for incoming apes. She wasn't sure it was the bonobos, but the longer the show stayed off the air, the more likely it seemed. Somebody at the studio, an interpreter or, more likely, Peter, had recognized the implications of Sam's statements and pulled the plug. Not only had Peter participated in blowing up the lab, but now he was going to consign them to a living death at a bio-medical facility.

Someone banged on her door. She shrieked, once, and the banging stopped. After a few seconds, a hesitant rapping took its place.

Isabel peeled back the covers and made her way to the door in darkness. She couldn't pretend she wasn't there, but the bolt was on, and hotel security was a minute or two away, at most. She put her eye to the peephole, which revealed John Thigpen, nose enlarged by the fish-eye lens, nostrils flaring in and out, leaning with one hand against the door frame. She swung the door open and ushered him in.

He staggered forth. She flicked on the ceiling light.

"What is it? What's wrong?"

He just stood there, looking bewildered, his eyes wild, not landing on anything. They finally focused on her. "Did I wake you up?"

"I was already awake," she said. "What is it? What happened?"

"I think I'm his father." His eyes were as wide as a lemur's.

"Whose?"

"That green-haired vegan eco-feminist."

"Nathan?"

John nodded, still panting.

"What on earth would make you think that?" she said.

"How many seventeen-year-old Pinegars can there be in the world?"

Isabel suddenly wondered whether she should have let him in. Was he drunk? He didn't smell like it, and she was preternaturally good at discerning alcohol on people's breath. Was he high? She examined him more closely—his pupils were the same size and not dilated.

He seemed to sense her apprehension. "I'm sorry. I shouldn't have come," he said, and while he continued to shiver, he no longer looked crazed. He just looked miserable and pathetic. He took a step toward the door.

"No, it's okay," Isabel said, touching his elbow. "Come, sit down. Tell me what's going on."

He reeled toward the couch, and she followed. As the tale of his long-ago indiscretion spilled out, Isabel ended up sitting beside him, facing him, legs tucked beneath her.

"I didn't even know if we'd done it," he said, "but apparently I knocked her up. Why didn't she just *say* something? I was stupid and a kid, but maybe if my parents or I had been in his life he wouldn't have turned out like this."

"He's not that bad," said Isabel.

"Yes, he is," said John.

"Yes. I suppose he is," Isabel conceded.

John dropped his head against the back of the couch and groaned.

"Okay. Look," she said, swinging her legs around and straightening up. "There's no point in panicking yet. You don't know for sure that he's yours."

"He's seventeen. He's a Pinegar. He grew up in New York City."

Isabel couldn't deny that he had a point. She got up and retrieved her computer. John sat like a splayed lump, a limp starfish flung over the left side of the couch, unmoving except for the occasional rise and fall of his Adam's apple.

"I'm sorry," he croaked as she typed. "I don't know what came over me."

"For what?"

"For dumping all this on you."

"It's okay," said Isabel. "Obviously you needed to talk to someone. I can understand why your wife wouldn't be your first choice."

"She's going to kill me. *Kill me.* What am I going to do?"

Isabel shook her head sympathetically, still typing.

John added, "I could have been a good dad, I think. I had a good role model. My dad is a good dad. What about your dad?"

"Gone," said Isabel.

"Oh God. I'm sorry."

"About what?" she said, still typing. Isabel glanced over quickly and realized where his mind had gone. "Oh. No, he's not dead. At least, I don't think he is. Just gone. He may not be my father anyway. That was part of the problem."

"I'm sorry," John said again.

"I'm not. I like knowing there's a chance I'm not related to him. Of course, I'd also like not to be related to my mother, but unfortunately there's no room for doubt there." She turned her laptop around so he could see the screen. "Here. DNA paternity testing. Super-expedited service. Twenty-four-hour turnaround. No blood samples needed. Email or phone results. We can order it right now, if you like."

He opened his eyes further, transforming from lemur to owl. He blinked a few times. "What kind of sample do I need?"

She handed him the computer. "A glass he's drunk from. Or a cigarette butt, or a single hair—apparently you can use it even if it's been dyed."

John looked around hopefully, as though a green hair might magically appear.

"He's never been in my room," Isabel said. "But I'll get a sample tomorrow. Today," she said, glancing at the window and realizing that morning was threatening to break at any second.

John stared at the online form. He began filling in the fields, timidly at first, and then so quickly his fingers tripped over themselves and he had to back up to make corrections. Isabel scootched over so she could see what he was doing. He was already punching in his credit card number.

As he prepared to leave, he stood awkwardly at the door. Finally, he dropped his chin and said, "Thank you."

"You're welcome." As he turned to leave, her own anxieties flooded back. What if this new crisis of his pushed hers from the spotlight? "You're still going to nail Faulks, right? Because now that *Ape House* is off the air, I can't even watch to see if they're okay. What if the baby isn't nursing properly? What if Makena gets an infection? What if they're still just eating cheeseburgers and M&M's?"

He turned back. "Absolutely. I'm sending my dispatch tonight. The issue will hit the stands late afternoon tomorrow."

"Thank God," she said. "Because you know what's at stake here, right? If the county seizes the apes, they've agreed to send them to the San Diego Zoo, where I found us temporary housing until I figure something else out. But if you don't expose him, and he gets to keep ownership, God only knows where they'll end up. . . ."

She realized she was clutching his arm, probably hard enough to hurt. She let go as soon as she noticed, and squeezed her eyes shut.

John folded her into a hug. "Don't worry," he said, and she felt his voice resonate through his chest. "I'm not going to let that happen."

To Isabel's astonishment, she believed him. She even allowed her arms to meet behind his back.

———

Almost as soon as John left her room, Isabel called Celia and ordered her to come and bring Nathan.

He was bedraggled, although he didn't look as bad as John. Isabel studied the bones of his face and the color of his eyes. He and John were about the same height, and while Nathan still had that stringy, gangly youth thing going on, he might fill out into a similar build. Certainly it was not impossible—

She suddenly became aware that he was returning her stare.

"Have you called your parents yet?" she said.

"No," he said. "And I'm not going to either."

"Listen, mister, you better make that court date. You understand?"

He shrugged, looking beleaguered.

"If you don't, how are you going to pay John back?"

"I don't know. Maybe get a credit card. Take out an advance . . ."

"Nathan. You're seventeen. You don't have a job. No one's going to give you a credit card."

Celia spun to face him. "Seventeen? You're *seventeen*? That's, like, jailbait!" She whacked him in the arm.

"I'm eighteen in two months," he muttered, rubbing his arm.

Celia addressed Isabel. "He told me he was nineteen." Her head whipped around, lightning bolts of displeasure forming between her eyes. "You told me you were nineteen!"

"I suggest you tuck him into his own sleeping bag tonight," said Isabel.

Nathan stuck his hands in his pockets and looked uncharacteristically subdued. Celia crossed her arms, stared straight ahead of her, and tapped her foot.

Isabel rubbed her temples. "When did you kids last eat?"

"The last time I ate was about noon yesterday," Celia answered. "Probably the same for him—*unless they fed you in jail*!" she said, throwing Nathan a scorching look.

"Celia, this isn't helping. Are eggs murder?" Isabel inquired, addressing Nathan.

He looked sideways, and said, "Technically not if they're unfertilized, but the conditions under which the laying hens are kept are—"

"Right," Isabel said brightly. "So unbuttered toast and orange juice for you. Celia?"

"You're ordering up?" asked Celia.

"The bar isn't open yet, and we can hardly go to the restaurant, can we?" she said, staring pointedly at Nathan, who studied the pattern on the carpet carefully.

"Two eggs over easy, wheat toast, and grapefruit if they have it," said Celia.

Isabel picked up the room phone.

What Isabel didn't add was that it was also infinitely easier to steal a glass from a room service tray than a restaurant. She just had to keep track of who drank from what.

Within an hour of collecting the glass from Isabel, John had dropped a package containing it and a swab from his own cheek into the FedEx box at the corner. Given the amount of sleep he'd had, John should have been the walking dead. Instead he was completely wired, worrying in stereo about potential fatherhood and his dispatch.

The paternity issue had his stomach in knots. He hadn't even managed a cup of coffee since staggering back to the Buccaneer from Isabel's room just before dawn.

Why hadn't Ginette told him? His life would have been so different—*all* their lives would have been so different. If he'd stayed with Ginette, there would have been no life with Amanda. And whether he'd stayed with Ginette or not, he would have had to drop out of college and find a job. Ginette could not possibly have made enough money waiting tables to support herself and a child, and yet she must have done exactly that. Unless she had married someone else, his child had grown up without a father—it didn't make a lick of difference that John hadn't known and therefore had no opportunity to do anything differently. It was Nathan who had suffered, Nathan who had grown up without the advantages of two parents, and John was going to make it up to him. He and Amanda were going to be a part of his life from now on. Of course, that led to the unpleasant proposition of telling Amanda—who was actively trying to conceive his child—that not only did he already have one, but that the existing child was a green-haired vegan juvenile delinquent.

This avalanche of fatherly responsibility had John hyperventilating again, clenching his hands into fists as he walked.

And what Isabel had said haunted him almost as much:

". . . where I found us temporary housing," she'd said.

Us.

They were as much family to her as any human had ever been to him. If Nathan actually was his son, even closer.

His dispatch was due by midnight, and although it promised to surpass Topher's wildest dreams, it would not contain the type of indisputable evidence that would make the FBI take him seriously. The *Weekly Times* had published too many unfounded stories in the past. If only he were still with the *Inky* . . .

He shook the thought from his head. He needed something solid on Faulks. He had no idea how, but for Isabel's sake, and for the sake of the apes, he was determined to come up with the final nail.

36

John pored over the contents of Peter Benton's inbox, chewing and picking his cuticles and regretting all the caffeine he'd downed. It was already creeping toward 11:30, and his dispatch was due at 12:00. It was written and ready to go, but he just couldn't make himself hit Send. He was seeking one last detail that would transform it from a piece of *Weekly Times* malevolent fluff to the news story of the year.

At 11:37 John's phone rang. It was Ivanka. "He's here," she shouted, competing with a deafening background of music and voices. "Very drunk, very mean, but I say I call, so I call. I no supposed to work tonight, but he ask for me. I stay long enough for lap dance, then I leave. Come if you like, but I think tonight is not good night for talk."

"Ivanka! I need you to do me a favor. Go where no one can hear you."

She did, and then listened as he pleaded his case.

"Sure," she said. "I can do that." John could practically hear the shrug that accompanied her statement.

The waiting was agony: John turned on the television and tried to watch. He paced, bit his nails, ran his hands through his hair, and scratched his scalp. He ran his hands up and down his arms, seeking something. When he went to the bathroom, he was startled by the image he saw in the mirror. He took several deep breaths while staring himself in the eyes. He smoothed his hair with wet hands, then went and sat on the edge of his bed. He turned the TV off as he passed it.

At 12:01, his phone rang. "I've got it," she said.

"Where are you?"

"In my room."

John hung up, leapt off his bed, and thrust his feet into his shoes. His phone rang again immediately.

"I'm coming right up," he said, hopping as he forced one recalcitrant heel into submission.

"You shouldn't be doing a damned thing but sending me my file," said Topher.

Before he could continue his rant, John said, "It will be late, it will be the most explosive thing you've ever published, and you will publish every word of it exactly as I wrote it."

"I'll be the judge of that," said Topher.

"Of course you will," said John. "And believe me, you'll do it."

Moments later John rapped on Ivanka's door. She opened it a crack and handed him a BlackBerry. "Katarina's shift starts in twenty-five minutes. Bring back in ten. She will take to Lost and Found."

John ran downstairs, clutching Ken Faulks's BlackBerry, beginning to forward himself all the settings, emails, and text messages before he even reached his room. The email application led to an anonymous proxy server, and contained the emails from Peter Benton. There was absolutely no question that he was in collusion with Faulks before, during, and after the explosion, and no question that Benton had tried to extort more money after the fact. There were other interesting nuggets as well, such as files that contained ratings and subscription information that conflicted dramatically with Faulks's public proclamations.

"Come on, come on," he said, watching the clock and checking his laptop. Although he had selected and forwarded them simultaneously, each file arrived separately and out of order—that, of course, didn't matter but he had to be sure he was in possession of every last piece of information before he took the thing back. When the correct number of messages showed up in his email, he returned his attentions to the BlackBerry and deleted all traces of the emails having been forwarded. Then he ran the BlackBerry back up to Ivanka.

She answered the door in a fluffy bathrobe. She was still in full makeup, but was removing hairpins, sliding them over the edge of her pocket, lining them up like staples.

"What took you so long?" she said.

John thrust the BlackBerry into her hands, grabbed her by the shoulders, and kissed the streak of blush on her powdered cheek. "Ivanka, you're the best."

A white stretch car pulled up beneath the balcony, pounding with Russian techno-pop.

"Katarina," Ivanka called over her shoulder.

Katarina emerged from the bathroom in pink vinyl go-go boots, sequined boy shorts, and a matching halter top. She plucked the BlackBerry from Ivanka's hands without slowing down, and pushed past John. Although she didn't say a word, he thought he saw a smirk.

"Katarina!" he called after her. "Wipe off the fingerprints before you hand it in!"

Katarina held the BlackBerry up over her shoulder by way of acknowledgment before elegantly descending the concrete stairs. The car door opened, the music grew louder, and then the door shut and the car pulled away.

Ivanka sauntered over to the bed and lay on it. She crossed her feet, which were encased in high-heeled slippers adorned with feathers. She lit a cigarette.

"Thanks again for your help, Ivanka," said John. "This is really huge."

"My pleasure," she said. She pointed her cigarette at a miniature fridge that was decorated with magnets and stick-on daisies. A brand-new turkey baster, still in its cellophane, rested on top. "Besides, if all goes well, I can retire. I am set for eighteen years."

"What?" John said helplessly.

"I always use condom," she explained. "This time, I keep. He thinks I'm too old for cougar. Well, maybe not too old for baby. Ha. That will teach."

———

It was 3:56 A.M. when John finally pressed Send, and the read receipt came back instantly.

Three minutes later, Topher called and with no preamble whatsoever said, "Holy shit. Is this real? Or did you make it up?"

"One hundred percent real."

"It's not the old 'sources said' routine?"

"The sources are real."

"Can you prove it?"

"Absolutely. But I'm not giving them up."

"What do you have? I want to see it."

"Yeah, I'll forward it, but I'm serious about protecting my sources. I'm not giving them up under any circumstances."

"Fine. What have you got?"

"Topher?"

"I hear you. We'll protect them. What do you have?"

"I have corresponding email archives from both Benton and Faulks proving that they were in contact before and after the explosion at the lab, that Benton was demanding more money after the fact, and that Faulks began bouncing his emails before finally rehiring him. And I have at least one expert who saw the bonobo identify one of Faulks's henchmen on TV as one of the people involved in the initial explosion. Somewhere, somebody has it on DVR, and I'll put money on Sam being able to pick him out of a lineup."

"Who is Sam?"

"One of the bonobos."

Topher whooped, called him a golden boy, told him to get drunk, treat himself, whatever, and hung up.

John called Amanda, who didn't answer, but then again, it was just after four in the morning, three, her time. "Hey, baby," he cooed into her voice mail. "I think maybe I've just managed to redeem myself as a journalist. This whole thing can't last much longer—it's going to blow wide open. I'll be home soon, and I can't wait to see you. I hope your writing is going well and the dog is settling in. I love you."

John undressed, turned off the lights, and crawled under the covers. He thought of Ivanka and her turkey baster. He thought of Makena nursing her new infant, of how tenderly she cradled it, nudging its tiny wrinkled face toward her nipple. He thought of Amanda's longing to have their own family—to be not just extensions of Fran and Tim, of Paul and Patricia. Suddenly it all made perfect sense. To be able to create life with the woman he loved was a miracle of nature, perhaps the deepest need he'd ever felt.

John slept until nearly two in the afternoon and would certainly have continued sleeping if someone weren't knocking insistently on his door. He opened it a crack and found Victor, the perpetually glistening fat man from the front office.

"A fax came," he said, thrusting a handful of crinkled papers at John.

"Thanks," said John, taking them. He closed the door.

The fax was a skewed black-and-white version of today's newly minted *Weekly Times*. The cover sheet read, "Didn't want you to have to wait. Real thing to follow soon. Best, Topher." Dead smack in the center of the cover was a most unflattering picture of Faulks (probably caught mid-blink). He was set against a mushroom cloud, beneath the headline PORN KING KONGED! Given the nature of the cover, John was a little apprehensive as he turned the pages, but Topher had indeed published his piece word for word. It was all there, from the title, "Language-Proficient Ape Fingers Faulks Associate in Laboratory Bombing," right down to the "Close sources have provided indisputable evidence that Peter Benton, former head scientist of the Great Ape Language Lab, conspired with Ken Faulks, media mogul turned pornographer, in a New Year's Day bombing that grievously injured another scientist and turned the six resident bonobo apes into prisoners of America's insatiable appetite for the phenomenon known as reality television."

He paused long enough to pull his jeans over his boxers, and then ran all the way to the Mohegan Moon in his undershirt, with no socks beneath his shoes, pages clutched to his chest.

"Can you meet me?" Isabel breathed into the phone.

Peter's response was immediate. "Of course. Where?"

"In the bar of the Mohegan Moon. Come as soon as you can. I can't believe you pulled it off. Thank you. Thank you, thank you, thank you."

"My God." He sounded stunned. "I can't wait to see you, Izzy."

"Me either," she said, staring at the pages of the fax, which were spread neatly on the desk in front of her.

Twenty minutes later, Isabel was sitting at a table near the center of the bar. Tables were easier to get now that *Ape House* was off the air. There were still a handful of reporters and casino patrons around, but it was no longer standing room only. Cat Douglas was at the corner of the bar, sipping a Campari and soda. She slid off her stool and headed toward Isabel, but when she met Isabel's gaze, she halted. Isabel stared her back into the corner.

When Peter came in, his eyes flitted about the room before landing on Isabel. He kissed her quickly on the cheek, and then took a seat. The chair screeched against the floor as he pulled it back, and he looked around apologetically.

"You look wonderful," he said as he settled himself.

"Thank you," she replied, conscious that the last time he'd seen her she was completely bald and missing five teeth. He seemed very different to her too, although she couldn't put a finger on it—he was dressed and groomed as he always had been, conservatively, neatly, and still exuded the same easy confidence.

The waiter came by and took his drink order—a double scotch on the rocks.

"So," he said, when the waiter left. "Here we are."

"Yes." She stared into her seltzer water, and stirred the little red straw. She pulled the wedge of lime from the side, squeezed it, and dropped it into the glass. The little burst of juice temporarily clouded the water. In her peripheral vision, she could see Cat Douglas watching closely.

Isabel smiled and held her hands out across the table. Peter took them.

"So now we get the apes back," she said. "I can hardly believe it." She blinked rapidly. "Sorry. It's been such a long road. I can't believe it's over."

Peter continued holding Isabel's hands, but his grip weakened. The waiter deposited a double scotch on ice in front of him. "Thank you," he said, glancing up at him.

"It is over, right?" said Isabel. She managed a tearful smile. "What you said the other day, about getting back to where we were, you meant it, right?"

"I love you, Isabel. I have always loved you."

"I'm talking about the apes, Peter. The apes are coming home with us, right?"

Peter downed his scotch without taking his eyes off her.

"You should order another one," said Isabel.

He glanced up and laughed. "You know what Shakespeare said about alcohol. It provoketh the desire, but taketh away the performance. And God knows, I've been without you for so long, I think—"

"It is not 'provoketh' or 'taketh,' you idiot." She stood up and leaned over the table. "When will you learn to *shut the hell up*!"

He leaned back.

She sat back down and reached into her purse, pulling out the papers, which she'd folded in half. She smoothed them against the table, calmly, folding backward against the original crease so they would lie flat. "I wish I could say I was sad about this, but nothing gives me greater pleasure than to inform you that your sorry ass is going to jail. You're going to be spending many years in a cell eight by eight by twelve feet. You're going to experience what it feels like to be kept in a cage by hostile people who don't care about you or your suffering, just like all those apes you experimented on at PSI."

Isabel slid the papers across the table. As he took and read them, she felt high. She felt higher still as she watched comprehension dawn on his face. When she stood up and announced, loudly, that this was hitting newsstands all across the country at this very moment, she saw the stricken look in Cat's eyes as she realized she'd been scooped, and thought she might swoon.

As John crossed the parking lot of the Buccaneer, Ivanka leaned over the balcony in a bathrobe and yelled, "Quick! Turn on TV!" John hurried to his room.

Topher McFadden was on the third station he turned to, surrounded by reporters and television cameras. His blond hair was rakishly wind-blown, his lavender dress shirt open at the top. Flashbulbs reflected off the lenses of his square glasses.

"This is the kind of story the *Weekly Times* takes pride in bringing to the public," he was saying. "It's the information they trust us to provide."

A buzz of voices rose around him. Topher scanned the faces and mi-crophones and pointed at someone. The other voices dropped off.

"How were you able to get this story ahead of all the major newspa-pers covering *Ape House*?"

"Our reporters are trained investigators who know how to dig down and get the facts. I personally selected John Thigpen for this assignment, and I've worked closely with him since his first dispatch. He has the background and tenacious investigative spirit needed to bring this story to light. He established relationships with the apes and their caretakers even before the bombing, and he used those contacts to discover what other reporters could not."

More shouting for attention, more jostling. Topher pointed at some-one else. The rest fell silent. "Yes," he said, inviting a question.

"Stories are swirling about a criminal investigation into the allega-tions in this story. Can you please comment?"

Once again the voices swelled. Topher held both hands up and closed his eyes, asking for quiet. When the chatter stopped, he said, "The final pieces of this puzzle fell into place just before our publication deadline. Since then, we have been cooperating with the authorities at the City of Lawrence Police Department, as well as with the FBI, and we will make our information available to the extent that we can while protecting our sources. What I can tell you is that the Doña Ana County Department of Animal Control took over the physical care of the bonobos this morning, and that a transport team from the San Diego Zoo is on its way at this very moment."

As the voices rose once again, shouting competing questions, Topher pointed to another reporter, acting every bit as though he were the President's press secretary.

"Apparently this story relies heavily on the word," said the woman, "if that's even the right term, of an ape who appeared to recognize one of Faulks's employees as involved in the laboratory bombing. Do you think the courts would consider evidence from an ape?"

Topher composed his tanned face into a look of deep concentration. "Keep in mind that these apes are proficient in human language, and while they might not be permitted to testify in a court of law, they can certainly testify in the court of public opinion. An interview with Katie Couric might prove interesting indeed. But Sam's opinion is far from the only evidence the *Weekly Times* uncovered."

"Faulks is a movie producer—was he responsible for the video statement that was released on the Internet?"

"Everything we're sure of, we printed. It seems likely that after the bombing the ELL saw an opportunity, took credit, and did what additional damage they could. But I'm sure the FBI will be happy to clarify as the investigation continues."

Someone in a suit leaned toward Topher and whispered in his ear. Topher nodded.

"Mr. McFadden!"

"Mr. McFadden!"

Topher raised a hand to indicate he was finished. "Thank you very much. You can expect further information in our next issue." He turned and disappeared into the crowd with his handlers. John stared at the screen, stunned. A news anchor poked her head into the frame and explained that the bonobos would be reunited with two of their former caretakers as soon as possible, and then, pending a veterinary exam, would begin their journey to San Diego.

37

By the next morning, John understood what it was like to be pursued by the media. He did not know how his cell phone number became so widely distributed, but both it and his room phone rang constantly. Other reporters, like Cat Douglas, simply showed up at his door.

"Hi, John," she said, smiling broadly with her head cocked. Her chestnut hair swung in what he assumed she thought was an appealing manner. "It's great to see you! I didn't even know you were—"

And then John shut the door. He gave others, such as Cecil, a few more minutes, but because what they really wanted to know was where and how he got the information, no one left happy. The FBI was interested in exactly the same question, and informed him that he could either give up his sources voluntarily, or else he could wait and be subpoenaed, but either way, give them up he would. John did not argue—nor did he tell them that no matter what they had planned for him, he was taking his sources to the grave.

He didn't have the option of not answering his phone, because he was expecting the DNA results any second. They were already past the promised twenty-four-hour turnaround.

"Hello?" he said, answering his phone for the forty-eighth time that day. At this point, he was leaving it plugged in all the time.

"Is this John Thigpen?" said a woman with an English accent. Although she was asking a question, her voice dipped down at the end.

"Yes. Who's this?"

"My name is Hilary Pinegar. It seems I owe you some money. Some girl named Celia was kind enough to call and tell me what was going on."

"Hilary Pinegar? You're Nathan's mother?" John sat on the edge of the bed.

"Yes. I'm very sorry for the trouble he's caused. He's a bit out of control at the moment. His father and I are hoping it's just a phase. Anyway, we're coming to Lizard to clear everything up, but regardless of that, I'd like to return your money as soon as possible."

"Hilary Pinegar," John said yet again.

"Yes," she said, sounding perplexed at having to confirm it yet again.

"Any relation to Ginette?"

There was a pause. "No. I'm sorry."

"Never mind," said John.

"Anyway," she continued, "if you could just let me know your address, I'll put a check in the mail straightaway."

As John hung up, he felt inexplicably hollow. Disappointed, even.

38

Eight policemen surrounded Isabel, creating a pod to help her navigate the crowd, which had grown even larger now that no one knew what was happening inside the house. As an officer unlocked the main door, the crowd fell silent, craning their necks to see what was going on.

Isabel stepped into the anteroom, then turned and nodded to the officer, who backed out and closed the door behind him.

Isabel looked around because this was the one room in the house that didn't have a camera and so she had never seen it. The room and doors were large enough to accommodate a forklift, and there were track marks and scuffs on the floor, scrapes and dents in the beige walls.

Isabel stared at the interior door and exhaled hard. This was it. She wondered if they already knew she was there.

She knelt on the floor so that she was face-level with the peephole, which was at the height of a squatting or knuckle-walking bonobo. She knocked. She heard loping on the other side of the door, and then silence. She knew she was being scrutinized, and so she smiled. Her hands and lips trembled in anticipation.

A shuffle, a deafening squeal, and the door was yanked open. Bonzi leapt through it and onto Isabel, flinging her arms around her, nearly knocking her backward. Lola jumped onto her head and clung to her face like an octopus claiming a scuba mask. Isabel heard thunderous galloping and joyous squealing and braced herself as the other apes threw themselves at her, on her, hugging her, patting her, pulling her by the arms.

"Lola! I can't breathe!" Isabel laughed, freeing one of her arms so she could pry Lola's belly away from her face. Lola arranged herself on the side of Isabel's head, but even then it was hard for Isabel to keep track of which ape was where, because they were leaping and squeaking and clinging to her.

Bonzi was insistently yanking her arm.

"All right, all right, I'll come in! But you have to let me," she said. Not one of them let go. Isabel crawled into the house, dragged by hairy black arms, draped in bonobos. She was nearly breathless with effort and laughter.

When the apes finally calmed down and settled into grooming Isabel and each other, Makena solemnly presented her infant.

It was a little girl. Isabel, who still had Lola clinging to her head, held the baby upright against her shoulder and looked into her black and crinkled face. The baby's eyes were round and shiny with excitement. She clutched the fabric of Isabel's shirt in her tiny fists, just as she had her mother's fur.

"Well hello, baby," Isabel said, her eyes brimming with tears. She turned to Makena. "You did a good job, Makena. She's beautiful. We're going to have to think of a name, aren't we?"

Sam hung back and watched while Mbongo pulled Isabel's leg out from under her. He removed her shoe and sock, and began to search between her toes. Bonzi crouched behind her, picking through her short hair and taking a particular interest in the area around her scar. Jelani examined her jaw and nose, then slipped his fingers into her mouth and removed her dental flipper.

"Jelani! Give me back my teeth!" Isabel said, laughing so hard she could barely speak. He responded by putting them in his own mouth and rubbing up against Makena, who then rubbed up against Sam.

Bonzi came around and squatted in front of Isabel. She brought her open hand to her temple and thrust it away, closing her fingers. She touched her fingers and thumb to her lips, and then to her ear.

BONZI GO HOME. HURRY ISABEL GO.

Isabel, who was still juggling babies, said, "We'll go home soon, Bonzi. It will be a different home, but it will be a good home, and I'm going to be there. I'm never leaving you again."

Bonzi spun and peeped, signing, KISS KISS, BONZI LOVE.

She stopped spinning and Isabel saw the gleam of intent in her eyes. Isabel laughed and puckered up as Bonzi inserted her face between the babies and pressed her pink whiskered lips against Isabel's.

39

John stood at the perimeter of the crowd and watched the huge white truck pull out. He lifted a hand in farewell, although he knew that Isabel and Celia were in the back with the apes and couldn't see him. It had happened fast: barriers were set up, the truck backed up to the door of the building, and the transfer was made. John had tried to call Isabel earlier in the day and wasn't surprised when she didn't answer. He knew she was busy with the apes, and the thought of their reunion made him long for Amanda.

When John checked out of the Buccaneer, Victor charged him for the bedspread he'd used to put out the flaming man. John didn't argue, since not only had Topher been calling him regularly to remind him that he was "the man," but his assistant had also arranged for John to fly home first-class. It was a nice surprise, but unnecessary, as John would have flapped his arms and flown himself if that's what it took. He left Amanda a jubilant message, and, because he was feeling goofy and happy, topped it off with a rendition of Ozzy Osbourne's "Mama, I'm Coming Home."

He pondered going to the Mohegan Moon for lunch, but decided to eat a package of Twizzlers from the vending machine instead. It didn't matter. Tonight he'd be dining in Amanda's kitchen—and then cleaning it.

On the airplane, as he prepared to turn off his cell phone, he noticed he had a message. It was his mother-in-law, begging him to call. Against his better judgment, he did.

"Hello, Fran. What's up?"

"What have you done to my daughter?" she demanded.

"What are you talking about?"

"She's not answering the phone. What did you do?"

John was about to say something vicious about how Amanda was probably screening Fran's calls, but then he realized that he also couldn't remember the last time he'd spoken to Amanda. The past few days had been a blur, but how could he not have noticed?

"How long since she last answered?" he asked.

"Three days. Something's going on. I can feel it. Mother's intuition."

What if Amanda had tried to change a ceiling lightbulb and fallen from a ladder? What if she was lying in a pool of her own blood right now, eyes glazed and hopeless, her phone on some faraway counter? What if that monstrous dog had torn her to shreds and left her with her face hanging off?

"I'm on the plane right now," he said. "I'll call you when I get home."

An airline attendant suddenly appeared in his face. "Sir?" she said, flashing a professional smile. "It's time to turn off your phone."

"Yes. Of course," he said. When she turned her back to address the other recalcitrant phone users, he twisted toward the wall in an effort to hide what he was doing and called Amanda.

"Hi, this is Amanda. Leave me a message and I'll get back to you as soon as I can."

With a growing sense of panic, John combed through his brain trying to come up with someone to call. Other than Sean, he knew none of her acquaintances or co-workers. He knew Sean's last name, of course. But even if Sean's number was listed, there were probably hundreds—if not thousands—of S. Greens in the L.A. telephone directory. John stared at the number pad of his cell phone as it dawned on him that he knew virtually nothing of Amanda's new life, or any of its potential dangers.

Helplessly, under the now-pointed glare of the flight attendant, John shut off his phone.

It was the first time in his life that John had flown first-class, but he didn't so much as recline his seat, never mind take advantage of the free beverages. He spent the entire flight staring at the topmost part of the road-kill toupée in front of him, his mind filled with terrifying images.

As the cab pulled up to the house, John noticed that the garage door was in the mostly-down position. The Jetta's wheels were visible through the crack, and there were fresh dog turds on the lawn. This last was promising.

He unlocked the door and went in.

"Amanda?"

There was no answer, although her purse was on the table by the door.

He went into the kitchen. There was no ladder and no pool of blood. There was nothing new at all, except two stainless-steel dog bowls on a large rubber mat.

As John mounted the stairs, the dog came into view one slice at a time: the first included ears and forehead, the next an unlikely mixture of pastel pinks and blues. John reached the top of the stairs and stared in disbelief. The poor thing was lying outside the closed washroom door, wearing an argyle sweater and a morose expression. It was hard to take an argyle-sweater-wearing dog seriously, even if it was a meth-lab dog, and so John approached the washroom. From inside he could hear scraping and scouring, banging and crashing.

"Amanda?"

John looked down at Booger, who didn't even lift his head. His eyebrows twitched with worry.

John opened the door. Amanda was on her knees beside the toilet wearing a paper face mask, shower cap, yellow rubber gloves up to her elbows, and garbage bags pulled over each leg and tied off at the thigh.

She was brandishing a can of Lysol and spraying violently in all directions. Sponges, rolls of paper towel, and other cleaning products surrounded her.

"Amanda?" he said.

"Don't run the water," she said without looking at him. "I'm soaking the elbow pipes with bleach." She turned the Comet can upside down and whacked the bottom, sending volcanic bursts of powder into the air. She sat bolt upright, coughing with her rubber forearm held up in front of the mask, then grabbed a brush from a bucket and began scrubbing the floor tiles vigorously.

"Amanda? What are you doing?"

"Did you know," she said, still not looking at him, "that all those places brushes and mops don't reach are just teeming with pathogens? Baseboards, drains, grout—and handles, they're the worst! Crawling with staph, strep, E. coli, MRSA, leptospirosis, hepatitis A, yersiniosis. And in public restrooms—did you know that most people flush with their feet, thereby leaving disgusting sidewalk germs on the toilet handles in addition to everything else? But the sink handles are *just as dirty*. And so are the doorknobs, because of people who don't wash at all— they leave all their filthy, disgusting germs on the handle for the next unsuspecting idiot, even if that idiot went to the effort of washing his hands. You have to sanitize them all . . ." She dropped the brush, picked up a can, and leaned into the tub. She sprayed the faucet and handles until they dripped with white froth.

"Amanda?"

"And don't get me started on the toxic mist of flushing. Never again will I keep a toothbrush in the same room as a toilet. It's a miracle we're not all dead."

"Amanda, please tell me what's going on."

She sat up on her knees, pulled down her mask, and glanced at him. After a pause, she said, "I will. After I take a shower." Then she reached over and shut the door in his face.

John stood in the hallway, staring at it. Then he went downstairs to wait.

A few minutes later, Amanda appeared in her robe and sank into the couch. She was pale as biscuit dough and had dark circles beneath her eyes. She had towel-dried her hair, which was already springing into coils.

"I'll get some coffee," he said.

He stayed in the kitchen while it brewed. He had no idea what had happened, and therefore no idea what to say. After the coffee burped and gurgled its way to an end, he poured a cup and added sugar. He thought better of the cream, as it had ripened into some sort of new, unnamed cheese product.

He deposited the steaming mug on the table in front of Amanda and took a seat across from her. She leaned forward, wrapped both hands around the mug, let go, and sat back without taking a sip.

"Amanda, baby, what's going on?"

"I got a job," she said, trying so hard to sound casual it broke his heart.

"Why? Doing what?"

"I'm writing a brochure about cleaning public restrooms. Next week I move on to the proper boiling of institutional uniforms and linens. After that, industrial kitchens."

John watched her closely. "Did something happen to the series?"

"No, John," she said fiercely. "Something happened to us. And since I don't get any money until and unless NBC commits to more episodes, I need something to live on. By the way, we have an offer on the house in Philly, so at least we won't have to wait too long to divvy that up."

Divvy it up? John stared at her, afraid to say anything. The dog crept around the corner and lay flush against the wall, eyes moving between John and Amanda.

She sighed and gave every appearance of having restored her calm. "So I went to the store a few days ago. Doesn't matter what for," she said, waving away the unasked question with her hand, "and our credit card was declined. Impossible, I said. I just paid the bill. But no, the clerk called the credit card company, and they insisted that we were maxed out."

John felt a sickness beyond anything he'd ever experienced. He knew what was coming.

"So I left everything at the counter and did the walk of shame back to the car. When I got home, I got online and looked at the activity on our account. You'll never guess what I found there."

There was a long silence. She swallowed hard and wiped her eyes. When she finally spoke, her voice was under tight control. "I have never cheated on you. Not once. So were the DNA results what you expected? Are congratulations in order? I won't even ask about the bail bond."

"Amanda," he said quietly, "I can explain."

"Ha!" she snorted, and then burst into gulping, sobbing tears. John moved as though to stand up and go to her. She held a hand up to stop him. "Please don't. Let me guess—she smokes, doesn't she? She's who was in your room right before I got there, wasn't she? Is this her dog too? Because she can't have him back. *She can't have him.*"

Booger slithered over and sat at her feet. He licked her hands and looked reproachfully at John.

"I hope she didn't smoke while she was pregnant," continued Amanda. "Is the baby all right?"

John took a deep breath. "There is no baby. There never was. There was a seventeen-year-old green-haired punk whose last name was Pinegar. I bailed him out of jail."

Amanda froze. Her hand stopped in the center of Booger's back. He turned to investigate and began nibbling an itch beneath the pastel diamonds of his sweater.

"Yes. Pinegar. I did the math, I thought I was his father. I'm not. His mother isn't even Ginette. His parents are sending a check for the bail bond."

"Ginette Pinegar? You thought you had a kid with Ginette Pinegar?"

"I don't know. How many Pinegars can there be in the world?" He leaned back against the cushions, feeling like someone was driving an ice pick into his frontal lobe.

"You never cheated on me?"

"Never. Never, ever, ever."

It was a few seconds before she launched herself, but launch herself she did, right over the coffee table and into his lap. Before he was really aware what was happening, she had her arms wrapped around his head and was weeping into his hair.

Later, when they were lying in a tangled heap of bedclothes and her air-dried corkscrew hair was spread on his chest and tickling his chin, she said, "One of those agents you sent my book to left a message today. She wants to talk tomorrow."

"That sounds promising."

"Maybe. I'm too superstitious to believe anything at this point."

After a moment of contemplation, John said, "Why is the dog wearing a sweater?"

"My mother has been sending things. He has quite the wardrobe."

"Your mother is knitting sweaters for the dog?"

"Yup."

John sighed. "We're going to be in so much trouble when we have a baby."

"Yup," said Amanda.

SIX MONTHS LATER

There was scattered clapping as the mayor took the oversized scissors from the presentation box and cut the ribbon that ran across the open gate. The red satin ends fluttered to the ground as photographers snapped away, including the one from *The Atlantic,* who had accompanied John. The mayor posed with Isabel, draping an arm around her shoulders and baring his teeth in a camera-ready smile. Celia hovered on the other side of him. He glanced at her, and his lips drooped for the briefest of moments. Then he recovered and put an arm around her as well.

John kept quiet when the other reporters began asking questions because he knew he would have a chance later. He stood off to the side with Gary Hanson, the architect who had designed the new facility, and Nathan Pinegar, whose parents had persuaded the judge in Lizard that helping to build the apes' new residence should count toward his community service. He looked happy and fit, his hair even more strikingly verdant than usual. John had a clear vision of Nathan and Celia, up late the night before, dyeing each other's hair for the occasion.

"Dr. Duncan, is it safe to say you're satisfied with the amount of the settlement?"

Isabel looked briefly over her shoulder, toward the thirty acres of Maui mountain property protected by a double fence. She turned back to the cameras. From the gleam in her eye and her tightly closed lips, John could tell she was trying to contain herself. She looked at the ground and cleared her throat. "The terms of the agreement prohibit my saying anything about the amount of the settlement," she said, "but the bonobos and I would like to express our eternal gratitude to the San Diego Zoo for their generous hospitality during the time it took for our new home to be built. I also want to thank Gary Hanson and his firm for donating their services to us, and for designing the most ape-friendly habitat I've ever seen outside of a jungle." She searched the crowd. For a brief moment, John thought she was seeking him. When her eyes landed on Gary, she finally allowed herself to smile, broadly and openly.

"Can you tell us more about your plans for the Great Ape Language Project?"

"We're in the process of vetting the best scientists in the field, and are committed to continuing our work on language acquisition and cognition in the tradition begun by the late Richard Hughes, who believed it's our duty to provide great apes with dignity, autonomy, and the quality of life they so obviously deserve."

"The press release mentioned your collaboration with the Children's Clinical Language Center in Boston. Can you expand on that?"

"There is strong evidence that nonverbal children benefit greatly by using alternative methods of expressing themselves, such as signing, and using lexigrams. We are sharing our data with the CCLC, and are excited about potential advances in this field."

"What are your feelings on the pending criminal trials?"

"I think people are innocent until proven guilty, and I have every confidence that justice will be served." Her eyes swept the crowd, smiling and making eye contact. "Thank you so much for coming." She folded her cheat sheets in half, slid them into her pocket, and motioned the inner circle—Celia, Nathan, Gary, John, and his photographer, Philippe—to follow her. The uniformed security guard shut the gate behind them, and the crowd outside began to disperse.

Isabel led the group down a dirt road that wound between swaying tropical trees and bushes with flowers so overwhelmingly fragrant they smelled like fruit on the verge of going off.

John fell into stride beside her. Her hair had grown enough that he could no longer see the scar. It would be years before it would swing against her back again, but her face was delicate and pretty, and the look suited her.

"I hear you were in the Congo," she said. "At the Lola ya Bonobo sanctuary."

"Yes. I got back last week."

"How was it?"

"Amazing. Almost surreal. We flew Air France from Paris. When we landed in Kinshasa, it was a completely different world. A troop of armed soldiers boarded our plane by the front, marched through, and got off at the back. There were plane carcasses all over the tarmac." John shook his head at the memory. "In the airport, chaos, and not of the organized kind. Fortunately, we had a 'protocol man' to negotiate bribes and get us through customs and immigration. If it weren't for him, I swear we'd still be there. And stripped of all our belongings."

"And how was the sanctuary?" she asked, looping an arm through his. The gesture was unexpected, and caused a tugging in John's chest.

"The road had potholes big enough to swallow the truck and we passed through a lot of poverty and dusty farmland, but the sanctuary itself is gorgeous. It's the old vacation home of Mobutu Sese Seko, the former dictator. There are ponds full of lilies, a river that rushes over a waterfall, and mosquitoes! They're like little stealth bombers"—he mimicked one with his free hand—"silent, painless, and deadly. Did you know there's a type of malaria that can kill you in four days flat?"

"Yup," said Isabel. "Falciparum malaria. I assume you had your prophylaxis?"

"And how. Hepatitis A and B, yellow fever, typhoid, tetanus, flu shots, meningitis, polio—even rabies, because of the feral dogs . . ." He shook his head. "I'm forgetting something."

"Malaria?" Isabel suggested.

"Right. Malaria," said John. "And we heard the bonobos as soon as we got there. They were all around us. They sounded like really loud birds. They came to check us out and immediately stole Philippe's camera. It was a group effort—one of them was hugging his legs while another unlatched the strap, and then a third grabbed the camera and made off with it. They took it up a tree and I seriously thought Philippe was going to cry. We eventually traded it for green apples, but not before the bonobos took about a dozen pictures. There's one we're going to run with the piece—it's of Philippe looking straight into the lens, pleading, his face contorted in pure desperation. It's brilliant."

Isabel threw her head back and laughed. "And completely typical of bonobos!" She sighed. "I want to go there someday."

"I'm sure you will."

"I'm sure I will too," she said, and she sounded so confident it made John sneak another look at her. She seemed so happy and relaxed. Even on the day they'd met, before the bombing, there had been something reserved and anxious about her. There was no sign of that now. The very way she moved her body was different. The old Isabel would never have taken his arm.

The stand of trees ended, revealing a clearing and a large blockish structure. At one end of it was a tall tower with walls made of netting. It was strung from top to bottom with fire hoses and hammocks, and was full of climbing structures, toys, and kiddie pools.

Isabel pulled her arm free of John's. "That's their outdoor play yard," she said, pointing to it with obvious pride. "They come and go as they please. They can also go into the forest if one of us goes with them. They love it. We plant specific treats in specific places. Like that"—she pointed to a tree—"always has a cooler beneath it with hard-boiled eggs, and that"—she pointed to another—"always has M&M's—sugar-free, of course. We're still undoing the damage from the pizza and cheeseburgers."

Immediately inside the structure was a large observation area, separated from the apes' living quarters by a curved wall of glass. The bonobos were nowhere to be seen, though Gary went to the glass and stood expectantly. Philippe joined him, his camera poised. Celia and Nathan stood slightly behind them, also staring into the apes' quarters.

"So, what do you think?" Isabel said, watching him expectantly.

"It's magnificent," said John. "Where are the bonobos?"

"They're in the group room. Probably watching reruns of *Ape House*. They're a bit obsessed with it."

"Did my package arrive?" he asked.

"I don't know," said Isabel. "Celia?"

"Yes," said Celia, whipping her fuchsia head around. "And it looks super yummy. Thanks, Pigpen."

John raised two fingers in a peace salute.

"What is it?" asked Isabel.

"A carrot cake," John said. "To celebrate the occasion."

He saw her hesitate. "Oh, I don't know . . ." she said.

"Amanda made it," he added quickly. "Organic carrots, sweetened with apple juice, and the icing is made with fat-free cream cheese. Here's a list of ingredients." He pulled a crumpled piece of paper from his pocket and handed it to Isabel.

Isabel laughed. "Oh, well, if Amanda made it . . ."

"Cool," said Celia. "We'll go tell them it's coming." She and Nathan disappeared into a corridor.

Isabel looked at her feet, and then back up at John. "I want to thank you."

"Oh, *pffft,* it was nothing," he said, waving a hand.

"It was not nothing. You spent ten days in jail on our behalf."

"A journalist protects his sources."

"Celia wanted to come forward," said Isabel. "I had to remind her that you were also protecting Joel, Jawad, and Ivanka."

"And you," he said.

"Yes, and me."

There was a pause as their eyes locked.

"So, um," he said in a lowered voice, "did I detect something going on with, um . . . ?" He inclined his head slightly toward Gary.

"Maybe. Kind of." Her cheeks went pink. "So," she said, tearing her gaze away, "how is Amanda?"

"The morning sickness has passed, and she no longer runs screaming from the room at the smell of coffee. . . ."

Isabel laughed. "That's good. When is the little one due?"

"In a little less than three months. Four days after Ivanka's, believe it or not."

"You must be excited."

"Excited and terrified in equal parts," he said, hoping his expression didn't betray the actual balance.

"And her new book!" Isabel clapped her hands in front of her. "I was so happy to hear about that. When is it coming out again?"

"Four months."

"I can't wait to read it. Will you tell her?"

"Of course."

"Also tell her I'm sorry about the series, unless that's a sore point."

"Not at all. She was delighted when they dropped it. She hated it and L.A. with all her considerable passion."

"And you? How are you doing?"

"I'm getting by. Also happy to be back in New York, even though our apartment is currently full of cats that Amanda is fostering for a local shelter, and because she's pregnant I get to do the kitty litter. That is, when Booger doesn't take care of it." John saw her shudder, and couldn't help adding, "Kitty-litter surprise. Yum. His favorite."

"Bleh," she said, scrunching up her face. Then she added, "So who does it while you're gone?"

"A roster of friends, backed up by a saintly neighbor."

After a moment of silence, Isabel glanced at Philippe. "*The Atlantic,* huh? That's pretty impressive."

"This is just a one-off, but still. Doing time seems to have done wonders for my career." He, too, glanced at Philippe. "If I'd known, I'd have held up a liquor store years ago."

Isabel laughed. "I hardly think that would have the same effect."

The bonobos burst into the observation area, peeping and squeaking, loping back and forth in front of the window. Philippe began clicking away.

Bonzi signed excitedly, GIMME GOOD TREAT! BONZI EAT GIMME YOU!

"The visitor brought it," said Isabel, pointing at John.

BONZI LOVE VISITOR!

Celia appeared on the apes' side of the glass with the cake. She had stuck a candle in the center of it. "Bonzi! Come here," she said. "There's a lighter in my pocket. Can you light the candle?"

Bonzi reached into Celia's pocket, pulled out a lighter, and deftly lit the candle. No sooner was it lit than Jelani rushed over and blew it out. He plucked it from the cake and sucked the icing from the end. Mbongo sat eyeing John suspiciously until Celia handed him a piece of cake.

"Do you like your treat? John brought it."

Mbongo pulled the perfectly formed marzipan carrots off the top of his piece and sucked them, studiously avoiding eye contact with John. Bonzi licked icing off her lips and came to the glass.

BONZI LOVE VISITOR. BUILD VISITOR NEST. KISS KISS.

She stood on the rim and pressed her lips against the glass. They smushed outward. The effect was of looking at an algae eater at work from the outside of a fish tank.

John hesitated for just a second, then said, "My apologies to whoever cleans the glass." As he approached, he saw Philippe swing his camera around to capture the moment. John lined himself up with Bonzi's lips and planted a big kiss on them.

AUTHOR'S NOTE

Right before I went on tour for *Water for Elephants,* my mother sent me an email about a place in Des Moines, Iowa, that was studying language acquisition and cognition in great apes. I had been fascinated by human-ape discourse ever since I first heard about Koko the gorilla (which was longer ago than I care to admit) so I spent close to a day poking around the Great Ape Trust's Web site. I was doubly fascinated—not only with the work they're doing, but also by the fact that there was an entire species of great ape I had never heard of. Although I had no idea what I was getting into, I was hooked.

During the course of my research, I was fortunate enough to be invited to the Great Ape Trust—not that that didn't take some doing. I was assigned masses of homework, including a trip to York University in Toronto for a crash course on linguistics. Even after I received the coveted invitation to the Trust, it didn't necessarily mean I was going to get to meet the apes: that part was up to them. Like John, I tried to stack my odds by getting backpacks and filling them with everything I thought an ape might find fun or tasty—bouncy balls, fleece blankets, M&M's, xylophones, Mr. Potato Heads, etc.—and then emailed the scientists, asking them to please let the apes know I was bringing "surprises." At the end of my orientation with the humans, I asked, with some trepidation, whether the apes were going to let me come in. The response was that not only were they letting me come in, they were insisting.

The experience was astonishing—to this day I cannot think about it without getting goose bumps. You cannot have a two-way conversation with a great ape, or even just look one straight in the eye, close up, without coming away changed. I stayed until the end of the day, when I practically had to be dragged out, because I was having so much fun. I was told that the next day Panbanisha said to one of the scientists, "Where's Sara? Build her nest. When's she coming back?"

Most of the conversations between the bonobos and humans in this book are based on actual conversations with great apes, including Koko, Washoe, Booey, Kanzi, and Panbanisha. After two years of research, I came away realizing that I have only seen the tip of the iceberg, and to anyone who wants to learn more, I highly recommend the following books as a starting point: *Kanzi: The Ape at the Brink of the Human Mind* by Sue Savage-Rumbaugh and Roger Lewin, and *Next of Kin: My Conversations with Chimpanzees* by Roger Fouts with Stephen Tukel Mills. You can also find information about bonobos at the Web sites for the Great Ape Trust (www.greatapetrust.org) and the Friends of Bonobos (www.friendsofbonobos.org).

Many of the ape-based scenes in this book are also based on fact—such as the Philadelphia Zoo fire, the gorilla (Binti Jua) who saved the fallen toddler, the types of experiments performed on chimpanzees and the conditions under which they were kept, the treatment and discarding of the Air Force chimps—although I have taken the fiction writer's liberty of fudging names, dates, and places. Many of the worst conditions have now been outlawed, but they demonstrate how we've traditionally treated our closest relatives—as "hairy test tubes," is how Dr. Fouts put it. We've come a long way, but given that all four species of great ape are either endangered or critically endangered, we still have a long way to go.

One of the places I did not disguise or rename is the Lola ya Bonobo sanctuary in the Democratic Republic of the Congo. They take in orphaned infants (usually sold as pets after their mothers are killed for bush meat), nurse them back to health, and when they're ready, release them back into the jungle. This, combined with ongoing education of the local people, is one of the wild bonobos' best hopes for survival.

One day, I'm going to be brave enough to visit Lola ya Bonobo. In the meantime, in response to Panbanisha's question, I'm coming back soon. Very soon. I hope you have my nest ready!

ACKNOWLEDGMENTS

So many people helped me with the writing of this book that I am sure I am going to forget some; to anyone whose name is missing, I apologize.

First, and most important, I want to thank the apes at the Great Ape Trust—Kanzi, Panbanisha, Matata, Nyota, Nathan, Elikya, Maisha, Azy, Knobi, and Allie—for inviting me into their home and allowing me a glimpse into their remarkable world. I also want to thank the humans there, both for facilitating my visit and for answering my many questions as the book progressed: Liz Rubert-Pugh, Sue Savage-Rumbaugh, Tyler Romine, Daniel Musgrave, Susannah Maisel, Heather Taylor, Sharon Mckee, T. J. Kaperbauer, Takashi Yoshida, Beth Dalbey, Bill Fields, and Al Setka.

To Jim Benson and Bill Greaves, the professors at York University who helped prepare me for my visit to the Trust and who never once uttered the words "rank lexical relation." Indeed, when I left your office, although I went to the bus stop, what I really wanted to do was head for the enrollment office. The chills I got when I listened to the recording of Kanzi and realized that he was uttering the words "bring water" were a precursor to the incredible experience that was my real-life conversations with the apes.

To Vanessa Woods, bonobo researcher at Duke University and a regular fixture at the Lola ya Bonobo Sanctuary in the Democratic Republic of the Congo, not just for her help with my questions and access to her gorgeous photographs, but also for her friendship to me and her unflagging devotion to bonobos.

To my writing group: Karen Abbott, Joshilyn Jackson, and Renee Rosen. Your patience, dedication, and astonishing willingness to respond positively to a DEAR ("Drop Everything And Read") despite your own deadlines is beyond what anyone could ever reasonably expect. You have provided daily—hourly—friendship. You have fed me strange martini-like concoctions with obscene names. You have consistently beaten me in poker and then done victory dances. You have listened to me moan, weep, and gnash my teeth, and you have, in multitudes of ways, made this a much better book. You are not just my critique partners, you are my dearest friends.

To Terence Bailey, Catherine DiCairano, Beth Helms, Kathryn Puffett, and the many other people who had a hand in shaping this story, for everything from critiques, pep talks, brainstorming sessions, and providing plausible medical dialogue—not to mention the occasional delivery of confit of fig and balsamic vinegar.

Thanks also to my children, who did not particularly help (and occasionally even hindered) my progress, but whom I thank nonetheless because they are the reason for everything.

To Emma Sweeney, my wonderful agent, and Cindy Spiegel, my amazing editor, for their guidance, support, love, and for helping me find the statue in the rough-hewn rock. I am also deeply indebted to Random House for giving me the support and time I needed to research and write this book.

And finally, to Bob: You are my best friend, my love, my partner in crime. You keep our world going when I cannot do anything but this. When I leap off a cliff, you pull me up by my bungee cord. When I'm hopeless, you give me hope. When I'm unlovable, you love me anyway. I can't fathom why you put up with me, but I'm eternally grateful that you do.

APE HOUSE

SARA GRUEN

A Reader's Guide

A Conversation with Sara Gruen

Random House Reader's Circle: When did you first become interested in writing a novel about human-ape interaction?

Sara Gruen: I've been following the progress of Koko the gorilla since 1980 and have always been fascinated by the concept of human-ape discourse. Right before I went on tour for *Water for Elephants,* my mother sent me an email with a link to the Great Ape Trust, and after I spent a few days poking around their site, I decided that I had to feature these amazing beings in my next book. Part of it was the language and cognition studies going on at the Trust, and part of it was this amazing species of great ape that I'd never heard of before.

RHRC: For your research, you spent time with the bonobos at Great Ape Trust. Can you describe some of the relationships you formed with the apes?

SG: I met Kanzi first. He's very outgoing and always willing to show off what he knows. Mostly he wants to play chase without actually running, so he picks two people (usually women) and orders them to chase each other in front of him. It's kind of like *Ape Baywatch*! He also likes to show off his keyboarding skills and converse on his lexigram board and ask for treats for his visitors—bonobos are very generous.

I met Panbanisha next, and, although she is arguably more language-competent than Kanzi, her brother, she is much more shy. I already knew through research that she didn't like cats, but she did like dogs, and also that she had two sons (one has since passed on), so I brought pictures of my dogs and my own kids as icebreakers, hoping she would want to speak to me. I showed her the dogs, and she didn't respond. Then I showed her a picture of the kids when they were little and all in a bubble bath, and she went to her lexigram board and said, "Babies washing bubbles." Because bonobo culture is matriarchal and infants enjoy such high status on the social hierarchy, being a mother gave me instant status. The day after I left, she said to one of the scientists, "Where's Sara? Build her nest. When's she coming back?"

I joined the whole family in a fruit-of-the-month club so they'd be reminded of me on a regular basis, but I needn't have worried. They have great memories. Since then I have had a tea party with Panbanisha in the forest, with tea that she brewed and cookies she selected, and generally just spent excellent girl time with her (we did our hair and makeup together). I've run back and forth for Kanzi many, many times and played tickle chase with Maisha and Nyota, the adolescent male bonobos, and they are better than any personal trainer. They will absolutely wear you out!

RHRC: You've described your conversations with the apes at the Trust as "life-changing." What was your most memorable conversation?

SG: The most memorable conversation was about a week after Easter when I went up to visit. Panbanisha put on purple lipstick and made tea and invited me to have a tea party in the forest. The apes are on diets on Tuesdays and Thursdays—when they eat only monkey chow—and on the other days they eat fruits, vegetables, fish, and tofu. But this was a Tuesday and so she took advantage of this and asked me if I had had an egg for breakfast. I said no, I hadn't. She said that the Easter bunny had been by the week earlier and had hidden eggs in the forest. And then she said, "I wish the bunny would come back." Five minutes later, the "Easter bunny" snuck out of the Trust and hid more eggs in the forest. So the most memorable conversation I've had with an ape involved an ape asking me what I had for breakfast and then segueing into requesting more Easter eggs. She was totally manipulating diet Tuesdays!

RHRC: Do bonobos understand fiction and stories? Do they (or could they) write? Would you consider sharing your work with them?

SG: In a very real sense they are already reading: The lexigrams on their board are symbols for spoken words, and Panbanisha has been known to write lexigrams on the floor in chalk. In the spring I took my manuscript with me on my visit, and when Panbanisha and I were having our tea party, I read some of the beginning to her, and she and Dr. Sue had a conversation about what the differences were between good visitors and bad visitors. Panbanisha knows the book is dedicated to her and pointed to her name on the page. The bonobos actually saw the book cover before I did! They absolutely understand when something is fiction: Panbanisha is fond of horror movies, and Kanzi cannot stand them, while Maisha prefers *Spiderman*.

RHRC: One of the most emotional parts of the book is when Isabel visits the research facility that used apes in experiments. Have you visited a lab like the one in your book?

SG: The section in which Isabel visits the biomedical lab was difficult to write because it is based on real experiments that have been carried out on great apes. I did not visit such a place—not only is it extremely difficult to gain entry, but I'm not sure I could have stood it. I am haunted just by knowing such a place exists and having seen pictures.

RHRC: Do you find it easier or more enjoyable to write animals than to write humans?

SG: I think I explore them equally. I just don't think I've had the desire yet to write a vicious animal—like a dog-gone-bad or anything—whereas I *do* feel that I need a balance of all types of humans. I just think I'm better equipped to make a study of human personality than to get into the minds of animals.

RHRC: The bonobos in *Ape House* are exploited by humans, even appearing on a reality TV show. What did you want to explore about our culture's fascination with reality TV?

SG: Reality TV and the culture of tabloid journalism boil down to voyeurism, and nobody would be interested in "celebutantes" if they stopped behaving badly. The world of Twitter and Facebook and gossip blogs has provided us with instant access to information about these people and fosters a false sense of intimacy with them, all while letting us maintain enough distance to tut-tut about their bad behavior. Gossip replaces real news. If an Olsen twin changes her hair color, it's likely to get more press than the damage the oil spill is doing to the Gulf. We are turning ourselves into a society with the attention span of hamsters.

RHRC: You studied English in college and started your career as a technical writer. Was there ever a point when you considered a career working with animals?

SG: Yes, when I was growing up I wanted to be a veterinarian. And I started thinking about doing language cognition when I heard about Koko. I corresponded with Penny Patterson, the researcher who taught American Sign Language to Koko, and I asked her what courses I should take in order to be able to do that. But then when I got to high school, I found that I was entirely incapable of even dissecting a worm, so that was out the window.

RHRC: Describe a typical day spent writing. Do you have any unusual writing habits?

SG: I start writing the second my kids leave for school and I finish when they get home. I perch like a bird at my desk (knees up under my chin, sitting on my feet—I've even been caught doing this on a yoga ball!). It takes me about an hour and a half to go through what I consider my "creative portal," and once I'm there, I'm often good for two thousand words. However, if I answer the phone or the door or talk to anyone, I need to spend that hour and a half again, so I've been known to hide behind the curtain from the mailman and other "intruders." I once got so desperate, I moved my desk into my closet and finished a book there.

RHRC: In the novel, journalist John Thigpen deals with newspapers downsizing, and his novelist wife, Amanda, struggles to get her book published. Did any of that come from personal experience?

SG: Well, the big, red "NO" written across my own query letter to agents made it into the book. I have a lot of writer friends and I just kind of boiled all of our horror stories into one horror-story melting pot, but I think it's a very accurate view of what a novelist has to go through because it's just so tough. If I had had any idea of the odds, I never would have tried it.

RHRC: Trying seems to have worked out quite well for you.

SG: Yes, I think this was a case of ignorance is bliss.

RHRC: What kind of animal person are you? Crazy cat lady? Adopter of homeless hamsters and injured snakes?

SG: All of the above! Except for the injured snakes. I did, however, leave an egg out for a visiting rat snake this summer.

RHRC: I'm assuming you must have a few animals of your own. What kind do you have?

SG: Currently, we have two dogs, four cats, two horses, and a goat. I say currently, because my stepdaughter is a vet with a soft heart and so you never know what's coming down the pipe . . .

Reading Group Questions and Topics for Discussion

1. The bonobos in *Ape House* are described as matriarchal, with Bonzi acting as the nurturing and intelligent "undisputed leader" (p. 6) of the group. Discuss how Bonzi's relationship with her family compares or contrasts with the various human characters' relationships with their own families. Consider Amanda's desire—and Ivanka's—to have children in your discussion.

2. What does the success of the show *Ape House* reveal about human society? Why do you think its audience finds it especially compelling? How does it compare to the other types of media discussed in the novel?

3. Why is Isabel so attached to the bonobos? What does she enjoy about their company (and that of Stuart, her late fish) that other people do not offer her? What prevents her from connecting at the beginning, and how does that change by the end?

4. Isabel says, "[The bonobos] know they're bonobos and they know we're human, but it doesn't imply mastery, or superiority" (p. 10). The bonobos are clearly sentient animals, demonstrating the use of both language and tools, two criteria often cited as proof of the separation between humans and other primates. What, then, actually separates us from them?

5. "At this moment, the story in his head was perfect. [John] also knew from experience that it would degenerate the second he started typing, because such was the nature of writing" (p. 215). John and Amanda are both writers who struggle to maintain integrity while making a living. Discuss the importance of writing, language, and creativity in the novel, as well as the compromises the characters are forced to accept.

6. In *Ape House,* Sara Gruen uses humor to reveal the many flaws of human society. Is this device effective for revealing human foibles? Did you identify with her portrayal of human behavior?

7. Which of the human characters in *Ape House* is most like a bonobo?

8. Contrast the physical and emotional transformations of Isabel and Amanda. What are the reasons for their change? How does it affect both of them and their relationships with the other characters?

9. Do you think the use of animals for research, even when it does not physically or emotionally harm them, is an inherent infringement upon the animal's free will, as the ELL would argue? Or is there a way for animal-related research to be beneficial to human society while also protecting and respecting the animals' rights? Discuss how *Ape House* explores the different sides of this issue.

10. Over the course of the novel, John grows increasingly concerned about the possibility of having fathered a child with Ginette Pinegar, while Isabel doesn't understand why a biological link to the boy should make a difference. For the bonobos, on the other hand, the concept of paternity is irrelevant. Discuss the way *Ape House* deals with family structures.

11. Compare the bonobos' behavior with that of the humans in the novel. Do you think of human behavior differently after reading the novel?

SARA GRUEN is the author of the #1 bestselling novel *Water for Elephants,* as well as the bestseller *Riding Lessons* and *Flying Changes.* She shares her North Carolina home with her own version of a blended family: a husband, three children, four cats, two dogs, two horses, and a goat. In order to write this novel, Gruen studied linguistics and a system of lexigrams so that she could communicate directly with the bonobos living at the Great Ape Trust in Des Moines, Iowa. She now considers them to be part of her extended family, and, according to the bonobos, the feeling is mutual.

www.saragruen.com

ABOUT THE TYPE

This book was set in Granjon, a modern recutting of a typeface pro-
duced under the direction of George W. Jones, who based Granjon's
design upon the letter forms of Claude Garamond (1480–1561). The
name was given to the typeface as a tribute to the typographic designer
Robert Granjon.